I0662953

The Hunters of the Hills

Joseph A. Altsheler

.

The Hunters of the Hills

Copyright © 2020 Bibliotech Press
All rights reserved

The present edition is a reproduction of previous publication of this classic work. Minor typographical errors may have been corrected without note, however, for an authentic reading experience the spelling, punctuation, and capitalization have been retained from the original text.

ISBN: 978-1-61895-771-9

FOREWORD

"The Hunters of the Hills" is the first volume of a series dealing with the great struggle of France and England and their colonies for dominion in North America, culminating with the fall of Quebec. It is also concerned to a large extent with the Iroquois, the mighty league known in their own language as the Hodenosaunee, for the favor of which both French and English were high bidders. In his treatment of the theme the author has consulted many authorities, and he is not conscious of any historical error.

CONTENTS

CHAPTER I
THE THREE FRIENDS

A canoe containing two boys and a man was moving slowly on one of the little lakes in the great northern wilderness of what is now the State of New York. The water, a brilliant blue under skies of the same intense sapphire tint, rippled away gently on either side of the prow, or rose in heaps of glittering bubbles, as the paddles were lifted for a new stroke.

Vast masses of dense foliage in the tender green of early spring crowned the high banks of the lake on every side. The eye found no break anywhere. Only the pink or delicate red of a wild flower just bursting into bloom varied the solid expanse of emerald walls; and save for the canoe and a bird of prey, darting in a streak of silver for a fish, the surface of the water was lone and silent.

The three who used the paddles were individual and unlike, none of them bearing any resemblance to the other two. The man sat in the stern. He was of middle years, built very powerfully and with muscles and sinews developed to an amazing degree. His face, in childhood quite fair, had been burned almost as brown as that of an Indian by long exposure. He was clothed wholly in tanned deerskin adorned with many little colored beads. A hatchet and knife were in the broad belt at his waist, and a long rifle lay at his feet.

His face was fine and open and he would have been noticed anywhere. But the eyes of the curious would surely have rested first upon the two youths with him.

One was back of the canoe's center on the right side and the other was forward on the left. The weight of the three occupants was balanced so nicely that their delicate craft floated on a perfectly even keel. The lad near the prow was an Indian of a nobler type than is often seen in these later days, when he has been deprived of the native surroundings that fit him like the setting of a gem.

The Indian, although several years short of full manhood, was tall, with limbs slender as was usual in his kind; but his shoulders were broad and his chest wide and deep. His color was a light copper, the tint verging toward red, and his face was illumined wonderfully by black eyes that often flashed with a lofty look of courage and pride.

The young warrior, Tayoga, a coming chief of the clan of the Bear, of the nation Onondaga, of the League of the Hodenosaunee,

1

known to white men as the Iroquois, was in all the wild splendor of full forest attire. His headdress, gustoweh, was the product of long and careful labor. It was a splint arch, curving over the head, and crossed by another arch from side to side, the whole inclosed by a cap of fine network, fastened with a silver band. From the crest, like the plume of a Roman knight, a cluster of pure white feathers hung, and on the side of it a white feather of uncommon size projected upward and backward, the end of the feather set in a little tube which revolved with the wind, the whole imparting a further air of distinction to his strong and haughty countenance.

The upper part of his body was clothed in the garment called by the Hodenosaunee gakaah, a long tunic of deerskin tanned beautifully, descending to the knees, belted at the waist, and decorated elaborately with the quills of the porcupine, stained red, yellow and blue and varied with the natural white.

His leggings, called in his own language giseha, were fastened by bands above the knees, and met his moccasins. They too were of deerskin tanned with the same skill, and along the seams and around the bottom, were adorned with the quills of the porcupine and rows of small, colored beads. The moccasins, ahtaquaoweh, of deerskin, were also decorated with quills and beads, but the broad belt, gagehta, holding in his tunic at the waist, was of rich blue velvet, heavy with bead work. The knife at his belt had a silver hilt, and the rifle in the bottom of the canoe was silver-mounted. Nowhere in the world could one have found a young forest warrior more splendid in figure, manner and dress.

The white youth was the equal in age and height of his red comrade, but was built a little more heavily. His face, tanned red instead of brown, was of the blonde type and bore an aspect of refinement unusual in the woods. The blue eyes were thoughtful and the chin, curving rather delicately, indicated gentleness and a sense of humor, allied with firmness of purpose and great courage. His dress was similar in fashion to that of the older man, but was finer in quality. He was armed like the others.

"I suppose we're the only people on the lake," said the hunter and scout, David Willet, "and I'm glad of it, lads. It's not a time, just when the spring has come and the woods are so fine, to be shot at by Huron warriors and their like down from Canada."

"I don't want 'em to send their bullets at me in the spring or any other time," said the white lad, Robert Lennox. "Hurons are not good marksmen, but if they kept on firing they'd be likely to hit at last. I don't think, though, that we'll find any of 'em here. What do you say, Tayoga?"

The Indian youth flashed a swift look along the green wall of forest, and replied in pure Onondaga, which both Lennox and Willet understood:

"I think they do not come. Nothing stirs in the woods on the high banks. Yet Onontio (the Governor General of Canada) would send the Hurons and the other nations allied with the French against the people of Corlear (the Governor of the Province of New York). But they fear the Hodenosaunee."

"Well they may!" said Willet. "The Iroquois have stopped many a foray of the French. More than one little settlement has thriven in the shade of the Long House."

The young warrior smiled and lifted his head a little. Nobody had more pride of birth and race than an Onondaga or a Mohawk. The home of the Hodenosaunee was in New York, but their hunting grounds and real domain, over which they were lords, extended from the Hudson to the Ohio and from the St. Lawrence to the Cumberland and the Tennessee, where the land of the Cherokees began. No truer kings of the forest ever lived, and for generations their warlike spirit fed upon the fact.

"It is true," said Tayoga gravely, "but a shadow gathers in the north. The children of Corlear wish to plow the land and raise corn, but the sons of Onontio go into the forest and become hunters and warriors with the Hurons. It is easy for the man in the woods to shoot down the man in the field."

"You put it well, Tayoga," exclaimed Willet. "That's the kernel in the nut. The English settle upon the land, but the French take to the wild life and would rather be rovers. When it comes to fighting it puts our people at a great disadvantage. I know that some sort of a wicked broth is brewing at Quebec, but none of us can tell just when it will boil over."

"Have you ever been to Quebec, Dave?" asked Robert.

"Twice. It's a fortress on a rock high above the St. Lawrence, and it's the seat of the French power in North America. We English in this country rule our selves mostly, but the French in Canada don't have much to say. It's the officials sent out from France who govern as they please."

"And you believe they'll attack us, Dave?"

"When they're ready, yes, but they intend to choose time and place. I think they've been sending war belts to the tribes in the north, but I can't prove it."

"The French in France are a brave and gallant race, Dave, and they are brave and gallant here too, but I think they're often more cruel than we are."

It was in David Willet's mind to say it was because the French had adapted themselves more readily than the English to the ways

3

of the Indian, but consideration for the feelings of Tayoga restrained him. The wilderness ranger had an innate delicacy and to him Tayoga was always a nobleman of the forest.

"You've often told me, Dave," said Lennox, "that I've French blood in me."

"There's evidence pointing that way," said Willet, "and when I was in Quebec I saw some of the men from Northern France. I suppose we mostly think of the French as short and dark, but these were tall and fair. Some of them had blue eyes and yellow hair, and they made me think a little of you, Robert."

Young Lennox sighed and became very thoughtful. The mystery of his lineage puzzled and saddened him at times. It was a loss never to have known a father or a mother, and for his kindest and best friends to be of a blood not his own. The moments of depression, however, were brief, as he had that greatest of all gifts from the gods, a cheerful and hopeful temperament.

The three began to paddle with renewed vigor. Gasna Gaowo, the canoe in which they sat, was a noble example of Onondaga art. It was about sixteen feet in length and was made of the bark of the red elm, the rim, however, being of white ash, stitched thoroughly to the bark. The ribs also were of white ash, strong and flexible, and fastened at each end under the rim. The prow, where the ends of the bark came together, was quite sharp, and the canoe, while very light and apparently frail, was exceedingly strong, able to carry a weight of more than a thousand pounds. The Indians surpassed all other people in an art so useful in a land of many lakes and rivers and they lavished willing labor upon their canoes, often decorating them with great beauty and taste.

"We're now within the land of the Mohawks, are we not, Tayoga?" asked Lennox.

"Ganeagaono, the Keepers of the Eastern Gate, rule here," replied the young warrior, "but the Hurons dispute their claim."

"I've heard that the Mohawks and the Hurons, who now fight one another, were once of the same blood."

"It is so. The old men have had it from those who were old men when they were boys. The Mohawks in a far, far time were a clan of the Wanedote, called in your language the Hurons, and lived where the French have built their capital of Quebec. Thence their power spread, and becoming a great nation themselves they separated from the Wanedote. But many enemies attacked them and they moved to the south, where they joined the Onondagas and Oneidas, and in time the League of the Hodenosaunee grew up. That, though, was far, far back, eight or ten of what the white men call generations."

4

"But it's interesting, tremendously so," said Robert, reflectively. "I find that the red races and the white don't differ much. The flux and movement have been going on always among them just as it has among us. Races disappear, and new ones appear."

"It is so, Lennox," said Tayoga gravely, "but the League of the Hodenosaunee is the chosen of Manitou. We, the Onundagaono, in your language Onondagas, Keepers of the Council, the Brand and the Wampum, know it. The power of the Long House cannot be broken. Onundagaono, Ganeogaono, Nundawaono (Senecas), Gweugwehono (Cayugas), Onayotekaono (Oneidas) and the new nation that we made our brethren, Dusgaowehono (Tuscaroras), will defend it forever."

Robert glanced at him. Tayoga's nostrils expanded as he spoke, the chin was thrown up again and his eyes flashed with a look of immeasurable pride. White youth understood red youth. The forest could be as truly a kingdom as cities and fields, and within the limits of his horizon Tayoga, a coming chief of the clan of the Bear, of the nation Onondaga, of the League of the Hodenosaunee, was as thoroughly of royal blood as any sovereign on his throne. He and his father and his father's father before him and others before them had heard the old men and the women chant the prowess and invincibility of the Hodenosaunee, and of that great league, the Onondagas, the Keepers of the Wampum, the Brand and the Council Fire, were in Tayoga's belief first, its heart and soul.

Robert had pride of race himself—it was a time when an ancient stock was thought to count for much—and he was sure that the blood in his veins was noble, but, white though he was, he did not feel any superiority to Tayoga. Instead he paid him respect where respect was due because, born to a great place in a great race, he was equal to it. He understood, too, why the Hodenosaunee seemed immutable and eternal to its people, as ancient Rome had once seemed unshakable and everlasting to the Romans, and, understanding, he kept his peace.

The lake, slender and long, now narrowed to a width of forty or fifty yards and curved sharply toward the east. They slowed down with habitual caution, until they could see what lay in front of them. Robert and Tayoga rested their paddles, and Willet sent the canoe around the curve. The fresh reach of water was peaceful too, unruffled by the craft of any enemy, and on either side the same lofty banks of solid green stretched ahead. Above and beyond the cliffs rose the distant peaks and ridges of the high mountains. The whole was majestic and magnificent beyond comparison. Robert and Tayoga, their paddles still idle, breathed it in and felt that

5

Manitou, who is the same as God, had lavished work upon this region, making it good to the eye of all men for all time.

"How far ahead is the cove, Tayoga?" asked Willet.

"About a mile," replied the Onondaga.

"Then we'd better put in there, and look for game. We've got mighty little venison."

"It is so," said Tayoga, using his favorite words of assent. Neither he nor Robert resumed the paddle, leaving the work for the rest of the way to the hunter, who was fully equal to the task. His powerful arms swept the broad blade through the water, and the canoe shot forward at a renewed pace. Long practice and training had made him so skillful at the task that his breath was not quickened by the exertion. It was a pleasure to Robert to watch the ease and power with which he did so much.

The lake widened as they advanced, and through a change in the color of the sky the water here seemed silver rather than blue. A flock of wild ducks swam near the edge and he saw two darting loons, but there was no other presence. Silence, beauty and majesty were everywhere, and he was content to go on, without speaking, infused with the spirit of the wilderness.

The cove showed after a while, at first a mere slit that only a wary eye could have seen, and then a narrow opening through which a small creek flowed into the lake. Willet, with swift and skillful strokes of the paddle, turned the canoe into the stream and advanced some distance up it, until he stopped at a point where it broadened into an expanse like a pool, covered partly with water lilies, and fringed with tall reeds. Behind the reeds were slanting banks clothed with dense, green foliage. It was an ideal covert, and there were thousands like it in the wonderful wilderness of the North Woods.

"You find this a good place, don't you, Tayoga?" said Willet, with a certain deference.

"It suits us well," replied the young Onondaga in his measured tones. "No man, Indian or white, has been here today. The lilies are undisturbed. Not a reed has been bent. Ducks that have not yet seen us are swimming quietly up the creek, and farther on a stag is drinking at its edge. I can hear him lapping the water."

"That was wonderful, Tayoga," said Willet with admiration. "I wouldn't have noticed it, but since you've spoken of it I can hear the stag too. Now he's gone away. Maybe he's heard us."

"Like as not," said Robert, "and he'd have been a good prize, but he's taken the alarm, and he's safe. We'll have to look for something else. Just there on the right you can see an opening among the leaves, Dave, and that's our place for landing."

Willet sent the canoe through the open water between the tall reeds, then slowed it down with his paddle, and the prow touched the bank gently.

The three stepped out and drew the canoe with great care upon the shore, in order that it might dry. The bank at that point was not steep and the presence of the deer at the water's edge farther up indicated a slope yet easier there.

"Appears to be a likely place for game," said Willet. "While the stag has scented us and gone, there must be more deer in the woods. Maybe they're full of 'em, since this is doubtful ground and warriors and white men too are scarce."

"But red scouts from the north may be abroad," said Robert, "and it would be unwise to use our rifles. We don't want a brush with Hurons or Tionontati."

"The Tionontati went into the west some years ago," said Tayoga, "and but few of their warriors are left with their kinsmen, the Hurons."

"But those few would be too many, should they chance to be near. We must not use our rifles. Instead we must resort to your bow and arrows, Tayoga."

"Perhaps waano (the bow) will serve us," said the young chief, with his confident smile.

"That being the case, then," said Willet, "I'll stay here and mind the canoe, while the pair of you boys go and find the deer. You're younger than I am, an' I'm willing for you to do the work."

The white teeth of Tayoga flashed into a deeper smile.

"Does our friend, the Great Bear, who calls himself Willet, grow old?" he asked.

"Not by a long sight, Tayoga," replied Willet with energy. "I'm no braggart, I hope, but you Iroquois don't call me Great Bear for nothing. My muscles are as hard as ever, and my wind's as good. I can lift more and carry more upon my shoulders than any other man in all this wilderness."

"I but jested with the Great Bear," said Tayoga, smiling. "Did I not see last winter how quick he could be when I was about to be cut to pieces under the sharp hoofs of the wounded and enraged moose, and he darted in and slew the animal with his long knife?"

"Don't speak of it, Tayoga. That was just a little matter between friends. You'd do as much for me if the chance came."

"But you've done it already, Great Bear."

Willet said something more in deprecation, and picking up the canoe, put it in a better place. Its weight was nothing to him, and Robert noticed with admiration the play of the great arms and shoulders. Seen now upon the land and standing at his full height

7

Willet was a giant, proportioned perfectly, a titanic figure fitted by nature to cope with the hardships and dangers of the wilderness.

"I'm thinking stronger than ever that this is good deer country," he said. "It has all the looks of it, since they can find here the food they like, and it hasn't been ranged over for a long time by white man or red. Tayoga, you and Robert oughtn't to be long in finding the game we want."

"I think like the Great Bear that we'll not have to look far for deer," said the Onondaga, "and I leave my rifle with you while I take my bow and arrows."

"I'll keep your rifle for you, Tayoga, and if I didn't have anything else to do I'd go along with you two lads and see you use the bow. I know that you're a regular king with it."

Tayoga said nothing, although he was secretly pleased with the compliment, and took from the canoe a long slender package, wrapped carefully in white, tanned deerskin, which he unrolled, disclosing the bow, waano.

The young Onondaga's bow, like everything he wore or used, was of the finest make, four feet in length, and of such powerful wood that only one of great strength and equal skill could bend it. He brought it to the proper curve with a sudden, swift effort, and strung it. There he tested the string with a quick sweeping motion of his hand, making it give back a sound like that of a violin, and seemed satisfied.

He also took from the canoe the quiver, gadasha, which was made of carefully dressed deerskin, elaborately decorated with the stained quills of the porcupine. It was two feet in length and contained twenty-five arrows, gano.

The arrows were three feet long, pointed with deer's horn, each carrying two feathers twisted about the shaft. They, like the bow and quiver, were fine specimens of workmanship and would have compared favorably with those used by the great English archers of the Middle Ages.

Tayoga examined the sharp tips of the arrows, and, poising the quiver over his left shoulder, fastened it on his back, securing the lower end at his waist with the sinews of the deer, and the upper with the same kind of cord, which he carried around the neck and then under his left arm. The ends of the arrows were thus convenient to his right hand, and with one sweeping circular motion he could draw them from the quiver and fit them to the bowstring.

The Iroquois had long since learned the use of the rifle and musket, but on occasion they still relied upon the bow, with which they had won their kingdom, the finest expanse of mountain and forest, lake and river, ever ruled over by man. Tayoga, as he strung his bow and hung his quiver, felt a great emotion, the spirit of his ancestors he would have called it, descending upon him. Waano and he fitted together and for the time he cherished it more than his rifle, the weapon that the white man had brought from another world. The feel of the wood in his hand made him see visions of a vast green wilderness in which the Indian alone roamed and knew no equal.

"What are you dreaming about, Tayoga?" asked Robert, who also dreamed dreams.

The Onondaga shook himself and laughed a little.

"Of nothing," he replied. "No, that was wrong. I was dreaming of the deer that we'll soon find. Come, Lennox, we'll go seek him."

"And while you're finding him," said Willet, "I'll be building the fire on which we'll cook the best parts of him."

Tayoga and Robert went together into the forest, the white youth taking with him his rifle, which, however, he did not expect to use. It was merely a precaution, as the Hurons, Abenakis, Caughnawagas and other tribes in the north were beginning to stir and mutter under the French influence. And for that reason, and because they did not wish to alarm possible game, the two went on silent foot.

No other human beings were present there, but the forest was filled with inhabitants, and hundreds of eyes regarded the red youth with the bow, and the white youth with the rifle, as they passed among the trees. Rabbits looked at them from small red eyes. A muskrat, at a brook's edge, gazed a moment and then dived from sight. A chipmunk cocked up his ears, listened and scuttled away.

But most of the population of the forest was in the trees. Squirrels chattering with anger at the invaders, or with curiosity about them, ran along the boughs, their bushy tails curving over their backs. A huge wildcat crouched in a fork, swelled with anger, his eyes reddening and his sharp claws thrusting forth as he looked at the two beings whom he instinctively hated much and feared more. The leaves swarmed with birds, robins and wrens and catbirds and all the feathered tribe keeping up an incessant quivering and trilling, while a distant woodpecker drummed portentously on the trunk of an old oak. They too saw the passing youths, but since no hand was raised to hurt them they sang, in their way, as they worked and played.

The wilderness spell was strong upon Tayoga, whose ancestors had lived unknown ages in the forest. The wind from the north as it rustled the leaves filled his strong lungs and made the great pulses leap. The bow in his hand fitted into the palm like a knife in its sheath. He heard the animals and the birds, and the sounds were those to which his ancestors had listened a thousand years and more. Once again he was proud of his heritage. He was Tayoga, a coming chief of the Clan of the Bear, of the nation Onondaga, of the League of the Hodenosaunee, and he would not exchange places with any man of whom he had heard in all the world.

The forest was the friend of Tayoga and he knew it. He could name the trees, the elm and the maple, and the spruce and the cedar and all the others. He knew the qualities of their wood and bark and the uses for which every one was best fitted. He noticed particularly the great maples, so precious to the Iroquois, from which they took sap and made sugar, and which gave an occasion and name to one of their most sacred festivals and dances. He also observed the trees from which the best bows and arrows were made, and the red elms and butternut hickories, the bark of which served the Iroquois for canoes.

When Tayoga passed through a forest it was not merely a journey, it was also an inspection. He had been trained from his baby frame, gaoseha, always to observe everything that met the human eye, and now he not only examined the trees, but also the brooks and the little ravines and the swell of the hills and the summits of the mountains that towered high, many miles away. If ever he came back there he would know the ground and all its marks.

His questing eye alighted presently upon the delicate traces of hoofs, and, calling Robert's attention, the two examined them with the full care demanded by their purpose.

"New," said Tayoga; "scarce an hour old."

"Less than that," said Robert. "The deer can't be far away."

"He is near, because there has been nothing to make him run. Here go the traces in almost a half circle. He is feeding and taking his time."

"It's a good chase to follow. The wind is blowing toward us, and he can take no alarm, unless he sees or hears us."

"It would be shame to an Onondaga if a deer heard him coming."

"You don't stand in any danger of being made ashamed, Tayoga. As you're to be the hunter, lead and I'll follow."

The Onondaga slipped through the undergrowth, and Robert, a skillful young woodsman also, came after with such care and lightness of foot that neither made a twig or leaf rustle. Tayoga always followed the traces. The deer had nibbled tender young shoots, but he had not remained long in one place. The forest was such an abundant garden to him that, fastidious as an epicure, he required the most delicate food to please his palate.

Tayoga stopped suddenly in a few minutes and raised his hand. Robert, following his gaze, saw a stag about a hundred yards away, a splendid fellow with head upraised, not in alarm, but to nuzzle some tender young leaves.

"I will go to the right," whispered the young warrior, "and will you, my friend, remain here?"

Robert nodded, and Tayoga slid silently among the bushes to secure a nearer and better position for aim. The Indian admired the stag which, like himself, fitted into the forest. He would not have hunted him for sport, nor at any other time would he have shot him, but food was needed and Manitou had sent the deer for that purpose. He was not one to oppose the will of Manitou.

The greatest bowman in the Northern wilderness crouched in the thicket, and reaching his right hand over his left shoulder, withdrew an arrow, which he promptly fitted to the string. It was a perfect arrow, made by the young chief himself, and the two feathers were curved in the right manner to secure the utmost degree of speed and accuracy. He fitted it to the string and drew the bow far back, almost to the head of the shaft. Now he was the hunter only and the spirit of hunting ancestors for many generations was poured into him. His eye followed the line of coming flight and he chose the exact spot on the sleek body beneath which the great heart lay.

The stag, with his head upraised, still pulled at the tender top of a bush, and the deceitful wind, which blew from him toward Tayoga, brought no warning. Nor did the squirrel chattering in the tree or the bird singing on the bough just over his head tell him that the hunter was near. Tayoga looked again down the arrow at the chosen place on the gleaming body of the deer, and with a sudden and powerful contraction of the muscles, bending the bow a little further, loosed the shaft.

The arrow flew singing through the air as swift and deadly as a steel dart and was buried in the heart of the stag, which, leaping upward, fell, writhed convulsively a moment or two, and died. The young Onondaga regarded his work a moment with satisfaction, and then walked forward, followed by his white comrade.

"One arrow was enough, Tayoga," said Robert, "and I knew before you shot that another would not be needed."

"The distance was not great," said Tayoga modestly. "I should have been a poor marksman had I missed."

He pulled his arrow with a great effort from the body of the deer, wiped it carefully upon the grass, and returned it to gadasha,

11

the quiver. Arrows required time and labor for the making, but unlike the powder and bullet in a rifle, they could be used often, and hence at times the bow had its advantage.

Then the two worked rapidly and skillfully with their great hunting knives, skinning and removing all the choicer portions of the deer, and before they finished they heard the pattering of light feet in the woods, accompanied now and then by an evil whine.

"The wolves come early," said Tayoga.

"And they're over hungry," said Robert, "or they wouldn't let us know so soon that they're in the thickets."

"It is told sometimes, among my people, that the soul of a wicked man has gone into the wolf," said Tayoga, not ceasing in his work, his shining blade flashing back and forth. "Then the wolf can understand what we say, although he may not speak himself."

"And suppose we kill such a wolf, Tayoga, what becomes of the wicked soul?"

"It goes at once into the body of another wolf, and passes on from wolf to wolf, being condemned to live in that foul home forever. Such a punishment is only for the most vile, and they are few. It is but the hundredth among the wicked who suffers thus."

"The other ninety-nine go after death to Hanegoategeh, the land of perpetual darkness, where they suffer in proportion to the crimes they committed on earth, but Hawenneyu, the Divine Being, takes pity on them and gives them another chance. When they have suffered long enough in Hanegoategeh to be purified he calls them before him and looks into their souls. Nothing can be hidden from him. He sees the evil thought, Lennox, as you or I would see a leaf upon the water, and then he judges. And he is merciful. He does not condemn and send to everlasting torture, because evil may yet be left in the soul, but if the good outweighs the bad the good shall prevail and the suffering soul is sent to Hawenneyugeh, the home of the just, where it suffers no more. But if the bad still outweighs the good then its chance is lost and it is sent to Hanishaonogeh, the home of the wicked, where it is condemned to torture forever."

"A reasonable religion, Tayoga. Your Hanegoategeh is like the purgatory, in which the Catholic church believes. Your God like ours is merciful, and the more I learn about your religion the more similar it seems to ours."

"I think your God and our Manitou are the same, Lennox, we only see him through different glasses, but our religion is old, old, very old, perhaps older than yours."

Although Tayoga did not raise his voice or change the inflection Robert knew that he spoke with great pride. The young Onondaga did not believe his religion resembled the white man's

12

but that the white man's resembled his. Robert respected him though, and knowing the reasons for his pride, said nothing in contradiction.

"The whining wolf is hungry," said Tayoga, "and since the soul of a warrior may dwell in his body I will feed him."

He took a discarded piece of the deer and threw it far into the bushes. A fearful growling, and the noise of struggling ensued at once.

"The wolf with the wicked soul in him may be there," said Robert, "but even so he has to fight with the other wolves for the meat you flung."

"It is a part of his fate," said Tayoga gravely. "Seeing and thinking as a man, he must yet bite and claw with beasts for his food. Now I think we have all of the deer we wish."

As they could not take it with them for tanning, they cut the skin in half, and each wrapped in his piece a goodly portion of the body to be carried to the canoe. Both were fastidious, wishing to get no stain upon their clothing, and, their task completed, they carefully washed their hands and knives at the edge of a brook. Then as they lifted up their burdens the whining and growling in the bushes increased rapidly.

"They see that we are going," said Tayoga. "The wolf even without the soul of a warrior in it knows much. It is the wisest of all the animals, unless the fox be its equal. The foolish bear and the mad panther fight alone, but the wolf, who is too small to face either, bands with his brothers into a league, even as the Hodenosaunee, and together they pull down the deer and the moose, and in the lands of the Ohio they dare to attack and slay the mighty bull buffalo."

"They know the strength of union, Tayoga, and they know, too, just now that they're safe from our weapons. I can see their noses poking already in their eagerness through the bushes. They're so hungry and so confident that they'll hardly wait until we get away."

As they passed with their burdens into the bushes on the far side of the little opening they heard a rush of light feet, and angry snarling. Looking back, Robert saw that the carcass of the stag was already covered with hungry wolves, every one fighting for a portion, and he knew it was the way of the forest.

CHAPTER II
ST. LUC

Willet hailed them joyfully when they returned.

"I'll wager that only one arrow was shot," he said, smiling.

"Just one," said Robert. "It struck the stag in the heart and he did not move ten feet from where he stood."

"And the Great Bear has the fire ready," said Tayoga. "I breathe the smoke."

"I knew you would notice it," said Willet, "although it's only a little fire yet and I've built it in a hollow."

Dry sticks were burning in a sunken place surrounded by great trees, and they increased the fire, veiling the smoke as much as possible. Then they broiled luscious steaks of the deer and ate abundantly, though without the appearance of eagerness. Robert had been educated carefully at Fort Orange, which men were now calling Albany, and Tayoga and the hunter were equally fastidious.

"The deer is the friend of both the red man and the white," said Willet, appreciatively. "In the woods he feeds us and clothes us, and then his horn tips the arrow with which you kill him, Tayoga."

"It was so ordered by Manitou," said the young Onondaga, earnestly. "The deer was given to us that we might live."

"And that being the case," said Willet, "we'll cook all you and Robert have brought and take it with us in the canoe. Since we keep on going north the time will come when we won't have any chance for hunting."

The fire had now formed a great bed of coals and the task was not hard. It was all cooked by and by and they stowed it away wrapped in the two pieces of skin. Then Willet and Tayoga decided to examine the country together, leaving Robert on guard beside the canoe.

Robert had no objection to remaining behind. Although circumstances had made him a lad of action he was also contemplative by nature. Some people think with effort, in others thoughts flow in a stream, and now as he sat with his back to a tree, much that he had thought and heard passed before him like a moving panorama and in this shifting belt of color Indians, Frenchmen, Colonials and Englishmen appeared.

He knew that he stood upon the edge of great events. Deeply sensitive to impressions, he felt that a crisis in North America was at

14

hand. England and France were not yet at war, and so the British colonies and the French colonies remained at peace too, but every breeze that blew from one to the other was heavy with menace. The signs were unmistakable, but one did not have to see. One breathed it in at every breath. He knew, too, that intrigue was already going on all about him, and that the Iroquois were the great pawn in the game. British and French were already playing for the favor of the powerful Hodenosaunee, and Robert understood even better than many of those in authority that as the Hodenosaunee went so might go the war. It was certain that the Indians of the St. Lawrence and the North would be with the French, but he was confident that the Indians of the Long House would not swerve from their ancient alliance with the British colonies.

Two hours passed and Willet and Tayoga did not return, but he had not expected them. He knew that when they decided to go on a scout they would do the work thoroughly, and he waited with patience, sitting beside the canoe, his rifle on his knees. Before him the creek flowed with a pleasant, rippling noise and through the trees he caught a glimpse of the lake, unruffled by any wind.

The rest was so soothing, and his muscles and nerves relaxed so much that he felt like closing his eyes and going to sleep, but he was roused by the sound of a footstep. It was so distant that only an ear trained to the forest would have heard it, but he knew that it was made by a human being approaching, and that the man was neither Willet nor Tayoga.

He put his ear to the earth and heard three men instead of one, and then he rose, cocking his rifle. In the great wilderness in those surcharged days a stranger was an enemy until he was proved to be otherwise, and the lad was alert in every faculty. He saw them presently, three figures walking in Indian file, and his heart leaped because the leader was so obviously a Frenchman.

His uniform was of the battalion Royal Roussillon, white faced with blue, and his hat was black and three-cornered, but face and manner were so unmistakably French that Robert did not think of his uniform, which was neat and trim to a degree not to be expected in the forest. He bore himself in the carelessly defiant manner peculiar to the French cadets and younger sons of noble families in North America at the time, an accentuation of the French at home, and to some extent a survival of the spirit which Richelieu partially checked. Even in the forest he wore a slender rapier at his belt, and his hand rested now upon its golden hilt.

He was about thirty years old, tall, slender, and with the light hair and blue eyes seen so often in Northern France, telling, perhaps, of Norman blood. His glance was apparently light, but Robert felt when it rested upon him that it was sharp, penetrating and hard to endure. Nevertheless he met it without lowering his own gaze. The man behind the leader was swart, short, heavy and of middle years, a Canadian dressed in deerskin and armed with rifle, hatchet and knife. The third man was an Indian, one of the most extraordinary figures that Robert had ever seen. He was of great stature and heavy build, his shoulders and chest immense and covered with knotted muscles, disclosed to the eye, as he was bare to the waist. All the upper part of his body was painted in strange and hideous designs which Robert did not recognize, although he knew the fashions of all the tribes in the New York and St. Lawrence regions. His cheek bones were unusually high even for an Indian and his gaze was heavy, keen and full of challenge. Robert judged that he belonged to some western tribe, that he was a Pottawatomie, an Ojibway or a Chippewa or that perhaps he came from the distant Sioux race.

He was conscious that all three represented strength, each in a different way, and he felt the gaze of three pairs of eyes resting upon him in a manner that contained either secret or open hostility. But he faced them boldly, a gallant and defiant young figure himself, instinct with courage and an intellectual quality that is superior to courage itself. The Frenchman who confronted him recognized at once the thinker.

"I bid you good day," said Robert politely. "I did not expect to meet travelers in these woods."

The Frenchman smiled.

"We are all travelers," he said, "but it is you who are our guest, since these rivers and mountains and lakes and forests acknowledge the suzerainty of my royal master, King Louis of France."

His tone was light and bantering and Robert, seeing the advantage of it, chose to speak in the same vein.

"The wilderness itself is king," he said, "and it acknowledges no master, save perhaps the Hodenosaunee. But I had thought that the law of England ran here, at least where white men are concerned."

He saw the eyes of the great savage flash when he mentioned the Hodenosaunee, and he inferred at once that he was a bitter enemy of the Iroquois. Some of the tribes had a hereditary hatred toward one another more ferocious than that which they felt against the whites.

The Frenchman smiled again, and swept his hand in a graceful curve toward the green expanse.

16

"It is true," he said, "that the forest is yet lord over these lands, but in the future I think the lilies of France will wave here. You perhaps have an equal faith that the shadow of the British flag will be over the wilderness, but it would be most unfitting for you and me to quarrel about it now. I infer from the canoe and the three paddles that you did not come here alone."

"Two friends are with me. They have gone into the forest on a brief expedition. They should return soon. We have food in abundance, a deer that we killed a few hours ago. Will you share it?"

"Gladly. Courtesy, I see, is not lost in the woods. Permit me to introduce ourselves. The chief is Tandakora of the Ojibways, from the region about the great western lake that you call Superior. He is a mighty warrior, and his fame is great, justly earned in many a battle. My friend in deerskin is Armand Dubois, born a Canadian of good French stock, and a most valiant and trustworthy man. As for me, I am Raymond Louis de St. Luc, Chevalier of France and soldier of fortune in the New World. And now you know the list of us. It's not so long as Homer's catalogue of the ships, nor so interesting, but it's complete."

His manner had remained light, almost jesting, and Robert judged that it was habitual with him like a cloak in winter, and, like the cloak, it would be laid away when it was not needed. The man's blue eyes, even when he used the easy manner of the high-bred Frenchman, were questing and resolute. But the youth still found it easier than he had thought to meet him in like fashion. Now he replied to frankness with frankness.

"Ours isn't and shouldn't be a hostile meeting in the forest, Chevalier de St. Luc," he said. "To you and your good friends I offer my greetings. As for myself, I am Robert Lennox, with two homes, one in Albany, and the other in the wilderness, wherever I choose to make it."

He paused a moment, because he felt the gaze of St. Luc upon him, very intent and penetrating, but in an instant he resumed:

"I came here with two friends whom you shall see if you stay with me long enough. One is David Willet, a hunter and scout, well known from the Hudson to the Great Lakes, a man to whom I owe much, one who has stood to me almost in the place of a father. The other I can truly call a brother. He is Tayoga, a young warrior of the clan of the Bear, of the nation Onondaga, of the League of the Hodenosaunee. My catalogue, sir, is just the same length as yours, and it also is complete."

The Chevalier Raymond Louis de St. Luc laughed, and the laugh was genuine.

"A youth of spirit, I see," he said. "Well, I am glad. It's a pleasure to meet with wit and perception in the wilderness. One prefers to talk with gentlemen. 'Tis said that the English are heavy, but I do not always find them so. Perhaps it's merely a slur that one nation wishes to cast upon another."

"It's scarcely correct to call me English," said Robert, "since I am a native of this country, and the term American applies more properly."

The eyes of St. Luc glistened.

"I note the spirit," he said. "The British colonies left to themselves grow strong and proud, while ours, drawing their strength from the King and the government, would resent being called anything but Frenchmen. Now, I'll wager you a louis against any odds that you'll claim the American to be as good as the Englishman anywhere and at any time."

"Certainly!" said Robert, with emphasis.

St. Luc laughed again and with real pleasure, his blue eyes dancing and his white teeth flashing.

"And some day that independence will cause trouble for the good British mother," he said, "but we'll pass from the future to the present. Sit down, Tandakora, and you too, Dubois. Monsieur Lennox is, for the present, our host, and that too in the woods we claim to be our own. But we are none the less grateful for his hospitality."

Robert unwrapped the venison and cut off large slices as he surmised that all three were hungry. St. Luc ate delicately but the other two did not conceal their pleasure in food. Robert now and then glanced a little anxiously at the woods, hoping his comrades would return. He did not know exactly how to deal with the strangers and he would find comfort in numbers. He was conscious, too, that St. Luc was watching him all the time intently, reading his expression and looking into his thoughts.

"How are the good Dutch burghers at Albany?" asked the chevalier. "I don't seek to penetrate any of your secrets. I merely make conversation."

"I reveal nothing," replied Robert, "when I say they still barter with success and enjoy the pleasant ways of commerce. I am not one to underrate the merchant. More than the soldier they build up a nation."

"It's a large spirit that can put the trade of another before one's own, because I am a soldier, and you, I judge, will become one if you are not such now. Peace, Tandakora, it is doubtless the friends of Monsieur Lennox who come!"

The gigantic Indian had risen suddenly and had thrust forward the good French musket that he carried. Robert had never beheld a more sinister figure. The lips were drawn back a little from his long white teeth and his eyes were those of a hunter who sought to kill for the sake of killing. But at the chiding words of St. Luc the tense muscles relaxed and he lowered the weapon. Robert was compelled to notice anew the great influence the French had acquired over the Indians, and he recognized it with dread, knowing what it might portend.

The footsteps which the savage had heard first were now audible to him, and he stood up, knowing that Tayoga and Willet were returning, and he was glad of it.

"My friends are here," he said.

The Chevalier de St. Luc, with his customary politeness, rose to his feet and Dubois rose with him. The Ojibway remained sitting, a huge piece of deer meat in his hand. Tayoga and Willet appeared through the bushes, and whatever surprise they may have felt they concealed it well. The faces of both were a blank.

"Guests have come since your departure," said Robert, with the formal politeness of the time. "These gentlemen are the Chevalier Raymond Louis de St. Luc, from Quebec, Monsieur Armand Dubois, from the same place, I presume, and Tandakora, a mighty Ojibway chief, who, it seems, has wandered far from his own country, on what errand I know not. Chevalier my friends of whom I spoke, Mr. David Willet, the great hunter, and Tayoga of the clan of the Bear, of the nation Onondaga, of the League of the Hodenosaunee, my brother of the forest and a great chief."

He spoke purposely with sonority, and also with a tinge of satire, particularly when he alluded to the presence of Tandakora at such a great distance from his tribe. But St. Luc, of course, though noticing it, ignored it in manner. He extended his hand promptly to the great hunter who grasped it in his mighty palm and shook it.

"I have heard of you, Mr. Willet," he said. "Our brave Canadians are expert in the forest and the chase, and the good Dubois here is one of the best, but I know that none of them can excel you."

Robert, watching him, could not say that he spoke without sincerity, and Willet took the words as they were uttered.

"I've had a long time for learning," he said modestly, "and I suppose experience teaches the dullest of us."

Robert saw that the Ojibway had now risen and that he and the Onondaga were regarding each other with a gaze so intent and fierce, so compact of hatred that he was startled and his great pulses began to beat hard. But it was only for an instant or two that the two warriors looked thus into hostile eyes. Then both sat down and their faces became blank and expressionless.

The gaze of St. Luc roved to the Onondaga and rested longest upon him. Robert saw the blue eyes sparkle, and he knew that the mind of the chevalier was arrested by some important thought. He could almost surmise what it was, but for the present he preferred to keep silent and watch, because his curiosity was great and natural, and he wondered what St. Luc would say next.

The Onondaga and the hunter sat down on a fallen tree trunk and inspected the others with a quiet but observant gaze. Each in his own way had the best of manners. Tayoga, as became a forest chief, was dignified, saying little, while Willet cut more slices from the deer meat and offered them to the guests. But it was the Onondaga and not St. Luc who now spoke first.

"The son of Onontio wanders far," he said. "It is a march of many days from here to Quebec."

"It is, Tayoga," replied St. Luc gravely, "but the dominions of the King of France, whom Onontio serves, also extend far."

It was a significant speech, and Robert glanced at Tayoga, but the eyes of the young chief were veiled. If he resented the French claim to the lands over which the Hodenosaunee hunted it was in silence. St. Luc paused, as if for an answer, but none coming he continued:

"Shadows gather over the great nations beyond the seas. The French king and the English king begin to look upon each other with hostile eyes."

Tayoga was silent.

"But Onontio, who stands in the French king's place at Quebec, is the friend of the Hodenosaunee. The French and the great Six Nations are friends."

"There was Frontenac," said Tayoga quietly.

"It was long ago."

"He came among us when the Six Nations were the Five, burned our houses and slew our warriors! Our old men have told how they heard it from their fathers. We did not have guns then, and our bows and arrows were not a match for the muskets of the French. But we have muskets and rifles now, plenty of them, the best that are made."

Tayoga's eyes were still veiled, and his face was without expression, but his words were full of meaning. Robert glanced at St. Luc, who could not fail to understand. The chevalier was still smooth and smiling.

"Frontenac was a great man," he said, "but he has been gathered long since to his fathers. Great men themselves make mistakes. There was bad blood between Onontio and the Hodenosaunee, but if the blood is bad must it remain bad forever? The evil was gone before you and I were born, Tayoga, and now the blood flows pure and clean in the veins of both the French and the Hodenosaunee."

"The Hodenosaunee and Corlear have no quarrel."

"Nor have the Hodenosaunee and Onontio. Behold how the English spread over the land, cut down the forests and drive away all the game! But the children of Onontio hunt with the Indians, marry with their women, leave the forests untouched, and the great hunting grounds swarm with game as before. While Onontio abides at Quebec the lands of the Hodenosaunee are safe."

"There was Frontenac," repeated Tayoga.

St. Luc frowned at the insistence of the Onondaga upon an old wound, but the cloud passed swiftly. In an instant the blue eyes were smiling once more.

"The memory of Frontenac shall not come between us," he said. "The heart of Onontio beats for the Hodenosaunee, and he has sent me to say so to the valiant League. I bring you a belt, a great belt of peace."

Dubois handed him a large knapsack and he took from it a beautiful belt of pure white wampum, uncommon in size, a full five feet in length, five inches wide, and covered with many thousands of beads, woven in symbolic figures. He held it up and the eyes of the Onondaga glistened.

"It is a great belt, a belt of peace," continued St. Luc. "There is none nobler, and Onontio would send no other kind. I give it to you, Tayoga."

The young warrior drew back and his hands remained at his sides.

"I am Tayoga, of the clan of the Bear, of the nation Onondaga, of the great League of the Hodenosaunee," he said, "but I am not yet a chief. My years are too few. It is a great matter of which you speak, St. Luc, and it must be laid before the fifty sachems of the allied tribes in the Long House. The belt may be offered to them. I cannot take it."

The flitting cloud passed again over the face of St. Luc, but he did not allow any change to show in his manner. He returned the splendid belt to Dubois, who folded it carefully and put it back in the great knapsack.

"Doubtless you are right, Tayoga," he said. "I shall go to the

Long House with the belt, but meantime we thank you for the courtesy of yourself and your friends. You have given us food when we were hungry, and a Frenchman does not forget."

"The Onondagas keep the council fire in their valley, and the sachems will gather there," said Tayoga.

"Where they will receive the belt of peace that I shall offer them," said St. Luc.

The Onondaga was silent. St. Luc, who had centered his attention upon Tayoga, now turned it to Robert.

"Mr. Lennox," he said, "we dwell in a world of alarms, and I am French and you are English, or rather American, but I wish that you and I could remain friends."

The frankness and obvious sincerity of his tone surprised Robert. He knew now that he liked the man. He felt that there was steel in his composition, and that upon occasion, and in the service to which he belonged, he could be hard and merciless, but the spirit seemed bright and gallant.

"I know nothing that will keep us from being friends," replied the lad, although he knew well what the Frenchman meant.

"Nor do I," said St. Luc. "It was merely a casual reference to the changes that affect us all. I shall come to Albany some day, Mr. Lennox. It is an interesting town, though perhaps somewhat staid and sober."

"If you come," said Robert sincerely, "I hope I shall be there, and it would please me to have you as a guest."

St. Luc gave him a sharp, examining look.

"I believe you mean it," he said. "It's possible that you and I are going to see much of each other. One can never tell what meetings time will bring about. And now having accepted your hospitality and thanking you for it, we must go."

He rose. Dubois, who had not spoken at all, threw over his shoulder the heavy knapsack, and the Ojibway also stood up, gigantic and sinister.

"We go to the Vale of Onondaga," said St. Luc, turning his attention back to Tayoga, "and as you advised I shall lay the peace belt before the fifty sachems of the Hodenosaunee, assembled in council in the Long House."

"Go to the southwest," said Tayoga, "and you will find the great trail that leads from the Hudson to the mighty lakes of the west. The warriors of the Hodenosaunee have trod it for generations, and it is open to the son of Onontio."

The young Indian's face was a mask, but his words and their tone alike were polite and dignified. St. Luc bowed, and then bowed to the others in turn.

"At Albany some day," he said to young Lennox, and his smile was very winning.

"At Albany some day," repeated Robert, and he hoped the prophecy would come true.

Then St. Luc turned away, followed by the Canadian, with the Indian in the rear. None of the three looked back and the last Robert saw of them was a fugitive gleam of the chevalier's white uniform through the green leaves of the forest. Then the mighty wilderness swallowed them up, as a pebble is lost in a lake. Robert looked awhile in the direction in which they had gone, still seeing them in fancy.

"How much does their presence here signify?" he asked thoughtfully.

"They would have the Hodenosaunee to forget Frontenac," replied Tayoga.

"And will the Six Nations forget him?"

"The fifty sachems in council alone can tell."

Robert saw that the young Onondaga would not commit himself, even to him, and he did not ask anything more, but the hunter spoke plainly.

"We must wake up those fat Indian commissioners at Albany," he said. "Those Dutchmen think more of cheating the tribes than they do of the good of either white man or red man, but I can tell you, Robert, and you too, Tayoga, that I'm worried about that Frenchman coming down here among the Six Nations. He's as sharp as a razor, and as quick as lightning. I could see that, and there's mischief brewing. He's not going to the Onondaga Valley for nothing."

"Tandakora, the Ojibway, goes with a heavy foot," said the Onondaga.

"What do you mean, Tayoga?" asked Willet.

"He comes of a savage tribe, which is hostile to the Hodenosaunee and all white men. He has seen three scalps which still grow on the heads of their owners."

"Which means that he might not keep on following St. Luc. Well, we'll be on our guard and now I don't see any reason why we should stay here longer."

"Nor I," said Robert, and, Tayoga agreeing with them, they returned the canoe to the stream, paddling back into the lake, and continuing their course until they came to its end. There they carried the canoe across a portage and launched it on a second lake as beautiful as the first. None of the three spoke much now, their minds being filled with thoughts of St. Luc and his companions.

They were yet on the water when the day began to wane. The green forest on the high western shore was touched with flame from the setting sun. Then the surface of the lake blazed with red light, and in the east the gray of twilight came.

"It will be night in half an hour," said Robert, "and I think we'd better make a landing, and camp."

"Here's a cove on the right," said Willet. "We'll take the canoe up among the trees, and wrap ourselves in our blankets. It's a good thing we have them, as the darkness is going to bring a chill with it."

They found good shelter among the trees and bushes, a small hollow protected by great trees and undergrowth, into which they carried the canoe.

"Since it's not raining this is as good as a house for us," said Willet.

"I think it's better," said Robert. "The odor of spruce and hemlock is so wonderful I wouldn't like to have it shut away from me by walls."

The Onondaga drew in deep inhalations of the pure, healing air, and as his black eyes gleamed he walked to the edge of the little hollow and looked out in the dusk over the vast tangled wilderness of mountain and lake, forest and river. The twilight was still infused with the red from the setting sun, and in the glow the whole world was luminous and glorified. Now the eyes of Tayoga, which had flashed but lately, gave back the glow in a steady flame.

"Hawenneyu, the Divine Being whom all the red people worship, made many great lands," he said, "but he spent his work and love upon that which lies between the Hudson and the vast lakes of the west. Then he rested and looking upon what he had done he was satisfied because he knew it to be the best in all the world, created by him."

"How do you know it to be the best, Tayoga?" asked Willet. "You haven't seen all the countries. You haven't been across the sea."

"Because none other can be so good," replied the Iroquois with simple faith. "When Hawenneyu, in your language the Great Spirit, found the land that he had made so good he did not know then to whom to give it, but in the greatness of his wisdom he left it to those who were most fitted to come and take it. And in time came the tribes which Tododaho, helped by Hayowentha, often called by the English Hiawatha, formed into the great League of the Hodenosaunee, and because they were brave and far-seeing and abided by the laws of Tododaho and Hayowentha, they took the land which they have kept ever since, and which they will keep forever."

24

"I like your good, strong beliefs, Tayoga," said the hunter heartily. "The country does belong to the Iroquois, and if it was left to me to decide about it they'd keep it till the crack of doom. Now you boys roll in your blankets. I'll take the first watch, and when it's over I'll call one of you."

But Tayoga waited a little until the last glow of the sun died in the west, looking intently where the great orb had shone. Into his religion a reverence for the sun, Giver of Light and Warmth, entered, and not until the last faint radiance from it was gone did he turn away.

Then he took from the canoe and unfolded eyose, his blanket, which was made of fine blue broadcloth, thick and warm but light, six feet long and four feet wide. It was embroidered around the edges with another cloth in darker blue, and the body of it bore many warlike or hunting designs worked skillfully in thread. If the weather were cold Tayoga would drape the blanket about his body much like a Roman toga, and if he lay in the forest at night he would sleep in it. Now he raked dead leaves together, spread the blanket on them, lay on one half of it and used the other half as a cover.

Robert imitated him, but his blanket was not so fine as Tayoga's, although he found it soft and warm enough. Willet sat on a log higher up, his rifle across his knees and gazed humorously at them.

"You two lads look pretty snug down there," he said, "and after all you're only lads. Tayoga may have a head plumb full of the wisdom of the wilderness, and Robert may have a head stuffed with different kinds of knowledge, but you're young, mighty young, anyhow. An' now, as I'm watching over you, I'll give a prize to the one that goes to sleep first."

In three minutes deep regular breathing showed that both had gone to the land of slumber, and Willet could not decide which had led the way. The darkness increased so much that their figures looked dim in the hollow, but he glanced at them occasionally. The big man had many friends, but young Lennox and Tayoga were almost like sons to him, and he was glad to be with them now. He felt that danger lurked in the northern wilderness, and three were better than two.

CHAPTER III
THE TOMAHAWK

Willet awakened Robert about two o'clock in the morning—it was characteristic of him to take more than his share of the work—and the youth stood up, with his rifle in the hollow of his arm, ready at once.

"Tayoga did more yesterday than either of us," said the hunter, "and so we'll let him sleep."

But the Onondago had awakened, though he did not move. Forest discipline was perfect among them, and, knowing that it was Robert's time to watch, he wasted no time in vain talk about it. His eyes closed again and he returned to sleep as the white lad walked up the bank, while the hunter was soon in the dreams that Tarenyawagon, who makes them, sent to him.

Robert on the bank, although he expected no danger, was alert. He had plenty of wilderness skill and his senses, naturally acute, had been trained so highly that he could discern a hostile approach in the darkness. The same lore of the forest told him to keep himself concealed, and he sat on a fallen tree trunk between two bushes that hid him completely, although his own good eyes, looking through the leaves, could see a long distance, despite the night.

It was inevitable as he sat there in the silence and darkness with his sleeping comrades below that his thoughts should turn to St. Luc. He had recognized in the first moment of their meeting that the young Frenchman was a personality. He was a personality in the sense that Tayoga was, one who radiated a spirit or light that others were compelled to notice. He knew that there was no such thing as looking into the future, but he felt with conviction that this man was going to impinge sharply upon his life, whether as a friend or an enemy not even Tarenyawagon, who sent the dreams, would tell, but he could not be insensible to the personal charm of the Chevalier Raymond Louis de St. Luc.

What reception would the fifty sachems give to the belt that the chevalier would bring? Would they be proof against his lightness, his ease, his fluency and his ability to paint a glowing picture of French might and French gratitude? Robert knew far better than most of his own race the immensity of the stake. He who roamed the forest with Tayoga and the Great Bear understood to the full the power of the Hodenosaunee. It was true, too, that the Indian commissioners at Albany had not done their duty and had given the Indians just cause of complaint, at the very moment when the great League should be propitiated. Yet the friendship between the Iroquois and the English had been ancient and strong, and he would not have feared so much had it been any other than St. Luc who was going to meet the sachems in council.

Robert shook his head as if the physical motion would dismiss his apprehensions, and walked farther up the hill to a point where he could see the lake. A light wind was blowing, and little waves of crumbling silver pursued one another across its surface. On the far side the bank, crowned with dense forest showing black in the dusk, rose to a great height, but the lad's eyes came back to the water, his heart missing a beat as he thought he saw a shadow on its surface, but so near the opposite shore that it almost merged with a fringe of bushes there.

Then he rebuked himself for easy alarm. It was merely the reflection from a bough above in the water below. Yet it played tricks with him. The shadow reappeared again and again, always close to the far bank, but there were many boughs also to reproduce themselves in the mirror of the lake. He convinced himself that his eyes and his mind were having sport with him, and turning away, he made a little circle in the woods about their camp. All was well. He heard a swish overhead, but he knew that it was a night bird, a rustling came, and an ungainly form lumbered through a thicket, but it was a small black bear, and coming back to the hollow, he looked down at his comrades.

Tayoga and Willet slept well. Neither had stirred, and wrapped in their blankets lying on the soft leaves, they were true pictures of forest comfort. They were fine and loyal comrades, as good as anybody ever had, and he was glad they were so near, because he began to have a feeling now that something unusual was going to occur. The shadows on the lake troubled him again, and he went back for another look. He did not see them now, and that, too, troubled him. It proved that they had been made by some moving object, and not by the boughs and bushes still there.

Robert examined the lake, his eyes following the line where the far bank met the water, but he saw no trace of anything moving, and his attention came back to the woods in which he stood. Presently, he crouched in dense bush, and concentrated all his powers of hearing, knowing that he must rely upon ear rather than eye. He could not say that he had really seen or heard, but he had felt that something was moving in the forest, something that threatened him.

His first impulse was to go back to the little hollow and awaken his comrades, but his second told him to stay where he was until the danger came or should pass, and he crouched lower in the undergrowth with his hand on the hammer and trigger of his rifle. He did not stir or make any noise for a long time. The forest, too, was silent. The wind that had ruffled the surface of the lake ceased, and the leaves over his head were still.

But he understood too well the ways of the wilderness to move yet. He did not believe that his faculties, attuned to the slightest alarm, had deceived him, and he had learned the patience of the Indian from the Iroquois themselves. His eyes continually pierced the thickets for a hostile object moving there, and his ears were ready to notice the sound of a leaf should it fall.

He heard, or thought he heard after a while, a slight sliding motion, like that which a great serpent would make as it drew its glistening coils through leaves or grass. But it was impossible for him to tell how near it was to him or from what point it came, and his blood became chill in his veins. He was not afraid of a danger seen, but when it came intangible and invisible the boldest might shudder.

The noise, real or imaginary, ceased, and as he waited he became convinced that it was only his strained fancy. A man might mistake the blood pounding in his ears or the beat of his own pulse for a sound without, and after another five minutes, taking the rifle from the hollow of his arm, he stood upright. Certainly nothing was moving in the forest. The leaves hung lifeless. His fancies had been foolish.

He stepped boldly from the undergrowth in which he had knelt, and a glimpse of a flitting shadow made him kneel again. It was instinct that caused him to drop down so quickly, but he knew that it had saved his life. Something glittering whistled where his head had been, and then struck with a sound like a sigh against the trunk of a tree.

Robert sank from his knees, until he lay almost fiat, and brought his rifle forward for instant use. But, for a minute or two, he would not have been steady enough to aim at anything. His tongue was dry in his mouth, and his hair lifted a little at his marvelous escape.

He looked for the shadow, his eyes searching every thicket; but he did not find it, and now he believed that the one who had sped the blow had gone, biding his time for a second chance.

Another wait to make sure, and hurrying to the hollow he awoke Tayoga and the hunter, who returned at once with him to the place where the ambush had miscarried.

"Ah!" said the Onondaga, as they looked about. "Osquesont! Behold!"

The blade of an Indian tomahawk, osquesont, was buried deep in the trunk of a tree, and Robert knew that the same deadly weapon had whistled where his head had been but a second before. He shuddered. Had it not been for his glimpse of the flitting shadow his head would have been cloven to the chin. Tayoga, with a mighty wrench, pulled out the tomahawk and examined it. It was somewhat heavier than the usual weapon of the type and he pronounced it of French make.

"Did it come from Quebec, Tayoga?" asked Willet.

"Perhaps," replied the young warrior, "but I saw it yesterday."

"You did! Where?"

"In the belt of Tandakora, the Ojibway."

"I thought so," said Robert.

"And he threw it with all the strength of a mighty arm," said the Onondaga. "There is none near us in the forest except Tandakora who could bury it so deep in the tree. It was all I could do to pull it out again."

"And seeing his throw miss he slipped away as fast as he could!" said Willet.

"Yes, Great Bear, the Ojibway is cunning. After hurling the tomahawk he would not stay to risk a shot from Lennox. He was willing even to abandon a weapon which he must have prized. Ah, here is his trail! It leads through the forest toward the lake!"

They were able to follow it a little distance but it was lost on the hard ground, although it led toward the water. Robert told of the shadow he had seen near the farther bank, and both Willet and Tayoga were quite sure it had been a small canoe, and that its occupant was Tandakora.

"It's not possible that St. Luc sent the Ojibway back to murder us!" exclaimed Robert, his mind rebelling at the thought.

"I don't think it likely," said Willet, but the Onondaga was much more emphatic.

"The Ojibway came of his own wish," he said. "While the sons of Onontio slept he slipped away, and it was the lure of scalps that drew him. He comes of a savage tribe far in the west. An Iroquois would have scorned such treachery."

Robert felt an immense relief. He had become almost as jealous of the Frenchman's honor as of his own, and knowing that

29

Tayoga understood his race, he accepted his words as final. It was hideous to have the thought in his mind, even for a moment, that a man who had appeared so gallant and friendly as St. Luc had sent a savage back to murder them.

"The French do not control the western tribes," continued Tayoga, "though if war comes they will be on the side of Onontio, but as equals they will come hither and go thither as they please."

"Which means, I take it," said the hunter, "that if St. Luc discovers what Tandakora has been trying to do here tonight he'll be afraid to find much fault with it, because the Ojibway and all the other Ojibways would go straight home?"

"It is so," said the Onondaga.

"Well, we're thankful that his foul blow went wrong. You've had a mighty narrow escape, Robert, my lad, but we've gained one good tomahawk which, you boys willing, I mean to take."

Tayoga handed it to him, and with an air of satisfaction he put the weapon in his belt.

"I may have good use for it some day," he said. "The chance may come for me to throw it back to the savage who left it here. And now, as our sleep is broken up for the night, I think we'd better scout the woods a bit, and then come back here for breakfast."

They found nothing hostile in the forest, and when they returned to the hollow the thin gray edge of dawn showed on the far side of the lake. Having no fear of further attack, they lighted a small fire and warmed their food. As they ate day came in all its splendor and Robert saw the birds flashing back and forth in the thick leaves over his head.

"Where did the Ojibway get his canoe?" he asked.

"The Frenchmen like as not used it when they came down from Canada," replied the hunter, "and left it hid to be used again when they went back. It won't be worth our while to look for it. Besides, we've got to be moving soon."

After breakfast they carried their own canoe to the lake and paddled northward to its end. Then they took their craft a long portage across a range of hills and launched it anew on a swift stream flowing northward, on the current of which they traveled until nightfall, seeing throughout that time no sign of a human being. It was the primeval wilderness, and since it lay between the British colonies on the south and the French on the north it had been abandoned almost wholly in the last year or two, letting the game, abundant at any time, increase greatly. They saw deer in the thickets, they heard the splash of a beaver, and a black bear, sitting on a tiny island in the river, watched them as they passed.

On the second day after Robert's escape from the tomahawk they left the river, made a long portage and entered another river, also flowing northward, having in mind a double purpose, to throw off the trail anyone who might be following them and to obtain a more direct course toward their journey's end. Knowing the dangers of the wilderness, they also increased their caution, traveling sometimes at night and lying in camp by day.

But they lived well. All three knew the importance of preserving their strength, and to do so an abundance of food was the first requisite. Tayoga shot another deer with the bow and arrow, and with the use of fishing tackle which they had brought in the canoe they made the river pay ample tribute. They lighted the cooking fires, however, in the most sheltered places they could find, and invariably extinguished them as soon as possible.

"You can't be too careful in the woods," said Willet, "especially in times like these. While the English and French are not yet fighting there's always danger from the savages."

"The warriors from the wild tribes in Canada and the west will take a scalp wherever there's a chance," said the young Onondaga.

Robert often noticed the manner in which Tayoga spoke of the tribes outside the great League. To him those that did not belong to the Hodenosaunee, while they might be of the same red race, were nevertheless inferior. He looked upon them as an ancient Greek looked upon those who were not Greeks.

"The French are a brave people," said the hunter, "but the most warlike among them if they knew our errand would be willing for some of their painted allies to drop us in the wilderness, and no questions would be asked. You can do things on the border that you can't in the towns. We might be tomahawked in here and nobody would ever know what became of us."

"I think," said Tayoga, "that our danger increases. Tandakora after leaving the son of Onontio, St. Luc, might not go back to him. He might fear the anger of the Frenchman, and, too, he would still crave a scalp. A warrior has followed an enemy for weeks to obtain such a trophy."

"You believe then," said Robert, "that the Ojibway is still on our trail?"

Tayoga nodded. After a moment's silence he added:

"We come, too, to a region in which the St. Regis, the Caughnawaga, the Ottawa and the Micmac, all allies of Onontio, hunt. The Ojibway may meet a band and tell the warriors we are in the woods."

31

His look was full of significance and Robert understood thoroughly.

"I shall be glad," he said, "when we reach the St. Lawrence. We'll then be in real Canada, and, while the French are undoubtedly our enemies, we'll not be exposed to treacherous attack."

They were in the canoe as they talked and Tayoga was paddling, the swiftness of the current now making the efforts of only one man necessary. A few minutes later he turned the canoe to the shore and the three got out upon the bank. Robert did not know why, but he was quite sure the reason was good.

"Falls below," said Tayoga, as they drew the canoe upon the land. "All the river drops over a cliff. Much white water."

They carried the canoe without difficulty through the woods, and when they came to the falls they stopped a little while to look at the descent, and listen to the roar of the tumbling water.

"I was here once before, three years ago," said Willet.

"Others have been here much later," said the Onondaga.

"What do you mean, Tayoga?"

"My white brother is not looking. Let him turn his eyes to the left. He will see two wild flowers broken off at the stem, a feather which has not fallen from the plumage of a bird, because the quill is painted, and two traces of footsteps in the earth."

"As surely as the sun shines, you're right, Tayoga! Warriors have passed here, though we can't tell how many! But the traces are not more'n a half day old."

He picked up the feather and examined it carefully.

"That fell from a warrior's scalplock," he said, "but we don't know to what tribe the warrior belonged."

"But it's likely to be a hostile trail," said Robert.

Tayoga nodded, and then the three considered. It was only a fragment of a trail they had seen, but it told them danger was near. Where they were traveling strangers were enemies until they were proved to be friends, and the proof had to be of the first class, also. They agreed finally to turn aside into the woods with the canoe, and stop until night. Then under cover of the friendly darkness they would resume their journey on the river.

They chose the heavily wooded crest of a low hill for the place in which to wait, because they could see some distance from it and remain unseen. They put the canoe down there and Robert and Tayoga sat beside it, while Willet went into the woods to see if any further signs of a passing band could be discovered, returning in an hour with the information that he had discovered more footprints.

"All led to the north," he said, "and they're well ahead of us.

32

There's no reason why we can't follow. We're three, used to the wilderness, armed well and able to take care of ourselves. And I take it the night will be dark, which ought to help us."

The Onondaga looked up at the skies, which were of a salmon color, and shook his head a little.

"What's the matter?" asked Robert.

"The night will bring much darkness," he replied, "but it will bring something else with it—wind, rain."

"You may be right, Tayoga, but we must be moving, just the same," said Willet.

At dusk they were again afloat on the river and, all three using the paddles, they sent the canoe forward with great speed. But it soon became apparent that Tayoga's prediction would be justified. Clouds trailed up from the southwest and obscured all the heavens. A wind arose and it was heavy and damp upon their faces. The water seemed black as ink. Low thunder far away began to mutter. The wilderness became uncanny and lonely. All save forest rovers would have been appalled, and of these three one at least felt that the night was black and sinister. Robert looked intently at the forest on either shore, rising now like solid black walls, but his eyes, unable to penetrate them, found nothing there. Then the lightning flamed in the west, and for a moment the surface of the river was in a blaze.

"What do you think of it, Tayoga?" asked Willet, anxiety showing in his tone, "Ought we to make a landing now?"

"Not yet," replied the Onondaga. "The storm merely growls and threatens at present. It will not strike for perhaps an hour."

"But when it does strike it's going to hit a mighty blow unless all signs fail. I've seen 'em gather before, and this is going to be a king of storms! Hear that thunder now! It doesn't growl any more, but goes off like the cracking of big cannon."

"But it's still far in the west," persisted Tayoga, as the three bent over their paddles.

The forest, however, was groaning with the wind, and little waves rose on the river. Now the lightning flared again and again, so fierce and bright that Robert, despite his control of himself, instinctively recoiled from it as from the stroke of a saber.

"Do you recall any shelter farther on, Tayoga?" asked the hunter.

"The overhanging bank and the big hollow in the stone," replied the Onondaga. "On the left! Don't you remember?"

"Now I do, Tayoga, but I didn't know it was near. Do you think we can make it before that sky over our heads splits wide open?"

"It will be a race," replied the young Iroquois, "but we three are strong, and we are skilled in the use of the paddle."

"Then we'll bend to it," said Willet. And they did. The canoe shot forward at amazing speed over the surface of the river, inky save when the lightning flashed upon it. Robert paddled as he had never paddled before, his muscles straining and the perspiration standing out on his face. He was thoroughly inured to forest life, but he knew that even the scouts and Indians fled for shelter from the great wilderness hurricanes.

There was every evidence that the storm would be of uncommon violence. The moan of the wind rose to a shriek and they heard the crash of breaking boughs and falling trees in the forest. The river, whipped continually by the gusts, was broken with waves upon which the canoe rocked with such force that the three, expert though they were, were compelled to use all their skill, every moment, to keep it from being overturned. If it had not been for the rapid and vivid strokes of lightning under which the waters turned blood red their vessel would have crashed more than once upon the rocks, leaving them to swim for life.

"That incessant flare makes me shiver," said Robert. "It seems every time that I'm going to be struck by it, but I'm glad it comes, because without it we'd never see our way on the river."

"Manitou sends the good and evil together," said Tayoga gravely.

"Anyhow," said Willet, "I hope we'll get to our shelter before the rain comes. Look out for that rock on the right, Robert!"

Young Lennox, with a swift and powerful motion of the paddle, shot the canoe back toward the center of the river, and then the three tried to hold it there as they sped on.

"Three or four hundred yards more," said Tayoga, "and we can draw into the smooth water we wish."

"And not a minute too soon," said Willet. "It seems to me I can hear the rain coming now in a deluge, and the waves on the river make me think of some I've seen on one of the big lakes. Listen to that, will you!"

A huge tree, blown down, fell directly across the stream, not more than twenty yards behind them. But the fierce and swollen waters tearing at it in torrents would soon bear it away on the current.

"Manitou was watching over us then," said Tayoga with the same gravity.

"As sure as the Hudson runs into the sea, he was," said Willet in a tone of reverence. "If that tree had hit us we and the canoe would all have been smashed together and a week later maybe the French would have fished our pieces out of the St. Lawrence."

Robert, who was farthest forward in the canoe, noticed that the cliff ahead, hollowed out at the base by the perpetual eating of the waters, seemed to project over the stream, and he concluded that it was the place in Tayoga's mind.

"Our shelter, isn't it?" he asked, pointing a finger by the lightning's flare.

Tayoga nodded, and the three, putting their last ounce of strength into the sweep of the paddles, sent the canoe racing over the swift current toward the haven now needed so badly. As they approached, Robert saw that the hollow went far back into the stone, having in truth almost the aspects of a cave. Beneath the mighty projection he saw also that the water was smooth, unlashed by the wind and outside the sweep of the current, and he felt immense relief when the canoe shot into its still depths and he was able to lay the paddle beside him.

"Back a little farther," said Tayoga, and he saw then, still by the flare of lightning, that the water ended against a low shelf at least six feet broad, upon which they stepped, lifting the canoe after them.

"It's all that you claimed for it, and more, Tayoga," said the hunter. "I fancy a ship in a storm would be glad enough to find a refuge as good for it as this is for us."

Tayoga smiled, and Robert knew that he felt deep satisfaction because he had brought them so well to port. Looking about after they had lifted up the canoe, he saw that in truth nature had made a good harbor here for those who traveled on the river, its waters so far never having been parted by anything but a canoe. The hollow went back thirty or forty feet with a sloping roof of stone, and from the ledge, whenever the lightning flashed, they saw the river flowing before them in a rushing torrent, but inside the hollow the waters were a still pool.

"Now the rain comes," said Tayoga.

Then they heard its sweep and roar and it arrived in such mighty volume that the surface of the river was beaten almost flat. But in their snug and well-roofed harbor not a drop touched them. Robert on the ledge with his back to the wall had a pervading sense of comfort. The lightning and the thunder were both dying now, but the rain came in a steady and mighty sweep. As the lightning ceased entirely it was so dark that they saw the water in front of them but dimly, and they had to be very careful in their movements on the ledge, lest they roll off and slip into its depths.

"Robert," said Willet in a whimsical tone, "one of the first things I tried to teach you when you were a little boy was always to be calm, and under no circumstances to let your calm be broken up when there was nothing to break it up. Now, we've every reason to be calm. We've got a good home here, and the storm can't touch us."

"I was already calm, Dave," replied Robert lightly. "I took your first lesson to heart, learned it, and I've never forgotten it. I'm so calm that I've unfolded my blanket and put it under me to soften the stone."

"To think of your blanket is proof enough that you're not excited. I'll do the same. Tayoga, in whose country is this new home of ours?"

"It is the land of no man, because it lies between the tribes from the north and the tribes from the south. Yet the Iroquois dare to come here when they choose. It's the fourth time I have been on this ledge, but before I was always with my brethren of the clan of the Bear of the nation Onondaga."

"Well, Tayoga," said Willet, in his humorous tone, "the company has grown no worse."

"No," said Tayoga, and his smile was invisible to them in the darkness. "The time is coming when the sachems of the Onondagas will be glad they adopted Lennox and the Great Bear into our nation."

Willet's laugh came at once, not loud, but with an inflection of intense enjoyment.

"You Onondagas are a bit proud, Tayoga," he said.

"Not without cause, Great Bear."

"Oh, I admit it! I admit it! I suppose we're all proud of our race—it's one of nature's happy ways of keeping us satisfied—and I'm free to say, Tayoga, that I've no quarrel at having been born white, because I'm so used to being white that I'd hardly know how to be anything else. But if I wasn't white—a thing that I had nothing to do with—and your Manitou who is my God was to say to me, 'Choose what else you'll be,' I'd say, and I'd say it with all the respect and reverence I could bring into the words, 'O Lord, All Wise and All Powerful, make me a strong young warrior of the clan of the Bear, of the nation Onondaga, of the League of the Hodenosaunee, hunting for my clan and fighting to protect its women and children, and keeping my word with everybody and trying to be just to the red races and tribes that are not as good as mine, and even to be the same to the poor white men around the towns that get drunk, and steal, and rob one another,' and maybe your Manitou who is my God would give to me my wish."

36

"The Great Bear has a silver tongue, and the words drop from his lips like honey," said Tayoga. But Robert knew that the young Onondaga was intensely gratified and he knew, too, that Willet meant every word he said.

"You'd better make yourself comfortable on the blanket, as we're doing, Tayoga," the youth said.

But the Onondaga did not intend to rest just yet. The wildness of the place and the spirit of the storm stirred him. He stood upon the shelf and the others dimly saw his tall and erect young figure. Slowly he began to chant in his own tongue, and his song ran thus in English:

> "The lightning cleaves the sky,
> The Brave Soul fears not;
> The thunder rolls and threatens,
> Manitou alone speeds the bolt;
> The waters are deep and swift,
> They carry the just man unhurt."
>
> "O Spirit of Good, hear me,
> Watch now over our path,
> Lead us in the way of the right,
> And, our great labors finished,
> Bring us back, safe and well,
> To the happy vale of Onondaga."

"A good hymn, Tayoga, for such I take it to be," said Willet. "I haven't heard my people sing any better. And now, since you've done more'n your share of the work you'd better take Robert's advice and lie down on your blanket."

Tayoga obeyed, and the three in silence listened to the rushing of the storm.

CHAPTER IV
THE INTELLIGENT CANOE

Lennox, Willet and Tayoga fell asleep, one by one, and the Onondaga was the last to close his eyes. Then the three, wrapped in their blankets, lay in complete darkness on the stone shelf, with the canoe beside them. They were no more than the point of a pin in the vast wilderness that stretched unknown thousands of miles from the Hudson to the Pacific, apparently as lost to the world as the sleepers in a cave ages earlier, when the whole earth was dark with forest and desert.

Although the storm could not reach them it beat heavily for long hours while they slept. The sweep of the rain maintained a continuous driving sound. Boughs cracked and broke beneath it. The waters of the river, swollen by the floods of tributary creeks and brooks, rose fast, bearing upon their angry surface the wreckage of trees, but they did not reach the stone shelf upon which the travelers lay.

Tayoga awoke before the morning, while it was yet so dark that his trained eyes could see but dimly the figures of his comrades. He sat up and listened, knowing that he must depend for warning upon his hearing, which had been trained to extreme acuteness by the needs of forest life. All three of them were great wilderness trailers and scouts, but Tayoga was the first of the three. Back of him lay untold generations that had been compelled to depend upon the physical senses and the intuition that comes from their uttermost development and co-ordination. Now, Tayoga, the product of all those who had gone before, was also their finest flower.

He had listened at first, resting on his elbow, but after a minute or two he sat up. He heard the rushing of the rain, the crack of splintering boughs, the flowing of the rising river, and the gurgling of its waters as they lapped against the stone shelf. They would not enter it he knew, as he had observed that the highest marks of the floods lay below them.

The sounds made by the rain and the river were steady and unchanged. But the intuition that came from the harmonious working of senses, developed to a marvelous degree, sounded a warning note. A danger threatened. He did not know what the

38

danger was nor whence it would come, but the soul of the Onondaga was alive and every nerve and muscle in his body was attuned for any task that might lie before him. He looked at his sleeping comrades. They did not stir, and their long, regular breathing told him that no sinister threat was coming to them.

But Tayoga never doubted. The silent and invisible warning, like a modern wireless current, reached him again. Now, he knelt at the very edge of the shelf, and drew his long hunting knife. He tried to pierce the darkness with his eyes, and always he looked up the stream in the direction in which they had come. He strained his ears too to the utmost, concentrating the full powers of his hearing upon the river, but the only sounds that reached him were the flowing of the current, the bubbling of the water at the edges, and its lapping against a tree or bush torn up by the storm and floating on the surface of the stream.

The Onondaga stepped from the shelf, finding a place for his feet in crevices below, the water rising almost to his knees, and leaned farther forward to listen. One hand held firmly to a projection of stone above and the other clasped the knife.

Tayoga maintained the intense concentration of his faculties, as if he had drawn them together in an actual physical way, until they bore upon one point, and he poured so much strength and vitality into them that he made the darkness thin away before his eyes and he heard noises of the water that had not come to him before.

A broken bough, a bush and a sapling washed past. Then came a tree, and deflecting somewhat from the current it floated toward the shelf. Leaning far over and extending the hand that held the knife, Tayoga struck. When the blade came back it was red and the young Onondaga uttered a tremendous war whoop that rang and echoed in the confines of the stony hollow.

Lennox and Willet sprang to their feet, all sleep driven away at once, and instinctively grasped their rifles.

"What is it, Tayoga?" exclaimed the startled Willet.

"The attack of the savage warriors," replied the Onondaga. "One came floating on a tree. He thought to slay us as we slept and take away our scalps, but the river that brought him living has borne him away dead."

"And so they know we're here," said the hunter, "and your watchfulness has saved us. Well, Tayoga, it's one more deed for which we have to thank you, but I think you'd better get back on the shelf. They can fire from the other side, farther up, and although it would be at random, a bullet or two might strike here."

The Onondaga swung himself back and all three flattened themselves against the rock. After Tayoga's triumphant shout there was no sound save those of the river and the rain. But Robert expected it. He knew the horde would be quiet for a while, hoping for a surprise the second time after the first one had failed.

"It was bold," he said, "for a single warrior to come floating down the stream in search of us."

"But it would have succeeded if Tayoga hadn't been awake," said the hunter. "One warrior could have knifed us all at his leisure."

"Where do you think they are now?"

"They must be crouched in the shelter of rocks. If they had nothing over them the storm would take the fighting spirit for the time out of savages, even wild for scalps. I'm mighty glad we have the canoe. It holds the food we need for a siege, and if the chance for escape comes it will bear us away. I think, Tayoga, I can see a figure stirring among the boulders on the other side farther up."

"I see two," said the Onondaga, "and doubtless there are others whom we cannot see. Keep close, my friends, I think they are going to fire."

A dozen rifles were discharged from a point about a hundred yards away, the exploding powder making red dots in the darkness, the bullets rattling on the stone cliff or sending up little spurts of water from the river. The volley was followed by a shrill, fierce war whoop, and then nothing was heard but the flowing of the river and the rushing of the rain.

"You are not touched?" said Tayoga, and Robert and Willet quickly answered in the negative.

"They don't know just which way to aim their guns," said Willet, "and so long as we keep quiet now they won't learn. That shout of yours, Tayoga, was not enough to tell them."

"But they must remember about where the hollow is, although they can't pull trigger directly upon it, owing to the darkness and storm," said Robert.

"That about sums it up, my boy," said the hunter. "If they do a lot of random firing the chances are about a hundred to one they won't hit us, and the Indians don't have enough ammunition to waste that way."

"I don't suppose we can launch the canoe and slip away in it?"

"No, it would be swamped by the rain and the flood. It's likely, too, that they're on watch for us farther down the stream."

"Then this is our home and fortress for an indefinite time, and, that being the case, I'm going to make myself as easy as I can."

40

He drew the blanket under his body again and lay on his elbow, but he held his rifle before him, ready for battle at an instant's notice. His feeling of comfort returned and with it the sense of safety. The bullets of the savages had gone so wild and the darkness was so deep that their shelter appeared to him truly as a fortress which no numbers of besiegers could storm.

"Do you think they'll try floating down the stream on trees or logs again, Tayoga?" he asked.

"No, the danger is too great," replied the Onondaga. "They know now that we're watching."

An hour passed without any further sign from the foe. The rain decreased somewhat in violence, but, as the wind rose, its rush and sweep made as much sound as ever. Then the waiting was broken by scattering shots, accompanied by detached war whoops, as if different bands were near. From their shelter they watched the red dots that marked the discharges from the rifles, but only one bullet came near them, and after chipping a piece of stone over their heads it dropped harmlessly to the floor.

"That was the one chance out of a hundred," said Willet, "and now we're safe from the next ninety-nine bullets."

"I trust the rule will work," said Robert.

"I wish you'd hold my left hand in a firm grip," said Willet.

"I will, but why?" returned the youth.

"If I get a chance I'm going to drag up some of that dead and floating wood and lay it along the edge of the shelf. In the dark the savages can't pick us off, but we'll need a barrier in the morning."

"You're right, Dave, of course. I'm sorry I didn't think of it myself."

"One of us thought of it, and that's enough. Hold my hand hard, Robert.

Don't let your grip slip."

By patient waiting and help from the others Willet was able to draw up two logs of fair size, and some smaller pieces which they placed carefully on the edge of the stone shelf. Lying flat behind them, they would be almost hidden, and now they could await the coming of daylight with more serenity.

A long time passed. The three ate strips of the deer meat, and Robert even slept for a short while. He awoke to find a further decrease in the rain, although the river was still rising, and Tayoga and Willet were of the opinion that it would stop soon, a belief that was justified in an hour. Robert soon afterward saw the clouds move away, and disclose a strip of dark blue sky, into which the stars began to come one by one.

41

"The night will grow light soon," said Tayoga, "then it will darken again for a little time before the coming of the day."

"And we've built our breastwork none too soon," said Willet. "There'll be so many stars by and by that those fellows can pick out our place and send their bullets to it. What do you think, Tayoga? Is it just a band taking the chance to get some scalps, or are they sent out by the Governor General of Canada to do wicked work in the forest and then be disowned if need be?"

"I cannot tell," replied the Onondaga. "Much goes on in the land of Onontio at Stadacona (Quebec). He talks long in whispers with the northern chiefs, and often he does not let his left ear know what the right ear hears. Onontio moves in the night, while Corlear sleeps."

"That may be so, Tayoga, but whether it's so or not I like our straightforward English and American way best. We may blunder along for a while and lose at first, but to be open and honest is to be strong."

"I did not say the ways of Corlear would prevail. It is not the talk of Corlear that will keep the Hodenosaunee faithful to the English side, but it is the knowledge of the fifty sachems that when Onontio is speaking in a voice of honey he is to be trusted the least."

Willet laughed.

"I understand, Tayoga," he said. "You're for us not because you have so much faith in Corlear, but because you have less in Onontio. Well, it's a good enough reason, I suppose. But all Frenchmen are not tricksters. Most of 'em are brave, and when they're friends they're good and true. About all I've got to say against 'em is that they're willing to shut their eyes to the terrible things their allies do in their name. But I've had a lot to do with 'em on the border, and you can get to like 'em. Now, that St. Luc we met was a fine upstanding man."

"But if an enemy, an enemy to be dreaded," said Tayoga with his usual gravity.

"I wouldn't mind that if it came to war. In such cases the best men make the best enemies, I suppose. He had a sharp eye. I could see how he measured us, and reckoned us up, but he looked most at Robert here."

"His sharp eye recognized that I was the most important of the three," said Robert lightly.

"Every fellow is mighty important to himself," said Willet, "and he can't get away from it. Tayoga, do you think you see figures moving on the other bank there, up the stream?"

"Two certainly, others perhaps, Great Bear," replied the Onondaga. "I might reach one with my rifle."

"Don't try it, Tayoga. We're on the defense, and we'll let 'em make all the beginnings. The sooner they shoot away their ammunition the better it will be for us. I think they'll open fire pretty soon now, because the night is growing uncommon bright. The stars are so big and shining, and there are so many of them they all look as if they had come to a party. Flatten yourselves down, boys! I can see a figure kneeling by a bowlder and that means one shot, if not more."

They lay close and Robert was very thankful now for the logs they had dragged up from the water, as they afforded almost complete shelter. The crouching warrior farther up the stream fired, and his bullet struck the hollow above their heads.

"A better aim than they often show," said Willet.

More shots were fired, and one buried itself in the log in front of Robert. He heard the thud made by the bullet as it entered, and once more he was thankful for their rude breastwork. But it was the only one that struck so close and presently the savages ceased their fire, although the besieged three were still able to see them in the brilliant moonlight among the bowlders.

"They're getting a bit too insolent," said the hunter. "Maybe they think it's a shorter distance from them to us than it is from us to them, and that our bullets would drop before they got to 'em. I think, Tayoga, I'll prove that it's not so."

"Choose the man at the edge of the water," said Tayoga. "He has fired three shots at us, and we should give him at least one in return."

"I'll pay the debt, Tayoga."

Robert saw the warrior, his head and shoulders and painted chest appearing above the stone. The distance was great for accuracy, but the light was brilliant, and the rifle of the hunter rose to his shoulder. The muzzle bore directly upon the naked chest, and when Willet pulled the trigger a stream of fire spurted from the weapon.

The savage uttered a cry, shot forward and fell into the stream. His lifeless body tossed like dead wood on the swift current, reappeared and floated by the little fortress of the three. Robert shuddered as he saw the savage face again, and then he saw it no more.

The savages uttered a shout of grief and rage over the loss of the warrior, but the besieged were silent. Willet, as he reloaded his rifle, gave it an affectionate little pat or two.

"It's a good weapon," he said, "and with a fair light I was sure I wouldn't miss. We've given 'em fair warning that they've got a nest of panthers here to deal with, and that when they attack they're taking risks. Can you see any of 'em now, Tayoga?"

"All have taken to cover. There is not one among them who is willing to face again the rifle of the Great Bear."

Willet smiled with satisfaction at the compliment. He was proud of his sharp-shooting, and justly so, but he said modestly:

"I had a fair target, and it will do for a warning. I think we can look for another long rest now."

The dark period that precedes the dawn came, and then the morning flashed over the woods. Robert, from the hollow, looking across the far shore, saw lofty, wooded hills and back of them blue mountains. Beads of rain stood on the leaves, and the wilderness seemed to emerge, fresh and dripping, from a glorious bath. Pleasant odors of the wild came to him, and now he felt the sting of imprisonment there among the rocks. He wished they could go at once on their errand. It was a most unfortunate chance to have been found there by the Indians and to be held indefinitely in siege. The flooded river would have borne them swiftly in their canoe toward the St. Lawrence.

"Mourning, Robert?" said Willet who noticed his face.

"For the moment, yes," admitted young Lennox, "but it has passed. I wanted to be going on this lively river and through the green wood, but since I have to wait I can do it."

"I feel the same way about it, and we're lucky to have such a fort as the one we are in. I think the savages will hang on here for a long while. Indians always have plenty of time. That's why they're more patient than white men. Like as not we won't get a peep out of them all the morning."

"Lennox feels the beauty of the day," said Tayoga, "and that's why he wants to leave the hollow and go into the woods. But if Lennox will only think he'll know that other days as fine will come."

The eye of the young Onondaga twinkled as he delivered his jesting advice.

"I'll be as patient as I can," replied Robert in the same tone, "but tomorrow is never as good as today. I wait like you and Dave only because I have to do so."

"In the woods you must do as the people who live there do," said the hunter philosophically. "They learn how to wait when they're young. We don't know how long we'll be here. A little more of the deer, Tayoga. It's close to the middle of the day now and we must keep our strength. I wish we had better water than that of a flooded and muddy river to drink, but it's water, anyhow."

44

They ate, drank and refreshed themselves and another long period of inaction followed. The warriors—at intervals—fired a few shots but they did no damage. Only one entered the hollow, and it buried itself harmlessly in their wooden barrier. They suffered from nothing except the soreness and stiffness that came from lying almost flat and so long in one position. The afternoon, cloudless and brilliant, waned, and the air in the recess grew warm and heavy. Had it not been for the necessity of keeping guard Robert could have gone to sleep again. The flood in the river passed its zenith and was now sinking visibly. No more trees or bushes came floating on the water. Willet showed disappointment over the failure of the besiegers to make any decided movement.

"I was telling you, Robert, a while ago," he said, "that Indians mostly have a lot of time, but I'm afraid the band that's cornered us here has got too much. They may send out a warrior or two to hunt, and the others may sit at a distance and wait a week for us to come out. At least it looks that way to a 'possum up a tree. What do you think of it, Tayoga?"

"The Great Bear is right," replied the Onondaga. "He is always right when he is not wrong."

"Come now, Tayoga, are you making game of me?"

"Not so, my brother, because the Great Bear is nearly always right and very seldom wrong. It is given only to Manitou never to be wrong."

"That's better, Tayoga. If I can keep up a high average of accuracy I'm satisfied."

Tayoga's English was always precise and a trifle bookish, like that of a man speaking a language he has learned in a school, which in truth was the case with the Onondaga. Like the celebrated Thayendanegea, the Mohawk, otherwise known as Joseph Brant, he had been sent to a white school and he had learned the English of the grammarian. Willet too spoke in a manner much superior to that of the usual scout and hunter.

"If the Indians post lines out of range and merely maintain a watch what will we do?" asked Robert. "I, for one, don't want to stay here indefinitely."

"Nor do any of us," replied Willet. "We ought to be moving. A long delay here won't help us. We've got to think of something."

The two, actuated by the same impulse, looked at Tayoga. He was very thoughtful and presently glanced up at the heavens.

"What does the Great Bear think of the sky?" he asked.

"I think it's a fine sky, Tayoga," Willet replied with a humorous inflection. "But I've always admired it, whether it's blue or gray or just black, spangled with stars."

Tayoga smiled.

"What does the Great Bear think of the sky?" he repeated. "Do the signs say to him that the coming night will be dark like the one that has just gone before?"

"They say it will be dark, Tayoga, but I don't believe we'll have the rain again."

"We do not want the rain, but we do want the dark. Tonight when the moon and stars fail to come we must leave the hollow."

"By what way, Tayoga?"

The Onondaga pointed to the river.

"We have the canoe," he said.

"But if they should hear or see us we'd make a fine target in it," said Robert.

"We won't be in it," said the Onondaga, "although our weapons and clothes will."

"Ah, I understand! We're to launch the canoe, put in it everything including our clothes, except ourselves, and swim by the side of it. Three good swimmers are we, Tayoga, and I believe we can do it."

The Onondaga looked at Willet, who nodded his approval.

"The chances will favor us, and we'd better try it," he said, "that is, if the night is dark, as I think it will be."

"Then it is agreed," said Robert.

"It is so," said Tayoga.

No more words were needed, and they strengthened their hearts for the daring attempt, waiting patiently for the afternoon to wane and die into the night, which, arrived moonless and starless and heavy with dark, as they had hoped and predicted. Just before, a little spasmodic firing came from the besiegers, but they did not deign to answer. Instead they waited patiently until the night was far advanced and then they prepared quickly for running the gauntlet, a task that would require the greatest skill, courage and presence of mind. Robert's heart beat hard. Like the others he was weary of the friendly hollow that had served them so well, and the murmuring of the river, as it flowed, invited them to come on and use it as the road of escape.

The three took off all their clothing and disposed everything carefully in the canoe, laying the rifles on top where they could be reached with a single swift movement of the arm. Then they stared up and down the stream, and listened with all their powers of hearing. No savage was to be seen nor did anyone make a sound that reached the three, although Robert knew they lay behind the rocks not so very far away.

46

"They're not stirring, Tayoga," whispered the hunter. "Perhaps they think we don't dare try the river, and in this case as in most others the boldest way is the best. Take the other end of the canoe, and we'll lift it down gently."

He and the Onondaga lowered the canoe so slowly that it made no splash when it took the water, and then the three lowered themselves in turn, sinking into the stream to their throats.

"Keep close to the bank," whispered the hunter, "and whatever you do don't make any splash as you swim."

The three were on the side of the craft next to the cliff and their heads did not appear above its side. Then the canoe moved down the stream at just about the speed of the current, and no human hands appeared, nor was any human agency visible. It was just a wandering little boat, set adrift upon the wilderness waters, a light shell, but with an explorer's soul. It moved casually along, keeping nearest to the cliff, the safest place for so frail a structure, hesitating two or three times at points of rocks, but always making up its mind to go on once more, and see where this fine but strange river led.

Luckily it was very dark by the cliff. The shadows fell there like black blankets, and no eye yet rested upon the questing canoe which kept its way, idly exploring the reaches of the river. Gasna Gaowo, this bark canoe of red elm, was not large, but it was a noble specimen of its kind, a forest product of Onondaga patience and skill. On either side near the prow was painted in scarlet a great eagle's eye, and now the two large red eyes of the canoe gazed ahead into the darkness, seeking to pierce the unknown.

The canoe went on with a gentle, rocking motion made by the current, strayed now and then a little way from the cliff, but always came back to it. The pair of great red eyes stared at the cliff so close and at the other cliff farther away and at the middle of the stream, which was now tranquil and unruffled by the wreckage of the forest blown into the water by the storm. The canoe also looked into one or two little coves, and seeing nothing there but the river edge bubbling against the stone, went on, came to a curve, rounded it in an easy, sauntering but skillful fashion, and entered a straight reach of the stream.

So far the canoe was having a lone and untroubled journey. The river widening now and flowing between descending banks was wholly its own, but clinging to the habit it had formed when it started it still hung to the western bank. The night grew more and more favorable to the undiscovered voyage it wished to make. Masses of clouds gathered and hovered over that particular river, as if they had some especial object in doing so, and they made the night so dark that the red eyes of the canoe, great in size though they were, could see but a little way down the stream. Yet it kept on boldly and there was a purpose in its course. Often it seemed to be on the point of recklessly running against the rocky shore, but always it sheered off in time, and though its advance was apparently casual it was moving down the stream at a great rate.

The canoe had gone fully four hundred yards when an Abenaki warrior on the far side of the river caught a glimpse of a shadow moving in the shadow of the bank, and a sustained gaze soon showed to him that it was a canoe, and, in his opinion, a derelict, washed by the flood from some camp a long distance up the stream. He watched it for a little while, and was then confirmed in his opinion by its motion as it floated lazily with the current.

The darkness was not too great to keep the Abenaki from seeing that it was a good canoe, a fine shell of Iroquois make, and canoes were valuable. He had not been able to secure any scalp, which was a sad disappointment, and now Manitou had sent this stray craft to him as a consolation prize. He was not one to decline the gifts of the gods, and he ran along the edge of the cliff until he came to a low point well ahead of the canoe. Then he put his rifle on the ground, dropped lightly into the stream, and swam with swift sure strokes for the derelict.

As the warrior approached he saw that his opinion of the canoe was more than justified. It had been made with uncommon skill and he admired its strong, graceful lines. It was not often that such a valuable prize came to a man and asked to be taken. He reached it and put one hand upon the side. Then a heavy fist stretched entirely over the canoe and struck him such a mighty blow upon the jaw that he sank senseless, and when he revived two minutes later on a low bank where the current had cast him, he did not know what had happened to him.

Meanwhile the uncaptured canoe sailed on in lonely majesty down the stream.

"That was a shrewd blow of yours, Dave," said Robert. "You struck fairly upon his jaw bone."

"It's not often that I fight an Indian with my fists, and the chance having come I made the most of it," said the hunter. "He may have been a sentinel set to watch for just such an attempt as we are making, but it's likely they thought if we made a dash for it we'd be in the canoe."

"It was great wisdom for us to swim," said Tayoga. "Another sentinel seeing the canoe may also think it was washed away somewhere and is merely floating on the waters. I can see a heap of underbrush that has gathered against a projecting point, and the current would naturally bring the canoe into it. Suppose we let it rest there until it seems to work free by the action of the water, and then go on down the river."

"It's a good idea, Tayoga, but it's a pretty severe test to remain under fire, so to speak, in order to deceive your enemy, when the road is open for you to run away."

"But we can do it, all three of us," said Tayoga, confidently.

A spit of high ground projected into the river and in the course of time enough driftwood brought by the stream and lodged there had made a raft of considerable width and depth, against which the canoe in its wandering course lodged. But it was evident that its stay in such a port would be but temporary, as the current continually pushed and sucked at it, and the light craft quivered and swayed continually under the action of the current.

The three behind the canoe thrust themselves back into the mass of vegetation, reckless of scratches, and were hidden completely for the time. Since he was no longer kept warm by the act of swimming Robert felt the chill of the water entering his bones. His physical desire to shiver he controlled by a powerful effort of the will, and, standing on the bottom with his head among the boughs, he remained quiet.

None of the three spoke and in a few minutes a warrior on the other side of the stream, watching in the bushes, saw the dim outline of the canoe in the darkness. He came to the edge of the water and looked at it attentively. It was apparent to him, as it had been to the other savage, that it was a stray canoe, and valuable, a fine prize for the taking. But he was less impulsive than the first man had been and at that point the river spread out to a much greater width. He did not know that his comrade was lying on the bank farther up in a half stunned condition, but he was naturally cautious and he stared at the canoe a long time. He saw that the action of the current would eventually work it loose from the raft, but he believed it would yet hang there for at least ten minutes. So he would have time to go back to his nearest comrade and return with him. Then one could enter the water and salvage the canoe, while the other stayed on the bank and watched. Having reached this wise conclusion he disappeared in the woods, seeking the second Indian, but before the two could come together the canoe had worked loose and was gone.

The three hidden in the bushes had watched the Indian as well as the dusk would permit and they read his mind. They knew that when he turned away he had gone for help and they knew equally well that it was time for the full power of the current to take effect.

"Shove it off, Tayoga," whispered Willet, "and I think we'd better help along with some strokes of our own."

"It is so," said Tayoga.

Now the wandering canoe was suddenly endowed with more life and purpose, or else the current grew much swifter. After an uneasy stay with the boughs, it left them quickly, sailed out toward the middle of the stream, and floated at great speed between banks that were growing high again. The friendly dark was also an increasing protection to the three who were steering it. The heavy but rainless clouds continued to gather over them, and the canoe sped on at accelerated speed in an opaque atmosphere. A mile farther and Willet suggested that they get into the canoe and paddle with all their might. The embarkation, a matter of delicacy and difficulty, was made with success, and then they used the paddles furiously.

The canoe, suddenly becoming a live thing, leaped forward in the water, and sped down the stream, as if it were the leader in a race. Far behind them rose a sudden war cry, and the three laughed.

"I suppose they've discovered in some way that we've fled," said Robert.

"That is so," said Tayoga.

"And they'll come down the river as fast as they can," said Willet, "but they'll do no more business with us. I don't want to brag, but you can't find three better paddlers in the wilderness than we are, and with a mile start we ought soon to leave behind any number of warriors who have to run through the woods and follow the windings of the stream."

"They cannot catch us now," said Tayoga, "and I will tell them so."

He uttered a war whoop so piercing and fierce that Robert was startled. It cut the air like the slash of a sword, but it was a long cry, full of varied meaning. It expressed satisfaction, triumph, a taunt for the foe, and then it died away in a sinister note like a threat for any who tried to follow. Willet laughed under his breath.

"That'll stir 'em, Tayoga," he said. "You put a little dart squarely in their hearts, and they don't like it. But they can squirm as much as they please, we're out of their reach now. Hark, they're answering!"

They heard a cry from the savage who had besieged them, but it was followed by a long silence. The three paddled with their utmost strength, the great muscles on their arms rising and falling with their exertions, and beads of perspiration standing out on their foreheads.

Hours passed. Mile after mile fell behind them. The darkness began to thin, and then the air was shot with golden beams from the rising sun. Willet, heaving an immense sigh of relief, laid his paddle across the canoe.

"The danger has passed," he said. "Now we'll land, put on our clothes and become respectable."

CHAPTER V
THE MOHAWK CHIEF

The canoe was passing between low shores, and they landed on the left bank, lifting out of the water the little vessel that had served them so well, and carrying it to a point some distance in the bushes. There they sat down beside it a while and drew long, deep and panting breaths.

"I don't want to repeat that experience soon," said Robert. "I think every muscle and bone in me is aching."

"So do mine," said Willet, "but they ache in a good cause, and what's of more importance just now a successful one too. Having left no trail the Indians won't be able to follow us, and we can rest here a long time, which compels me to tell you again to put on your clothes and become respectable."

They were quite dry now, and they dressed. They also saw that their arms and ammunition were in order, and after Willet had scouted the country a bit, seeing that no human-being was near, they ate breakfast of the deer meat and felt thankful.

"The aches are leaving me," said Willet, "and in another half-hour I'll be the man I was yesterday. Not I'll be a better man. I've been in danger lots of times and always there's a wonderful feeling of happiness when I get out of it."

"That is, risk goes before real rest," said Robert.

"That's about the way to put it, and escaping as we've just done from a siege, this dawn is about the finest I've ever seen. Isn't that a big and glorious sun over there? I suppose it's the same sun I've been looking at for years, but it seems to me that it has a new and uncommonly splendid coat of gilding this morning."

"I think it was put on to celebrate our successful flight," said Robert. "It's not only a splendid sun, Dave, but it's an uncommonly friendly one too. I can look it squarely in the eye for just a second and it fairly beams on me."

"My brothers are right," said Tayoga gravely. "If it had not been the will of Manitou for us to escape from the trap that had been set for us the sun rising newly behind the mountains would not smile upon us."

"I take that as allegorical," said Robert. "We see with our souls, and our eyes are merely the mirrors through which we look. Seeing, or at least the color of it, is a state of mind."

Tayoga followed him perfectly and nodded.

"You are getting too deep," interrupted the hunter. "Let's be satisfied with our escape. Here, each of you take another piece of venison. I'm glad you still have your bow and arrows, Tayoga, because it won't be long before we'll have to begin looking for another deer."

"The woods swarm with game. It will not be difficult to find one," said Tayoga.

"But for the present I think we'd better lie close. Of course the chief danger of attack from those savages has passed, but we're some distance from Canada, and it's still doubtful ground. Another wandering band may run upon us and that Ojibway, Tandakora, will never quit hunting us, until a bullet stops him. He has a terrible attack of the scalp fever. We want to make good time on our journey, but we mustn't spoil everything by trying to go too fast."

"It might be wise for us to remain the entire day in the forest," replied the Onondaga. "After the great and long trial of our strength last night, we need much rest. And tonight we can make speed on the river again. What says Lennox?"

"I'm for it," replied Robert, "but I suggest that we go deeper into the forest, taking the canoe with us, and hide our trail. I think I see the gleam of water to our right and if I'm correct it means a brook, up which we can walk carrying the canoe with us."

"A good idea, Robert," said Willet. "Suppose you look first and see if it's really a brook."

The lad returned in a moment or two with a verification. The water of the little stream was clear, but it had a fine sandy bottom on which footprints were effaced in a few seconds. They waded up it nearly a mile until they came to stony ground, when they left the brook and walked on the outcrop or detached stones a considerable distance, passing at last through dense thickets into a tiny open space. They put the canoe down in the center of the opening, which was circular, and stretched their own bodies on the grass close to the bushes, through which they could see without being seen.

"That trail is well hidden," said Willet, "or rather it's no trail at all. It's just about as much trace as a bird leaves, flying through the air."

"Do you know where we are, Dave?" asked Robert.

"We're not so far from the edge of the wilderness. Before long the land will begin to slope down toward the St. Lawrence. But it's all wild enough. The French settlements themselves don't go very far back from the big river. And the St. Lawrence is a mighty stream, Robert. I reckon there's not another such river on the globe. The

53

Mississippi I suppose is longer, and carries more volume to the sea, but the St. Lawrence is full of clear water, Robert, think of that! Most all the other big rivers of the world, I hear, are muddy and yellow, but the St. Lawrence, being the overflow of the big lakes, is pure. Sometimes it's blue and sometimes it's green, according to the sunlight or the lack of it, and sometimes it's another color, but always it's good, fresh water, flowing between mighty banks to the sea, the stream getting deeper and deeper and broader and broader the farther it goes, till beyond Quebec it's five and then ten miles across, and near the ocean it's nigh as wide as Erie or Ontario. I'm always betting on the St. Lawrence, Robert. I haven't been on all the other continents, but I don't believe they can show anything to beat it."

"Have you seen much of the big lakes, Dave?"

"A lot of Erie and Ontario, but not so much of those farther west, Michigan, Huron and Superior, although they're far bigger and grander. Nothing like 'em in the lake line in this world. We don't know much about Superior, but I gather from the Indians that it's nigh to four hundred miles long, and maybe a hundred and fifty miles across in the middle. What a power of water! That's not a lake! It's a fresh-water sea. I've seen Niagara, too, Robert, where the river comes tumbling over two mighty cliffs, and the foam rises up to the sky, and the rainbow is always arching over the chasm below. It's a tremendous sight and it keeps growing on you the longer you look at it. The Indians, who like myths and allegories, have a fine story about it. They say that Heno, to whom Manitou gave charge of the thunderbolt, once lived in the great cave or hollow behind the falls, liking the damp and the eternal roar of the waters. And Manitou to help him keep a watch over all the thunderbolts gave him three assistants who have never been named. Now, the nations of the Hodenosaunee call themselves the grandchildren of Heno, and when they make invocation to him they call him grandfather. But they hold that Heno is always under the direction of Hawenneyu, the Great Spirit, who I take it is the same in their minds as Manitou. The more you learn of the Indians, and especially of the Hodenosaunee, Robert, the more you admire the beauty and power of their minds."

Willet spoke with great earnestness, his own mind through the experiences of many years being steeped in forest lore and imagery. Robert, although he knew less of Indian mythology, nevertheless knew enough to feel for it a great admiration.

"I studied the myths of the Greeks and Romans at Albany," he said, "and I don't see that they were very much superior to those of the Indians."

"Maybe they weren't superior at all," said Willet, "and I don't believe the Greeks and Romans ever had a country like the one in which we are roaming. The Book says God made the world in six days, and I think He must have spent one whole day, and His best day, too, on the country in here. Think of the St Lawrence, and all the big lakes and middle-sized lakes and little lakes, and the Hudson and the other splendid rivers, and the fine mountains east of the Hudson and west of it, and all the grand valleys, and the great country of the Hodenosaunee, and the gorgeous green forest running hundreds and hundreds of miles, every way! I tell you, Robert--and it's no sacrilege either--after He did such a splendid and well-nigh perfect job He could stop for the night and call it a good and full day's work. I reckon that nowhere else on the earth's surface are so many fine and wonderful things crowded into one region."

He took a deep breath and gazed with responsive eyes at the dim blue crests of the mountains.

"It's all that you call it," said Robert, whose soul was filled with the same love and admiration, "and I'm glad I was born within its limits. I've noticed, Dave, that the people of old lands think they alone have love of country. New people may love a new land just as much, and I love all this country about us, the lakes, and the rivers, and the mountains and the valleys and the forests."

He flung out his arms in a wide, embracing gesture, and he, too, took deep long breaths of the crisp air that came over the clean forest. Tayoga smiled, and the smile was fathomless.

"I, Tayoga, of the clan of the Bear, of the nation Onondaga, of the great League of the Hodenosaunee, can rejoice more than either of you, my white friends," he said, "because I and my fathers for ages before me were born into this wonderful country of which you speak so well, but not too well, and much of it belongs to the Hodenosaunee. The English and the French are but of yesterday. Tododaho lighted the first council fire in the vale of Onondaga many generations before either came across the sea."

"It's true, Tayoga," said Willet, "and I don't forget it for a moment. All of us white people, English, French, Dutch, Germans and all other breeds, are mere newcomers, and I'm not one ever to deny the rights of the Hodenosaunee."

"I know that the Great Bear is always our friend," said the young Onondaga, "and Lennox too, no less."

"I am, Tayoga," said Robert fervently.

The white lad went to sleep by and by, the others to follow in their turn, and when he woke it was afternoon. About midway of his comrade's nap Tayoga had gone to sleep also, and now Willet followed him, leaving Robert alone on guard.

His eyes could pierce the bushes, and for some distance beyond, and he saw that no intruder had drawn near. Nor had he expected any. The place was too remote and well hidden, and the keenest warriors in the world could not follow a vanished trail.

He ate two or three strips of the deer meat, walked around the complete circle of the opening, examining the approaches from every side, and having satisfied himself once more that no stranger was near, returned to his place on the grass near his comrades, full of the great peace that can come only to those of sensitive mind and lofty imagination. His sleep had rested him thoroughly. The overtaxed muscles were easy again, and with the vast green forest about him and the dim blue mountains showing on the horizon, he felt all the keen zest of living.

He was glad to be there. He was glad to be with Tayoga. He was glad to be with Willet and he was glad to be going on the important mission which the three hoped to carry out, according to promise, no matter what dangers surrounded them, and that there would be many they already had proof. But, for the present, at least, there was nothing but peace.

He lay on his back and stared up at the blue sky, in which clouds fleecy and tiny were drifting. All were going toward the northeast and that way the course of himself and his comrades lay. If Manitou prospered them, they would come to the Quebec of the French, which beforetime had been the Stadacona of old Indian tribes. That name, Quebec, was full of significance to him. Standing upon its mighty rock, it was another Gibraltar. It told him of the French power in North America, and he associated it vaguely with young officers in brilliant uniforms, powdered ladies, and all the splendor of an Old World court reproduced in the New World. St. Luc had come from there, and with his handsome face and figure and his gay and graceful manner he had typified the Quebec of the chevaliers, which the grave and solid burghers of Albany regarded with dread and aversion and yet with a strange sort of attraction.

He did not deny to himself that he too felt the attraction. An unknown kinship with Quebec, either in blood or imagination, was calling. He wondered if he would see St. Luc there, but on reflection he decided that it was impossible. The mission of the chevalier to the Hodenosaunee would require a long absence. He might arrive in the vale of Onondaga and have to wait many days before the fifty sachems should decide to meet in council and hear him.

But Robert believed that if St. Luc should appear before the fifty he would prove to be eloquent, and he would neglect no artifice of word and manner to make the Hodenosaunee think the French power at Quebec invincible. He would describe the great deeds of the French officers and soldiers. He would tell them of that glittering court of Versailles, and perhaps he would make them think their salvation depended upon an alliance with France.

Robert was sorry for the moment that his mission was taking him to Quebec and not to the vale of Onondaga, where Willet and he--and Tayoga too--could appear before the sachems as friends true and tested, and prove to them that the English were their good and natural allies. They would recall again what Frontenac had done. They would dwell upon the manner in which he had carried sword and fire among the Six Nations, then the Five, and they would keep open the old wound that yet rankled.

It was a passing wish. The Iroquois would remain faithful to their ancient allies, the English. The blood that Frontenac had shed would be forever a barrier between the Long House and the Stadacona that was. Once more Quebec filled his eye, and he gazed into the northeast where the French capital lay upon its mighty and frowning rock. His curiosity concerning it increased. He wanted to see what kind of city it was, and he wanted to see what kind of a man the Marquis Duquesne, the Governor-General of Canada, was. Well, he would be there before many days and he would see for himself. He and his comrades already had been triumphant over a danger so great that nothing could stop them now. He felt all the elation and certainty that came from a victory over odds.

He rose, parted the bushes and made another tour of the region about their covert. When he was at a point about a hundred yards away he fancied that he heard a sound in a thicket a considerable distance ahead. Promptly taking shelter behind a large tree, he used both eyes and ears, watching the thicket closely, and listening for any other sound that might come.

He heard nothing else but his keen eyes noted a bush swaying directly into the teeth of the wind, a movement that could not occur unless something alive in the thicket caused it. He slid his rifle forward and still watched. Now the bush shook violently, and an awkward black figure, shooting out, ran across the open. It was only a bear, and he was about to resume his circling walk, but second thought told him that the bear was running as if he ran away from an object of which he was afraid, and there was nothing in the northern forests except human beings to scare a bear.

He settled back in his shelter and resumed his watch in the thicket, leaving the bear to run where he pleased, which he did, disappearing with a snort in another thicket. A full ten minutes passed. Robert had not stirred. He was crouched behind the tree, blending with the grass, and he held his rifle ready to be fired in an instant, should the need arise.

The bush that had moved against the wind had ceased stirring long since, but now he saw another shaking and it, too, paid no attention to the laws of nature, defying the wind as the first had done. Robert concentrated his gaze upon it, thankful that he had not made the black bear the original cause of things, and presently he saw the feathered head of an Indian appear among the leaves. It was only a glimpse, he did not see the body or even the face of the warrior, but it was enough. Where one warrior was another was likely to be in those northern marches, the most dangerous kind of neutral ground.

He began to slide away, keeping the big tree trunk between him and the thicket, using all the arts of the forest trailer that he had learned by natural aptitude and long practice. He went back slowly, but the grass stems moved only a little as he went, and he was confident that he not only had not been seen, but would not be seen. Yet he scarcely dared to breathe--until he reached the bushes inclosing the opening in which his comrades lay.

He paused a few moments before waking the others and filled his lungs with air. He was surprised to find that the hands holding his rifle were damp with perspiration, and he realized then how great the brief strain had been. Suppose he had not seen the Indian in the bush, and had been ambushed while on his scouting round! Or suppose he had stayed with his comrades and had been ambushed there! But neither had happened, and, taking Willet by the shoulder, he shook him, at the same time whispering in his ear to make no noise. The hunter, his trained faculties at once awake and on guard, sat up quietly, and Tayoga, who seemed to awake instinctively at the same time, also, sat up.

"What is it, Robert?" whispered Willet.

"An Indian in the bush about two hundred yards away," replied the youth. "I merely saw his hair and the feather in it, but it's safe to assume that he's not the only one."

"That is so," said Tayoga. "A warrior does not come here alone."

"It can't be the band we beat off when we were in the hollow," said Willet confidently. "They must be far south of us, even if they haven't given up the chase."

"It is so, Great Bear," said Tayoga. "Was the warrior's head bare, Lennox, or did he have the headdress, gustoweh, like mine?"

58

"I think," replied Robert, "that the feather projected something like yours, perhaps from a cross-splint."

"Could you tell from what bird the feather came?"

"Yes, I saw that much. It was the plume of an eagle."

Tayoga mused a moment or two. Then he put two fingers to his mouth and blew between them a mellow, peculiar whistle, much like the notes of a deep-throated forest bird. He waited half a minute and a reply exactly similar came.

"These," said Tayoga, "are our people," and rising and parting the bushes, he walked, upright and fearless, toward the thicket in which Robert had seen the warrior. Robert and Willet, influenced by boldness as people always are, followed him with confidence, their rifles not thrust forward, but lying in the hollows of their arms.

A dozen warriors issued from the thicket, at their head a tall man of middle age, open and noble in countenance and dignified in bearing.

"These be Mohawks, Ganeagaono, the Keepers of the Eastern Gate," said Tayoga, "and the sachem Dayohogo, which in English means, At the Forks, leads them. He is a great man, valiant in battle and wise in council. His words have great weight when the fifty sachems meet in the vale of Onondaga to decide the questions of life and death."

He paused and bent his head respectfully before the man of superior age, and, as yet, of superior rank. A look of pleasure appeared upon the face of the Mohawk chief when he saw the young Onondaga.

"It is Tayoga of the clan of the Bear, of the nation Onundagaono (Onondaga)," he said.

"It is so, Dayohogo of the clan of the Wolf, of the nation Ganeagaono (Mohawk)," replied Tayoga. "Thou of the Keepers of the Eastern Gate and my father, Daatgadose, of the Keepers of the Council Fire, have been friends since they stood at the knees of their mothers, and we too are friends, Dayohogo."

"You speak true words, Tayoga," said the chief, looking with an appraising eye upon the handsome face and athletic figure of the young Onondaga. "And the white people with you? One I know to be the Great Bear who calls himself Willet, but the boy I know not."

"His name is Lennox, O Dayohogo. He is the true friend of the Great Bear, of Tayoga and of the Hodenosaunee. He has within the last two days, standing beside us, fought a valiant battle against the Abenakis, the Hurons, the St. Regis and warriors of the other savage tribes that call themselves the allies of Onontio."

Robert felt the penetrating eye of the Mohawk chief upon him.

59

But the gaze of the Indian was friendly, and while he felt admiration for Tayoga he felt equal approval of Lennox.

"You have fought against odds and you have come away safe," he said.

"None of us received any hurt," replied Tayoga, modestly, "but we slew more than one of those who attacked. It was in a gorge of the river far back, and we escaped in the night, swimming with our canoe. Now we rest here, and truly, Dayohogo, we are glad to see you and your warriors. The forest has become safe for us. We have part of a deer left, and we ask you to share it with us."

"Gladly," said Dayohogo. "We bring venison and corn meal, and we will have food together."

His warriors were stalwart men, armed well, and they had no fear of any foe, lighting a fire in the open, warming their deer meat and making bread of their corn meal. The three ate with them, and Robert felt that they were among friends. The Mohawks not only had Frontenac to remember, but further back Champlain, the French soldier and explorer, who had defeated them before they knew the use of firearms. He felt that Duquesne at Quebec would have great difficulty in overcoming the enmity of this warlike and powerful red nation, and he resolved to do what he could to keep them attached to the British cause. It might be only a little, but a little many times amounted to much.

Dayohogo and his warriors had been on a scout toward the north to the very borders of the French settlements, and the chief told the three that an unusual movement was going on there. Regular soldiers were expected soon from France. War belts and splendid presents had been sent to the tribes about the Great Lakes, both to the north and to the south, and Onontio was addressing messages of uncommon politeness to his brethren, the valiant Ganeagaono, otherwise the Mohawks, the Keepers of the Eastern Gate.

"And do the Mohawk chiefs listen to the words of Onontio?" asked Robert anxiously.

Dayohogo did not reply at once. He looked at the green woods. Birds, blue or gray or brown, were darting here and there in the foliage, and his eye rested for a moment on a tiny wren.

"The voice of Onontio is the voice of a bird chattering in a tree," he said. "In the day of my father's father's father the children of Onontio, under Champlain, came with guns, which were strange to us, and with presents they induced the Adirondack warriors to help them. They came up the great lake which the white people call Champlain, then they crossed to Ticonderoga, near the outlet of the

60

lake, Saint Sacrement, and fell upon two hundred warriors of the Ganeagaono, who then knew only the bow and arrow and the war club, and slew many of them. It was four generations ago, but we do not forget. Then when my father was a young warrior Frontenac came with a host of white soldiers and the Canadian Indians and killed the warriors and laid waste with fire the lands of the Five Nations, now the Six. Can the Hodenosaunee forget?"

The chief gloomed into the fire, and his eyes flashed with the memory of ancient wrongs.

"Onontio has sent belts to the Ganeagaono also, has he not?" asked Robert.

The eyes of the chief flashed again.

"He has tried to do so," he replied, "but the Ganeagaono are loyal to their brethren of the Hodenosaunee since Tododahoe first found the sacred wampum on the shore of the lake, Chautauqua. Our three clans, the Turtle, the Wolf and the Bear, met in our largest village south of the river, Ganeagaono (Mohawk), and listened to the bearers of the belts. Then we sent them back to Onontio, telling them if they wished to be heard further they must bring the belt to the council of all the sachems of the Hodenosaunee in the vale of Onondaga."

"The other nations of the Hodenosaunee," said Tayoga, "have always known that the Ganeagaono would do no less. The Keepers of the Eastern Gate have never departed by the width of a single hair from their obligations."

Dayohogo turned his gloomy face upon the Onondaga youth, and it was lighted up suddenly by a smile of appreciation and pleasure.

"Tayoga of the Onundagaono," he said in measured tones, "you have spoken well. The Onundagaono, the Keepers of the Council Fire, and the Ganeagaono, the Keepers of the Eastern Gate, be the first tribes of the Hodenosaunee, and better it be for a warrior of either to burn two days and two nights in the fire than to violate in the least the ancient customs and laws of the Hodenosaunee."

"Before we had the fight with the savage band," said Robert, "we met a Frenchman, the Chevalier Raymond Louis de St. Luc, who was going to the vale of Onondaga with belts from Onontio. St. Luc is a brave man, a great orator, and his words will fall, golden and sweet like honey, on the ears of the fifty chiefs. He will say that Champlain and Frontenac belonged to an ancient day, that the forests have turned green and then turned red a hundred and fifty times since Champlain and sixty times since Frontenac. He will say

61

that what they did was due to a false wind that blew between the French and the Hodenosaunee, hiding the truth, and making friends see in the faces of friends the faces of enemies. He will say that a true wind blows now, and that it has blown away all the falsehoods. He will say that Onontio is a better friend than Corlear to the Hodenosaunee, and far more powerful."

The veteran Mohawk chief looked at young Lennox, and again his gaze was one of approval, also of comprehension.

"My young white friend is already a great warrior," he said. "What he did with Tayoga and the Great Bear proves it, but great as he is he is even greater in the council. The words of the son of Onontio, St. Luc, may drip from his lips like honey, but the speech of Lennox is the voice of the south wind singing among the reeds. Lennox will be a great orator among his people."

Robert blushed, and yet his heart was beating at the praise of Dayohogo, obviously so sincere. He felt with a sudden instinctive rush of conviction that the Mohawk was telling him the truth. It was an early and partial display of the liquid and powerful speech, which afterward gave him renown in New York and far beyond, and which caused people everywhere to call him the "Golden Mouthed." And he was always eager to acknowledge that much of its strength came from the lofty thought and brilliant imagery shown by many of the orators of the nations of the Hodenosaunee, with whom so much of his youth was spent.

"I only spoke the thought that was in my mind, Dayohogo," he said modestly.

"Wherein is the beginning of great speech," said the sachem sagely. "When Lennox returns from the journey on which he is now going it would be fit for him to go to the vale of Onondaga and meet St. Luc in debate before the fifty sachems."

Robert's heart leaped again. It was like a call to battle, and now he knew what his great aim in life should be. He would strive with study and practice to make himself first in it, but, for the present, he had other thoughts and purpose. Willet, however, took fire too from the words of the Mohawk chief.

"I've noticed before, Robert," he said, "that you had the gift of tongues, and we'll make a great orator of you. In times such as ours a man of that kind is needed bad. Maybe what Dayohogo thinks ought to be, will be, and you will yet oppose St. Luc before the fifty sachems in the vale of Onondaga."

"It would be well," said Dayohogo thoughtfully, "because the men at Albany still give the Hodenosaunee trouble, making a promise seem one thing when it is given, and another when the time to keep it comes."

"I know, Dayohogo!" exclaimed Willet, vehemently. "I know how those sleek traders who are appointed to deal with you cheat you out of your furs and try to cheat you out of your lands! But be patient a little longer, you who have been patient so long. Word has come from England that the King will remove his commissioners, and make Sir William Johnson his Indian agent for all North America."

The eyes of Dayohogo and his warriors glistened.

"Is it true?" he asked. "Is Waraiyageh (Johnson) to be the one who will talk with us and make the treaties with us?"

"I know it to be a fact, Dayohogo."

"Then it is well. We can trust Waraiyageh, and he knows that he can trust us. Where our trail runs to Kolaneha (Johnstown) on a hill not far from our tower castle he has built a great house, and I and my brother chiefs of all the three clans the Wolf, the Bear and the Turtle, have been there and have received presents from him. He is the friend of the Ganeagaono, and he knew that he could build a house among us and live there in peace, with our warriors to guard him."

The news that Johnson would be the King's Indian agent had an electric effect upon the Mohawks. Whether he talked English or Iroquois he talked a language they understood, and his acts were comprehensible by them. He had their faith and he never lost it.

Some of the hunters went out, and, the woods being full of game, they quickly shot another deer. Then the warriors still feeling in their strength that they had nothing to dread from enemies, built high the fire, cut up the deer, cooked it and made a great feast. The good feeling that existed between the Mohawks and the two whites increased. Robert unconsciously began to exercise his gift of golden speech. He dwelt upon the coming appointment of Waraiyageh, their best friend, to deal in behalf of the King with the Hodenosaunee, and he harped continually upon Champlain and Frontenac. He made them seem to be of yesterday, instead of long ago. He opened the old wounds the Mohawks had received at the hands of the French and made them sting and burn again. He dwelt upon the faith of the English, their respect for the lands of the Hodenosaunee and the ancient friendship with the Six Nations. He had forgotten the words of Dayohogo that he would be a great orator, but five minutes after they were spoken he was justifying them.

Tayoga and Willet glanced at each other, but remained silent. Young Lennox was saying enough for all three. Dayohogo did not take his eyes from the speaker, following all his words, and the

63

warriors, lying on their elbows, watched him and believed what he said. When he stopped the chief and all the warriors together uttered a deep exclamation of approval.

"You are called Lennox," said Dayohogo, "and after the white custom it is the only name that you have ever had, but we have a better way. When a warrior distinguishes himself greatly we give him a new name, which tells what he has done. Hereafter, Lennox, you will be known to the Ganeagaono as Dagaeoga, which is the name of a great chief of the clan of the Turtle, of our nation."

"I thank you much, Dahoyogo," said Robert, earnestly, knowing that a high honor was conferred upon him. "I shall try to deserve in some small way the great name you have conferred upon me."

"One can but do his best," said the Mohawk gravely.

But Willet rejoiced openly in the distinction that had been bestowed upon his young comrade, saying that some day it might be carried out with formal ceremonies by the Mohawk nation, and was a fact of great value. To be by adoption a son of any nation of the Hodenosaunee would be of enormous assistance to him, if he negotiated with the League in behalf of the English colonists. But to be adopted by both Onondagas and Mohawks gave him a double power.

Robert had already been influenced powerfully by Tayoga, the young Onondaga, and now the words of Dayohogo, the Mohawk, carried that influence yet further. He understood as few white men did the power of the Hodenosaunee and how its nations might be a deciding factor in the coming war between French and English, just as he understood long after that war was over their enormous weight in the new war between the Americans and English, and he formed a resolution as firm as tempered steel that his main effort for many years to come should be devoted to strengthening the ties that connected the people of New York and the great League.

The afternoon went on in pleasant talk. The Indians, among themselves or with those whom they knew from long experience to be good friends, were not taciturn. Robert told the Mohawks that they were going to Quebec, and Dayohogo expressed curiosity.

"It is the story in our nation, and it is true," he said, "that generations ago we held the great rock of Stadacona, and that the first Frenchman, Cartier, who came to Canada, found us there, and drove us away with firearms, which we had never seen before, and which we did not know how to meet. It is said also by our old men that we had a town with palisades around it at Hochelaga (Montreal), but whether it is true or not I do not know. It may be that it was a town of the Wanedote (Hurons), our enemies. And yet the Wanedote are of our blood, though far back in the past we split asunder, and now they take the peace belts of the French, while we take those of the English."

"And the capital of the French, which they call Quebec, and which you call Stadacona, stands on land which really belongs to the Mohawks," said Robert meaningly.

Dayohogo made no answer, but gloomed into the fire again. After a while he said that his warriors and he must depart. They were going toward Ticonderoga, where the French had built the fort, Carillon, within the territory of the Mohawks. He had been glad to meet Tayoga, the Great Bear, and the new young white chief, Dagaeoga, whose speech was like the flowing of pleasant waters. It was a favoring wind that had brought them together, because they had enjoyed good talk, and had exchanged wise counsel with one another. Robert agreed with him in flowery allegory and took from the canoe where it had been stored among their other goods a present for the chief--envoys seldom traveled through the Indian country without some such article for some such occasion.

It was gajewa, a war club, beautifully carved and polished, made of ironwood about three feet long, and with tufts of brilliant feathers at either end. Inserted at one end was a deer's horn, about five inches in length, and as sharp as a razor. While it was called a war club, it was thus more of a battle ax, and at close range and wielded by a powerful arm it was a deadly weapon. It had been made at Albany, and in order to render it more attractive three silver bands had been placed about it at equal intervals.

It was at once a weapon and a decoration, and the eyes of Dayohogo glistened as he received it.

"I take the gift, Dagaeoga," he said, "and I will not forget."

Then they exchanged salutations, and the Mohawks disappeared silently in the forest.

CHAPTER VI
THE TWO FRENCHMEN

When the three were left alone in the glade the hunter turned to young Lennox.

"You've done good work today, Robert," he said. "I didn't know you had in you the makings of an orator and diplomatist. The governor of New York did better than he knew when he chose you for one of this mission."

Robert blushed again at praise and modestly protested.

"Lennox has found that for which he is best fitted," said Tayoga, slyly.

"If I'm to talk without end I'll do my best," said Robert, laughing, "and I suggest that we resume our journey now. There doesn't appear to be any further danger from the Indians who besieged us."

"You're right about it, Robert," said the hunter. "The coming of the Mohawks has put a barrier between us and them. I've an idea that Dayohogo and his warriors won't go far toward Ticonderoga, but will soon turn south to meet those savages and acquire a few scalps if they can, and if they do meet 'em I hope they'll remove that Ojibway, Tandakora, who I think is likely to make us a lot of trouble."

Willet never spoke of the Iroquois as "savages," but he often applied the term to the Canadian and Western Indians. Like Robert, he regarded those who had built up the great political and military power of the Hodenosaunee as advanced, and, in a sense, civilized nations.

"I think my friend, the Great Bear, is right," said Tayoga. "Unless Tandakora and his band have gone toward the west it is likely that Dayohogo will meet them, and they cannot stand before the Mohawks."

"I think it more probable," said Robert, "that after the failure to destroy us Tandakora went back to St. Luc, giving a false explanation of his absence or none at all, just as he pleased."

"It may be so," said Tayoga, "but I have another opinion."

While they talked they were taking the canoe from its shelter, and then they bore it down to the river again, putting it back into the stream and listening with pleasure to the gurgle of the water by its sides.

"Paddling isn't the easiest work in the world," said Willet with satisfaction, "but when you're used to it your muscles can stand it a long time, and it's far ahead of walking. Now, ho for Canada!"

"Ho for Canada!" said Robert, and the three paddles flashed again in the clear water. The canoe once more became a live thing and shot down the stream. They were still in the wilderness, racing between solid banks of green forest, and they frequently saw deer and bear drinking at the edge of the river, while the foliage was vivid with color, and musical with the voices of singing birds.

Robert had a great elation and he had reason to be satisfied with himself. They had triumphed over the dangers of the gorge and savage siege, and he had sowed fruitful seed in the mind of Dayohogo, the powerful Mohawk chief. He had also come to a realization of himself, knowing for the first time that he had a great gift which might carry him far, and which might be of vast service to his people.

Therefore, the world was magnificent and beautiful. The air of forest and mountain was keen with life. His lungs expanded, all his faculties increased in power, and his figure seemed to grow. Swelling confidence bore him on. He was anxious to reach Quebec and fulfill his mission. Then he would go back to the vale of Onondaga and match himself against the clever St. Luc or any other spokesman whom the Marquis Duquesne might choose to send.

But his golden dreams were of Quebec, which was a continuous beacon and lure to him. Despite a life spent chiefly in the woods, which he loved, he always felt the distant spell of great capitals and a gorgeous civilization. In the New World Quebec came nearer than any other city to fulfilling this idea. There the nobles of France, then the most glittering country in the world, came in silks and laces and with gold hilted swords by their sides. The young French officers fought with a jest on their lips, but always with skill and courage, as none knew better than the British colonials themselves. There was a glow and glamor about Quebec which the sober English capitals farther south did not have. It might be the glow and glamor of decay, but people did not know it then, although they did know that the Frenchman, with his love of the forest and skill in handling the Indians, was a formidable foe.

"When do you think we'll reach the St. Lawrence, Dave?" he asked.

"In two or three days if we're not attacked again," replied the hunter, "and then we'll get a bigger boat and row down the river to Quebec."

"Will they let us pass?"

"Why shouldn't they? There's no war, at least not yet."

"That battle back there in the gorge may not have been war, but it looked precisely like it."

The hunter laughed deep in his throat, and it was a satisfied laugh.

"It did look like it," he said, "and it was war, red war, but nobody was responsible for it. The Marquis Duquesne, the Governor General of Canada, who is Onontio to our Iroquois, will raise his jeweled hand, and protest that he knew nothing about those Indians, that they were wild warriors from the west, that none of his good, pious Indians of Canada could possibly have been among them. And the Intendant, Francois Bigot, the most corrupt and ambitious man in North America, will say that they obtained no rifles, no muskets, no powder, no lead from him or his agents. Oh, no, these fine French gentlemen will disown the attack upon us, as they would have disavowed it, just the same, if we had been killed. I want to warn you, Robert, and you, Tayoga, that when you reach Quebec you'll breathe an air that's not that of the woods, nor yet of Albany or New York. It's a bit of old Europe, it's a reproduction on a small scale of the gorgeous Versailles over there that's eating the heart out of France. The Canadian Frenchman is a good man, brave and enduring, as I ought to know, but he's plundered and fooled by those people who come from France to make fame or quick fortunes here."

He spoke with earnestness, but not as a hunter. Rather he seemed now to Robert, despite his forest dress, to be a man of the world, one who understood cities as well as the wilderness.

"I don't know all your life, Dave," said young Lennox, "but I'm quite sure you know a great deal more than you would have people to think. Sometimes I believe you've been across the great water."

"Then you believe right, Robert. I never told you in so many words before, but I've been in Europe. I'll talk to you about it another time, not now, and I'll choose where and when."

He spoke so positively that Robert did not pursue the topic, knowing that if the hunter wished to avoid it he had good reasons. Yet he felt anew that David Willet, called the Great Bear by the Iroquois, had not spent his whole life in the woods and that when the time came he could tell a tale. There was always the fact that Willet spoke excellent English, so unlike the vernacular of the hunters.

The afternoon was waning fast. The sun was setting in an ocean of fire that turned the blue line of the mountains in the east to red. The slope of the land made the current of the river much swifter, and Robert and Willet drew in their paddles, leaving the work to Tayoga alone, who sat in the prow and guided their light craft with occasional strokes, letting the stream do the rest.

There was no more expert canoeman than Tayoga in the whole northern wilderness. A single sweep of his paddle would send the canoe to any point he wished, and apparently it was made without effort. There was no shortening of the breath nor any sudden and violent movement of his figure. It was all as smooth and easy as the flowing of the water itself. It seemed that Tayoga was doing nothing, and that the canoe once more was alive, the master of its own course.

The ocean of fire faded into a sea of gray, and then black night came, but the canoe sped on in the swift current toward the St. Lawrence. It was still the wilderness. The green forest on either side of the stream was unbroken. No smoke from a settler's chimney trailed across the sky. It was the forest as the Indian had known it for centuries. Robert, sitting in the center of the canoe, quit dreaming of great cities and came back to his own time and place. He felt the majesty of all that surrounded him, but he was not lonely, nor was he oppressed. Instead, the night, the great forest, the swift river and the gliding canoe appealed to his sensitive and highly imaginative mind. He was uplifted and he felt the confidence and elation that contribute so much to success.

It was characteristic of the three, so diverse in type, and yet knitted so closely together in friendship, that they would talk much at times and at other times have silence long and complete. Now, neither spoke for at least three hours. Tayoga, in the prow, made occasional strokes of his paddle, but the current remained swift and the speed of the canoe was not slackened. The young Onondaga devoted most of his time to watching. Much wreckage from storms or the suction of flood water often floated on the surface of these wild rivers, and his keen eyes searched for trunk or bough or snag. They also scanned at intervals the green walls speeding by on either side, lest they might pass some camp fire and not notice it, but finding no lighter note in the darkness he felt sure that no hostile bands were near.

About midnight the force of the current began to abate and Robert and Willet used the paddles. The darkness also thinned. The rainless clouds drifted away and disclosed a full moon, which turned the dusk of the water to silver. The stars came out in cluster after cluster and the skies became a shining blue. The wilderness revealed itself in another and splendid phase, and Robert saw and admired.

"How long will we go on, Dave?" The words were his and they were the first to break the long silence.

"Until nearly daylight," replied Willet. "Then we can land, take the canoe into the bushes and rest. What do you say, Tayoga?"

"It is good," replied the Onondaga. "We are not weary, because the river, of its own accord, has borne us on its bosom, but we must sleep. We would not wish to appear heavy of eye and mind before the children of Onontio."

"Well spoken, Tayoga," said the hunter. "An Iroquois chief knows that appearance and dignity count, and you were right to remind us of it. I think that by the next sunset we'll be meeting French, not the Canadian French that they call habitants, but outposts made up mostly of officers and soldiers from France. They'll be very curious about us, naturally so, and since your new friend Dayohogo has announced that you are a great orator, you can do most of the talking and explaining, Robert."

"I'll talk my best," replied young Lennox. "Nobody can do more."

As agreed, they drew the canoe into the bushes shortly before daylight, and slept several hours. Then they returned to the river and resumed their journey. By the middle of the afternoon they saw signs of habitation, or at least of the presence of human beings. They beheld two smokes on the right bank, and one on the left, trailing black lines against the blue of the sky, but they were all far away, and they did not care to stop and determine their origin.

Shortly before sunset they saw a camp fire, very close on the eastern shore, and as they drew near the figures of men in uniform were visible against the red glow.

"I think we'd better draw in here," said Robert. "This is undoubtedly an outpost, and, likely, an officer of some importance is in charge. Ours is a mission of peace, and we want to placate as many people as we can, as we go."

"It is so," said Tayoga, making a sweep or two of the paddle, and sending the canoe in a diagonal line toward the designated shore.

Two men in blue uniforms with white facings walked to the edge of the water and looked at them with curiosity. Robert gave them a gaze as inquiring as their own, and after the habit of the forest, noted them carefully. He took them to be French of France. One was about forty years of age, rather tall, built well, his face browned by forest life. He had black, piercing eyes and a strong hooked nose. A man of resolution but cold of heart, Robert said to himself. The other, a little smaller, and a little younger, was of much the same type. The uniforms of both were fine and neat, and they bore themselves as officers of importance. Like St. Luc, they fortified Robert's opinion of what he was going to find at Quebec.

Neither of the men spoke until the canoe touched the shore, and its three occupants sprang out. Then they bowed politely, though Robert fancied that he saw a trace of irony in their manner, and the elder said in good English:

"Good evening, gentlemen."

"Good evening, Messieurs," said Robert, remembering that he was to be spokesman. "We are English."

"I can see readily that two of you are."

"The third, Tayoga, the son of a great Onondaga chief, is English also at heart."

The lips of the Frenchman curled ever so little. Robert saw at once that he challenged his assertion about Tayoga, but he did not seem to notice it, as he expected that his comrades and himself would be guests in the French camp.

"I have mentioned Tayoga," he said, "but I will introduce him again. He is of the clan of the Bear, of the nation Onondaga, of the great League of the Hodenosaunee. I also present Mr. David Willet, a famous scout and hunter, known to the Indians, and perhaps to some of the French, too, as the Great Bear. My own name is Robert Lennox, of Albany and New York, and I have done nothing that is descriptive of me, but I bear important letters from the Governor of New York to Quebec, to be delivered to the Marquis Duquesne, the Governor General of Canada."

"That, young sir, is no slight mission," said the elder man, "and it is our good fortune to speed you on your way. My friend is the Chevalier Francois de Jumonville, one of France's most gallant officers, and I am Auguste de Courcelles, a colonel by fortune's favor, in the service of His Majesty, King Louis."

"I am sure," said Robert, "that it is not chance or the favor of fortune that has given you such important rank. Your manner and presence are sufficient assurance to me that you have won your rank with your own merits."

De Courcelles laughed a little, but it was a pleased laugh.

"You have a more graceful tongue than most of the English," he said, "and I could almost believe you had been at court."

"No nearer a court than Albany or New York."

"Then, sir, your credit is all the greater, because you have acquired so much with so little opportunity."

Robert bowed formally and Colonel de Courcelles bowed back in the same manner.

71

"The roads from Albany to Quebec are but trails," said de Courcelles, "but I hope your journey has been easy and pleasant."

Willet gave Robert a warning glance, and the lad replied:

"Fairly pleasant. We have met a slight obstacle or two, but it was not hard to remove them."

De Courcelles lifted his eyebrows a little.

"'Tis reported," he said, "that the savages are restless, that your English governors have been making them presents, and, as they interpret them, 'tis an inducement for them to take up the tomahawk against our good Canadians. Oh, don't be offended, Mr. Lennox! I have not said I believe such tales. Perhaps 'tis but the tongue of scandal wagging in this way, because it must wag in some way."

Robert believed much meaning underlay the man's words, and he made rapid surmises. Was de Courcelles trying to draw him out? Did he know of the attack made upon them at the hollow beside the river? Did he seek to forestall by saying the English were corrupting the Indians and sending them forth with the tomahawk? All these questions passed swiftly in his mind, but the gift discovered so newly came to his aid. His face expressed nothing, and smiling a little, he replied:

"The tongue of scandal, sir, does indeed wag wildly. The Governor of New York seeks at all times to keep peace among the Indians, and the fact that I am bearing letters from him to the Marquis Duquesne is proof of his good intentions."

"I accept your professions," said de Courcelles, "as I trust you will accept my own assurances of amity and good faith. Why should we discuss politics, when we are well met here in the woods? We have a fairly good camp, and it's at your service. If I may judge by appearances your journey has been attended by some hardships."

"You infer correctly," replied Robert, "and we shall be glad indeed to share your fire and food with you."

De Courcelles and Jumonville led the way to a large camp fire around which at least fifty French, Canadians and Indians were seated. All the French and Canadians were in uniform, and the Canadians, although living in a colder climate, had become much darker than the parent stock. In truth, many of them were quite as dark as the Indians.

These Canadians of the French stock were, for the present, silent men, and Robert regarded them with the deepest interest. Those who were not in uniform wore long frock coats of dark gray or dark brown, belted at the waist with a woolen sash of bright colors, decorated heavily with beads. Trousers and waistcoats were of the same material as the coats, but their feet were inclosed in Indian moccasins, also adorned profusely with beads. They wore long hair in a queue, incased in an eel-skin, and with their swarthy complexions and high cheek bones they looked like wild sons of the forest to Robert. Tayoga, the Onondaga, was to him a more civilized being. All the Canadians were smoking short pipes, and, while they did not speak, their black eyes, restless with eager curiosity, inspected the strangers.

The Indians in de Courcelles' party were of two types, the converted Indians of Canada, partly in white man's costume, and utterly savage Indians of the far west, in very little costume at all, one or two of them wearing only the breech cloth. The looks they bestowed upon Robert and his comrades were far from friendly, and he wondered if any Ojibway, a warrior who perhaps owned Tandakora as a chief, was among them. They were sitting about the fire and none of them spoke.

"We cannot offer you a banquet," said de Courcelles, "but we can give you variety, none the less. This portion of His Majesty's territory is a wilderness, but it provides an abundance of fish and game."

Robert believed that he had alluded purposely to the territory as "His Majesty's," and, his mind challenging it instantly, he was about to reply that in reality it was the northern part of the Province of New York, but his second and wiser thought caused him to refrain. He would enter upon no controversy with the older man, especially when he saw that the latter wished to draw him into one. De Courcelles, seeing that his lead was not followed, devoted himself to hospitality.

"We have venison, beaver tail, quail, good light bread and some thin red wine," he said. "You Americans or English--which shall I call you?"

"Either," replied Robert, "because we are both."

"Then English it shall be for the present, because you are under that flag. I was going to say that you are somewhat hostile to wine, which we French love, and which we know how to drink in moderation. In some respects we are a people of more restraint than you are. The slow, cold English mind starts with an effort, but when it is started it is stopped with equal difficulty. You either do too little or too much. You lack the logic and precision of the Frenchman."

Robert smiled and replied lightly. Having avoided controversy upon one point, he was of no mind to enter it upon another, and de Courcelles, not pressing a third attack, entered with Jumonville upon his duties as host. Both were graceful, easy, assured, and they

73

fulfilled Robert's conception of French officers, as men of the world who knew courts and manners. It was a time when courts were more important than they are today, and they were recognized universally as the chief fountains from which flowed honor and advancement.

Robert did not like them as well as St. Luc, but he found a certain charm in their company. They could talk of things that interested him, and they exerted themselves, telling indirectly of the glories of Quebec and alluding now and then to the greater splendors of Paris and Versailles. It was a time when the French monarchy loomed as the greatest power in the world. The hollowness and decay of the House of Bourbon were not yet disclosed, even to the shrewdest observers, and a spell was cast upon all the civilized nations by the gorgeous and glittering world of fashion and the world of arms. The influence reached even into the depths of the vast North American wilderness and was felt by Robert as he sat beside the camp fire in the savage woods with the Frenchmen.

He drank a little of the red wine, but only a very little, and Tayoga would not touch it at all. Willet took a small leather cup of it, but declined a second. The food was good, better cooked than it usually was among the English colonists, where the table was regarded as a necessity, and in no particular as a rite. Robert, despite his habitual caution, found his heart warming toward his French hosts. It could not be possible that the Indians had been set upon his comrades and himself by the French! The warmth of his heart increased when one of the Canadians took a violin from a cloth cover and began to play wailing old airs. Like so many others, Robert was not made melancholy by melancholy music. Instead, he saw through a pleasing glow and the world grew poetic and tender. The fire sank and Americans, French, Canadians and Indians listened with the same silent interest. Presently the violinist played a livelier tune and the habitants sang to the music:

> "Malbrouck, s'en va t-en guerre
> Mironton, mironton, mirontaine;
> Malbrouck s'en va t-en guerre
> Ne sait quand reviendra."

Then he left Malbrouck, and it was:

> "Hier sur le pont d'Avignon
> J'ai oui chanter la belle
74

Lon, la,
J'ai oui chanter la belle
Elle chantait d'un ton si doux
   Comme une demoiselle
   Lon, la,
   Comme une demoiselle."

The Canadians sang well, particularly in "The Bridge of Avignon," and the dying fire, the black woods around them and the sighing wind created an effect that no stage scenery could ever have given it. When the last note melted with the wind de Courcelles sighed a little and stared into the sinking fire.

"It is a fair country, sweet France," he said; "I myself have stood upon the bridge of Avignon, and I have watched the pretty girls. It may be that I have had a kiss or two, but all that is far away now. This is a bolder country than France, Mr. Lennox, larger, more majestic, but it is wild and savage, and will be so for many years to come. Nor can the rules that apply to old and civilized Europe apply here, where the deeds of men, like the land, are wilder, too."

Robert was conscious of some meaning in his words, perhaps a trace of apology for a deed that he had done or would do, but in the mind of young Lennox men's standards should be the same, whether in the wilderness of New York and Canada or in the open fields of France and England. De Courcelles, thoughtful for a moment, turned suddenly to the man with the violin and cried:

"Play! Play again!"

The man played quaint old airs, folk songs that had been brought from Normandy and Brittany, and the habitants sang them in low voices or rather hummed them in the subdued manner that seemed fitting to the night, since the black shadows were creeping up closer, leaving only the fire, as a core of light with the dusky figures around it. During all the talk the Indians had been silent. They had eaten their food and remained now, sitting in Turkish fashion, the flickering flames that played across their faces giving to them a look sinister and menacing to the last degree.

The Frenchmen, too, fell silent, as if their courtesy was exhausted and conversation had become an effort. The last of the old French airs was finished, and the player put his violin away. Jumonville, who had spoken but little, threw a fresh stick on the fire and looked at the black wall of circling forest.

"I can never get quite used to it," he said. "The wilderness is so immense, so menacing that when I am in it at night a little shiver will come now and then. I suppose our remote ancestors who lived in caves must have had fear at their elbows all their lives."

"Very likely," said de Courcelles, thoughtfully, staring into the coals. "It isn't strange that many people have worshiped fire as God. Why shouldn't they when it brings light in the dark, and lifts up our souls, when it warms us and makes us feel strong, when it cooks our food and when in the earlier day it drove away the great wild animals, with which man was not able to fight on equal terms?"

"I am not one to undervalue fire," said Robert.

"Few of us do in the forest. The night grows chill, but two of our good Canadians will keep the coals alive until morning. And now I suppose you are weary with your day's travels and wish sleep. I see that you have blankets of your own or I should offer you some of ours."

Tayoga had been sitting before the fire, as silent as the Canadian Indians, his rifle across his knees, his eyes turned toward the blaze. The glow of the flames fell upon him, disclosing his lofty countenance, his splendidly molded figure, and his superiority to the other Indians, who were not of the Hodenosaunee and who to him were, therefore, as much barbarians as all people who were not Greeks were barbarians to the ancient Greeks. Not a word of kinship or friendship had passed between him and them. For him, haughty and uncompromising, they did not exist. For a long time his deep unfathomable eyes had never turned from the fire, but now he rose suddenly and said:

"Someone comes in the forest!"

De Courcelles looked up in surprise.

"I hear nothing," he said.

"Someone comes in the forest!" repeated Tayoga with emphasis.

De Courcelles glanced at his own Indians. They had not yet moved, but in a moment or two they too rose to their feet, and then he knew that the Onondaga was right. Now Robert also heard a moccasined and light footstep approaching. A darker shadow appeared against the darkness, and the figure of an Indian, gigantic and sinister, stepped within the circle of the firelight.

It was Tandakora, the Ojibway.

Chapter VII
New France

The huge and savage warrior had never looked more malignant. His face and his bare chest were painted with the most hideous devices, and his eyes, in the single glance that he cast upon Robert and his comrades, showed full of black and evil passions. Then, as if they were no longer present, he stalked to the fire, took up some cooked deer meat that lay beside it, and, sitting down Turkish fashion like the other Indians, began to eat, not saying a word to the Frenchmen.

It was the action of a savage of the savages, but Robert, startled at first by the unexpected appearance of such an enemy, called to his aid the forest stoicism that he had learned and sat down, calm, outwardly at least. The initiative was not his now, nor that of his comrades, and he glanced anxiously at de Courcelles to see how he would take this rude invasion of his camp. The French colonel looked at Tandakora, then at Jumonville, and Jumonville looked at him. The two shrugged their shoulders, and in a flash of intuition he was convinced that they knew the Ojibway well.

Whatever anger de Courcelles may have felt at the manners of the savage he showed none at all. All the tact and forbearance which the French used with such wonderful effect in their dealings with the North American Indians were summoned to his aid. He spoke courteously to Tandakora, but, as his words were in the Ojibway dialect, Robert did not understand them. The Indian made a guttural reply and continued to gnaw fiercely at the bone of the deer. De Courcelles still took no offense, and spoke again, his words smooth and his face smiling. Then Tandakora, in his deep guttural, spoke rapidly and with heat. When he had finished de Courcelles turned to his guests, and with a deprecatory gesture, said:

"Tandakora's heart burns with wrath. He says that you attacked him and his party in the forest and have slain some of his warriors."

"Tandakora lies!"

It was the Onondaga who spoke. His voice was not raised, but every syllable was articulated clearly, and the statement came with the impact of a bullet. The tan of de Courcelles' face could not keep a momentary flush from breaking through, but he kept his presence of mind.

"It is easy enough to call a man a liar," he said, "but it is another thing to prove it."

"Since when," said Tayoga, haughtily, "has the word of an Ojibway, a barbarian who knows not the law, been worth more than that of one who is a member of the clan of the Bear, of the nation Onondaga, of the great League of the Hodenosaunee?"

He spoke in English, which Robert knew the Ojibway understood and which both Frenchmen spoke fluently. The great hand of Tandakora drifted down toward the handle of his tomahawk, but Tayoga apparently did not see him, his fathomless eyes again staring into the fire. Robert looked at Willet, and he saw the hunter's eye also fall upon the handle of his tomahawk, a weapon which he knew the Great Bear could hurl with a swiftness and precision equal to those of any Indian. He understood at once that Tayoga was protected by the hunter from any sudden movement by the Ojibway and his great strain relaxed.

De Courcelles frowned, but his face cleared in an instant. Robert, watching him now, believed he was not at all averse to a quarrel between the Onondaga and the Ojibway.

"It is not a question for me to decide," he replied. "The differences of the Hodenosaunee and the western tribes are not mine, though His Majesty, King Louis of France, wishes all his red brethren to dwell together in peace. Yet I but tell to you, Tayoga, what Tandakora has told to me. He says that you three attacked him and peaceful warriors back there in a gorge of the river, and slew some of his comrades."

"Tandakora lies," repeated Tayoga in calm and measured tones. "It is true that warriors who were with them fell beneath our bullets, but they came swimming in the night, seeking to murder us while we slept, and while there is yet no war between us. An Onondaga or a Mohawk or any warrior of the Hodenosaunee hates and despises a snake."

The words, quiet though they were, were fairly filled with concentrated loathing. The eyes of the huge Ojibway flashed and his clutch on the handle of his tomahawk tightened convulsively, but the fixed gaze of the hunter seemed to draw him at that moment. He saw that Willet's eyes were upon him, that every muscle was attuned and that the tomahawk would leap from his belt like a flash of lightning, and seeing, Tandakora paused.

The two Frenchmen looked at Tayoga, at Tandakora and at Willet. Then they looked at each other, and being acute men with a full experience of forest life, they understood the silent drama.

"I don't undertake to pass any judgment here," said de Courcelles, after a pause. "It is the word of one warrior against another, and I cannot say which is the better. But since you are going to the Marquis Duquesne at Quebec, Mr. Lennox, the matter may be laid before him, and it is for those who make charges to bring proof."

The words were silky, but Robert saw that they were intended to weave a net.

"We are on an official mission from the Governor of the Province of New York to the Governor General of Canada," he said. "We cannot be tried at Quebec for an offense that we have never committed, and for our commission of which you have only the word of a barbarian who twice tried to murder us."

The hand of Tandakora on the handle of his tomahawk again made a convulsive movement, but the gaze of the hunter was fixed upon him with deadly menace, and another hand equally as powerful and perhaps quicker than his own was clutched around the handle of another tomahawk. Again the Ojibway paused and chose the way of peace.

"Patience, Tandakora," said Jumonville, taking the initiative for the first time. "If you have suffered wrongs Onontio will avenge them. His eye sees everything, and he does not forget his children of the western forests."

"When we first saw him," said Robert, "he was with the Chevalier Raymond Louis de St. Luc, who was going with belts from the Marquis Duquesne to the council of the fifty chiefs in the vale of Onondaga. Now he has come on another course, and is here far from the vale of Onondaga."

"We will dismiss the matter," said de Courcelles, who evidently was for peace also. "Since you and your friends are our guests, Mr. Lennox, we cannot treat you except as such. Take to your blankets and you rest as safely with us as if you were sleeping in your own town of Albany."

Willet removed his hand from the handle of his tomahawk, and, rising to his full height, stretched himself and yawned.

"We accept your pledge in the spirit in which it is given, Colonel de Courcelles," he said, "and being worn from a long day and long toil I, for one, shall find sweet slumber here on the leaves with a kindly sky above me."

"Then, sir, I bid you a happy good night," said Colonel de Courcelles.

Without further ado the three folded their blankets them and fell asleep on the leaves.

Robert, before closing his eyes, had felt assured that no harm would befall them while they were in the camp of de Courcelles, knowing that the French colonel could not permit any attack in his own camp upon those who bore an important message from the Governor of New York to the Governor General of Canada. Hence his heart was light as he was wafted away to the land of slumber, and it was light again when he awoke the next morning at the first rays of dawn.

Tayoga and Willet still slept, and he knew that they shared his confidence, else these wary rovers of the woods would have been watching rather than sleeping. Jumonville also was still rolled in his blankets, but de Courcelles was up, fully dressed, and alert. Several of the Canadians and Indians were building a fire. Robert's questing eye sought at once for the Ojibway, but he was gone, and the youth was not surprised. His departure in the night was a relief to everybody, even to the French, and Robert felt that an evil influence was removed. The air that for a space the night before had been poisonous to the lungs was now pure and bracing. He took deep breaths, and his eyes sparkled as he looked at the vast green forest curving about them. Once more he felt to the full the beauty and majesty of the wilderness. Habit and use could never dull it for him.

De Courcelles turned upon him a frank and appreciative eye. Robert saw that he intended to be pleasant, even genial that morning, having no reason for not showing his better side, and the lad, who was learning not only to fence and parry with words, but also to take an intellectual pleasure in their use, was willing to meet him half way.

"I see, Mr. Lennox," said de Courcelles gayly, "that you are in a fine humor this morning. Your experience with the Ojibway has left no ill results. He departed in the night. One can never tell what strange ideas these savages will take into their heads."

"I have forgotten it," said Robert lightly. "I knew that a French gentleman could not take the word of a wild Ojibway against ours."

De Courcelles gave him a sharp glance, but the youth's face was a mask.

"At least," he said, "the matter is not one of which I could dispose. Nor can any government take note of everything that passes in a vast wilderness. I, too, shall forget it. Nor is it likely that it will ever be taken before the Marquis Duquesne. Come, our breakfast will soon be ready and your comrades are awakening."

Robert walked down to a small brook, bathed his face, and returned to find the food ready. He did not wholly trust either de Courcelles or Jumonville, but their manners were good, and it was quite evident that they no longer wished to interfere with the progress of the mission. Tayoga and Willet also seemed to have forgotten the episode of the night before, and asked no questions about Tandakora. After breakfast, the three put their canoe back in the river, and thanking their hosts for the courtesy of a night in their camp, shot out into the stream. De Courcelles and Jumonville, standing on the bank, waved them farewell, and they held their paddles aloft a moment or two in salute. Then a bend shut them from view.

"I don't trust them," said Robert, after a long silence. "This is our soil, but they march over it and calmly assume that it's their own."

"King George claims it, and King Louis claims it, too," said Willet in a whimsical tone, "but I'm thinking it belongs to neither. The ownership, I dare say, will not be decided for many a year. Now, Tayoga, what do you think has become of that demon, Tandakora?"

The Onondaga looked at the walls of foliage on either side of the stream before answering.

"One cannot tell," he said in his precise language of the schools. "The mind of the Ojibway is a fitful thing, but always it is wild and lawless. He longs, night and day, for scalps, and he covets ours most. It is because we have defeated the attempts he has made already."

"Do you think he has gone ahead with the intention of ambushing us? Would he dare?"

"Yes, he would dare. If he were to succeed he would have little to fear. A bullet in one of our hearts, fired from cover on the bank, and then the wilderness would swallow him up and hide him from pursuit. He could go to the country around the last and greatest of the lakes, where only the white trapper or explorer has been."

"It gives me a tremendously uncomfortable feeling, Tayoga, to think that bloodthirsty wretch may be waiting for a shot at us. How are we to guard against him?"

"We must go fast and watch as we go. Our eyes are keen, and we may see him moving among the trees. The Ojibway is no marksman, and unless we sit still it is not likely that he can hit us."

Tayoga spoke very calmly, but his words set Robert's heart to beating, understanding what an advantage Tandakora had if he sought to lie in ambush. He knew that the soul of the Ojibway was full of malice and that his craving for scalps was as strong as the Onondaga had said it was. Had it been anyone else he would not follow them, but Robert foresaw in Tandakora a bitter and persistent enemy. Both he and Willet, feeling the wisdom of Tayoga's advice, began to paddle faster. But the hunter presently slowed down a little.

"No use to take so much out of ourselves now that we'll just creep along later on," he said.

"The temptation to go fast is very strong," said Robert. "You feel then that you're really dodging bullets."

Tayoga was looking far ahead toward a point where the stream became much narrower and both banks were densely wooded, as usual.

"If Tandakora really means to ambush us," he said, "he will be there, because it offers the best opportunity, and it is a place that the heart of a murderer would love. Suppose that Dagaeoga and I paddle, and that the Great Bear rests with his rifle across his knees ready to fire at the first flash. We know what a wonderful marksman the Great Bear is, and it may be Tandakora who will fall."

"The plan, like most of yours, is good, Tayoga," said Willet. "The Lord has given me some skill with the rifle, and I have improved it with diligent practice. I think I can watch both sides of the stream pretty well, and if the Ojibway fires I can fire back at the flash. We'll rely upon our speed to make his bullet miss, and anyway we must take the chance. You lads needn't exert yourselves until we come to the narrow part of the stream. Then use the paddles for your lives."

Robert found it hard to be slow, but his will took command of his muscles and he imitated the long easy strokes of Tayoga. As the current helped much, their speed was considerable, nevertheless. The river flowed, a silver torrent, in the clear light of the morning, a fish leaping up now and then in the waters so seldom stirred by any strange presence. The whole scene was saturated with the beauty and the majesty of the wilderness, and to the eye that did not know it suggested only peace. But Robert often lifted his gaze from the paddle and the river to search the green thickets on either side. They were only casual glances, Willet being at once their sentinel and guard.

The great hunter was never more keenly alert. His thick, powerful figure was poised evenly in the canoe, and the long-barreled rifle lay in the hollow of his arm, his hand on the lock and his finger on the trigger. Eyes, trained by many years in the forest, searched continually among the trees for a figure that did not belong there, and, at the same time, he listened for the sound of any movement not natural to the wilderness. He felt his full responsibility as the rifleman of the fleet of one canoe, and he accepted it.

"Lads," he said, "we're approaching the narrowest part of the river. It runs straight, I can see a full mile ahead, and for all that distance it's not more than thirty yards from shore to shore. Now use the strength that you've been saving, and send the canoe forward like an arrow. Those are grand strokes, Tayoga! And yours too, Robert! Now, our speed is increasing! We fairly fly! Good lads! I knew you were both wonderful with the paddle, but I did not know you were such marvels! Never mind the woods, Robert, I'm watching 'em! Faster! A little faster, if you can! I think I see something moving in a thicket on our right! Bang, there goes his rifle! Just as I expected, his bullet hit the water twenty feet from us! And bang goes my own rifle! How do you like that, my good friend Tandakora?"

"Did you make an end of him?" asked Robert breathlessly.

"No," replied the hunter, although his tone was one of satisfaction. "I had to shoot when I saw the flash of his rifle, and I had only a glimpse of him. But I saw enough to know that my bullet took him in the shoulder. His rifle fell from his hand, and then he dropped down in the underbrush, thinking one of you might snatch up a weapon and fire. No, I didn't make an end of him, Robert, but I did make an end of his warfare upon us for a while. That bullet must have gone clean through his shoulder, and for the present at least he'll have to quit scalp hunting. But how he must hate us!"

"Let him hate," said Robert. "I don't care how much his hate increases, so long as he can't lie in ambush for us. It's pretty oppressive to have an invisible death lurking around you, unable to fend it off, and never knowing when or where it will strike."

"But we did fend it off," said the big hunter, as he reloaded the rifle of which he had made such good use. "And now I can see the stream widening ahead of us, with natural meadows on either side, where no enemy can lay an ambush. Easy now, lads! The danger has passed. That fiend is lying in the thicket binding up his wounded shoulder as best he can, and tomorrow we'll be in Canada. Draw in your paddles, and I'll take mine. You're entitled to a rest. You couldn't have done better if you had been in a race, and, after all, it was a race for life."

Robert lifted his paddle and watched the silver bubbles fall from it into the stream. Then he sank back in his seat, relaxing after his great effort, his breath coming at first in painful gasps, but gradually becoming long and easy.

"I'm glad we'll be in Canada tomorrow, Dave," he said, "because the journey has surely been most difficult."

"Pretty thick with dangers, that's true," laughed the hunter, "but we've run past most of 'em. The rest of the day will be easy, safe and pleasant."

His prediction came true, their journey on the river continuing without interruption. Two or three times they saw distant smoke rising above the forest, but they judged that it came from the camp fires of hunters, and they paid no further attention to it. That night they took the canoe from the river once more, carrying it into the woods and sleeping beside it, and the next day they entered the mighty St. Lawrence.

"This is Canada," said Willet. "Farther west we claim that our territory comes to the river and that we have a share in it. But here it's surely French by right of long occupation. We can reach Montreal by night, where we'll get a bigger boat, and then we'll go on to Quebec. It's a fine river, isn't it, Robert?"

"So it is," replied Robert, looking at the vast sheet of water, blue then under a perfectly blue sky, flowing in a mighty mass toward the sea. Tayoga's eyes sparkled also. The young warrior could feel to the full the splendors of the great forests, rivers and lakes of his native land.

"I too shall be glad to see Stadacona," he said, "the mighty rock that once belonged to a nation of the Hodenosaunee, the Mohawks, the Keepers of the Eastern Gate."

"It is the French who have pressed upon you and who have driven you from some of your old homes, but it is the English who have respected all your rights," said Robert, not wishing Tayoga to forget who were the friends of the Hodenosaunee.

"It is so," said the Onondaga.

Taking full advantage of the current, and sparing the paddles as much as they could, they went down the stream, which was not bare of life. They saw two great canoes, each containing a dozen Indians, who looked curiously at them, but who showed no hostility.

"It's likely they take us for French," said Willet. "Of what tribe are these men, Tayoga?"

"I cannot tell precisely," replied the Onondaga, "but they belong to the wild tribes that live in the regions north of the Great Lakes. They bring furs either to Montreal or Quebec, and they will carry back blankets and beads and guns and ammunition. Above the Great Lakes and running on, no man knows how far, are many other vast lakes. It is said that some in the distant north are as large as Erie or Ontario or larger, but I cannot vouch for it, as we warriors of the Hodenosaunee have never been there, hearing the tales from warriors of other tribes that have come down to trade."

"It's true, Tayoga," said Willet. "I've roamed north of the Great Lakes myself, and I've met Indians of the tribes called Cree and Assiniboine, and they've told me about those lakes, worlds and worlds of 'em, and some of 'em so big that you can paddle days without reaching the end. I suppose there are chains and chains of lakes running up and down a hollow in the middle of this continent of ours, though it's only a guess of mine about the middle. Nobody knows how far it is across from sea to sea."

"We better go in closer to the shore," said Tayoga. "A wind is coming and on so big a river big waves will rise."

"That's so, Tayoga," said Willet. "A little bark canoe like ours wasn't made to fight with billows."

They paddled near to the southern shore, and, being protected by the high banks, the chief force of the wind passed over their heads. In the center of the stream the water rose in long combers like those of the sea, and a distant boat with oarsmen rocked violently.

"Hugging the land will be good for us until the wind passes," said Willet. "Suppose we draw in among those bushes growing in the edge of the water and stop entirely."

"A good idea," said Robert, who did not relish a swamping of the canoe in the cold St. Lawrence.

A few strokes of the paddle and they were in the haven, but the three still watched the distant boat, which seemed to be of large size, and which still kept in the middle of the stream.

"It has a mast and can carry a sail when it wishes," said Willet, after a long examination.

"French officers are in it," said Tayoga.

"I believe you are right, boy. I think I caught the glitter of a uniform."

"And the boat has steered about and is coming this way, Great Bear. The French officers no doubt have the glasses that magnify, and, having seen us, are coming to discover what we are."

"Correct again, Tayoga. They've turned their prow toward us, and, as we don't want to have even the appearance of hiding, I think we'd better paddle out of the bushes and make way slowly again close to the shore."

A few sweeps of the paddle and the canoe was proceeding once more down the St. Lawrence, keeping in comparatively quiet waters near the southern side. The large boat was approaching them fast, but they pretended not to have seen it.

"Probably it comes from Hochelaga," said Tayoga.

"And your Hochelaga, which is the French Montreal, was Iroquois once, also," said Robert.

"Our fathers and grandfathers are not sure," replied Tayoga. "Cartier found there a great village surrounded by a palisade, and many of our people think that a nation of the Hodenosaunee, perhaps the Mohawks, lived in it, but other of our old men say it was a Huron town. It is certain though that the Hodenosaunee lived at Stadacona."

"In any event, most of this country was yours or races kindred to yours owned it. So, Tayoga, you are traveling on lands and waters that once belonged to your people. But we're right in believing that boat has come to spy us out. I can see an officer standing up and watching us with glasses."

"Let 'em come," said Willet. "There's no war--at least, not yet--and there's plenty of water in the St. Lawrence for all the canoes, boats and ships that England and France have."

"If they hail us," said Robert, "and demand, as they probably will, what we're about, I shall tell them that we're going to the Marquis Duquesne at Quebec and show our credentials."

The large boat rapidly came nearer, and as men on board furled the sail others at the oars drew it alongside the little canoe, which seemed a mere cork on the waves of the mighty St. Lawrence. But Robert, Tayoga and Willet paddled calmly on, as if boats, barges and ships were everyday matters to them, and were not to be noticed unduly. A tall young man standing up in the boat hailed them in French and then in English. Robert, watching out of the corner of his eye, saw that he was fair, like so many of the northern French, that he was dressed in a uniform of white with violet facings, and that his hat was black and three-cornered. He learned afterward that it was the uniform of a battalion of Languedoc. He saw also that the boat carried sixteen men, all except the oarsmen being in uniform.

"Who are you?" demanded the officer imperiously.

Robert, to whom the others conceded the position of spokesman, had decided already that his course should be one of apparent indifference.

"Travelers," he replied briefly, and the three bent to their paddles.

"What travelers are you and where are you going?" demanded the officer, in the same imperious manner.

The wash of the heavy boat made the frail canoe rock perilously, but its three occupants appeared not to notice it. Using wonderful skill, they always brought it back to the true level and maintained a steady course ahead. On board the larger boat the oarsmen, rowing hard, kept near, and for the third time the officer demanded:

"Who are you? I represent the authority of His Majesty, King Louis of France, upon this river, and unless you answer explicitly I shall order my men to run you down."

"But we are messengers," said Robert calmly. "We bear letters of great importance to the Marquis Duquesne at Quebec. If you sink us it's likely the letters will go down with us."

"It's another matter if you are on such a mission, but I must demand once more your names."

"The highest in rank among us is the young chief, or coming chief, Tayoga, of the clan of the Bear, of the nation Onondaga, of the great League of the Hodenosaunee. Next comes David Willet, a famous hunter and scout, well known throughout the provinces of New York and Massachusetts and even in Canada, and often called by his friends, the Iroquois, the Great Bear. As for me, I am Robert Lennox, of Albany and sometimes of New York, without rank or office."

The officer abated his haughty manner. The answer seemed to please him.

"That surely is explicit enough," he said. "I am Louis de Galisonniere, a captain of the battalion Languedoc, stationed for the present at Montreal and charged with the duty of watching the river for all doubtful characters, in which class I was compelled to put the three of you, if you gave no explanations."

"Galisonniere! That is a distinguished name. Was there not a Governor General of Canada who bore it?"

"A predecessor of the present Governor General, the Marquis Duquesne. It gives me pride to say that the Count de Galisonniere was my uncle."

Robert saw that he had found the way to young Galisonniere's good graces through his family and he added with the utmost sincerity, too:

"New France has had many a great Governor General, as we of the English colonies ought to know, from the Sieur de Roberval, through Champlain, Frontenac, de Beauharnais and on to your uncle, the Count de Galisonniere."

Willet and the Onondaga gave Robert approving looks, and the young Frenchman flushed with pleasure.

"You have more courtesy and appreciation for us than most of the Bostonnais," he said. "I would talk further with you, but conversation is carried on with difficulty under such circumstances. Suppose we run into the first cove, lift your canoe aboard, and we'll take you to Montreal, since that's our own port of destination."

Robert agreed promptly. He wished to make a good impression upon de Galisonniere, and, since the big boat was now far safer and more comfortable than the canoe, two ends would be served at the same time. Willet and the Onondaga also nodded in acquiescence, and a mile or two farther on they and the canoe too went aboard de Galisonniere's stout craft. Then the sail was set again, they steered to the center of the stream and made speed for Montreal.

CHAPTER VIII
GUESTS OF THE ENEMY

Captain Louis de Galisonniere proved to be a genial host, pleased with his guests, pleased with himself, and pleased with the situation. Brave and alert, he had also a certain amount of vanity which Robert had tickled. It was not for nothing that he was a nephew of Count de Galisonniere, once Governor General of Canada, rank and birth counting for so much then with the French nation, and it was not for nothing, either, that he had won his captaincy by valiant and diligent service of his own. So it afforded him great satisfaction to be hospitable now, and also to patronize slightly these men from the south, with whom in all probability New France would be at war before another year had passed. It was well also to impress the Onondaga, whom his vigilant mind recognized at once as a youth of station. None knew better than de Galisonniere the power and importance of the Iroquois, and how they might tip the scale in a great war between the French and British colonies.

His boat, which he proudly called the Frontenac, after the early and great Governor General of Canada, was equipped with supplies needed on trips between ports on the St. Lawrence. After providing stools for his guests, he offered them the light wine of France, even as de Courcelles had done, but Robert and Tayoga declined, although Willet accepted a glass.

"We appreciate your courtesy," said Robert, "but we descendants of the English in America do not take much to wine. I find that my head is much better without it."

"The intoxicating drinks of the white men are not good for the red race," said Tayoga gravely. "The warriors of the Hodenosaunee are able to fight anything else, but strong liquors take away their brains and make them like little children who fly into passions over trifles."

De Galisonniere looked with great interest at the young Onondaga, being impressed by the dignity of his manner and the soberness of his speech.

"You speak perfect English," he observed.

"I learned it in a white man's school at Albany," said Tayoga. "Lennox was my comrade there, just as he has been in the woods."

"You will see a much greater town than Albany when you

arrive at Quebec. You will see a noble city, on a noble site, an impregnable fortress, guarded by the most valiant troops in the world. For its like you would have to cross the sea to our old land of France."

"I have heard much of Stadacona, which you call Quebec," said Tayoga, without any alteration of tone. "Our old men speak often of it, when it belonged to our brethren, the Ganeagaono, known to you as the Mohawks, who never sold or ceded it to anybody."

De Galisonniere's face fell a little, but he recovered himself quickly.

"That was generations ago," he said, "and time makes many shifts and changes. There is a flux and efflux of all people, including the white, like the ceaseless movement of sand upon a beach."

The Onondaga was silent, but Robert saw that he did not unbend, and de Galisonniere, feeling that it was unwise to pursue the topic, turned his attention to the mighty river and its lofty wooded banks.

"I don't believe there's another river in the world the equal of this giant French stream of ours," he said.

"Our noble British river, the Hudson, has much to say for itself," said Robert.

"A grand river, in truth. I have seen it, but large and splendid as it is it lacks the length and size of the St. Lawrence."

"It is beyond question a noble stream to travel on. One makes greater speed here and suffers less hardship than in the forest."

"I am glad that I can take you to Montreal."

"Your hospitality to us, Captain de Galisonniere, is appreciated. I have found French officers courteous and ready to share with us all they had. You are not the first whom we have met on this journey. We encountered far down in our province of New York the Chevalier Raymond de St. Luc."

"St. Luc! St. Luc! The very flower of French chivalry! He is a relative of the famous La Corne de St. Luc, of whom you have doubtless heard, and at Quebec he is considered a model of all the qualities that make a soldier and a gentleman."

"He made a like impression upon me. Farther north we were so fortunate as to meet more of your countrymen, Colonel de Courcelles and Captain de Jumonville."

"I know them both! Brave officers!" said de Galisonniere.

But he turned away the conversation from the Frenchmen who had gone down into territory that Robert considered a portion of the Province of New York, and the lad surmised that, knowing a good deal about the nature of their errands, he feared lest he might reveal something through chance allusions. Instead, he talked of the St. Lawrence, Montreal, and the glories of Quebec to which he hoped he might return soon. He addressed most of his talk to Robert, but he spoke at times to Willet and Tayoga, both of whom responded briefly. The wind meanwhile remained strong, and it was not necessary to use the oars, the large sail carrying them swiftly toward Montreal. Robert, while talking with de Galisonniere, watched eagerly the two shores, seeing the smoke rise from the stout log houses of the Canadians, and once the tall steeple of a church dominating a little village, and seeming out of all proportion to the congregation that surrounded it.

"Yes, the church is very powerful with us," said de Galisonniere, following his eyes and noting his expression. "It suits our people, particularly our good Canadian French. Our priests are patriotic, brave, self-sacrificing, and are a power in our dealings with the Indians."

"I know it," said Robert.

At night they reached Montreal, then much inferior in size and importance to Quebec, the canoe was lifted from the Frontenac, and after many exchanges of courtesies, the three went to an inn.

"If chance offers," said Robert, "we shall be glad to help you as you have helped us."

"One never knows," said de Galisonniere. "You and I need not conceal from each other that there is much talk of war between England and France, which, of course, would mean war also between the English and French colonies. If it comes, and come it will, I think, I trust that no ill luck will befall you upon the battlefield."

"And I wish you as well," said Robert, sincerely.

The canoe was left in trustworthy hands, it being their purpose to sell it on the morrow and buy a larger boat, and they walked through the streets of this town of Hochelaga toward their inn. There were other Indians on the street--French Indians they were called to distinguish them from those who formed a British alliance--but none could be compared with Tayoga, arrayed in the full splendor of a coming chief of the clan of the Bear, of the nation Onondaga, of the League of the Hodenosaunee. Never had he borne himself more haughtily, never had his height appeared greater or his presence grander. Robert, looking at him, felt that if St. Luc was the very flower of French chivalry, this young comrade of his was to an even greater degree the very spirit and essence of all that was best in the great League of the Hodenosaunee.

The Indians--Hurons, Abenakis, St. Regis, Ottawas, and warriors from farther west--watched Tayoga with fascinated eyes. They knew perfectly well who the tall youth was, that he belonged to the great Iroquois league, and they knew, too, in their secret hearts that he had the superiority which Onondaga, Mohawk and their allied nations claimed. Hence, while their looks sometimes expressed an unwilling admiration, they were also charged always with hostility and hate. But Tayoga apparently took no notice. Once more he was the Greek to whom all outer peoples were barbarians.

"I don't think the French can make much progress with him," whispered Willet to Robert. "As the Indian has no written language, his memory is long. When we reach Quebec he'll never forget for an instant that it was once Stadacona, a village of the Mohawks, the Keepers of the Eastern Gate, and one of the great nations of the Hodenosaunee."

"No, he will not," said Robert, "and look who is waiting to meet us!"

Standing before a low house, which was crowded with the goods of a fur trader, were a half-dozen Indians, wild and savage in looks to the last degree, and in the center was one whose shoulder was bound tightly with a great roll of deerskin. In stature he rose far above the other warriors, and he had a thickness in proportion. The hate that the rest had shown when they looked upon Tayoga was nothing to his, which was the very concentrated essence of all malice.

"Our good friend, Tandakora, despite his wound seems to have arrived ahead of us," said Willet to Robert.

"Yes, and he shows very clearly that he would like to give Tayoga to the torture with himself as torturer, and yet he must know that it was you who put the bullet through his shoulder."

"Quite true, Robert, but he resents the Onondaga more than he does us. We are strangers, aliens to him, and he makes no comparisons with us, but Tayoga is an Indian like himself, whom he has fought against, and against whom he has failed. Watch us pass. For Tayoga, Tandakora will not exist, and it will instill more poison into the heart of the Ojibway."

Willet was a good prophet. The Onondaga walked within five feet of the Ojibway, but he did not show by the slightest sign that he was aware of the existence of Tandakora. The entire little drama, played by the children of the forest, was perfectly clear. Tandakora was dirt under the feet of Tayoga, and Tandakora felt that it was so. His heart burned within him and a twinge through his shoulder added to his anger. Yet he was powerless there in Montreal with the

French troops about, and he could merely glare impotently while the three walked by ignoring his existence. But they did not forget him, and each in his heart resolved to be on watch against treacherous attack.

They found on the slope of a high hill the inn to which de Galisonniere had recommended them, and obtained quarters for the night. Monsieur Jolivet, the proprietor, had lodged Indians before, great chiefs treating with the French Government, and he did not think it strange that Tayoga should come there. In truth, Monsieur Jolivet was a thrifty man who despised no patronage for which the pay was assured, and since peace still existed between France and Great Britain he was quite willing to entertain any number of Bostonnais at his most excellent inn on the slope of a high hill overlooking the St. Lawrence. Willet had shown him the color of gold, and from natural ability and long experience as an innkeeper being a shrewd reader of faces he was sure that his three unusual guests could be trusted.

Willet knew Canada better than Robert, and now he acted as spokesman.

"We will sleep here only one night," he said, "because early tomorrow morning we take boat for Quebec. We three will occupy one large room. You have such a room with three beds, have you not?"

"I have the room," responded Monsieur Jolivet promptly, "and the beds can be put in it at once. Then all will be arranged quickly by Lizette and Marie, the maids. Will you permit my man, Francois, to carry your weapons to the chamber now?"

"I think not," replied Willet, giving his rifle an affectionate look. "I've lived so long with this good old rifle of mine that we hate to be parted even for an hour. Tayoga and Mr. Lennox are younger than I am, but they're beginning to feel the same way about their arms. If you don't mind, Monsieur Jolivet, we'll keep our weapons with us."

"Ah, I see, sir, that you're a man of sentiment," said Monsieur Jolivet, laughing and rubbing his hands. "It is well that one can feel it in this rough world of ours. But will Monsieur see a young officer who has come from the commandant? Merely a little inquiry about your identity and an examination of your papers, if you have any. It's according to our custom, and it's just a formality, nothing more."

Robert knew that it was far from being a formality, but his comrades and he had nothing to fear, as their mission was duly accredited and they carried the letters to the Marquis Duquesne.

The young officer, a Frenchman of Canadian birth, entered presently, and with the courtesy characteristic of the French race, a trait that Robert liked, asked for an account of themselves, which was given readily. As usual the effect of the letters addressed to the Marquis Duquesne was magical, and, as the officer withdrew, he tendered them all the help he could give for a speedy and pleasant voyage to Quebec.

Monsieur Jolivet gave them a supper in his best style. Although a native of New France he was of Provencal blood, and he had a poetic strain. He offered to his guests not an excellent inn alone, but a magnificent view also, of which he made full use. The evening being warm with a soft and soothing wind, Marie and Lizette set the table in a little garden, in which early flowers were blooming already, offering delicate colors of pink and rose and pale blue. The table was spread with a white cloth, and silver and china were not lacking. The eyes of Robert, who had a fastidious taste, glistened.

"Monsieur Jolivet may be our enemy or not," he said, "but I like him. It is not often that one can dine at such an inn, with such a view of mountain, forest and magnificent river. In truth, the French do some things well."

"They surpass us in the matter of inns," said Willet. "They think more about it--and take more trouble. I'm sorry we have to quarrel with the French. They're good people, though they haven't been oversqueamish in the use of savages against us, and they're really responsible for the cruelties done by the painted demons."

He spoke freely of red "savages" before Tayoga, knowing that the young Onondaga would never think of applying the word to himself. Willet had shown too often that he considered the people of the Hodenosaunee the equals of anybody. Then he took their three rifles, laid them together on the grass by the side of a graveled walk and, looking at the vast expanse of mountain, forest and river, drew a deep breath.

"It's not much like fighting for our lives back there in the gorge, is it, Robert?" he asked. "It's a strange world here in America. We're lying in a rocky hollow one day, shooting at people who are shooting at us, and both sides shooting to kill, and two or three days later we're sitting at an inn in a town, eating off silver and china."

"It's a quick and pleasant transformation," said Robert, appreciatively.

He would have called it supper, but in Montreal it was dinner, and it was served by Lizette and Marie. There was fish from the St. Lawrence, chicken, beef, many vegetables, good white bread and coffee, all prepared in the excellent manner characteristic of Monsieur Jolivet's famous inn. Tayoga ate abundantly but delicately. He had learned the use of knife and fork at the school in Albany, and, like Robert, he was fastidious at the table.

Monsieur Jolivet, after his manner, gave them much of his own presence. One must be polite to the Bostonnais at such a time. He discoursed quite freely of Montreal, and of its advantages as a great trading post with the Indians, who already brought there vast quantities of furs. It would become one of the greatest and most brilliant jewels in the French crown, second perhaps only to Paris. But for the present, the chief glory of New France could be seen only at Quebec Ah, when the Bostonnais arrived there they would behold great lords and great ladies!

The three listened, each interested in his own way. Robert's fancy saw the silken splendor of a vice-regal court, and, anxious to know the larger world, he was more glad than ever that he had come upon this errand, dangerous though it had proved to be.

They sat a while after the dinner was over, looking down at the town and the great view beyond, a clear moon and brilliant stars casting a silver light which illuminated almost like the day. They saw lights gleaming in houses, and now and then shadowy figures passing. Out in the river a boat with a mast rocked in the current, and Robert believed it was the Frontenac of Louis de Galisonniere.

As the dusk thickened over the great river, the island, the hills and the forest, Hochelaga seemed very small, and the inn of the excellent Monsieur Jolivet was just a tiny point of light in all that vast darkness. It shone, nevertheless, by contrast, and was a little island of warmth and comfort in the sea of the wilderness. Monsieur Jolivet, who was deeply interested in the Bostonnais and the proud young Iroquois, talked freely. Under his light and chattering manner lay great powers of perception, and he saw that he had guests of quality, each in his own way. The hunter even was not an ordinary hunter, but, as Monsieur Jolivet judged, a man of uncommon intellectual power, and also of education. He would discover as much about them as he could, for his own personal gratification, because he might give valuable information to the commandant at Montreal, who was his friend, and because later on he might speak a useful word or two in the ear of Louis de Galisonniere, whom he knew well and whose good opinion he valued.

Robert, who was in a cheerful mood and who wished to exercise his gift of golden speech, met him half way, and enlarged upon the splendor and power of Britain, the great kingdom that bestrode the Atlantic, seated immovable in Europe, and yet spreading through her colonies in America, increasing and growing mightier all the time. It was soon a test of eloquence between him and Monsieur Jolivet, in which each was seeking to obtain from the other an expression of the opinion that swayed his country. The Onondaga was silent, and the hunter spoke only a word or two, but each listened intently to the dialogue, which, however earnest it might be, never went beyond the bounds of good humor.

"I cannot make you see the truth," said Monsieur Jolivet, at last, smiling and spreading his hands. "I cannot convince you that France is the first of nations, the nation of light and learning and humanity, and yet it is so. And seated here upon the St. Lawrence we shall build up another France, the New France of America, which will shed light upon you English or Bostonnais down below, and teach you the grace and beauty of civilization."

"We should be willing to learn from any who can teach us," said Robert, "and such a willingness I claim is a chief merit of us English who are born in America, or Bostonnais, as you would call us."

Monsieur Jolivet once more spread out his hands in deprecation.

"We argue in vain," he said. "But now Lizette comes with the coffee, which is one of the most glorious triumphs of my inn. Does the young chief drink coffee?"

"Yes," replied Robert, "he learned at Albany all the white man's habits."

After the coffee they rose from the table and mine host prepared to show them to their room. The darkness had thickened meanwhile and glimpses of the river and the hills were faint. The little garden was enclosed by three walls of darkness, being lighted on the side where it joined the inn. Yet Robert thought he saw a shifting figure blacker than the shadows in which it moved.

Marie and Lizette took away the silver and china and Monsieur Jolivet went ahead to show them to their room. Then something whistled in the darkness, and an arrow buried to the head of the barb stood out in the rear wall of the inn. The three seized their rifles, but the darker shadow in the shadows was gone. Tayoga broke off the arrow level with the wall, and threw the shaft into the garden.

"It was Tandakora," he said, "seeking revenge. But since the arrow has sped wrong he will not loose another shaft tonight. If it had not been for his wounded shoulder the arrow might have gone true. It was a treacherous deed, worthy of the savage Ojibway."

"I hope the time will come," said Willet, "when I shall send a bullet not through Tandakora's shoulder, but through his heart. I don't love the shedding of blood, but the forest will be a better forest without him. Meanwhile, say nothing, lads. Monsieur Jolivet is coming back, but don't mention the arrow to him. He may find the head of it later on in the wall, and then he can wonder about it as much as he pleases."

Mine host bustled back. The foul and treacherous attempt, the breaking off of the arrow, and the comment upon it had taken less than a minute, and, good observer though he was, he noticed nothing unusual in the appearance of his guests. They carried their rifles in their hands, but many visitors to Montreal did the same, and as they were beautiful weapons they might well guard against their loss.

"Follow me, my Bostonnais," he said lightly. "I have the great room with three beds for you, and I trust that you have enjoyed the dinner."

"We have enjoyed it greatly, all of it, Monsieur Jolivet, and especially the dessert," replied Robert with meaning.

"Ah, the pastry," said Monsieur Jolivet, clasping his hands. "It is Marie who made it. It is the gift that she has, and I shall tell her of your praise."

But Robert was not thinking of the pastry. It was of the arrow that he spoke as dessert, although the excellent Monsieur Jolivet was destined never to know the hidden significance of his words. The room which he showed them with so much pride was a large apartment worthy of their praise, having a polished, shining floor of oak, with furs spread here and there upon it, and a low ceiling crossed with mighty beams also of oak. Robert looked at the windows, three in number, and he saw with satisfaction that they had heavy shutters. Monsieur Jolivet's glance followed his own, and he said:

"The shutters are for use in the winter, when the great colds come, and the fierce winds rage. But you, messieurs, who live so much in the forest, will, of course, prefer to keep them wide open tonight."

Robert murmured assent, but when Monsieur Jolivet departed, wishing them a polite good night, he looked at his comrades.

"We are used to air," said Willet, "and lots of it, but those shutters will be closed until morning. As Tayoga truly said, he will hardly dare another arrow, but we mustn't take any risk, however small."

Tayoga nodded approval, and drawing the shutters close, they fastened them. Then they undressed and lay down upon their beds, but each prepared to sleep with his rifle beside him.

"The catches on those shutters are good and strong," said Willet, "and Tandakora, even if he should come again, won't try to break them. It wouldn't suit the purposes of the French for a warrior of a tribe allied with them to be caught trying to murder English visitors, and, that being the case, I expect to go to sleep soon and sleep well."

He was as good as his word. Robert, who blew out the candle, soon heard his regular breathing. Tayoga, who was used to rooms, the Iroquois themselves having strong log houses, quickly followed him in slumber, but young Lennox was not able to compose his nerves for a little while. He was perhaps more sensitive and imaginative than his comrades, or the close air may have kept him awake. He could not help feeling that Tandakora was outside trying the fastenings of the shutters, and at last rising, he walked on tiptoe and listened at every window in turn. He heard nothing without but the breathing of the gentle wind, and then, knowing that it had been only his vivid fancy, he went back to bed and slept soundly.

"Wake up, Robert, and breathe this air! After our having been sealed up in a room all night the breeze is heavenly."

The shutters were thrown back, and the hunter and Tayoga, fully dressed, stood by the windows. The air, fresh, life-giving, coming over the great forests and the mighty river, was pouring into the room in streams, and Tayoga and Willet were facing it, in order that they might receive it straight upon their foreheads. Robert joined them, and soon felt as if he had been created anew and stronger.

"I'll never again sleep in a room closed tight and hard," said Willet, "not even to protect my life. I've roamed the free woods for so many years that I think another such experience would make me choke to death."

"I'm not in love with it myself," said Robert, "but it makes the world outside look all the grander and all the more beautiful."

At their wish breakfast was served for them by Monsieur Jolivet in the garden, Willet insisting that for the present he could not stay any longer in a house. Robert from his seat could see the end of the broken barb embedded in the wall, but neither mine host nor any of his assistants had yet noticed it.

Monsieur Jolivet was pleased that they should have such a brilliant day to begin their journey to Quebec, and he was telling them where they could sell their canoe and buy a good boat when

Louis de Galisonniere appeared in the garden and presented them the compliments of the morning. He looked so trim and so gay that he brought with him a cheerful breeze, and the three felt the effect of it, although they wondered at the nature of his errand there. Robert invited him to join them at breakfast and he accepted their invitation, taking a roll and butter and a cup of coffee after the French custom which even then prevailed.

"I see that you've slept well," he said, "and that the inn of Monsieur Jolivet is as kind to the Bostonnais as it is to the French and the Canadians."

"Its hospitality to us could be no finer if we came from Paris itself, instead of the Province of New York," said Robert. "Our stay in Canada has been short, but most interesting."

Monsieur Jolivet had gone into the inn, and de Galisonniere said:

"Montreal is a fine town and I would not depreciate it in the presence of our host, but as I have told you before, our Quebec to which you are going is the true glory of New France. My knowledge that you're going there is the reason why I've come here this morning."

"How is that?" asked Robert

"Because I received orders last night to depart in the Frontenac for Quebec, a journey that I undertake with great willingness, since it takes me where I wish to go. I have also the authority of the commandant to ask your presence as guests for the voyage on board my vessel. Until we French and you English actually go to war we might as well be friends."

Robert glanced at Tayoga and Willet and they nodded slightly. Then he replied warmly that they accepted the invitation and would go with much pleasure in the Frontenac. After breakfast they sold the canoe and embarked presently, having first said goodby to Monsieur Jolivet, who with his best napkin, waved them farewell.

Robert was more than pleased at their good luck. The Frontenac offered them a better passage than any boat they could buy and have to row perhaps with their own strength. Moreover, they were already on excellent terms with de Galisonniere, and it would be a good thing for them to arrive at Quebec in his company.

A strong wind was blowing, and the Frontenac moved swiftly over the surface of the great stream which was like liquid green glass that morning. The three had put their weapons, including Tayoga's bow and arrows, in the cabin, and they sat on deck with de Galisonniere, who looked with pride at the magnificent river which was the very artery of life in the New France of the chevaliers.

Robert's own heart throbbed as he knew that this last stage of their journey would take them to famous Quebec.

"If the St. Lawrence didn't freeze over for such a long period," said de Galisonniere, "this region would become in time the greatest empire in the world."

"But isn't that a huge 'if'?" asked Robert, laughing.

De Galisonniere smiled.

"It is," he said, "but New France is the chief jewel in the French crown, nevertheless. In time the vice-regal court at Quebec will rule an empire greater than that of France itself. Think of the huge lakes, the great rivers, the illimitable forests, beyond them the plains over which the buffalo herds roam in millions, and beyond them, so they say, range on range of mountains and forests without end."

"I have been thinking of them," said Robert, "but I've been thinking of them in a British way."

De Galisonniere laughed again and then grew serious.

"It's natural," he said, "that you should think of them in a British way, while I think of them in a French way. I suppose we shall have war, Mr. Lennox, but doesn't it seem strange that England and France should fight about American territory, when there's so much of it? Here's a continent that civilized man cannot occupy for many generations. Both England and France could be hidden away in its forests, and it would take explorers to find them, and yet we must fight over a claim to regions that we cannot occupy."

Robert decided then that he liked young de Galisonniere very much. Some such thoughts had been passing through his own mind, and he was glad that he could talk frankly about the coming war with one who would be on the other side, one who would be an official but not a personal enemy. As the Frontenac slid on through the tumbling green current they talked earnestly. Willet, sitting near, glanced at them occasionally, but he too had plenty of thoughts of his own, while Tayoga, saying nothing, gazed at the high green southern shore. This, so the old men said, had once been the land of the Mohawks, one of the great nations of the Hodenosaunee, and now the children of Onontio, who had come with firearms against bows and arrows, spoke of it as theirs since Manitou first made the land rise from the deep. Tayoga was silent but he had many thoughts, and they were thoughts that came to him often and stayed long.

"De Courcelles and Jumonville, whom you met in the forest," said de Galisonniere, at length, "arrived in Montreal early last night, and after a stay of only two or three hours sailed in a schooner for Quebec."

"Did you see them at all while they were in Montreal?" asked Robert, who seemed to detect significance in the young Frenchman's tone.

"Only for a few moments," replied de Galisonniere, and Robert, judging that he wished to avoid more talk on the subject, made no further reference to de Courcelles. But the knowledge that he had gone on ahead to Quebec troubled him. De Courcelles was not so young and frank as de Galisonniere, nor did he seem to have the fine soul and chivalric spirit of St. Luc. Robert felt the three had cause to fear him.

But the journey down the St. Lawrence continued without serious delay, although the wind failed now and then and they took to the oars. It was a voyage full of variety and interest to Robert. He slept that night with his comrades on the deck of the Frontenac, and the next morning he found a strong wind again blowing.

In time they approached Quebec, and saw the increasing signs of population that betokened proximity to what was then in the eyes of North Americans a great capital. On either shore they saw the manor houses of the seigneurs, solid stone structures, low, steep of roof and gabled, with clustering outhouses, and often a stone mill near by. The churches also increased in numbers, and at one point the Frontenac stopped and took on a priest, a tall strongly built man of middle years, with a firm face. De Galisonniere introduced him as Father Philibert Drouillard, and Robert felt his penetrating gaze upon his face. Then it shifted to Willet and Tayoga, resting long upon the Onondaga.

Robert, knowing the great power of the church in Canada, was curious about Father Drouillard, whom he knew at once to be no ordinary man. His lean ascetic face seemed to show the spirit that had marked Jogues and Goupil and those other early priests whom no danger nor Indian torture could daunt. But he was too polite to ask questions, feeling that time would bring him all the information he wanted, in which he was right, as de Galisonniere said later in the day when Father Drouillard was sitting in the little cabin out of hearing:

"A man of influence at Quebec. He has no parish, nor seems to wish any, but he is deep in the councils of the Church. It is known, too, that he corresponds with Rome, with the Holy Father himself, 'tis said, and there are men high in office at Quebec who wish that he might be called from New France back to the old land. Francois Bigot, the Intendant, does not love him, nor does anyone of the group about Bigot, neither his commissary general, Cadet, nor Pean, the Town Mayor of Quebec, nor Descheneaux, nor the others of that group. It's a gorgeous life that our own court circle leads at Quebec, and at the great Chateau Bigot, in the midst of its walks and flowers and gardens. I don't know why I'm telling you these things, Mr. Lennox! It seems they should be the very last to say to one's official enemy, but I can't feel that I'm doing anything wrong when I do tell them to you."

His bright face was in gloom for a few moments, and Robert, quick in perception, had a sudden feeling that this brilliant Quebec, enveloped in so much color and glamour, might not be so sound within as the English towns to the south, despite their wrangling. But it merely increased his anxiety to see Quebec. Life would be all the more complex there.

The great river spread before them, blue now under a dazzling blue sky, and the stout Frontenac left a long white trailing wake. A stone house, larger than usual, showed through the green foliage on the south bank. Father Drouillard gazed at it, and his face darkened. Presently he arose and shook his hand towards the house, as if he were delivering a curse.

"The chateau that you see belongs to the young Count Jean de Mezy, a friend of the Intendant, Bigot. Sometimes they come from their revels at Beaumanoir to the Chateau de Mezy, and continue them there. Now you can see why Father Drouillard, who sympathizes with our honnetes gens, delivers his malediction."

The priest returned to his seat, and averted his face. An hour later the mighty rock of Quebec rose before them.

CHAPTER IX
AT THE INN

When Quebec came into view Robert stood up and looked long at the great rock and the town that crowned it, hung on its slopes and nestled at the foot of the cliffs below. Brilliant sunshine gilded its buildings of stone and gray wood, and played like burnished gold on the steeples of its many churches. In the distance the streets leading up the steep cliffs looked like mere threads, but in the upper town the great public buildings, the Intendant's Palace, the Cathedral, Notre Dame de la Victoire, the convents of the Ursuline Nuns and the Recollet Friars, the Bishop's Palace, and others raised for the glory and might of France, were plainly visible.

In more than one place he saw the Bourbon lilies floating and from the little boat on which he stood in the stream it looked like a grim and impregnable fortress of the Old World. The wonderful glow of the air, and the vast river flowing at its feet, magnified and colored everything. It was a city ten times its real size and the distance turned gray wood to gray stone. Everything was solid, immovable, and it seemed fit to defy the world.

Robert felt a catch in his breath. He had often seen Quebec, great and beautiful, in his dreams, but the reality was equal to it and more. To the American of that day Quebec was one of the vital facts of life. From that fortress issued the daring young French soldiers of fortune who led the forays against New York and New England. It was the seat of the power that threatened them continually. Many of the Bostonnais, seized in their fields, had been brought here as prisoners to be returned home only after years, or never. From this citadel, too, poured the stream of arms and presents for the Indians who were to lie in ambush along the English border, or to make murderous incursions upon the villages. From it flowed the countless dangers that had threatened the northern provinces almost continually for a century and a half. The Bostonnais themselves, mark of the initiative and energy that were to distinguish them so greatly later on, made a mighty effort against it, and doubtless would have succeeded, had they been allowed to carry the fight to a finish.

No man from New York or New England could look upon it without a mingling of powerful emotions. It was the Carthage to their Rome. He admired and yet he wished to conquer. He felt that permanent safety could never come to the northern border until the Bourbon lilies ceased to float over the great fortress that looked down on the St. Lawrence. Robert was not the only one who felt strong emotion. Tayoga stood beside him, his nostrils expanding and his gaze fierce:

"Stadacona!" he said under his breath, "Stadacona of the Ganeagaono, our great brother nation!"

But the emotion of de Galisonniere was of pleasure only. His eyes sparkled with joy and admiration. He was delighted to come back to Quebec, the gay city that he beheld through the eyes of youth and glowing recollections. He knew the corruption and wickedness of Bigot and of Cadet and of Pean and of the whole reckless circle about the Intendant, but Quebec, with its gallant men and its beautiful women; its manners of an Old World aristocracy and its air of a royal court, had many pleasures, and why should youth look too far into the future?

And yet another stood up and looked at Quebec, with emotions all his own, and unlike those of the three who were so young. Father Drouillard, tall in his black robe, gazed fixedly at the rock, and raised his hand in a gesture much like that with which he had cursed the chateau of Count Jean de Mezy. His eyes were set and stern, but, as the sun fell in floods of burnished gold on the cathedral and the convents, his accusing look softened, became sad, then pitying, then hopeful.

"A wonderful sight, Father Drouillard," said Willet, who stood at his elbow and who also gazed at Quebec with feelings quite his own. "I've seen it before, but I can never see it too often."

"Mr. Willet," said the priest, "you and I are greater in years than these youths, and perhaps for that reason we can look farther into the future. Youth fears nothing, but age fears everything. You come to Quebec now in peace, and I trust that you may never come in war. I can feel, nay I can see the clouds gathering over our two lands. Why should we fight? On a continent so vast is there not room enough for all?"

"Room and to spare," replied the hunter, "but as you say, Father Drouillard, you and I have lived longer than these youths, and age has to think. If left to themselves I've no doubt that New France and the English colonies could make a lasting peace, but the intrigues, the jealousies and the hates of the courts at London and Paris keep our forests, four thousand miles away, astir. When the Huron buries his arrow in the heart of a foe the motive that sent him to the deed may have had its start in Europe, but the poor savage never knows it."

103

The priest sighed, and looked at Willet with an awakened curiosity.

"I see that you're a man of education," he said, "and that you think. What you say is true, but the time will come when other minds than those of vain and jealous courtiers will sway the fortunes of all these vast regions. I have asked you nothing of your mission in Quebec, Mr. Willet, but I hope that I will see you again before you return."

"I hope so too," said the hunter sincerely.

The Frontenac now drew in to a wharf between the Royal Battery and the Dauphin's Battery, and Robert was still all eyes for the picturesque sights that awaited him in the greatest French town of the New World. De Galisonniere was hailed joyously by young officers and he made joyous replies. Robert, as they landed, saw anew and in greater detail the immense strength of Quebec.

He beheld the line of huge earthworks that Frontenac had built from the river St. Charles to Cape Diamond, and he saw the massive redoubts lined with heavy cannon. Now, he wondered at the boldness of the New Englanders who had assailed the town with so much vigor, and who might have taken it.

"I recommend to you," said de Galisonniere, "that you go to the Inn of the Eagle in the Upper Town. It is kept by Monsieur Berryer, who as a host is fully equal to Monsieur Jolivet of Montreal, and the merits of Monsieur Jolivet are not unknown to you."

"They are not," said Robert heartily, "and we may thank you, Captain de Galisonniere, for your great courtesy in bringing us from Montreal. We can only hope for a time in which we shall be able to repay your kindness."

After they had slipped some silver pieces to the boatmen and had said farewell to Captain de Galisonniere, they took their way up a steep street, a swarthy French-Canadian porter carrying their baggage. Here, as at Montreal, the most attention was attracted by Tayoga, and, if possible, the young Onondaga grew more haughty in appearance and manner. His moccasined feet spurned the ground, and he gazed about with a fierce and defiant eye.

Robert knew well what was stirring the spirit of the Onondaga. This was not the Quebec of the French, it was the Stadacona of the Mohawks, the great brother nation of the Onondagas, and the French here were but interlopers and robbers.

But Robert soon lost thought of Tayoga as he looked at the crowded city, and its mingling of the splendid and the squalid, its French and French-Canadians, its soldiers and priests and civilians and Indians, its great stone houses, and its wooden huts, its young officers in fine white uniforms and its swarthy habitants in brown homespun. Albany had its Dutch, and New York had its Dutch, too, and people from many parts of Europe, but Quebec was different, something altogether new, without a trace of English or Dutch about it, and, for that reason, it made a great appeal to his curiosity.

A light open carriage drawn by two stout ponies passed them at an amazing pace considering the steepness of the street, and they saw in it a florid young man in a splendid costume, his powdered hair tied in a queue.

"De Mezy," said the priest, who was just behind them.

Then they knew that it was the young man, the companion of Bigot in his revels, against whose chateau Father Drouillard had raised his threatening hands. Now the priest spoke the name with the most intense scorn and contempt, and Robert, feeling that he might encounter de Mezy again in this pent-up Quebec, gazed at his vanishing figure with curiosity. They had their gay blades in New York and Albany and even a few in Boston of the Puritans, but he had not seen anybody like de Mezy.

"It is such as he who are pulling down New France," murmured Father Drouillard.

A moment or two later the priest said farewell and departed in the direction of the cathedral.

"There goes a man," said Willet, as he looked after the tall figure in the black robe. "I don't share in the feeling of church against church. I don't see any reason why Protestant should hate Catholic and Catholic should hate Protestant. I've lived long enough and seen enough to know that each church holds good men, and unless I make a big mistake, and I don't think I make any mistake at all, Father Drouillard is not only a good man, but he has a head full of sense and he's as brave as a lion, too."

"Lots of priests are," said Robert. "Nobody ever endured the Indian tortures better than they. And what's the figure over the doorway, Dave?"

"That, Robert, is Le Chien d'Or, The Golden Dog. It's the sign put up by Nicholas Jaquin, whom they often called Philibert. This is his warehouse and he was one of the honnetes gens that we've been talking about. He fought the corrupt officials, he tried to make lower prices for the people, and beneath his Golden Dog he wrote:"

> "Je suis un chien qui ronge l'os,
> En le rongeant je prends mon repos;
> Un jour viendra qui n'est pas venu,
> Que je mordrai qui m'aura mordu."

105

"That is, some day the dog will bite those who have bitten him?"

"That's about it, Robert, and I suppose it generally comes true. If you keep on striking people some of them in time will strike you and strike you pretty hard."

"And does Philibert still run his warehouse beneath his sign of the Golden Dog?"

"No, Robert. He was too brave, or not cautious enough, and they assassinated him, but there are plenty of others like him. The French are a brave and honest people, none braver or more honest. I tell you so, because I know them, but their government is corrupt through and through. The House of Bourbon is dying of its own poison. It may seem strange to you, hearing me say it here in the Western world, so far from Versailles, but I'm not the only one who says so."

"But I like Quebec," said Robert. "I haven't seen another city that speaks to the eye so much."

They were now well into the Upper Town, and the porter guided them to the Inn of the Eagle, where Monsieur Paul Berryer, the host, gave them a welcome, and from whom they learned that the Governor General, the Marquis Duquesne, was absent in the east, but would return in two or three days. Robert was not sorry for the delay, as it would give them a chance to see the city, and perhaps, through de Galisonniere, make acquaintances among the French officers.

They were able to secure a large room with three beds, and both Robert and Willet drew from their small store of baggage suits quite in the fashion, three-cornered hats, fine coats and waistcoats, knee breeches, stockings and buckled shoes, and as a last and crowning triumph they produced handsome small swords or rapiers that they buckled to their belts.

"That canoe of ours wasn't large, but it brought a lot in it," said the hunter.

Robert surveyed himself in a small glass, and his clothes brought great pride. A chord in his nature responded to splendor of raiment, and the surroundings of the great world. Quebec might be corrupt but he could not hide from himself his immense interest in it. He noticed, too, that Willet wore his fine costume naturally.

"It's not the first time that you've been in such clothes, Dave," he said, "and it's not the first time that you've been in a society like that which makes its home in Quebec."

"No, it is not," replied Willet, "and some time, Robert, I'll tell you about those days, but not now."

106

Tayoga remained in his dress of a young Indian chief. Even if he had had any other he would not have put it on, and the fine deerskin and the lofty headdress became him and stamped him for what he was, a prince of the forest. He held in his heart, too, a deeper feeling against the French than any that animated either Robert or Willet. He could not forget that this was not Quebec, but Stadacona of the Ganeagaono, whose rights were also the rights of the other nations of the Hodenosaunee, and it was here that Frontenac, who had slaughtered the Iroquois, had made his home and fortress. The heart of Tayoga of the clan of the Bear of the nation Onondaga, of the great League of the Hodenosaunee, burned within him and the blood in his veins would not grow cool.

"I suppose, Dave," said Robert, "since we have to wait two days for the Marquis Duquesne, that we might go forth at once and begin seeing the town."

"Food first," said the hunter. "We've come a long journey on the river and we'll test the quality of the, inn."

It was too cool for the little terrace that adjoined the Inn of the Eagle, and Monsieur Berryer had a table set for them in the great dining-room, which had an oaken floor, oaken beams and much china and glass on shelves about the walls, the whole forming an apartment in which the host took a just pride. It was gayer and brighter than the inns of Albany and New York, and again Robert found his spirit responding to it.

A fire of light wood that blazed and sparkled merrily burned in a huge stone fireplace at the end of the room, and its grateful warmth entered into Robert's blood. He suddenly felt a great exaltation. He was glad to be there. He was glad that Tayoga and Willet were with him. He was glad that they had encountered dangers on their journey because they had won a triumph in overcoming them, and by the very act of victory they had increased their own strength and confidence. His sensitive, imaginative nature, easily kindled to supreme efforts, thrilled with the thoughts of the great deeds they might do.

His pleasure in the company and the atmosphere increased. Everything about him made a strong appeal to good taste. At the end of the room, opposite the fireplace, stood a vast sideboard, upon which china and glass, arranged in harmonious groups, shone and glittered. The broad shelves or niches in the walls held much cut glass, which now and then threw back from many facets the ruddy light of the fire. Before sitting down, they had dipped their hands in a basin of white china filled with water, and standing beside the door, and that too had pleased Robert's fastidious taste.

At their table each of the three found an immaculate white napkin, a large white china plate and goblet, knife, fork and spoon, all of silver, polished to the last degree. Again Robert's nature responded and he looked at himself in his fine dress in the glittering silver of the goblet. Then his right hand stole down and caressed the hilt of his rapier. He felt himself very much of a gentleman, very much of a chevalier, fit to talk on equal terms with St. Luc, de Galisonniere or the best French officer of them all. And Willet, wearing his costly costume with ease, was very much of a gentleman too, and Tayoga, dressed as the forest prince, was in his own way, and quite as good a way, as much of a gentleman as either.

At least a dozen others were in the great room, and many curious eyes were upon the three visitors from the south. It was likely that the presence of such marked figures as theirs would become known quickly in Quebec. They had shown the papers bearing their names at the gate by which they had entered, and doubtless the news of their arrival had been spread at once by the officer in command there. Well, they would prove to the proud chevaliers of Quebec how the Bostonnais could bear themselves, and Robert's pulses leaped.

They were served by an attentive and quiet waiter, and the three, each in his own way, watched everything that was going on. They were aware that not all would be as friendly as de Galisonniere or Father Drouillard, but they were fully prepared to meet a challenge of any kind and uphold the honor of their own people. Robert was hoping that de Galisonniere might come, as he had recommended the inn to them. He did not appear, but the others who did so lingered and young Lennox knew that it was because of the three, who received many hostile glances, although most were intended for the Onondaga. Robert was aware, too, that if the Iroquois had lost this Stadacona of the Mohawks and had been ravaged by Frontenac, they had taken a terrible revenge upon the French and their chief allies, the Hurons. For generations the Hodenosaunee had swept the villages along the St. Lawrence with fire and tomahawk, slaying and capturing their hundreds. But to Tayoga it was and always would be the French who had struck first, and the vital fact remained that they lived upon land upon which the Iroquois themselves had once lived, no man knew how long.

Robert saw that the looks were growing more menacing, although the good Monsieur Berryer glided among his guests, and counseled caution.

"Take no notice," said Willet in a low tone. "The French are polite, and although they may not like us they will not molest us."

Robert followed his advice. Apparently he had no thought

except for his food, which was delicate, but his ears did not miss any sound that could reach them. He understood French well, and he caught several whispers that made the red come to his cheeks. Doubtless they thought he could not speak their language or they would have been more careful.

Half way through the dinner and the door was thrown open, admitting a gorgeous figure and a great gust of words. It was a young man in a brilliant uniform, his hair long, perfumed, powdered and curled, and his face flushed. Robert recognized him at once as that same Count Jean de Mezy who had passed them in the flying carriage. Behind came two officers of about the same age, but of lower rank, seeking his favor and giving him adulation.

His roving eye traveled around the room, and, resting upon the three guests, became inflamed.

"Ah, Nemours, and you, Le Moyne," he said, "look there and behold the two Bostonnais and the Iroquois of whom we have heard, sitting here in our own Inn of the Eagle!"

"But there is no war, not as yet," said Nemours, although he spoke in an obsequious tone.

"But it will come," said de Mezy loudly, "and then, gentlemen, this lordly Quebec of ours, which has known many English captives, will hold multitudes of them."

There were cries of "Silence!" "Not so loud!"

"Don't insult guests!" but de Mezy merely laughed and said: "They don't understand! The slow-witted English never know any tongue but their own."

The red flush in Robert's face deepened and he moved angrily.

"Quiet, boy! Quiet!" whispered the hunter. "He wants a quarrel, and he is surrounded by his friends, while we're strangers in a strange land and a hostile city. Take a trifle of the light white wine that Monsieur Berryer is pouring for you. It won't hurt you."

Robert steadied himself and sipped a little. De Mezy and his satellites, Nemours and Le Moyne, sat down noisily at a table and ordered claret. De Mezy gave the cue. They talked of the Bostonnais, not only of the two Bostonnais who were present, but of the Bostonnais in all the English colonies, applying the word to them whether they came from Massachusetts or New York or Virginia. Robert felt his pulses leaping and the hunter whispered his warning once more.

De Mezy evidently was sincere in his belief that the three understood no French, as he continued to talk freely about the English colonies, the prospect of war, and the superiority of French troops to British or American. Meanwhile he and his two satellites drank freely of the claret and their faces grew more flushed. Robert could stand it no longer.

"Tayoga," he said clearly and in perfect French, "it seems that in Quebec there are people of loose speech, even as there are in Albany and New York."

"Our sachems tell us that such is the way of man," said the Onondaga, also in pure French. "Vain boasters dwell too in our own villages. For reasons that I do not know, Manitou has put the foolish as well as the wise into the world."

"To travel, Tayoga, is to find wisdom. We learn what other people know, and we learn to value also the good that we have at home."

"It is so, my friend Lennox. It is only when we go into strange countries and listen to the tongues of the idle and the foolish that we learn the full worth of our own."

"It is not wise, Tayoga, to give a full rein to a loose tongue in a public place."

"Our mothers teach us so, Lennox, as soon as we leave our birch bark cradles."

Willet had raised his hand in warning, but he saw that it was too late. The young blood in the veins of both Tayoga and Robert was hot, and the Iroquois was stirred not less deeply than the white man.

"The sachems tell us," he said, "that sometimes a man speaks foolish words because he is born foolish, again he says them at times because his temper or drink makes him foolish, or he may say them because it is his wish to be foolish and he has cultivated foolish ways all his life. This last class is the worst of all, Lennox, my friend, but there is a certain number of them in all lands, as one finds when one travels."

The Onondaga spoke with great clearness and precision in his measured school French and a moment of dead silence followed. Then Robert said:

"It is true, Tayoga. The chiefs of the Hodenosaunee are great and wise men. They have lived and seen much, and seeing they have remembered. They know that speech was given to man in order that he might convey his thoughts to another, and not that he might make a fool of himself."

An angry exclamation came from the table at which de Mezy sat, and his satellites, Nemours and Le Moyne, swept the three with looks meant to be contemptuous. Monsieur Berryer raised deprecating hands and was about to speak, but, probably seeing that both hands and words would be of no avail, moved quietly to one side. He did not like to have quarrels in his excellent Inn of the Eagle, but they were no new thing there, for the gilded youth of Quebec was hot and intemperate.

"But when a man is foolish in our village," resumed Tayoga, "and the words issue from his mouth in a stream like the cackling of a jay bird, the chiefs do not send warriors to punish him, but give him into the hands of the old women, who bind him and beat him with sticks until they can beat sense back into him."

"A good way, Tayoga, a most excellent way," said Robert. "People who have reached the years of maturity pay no attention to the vaporings and madness of the foolish."

He did not look around, but he heard a gusty exclamation, the scrape of a chair on the floor, and a hasty step. Then he felt a hot breath, and, although he did not look up, he knew that de Mezy, flushed with drink and anger, was standing over him. The temperament that nature had given to him, the full strength of which he was only discovering, asserted itself. He too felt wrath inside, but he retained all the presence of mind for which he afterward became famous.

"Shall we go out and see more of the city, Tayoga?" he asked.

"Not until I have had a word with you, young sprig of a Bostonnais," said de Mezy, his florid face now almost a flaming red.

"Your pardon, sir," said Robert, with his uncommon fluency of speech, "I have not the advantage of your acquaintance, which, no doubt, is my loss, as I admit that there are many good and brave men whom I do not know."

"I am Jean de Mezy, a count of France, a captain in the army of King Louis, and one of the most valued friends of our able Intendant, Francois Bigot."

"I have heard of France, of course, I have heard, equally of course, of His Majesty, King Louis, I have even heard of the Intendant, Francois Bigot, but, and sorry I am to say it, I have never heard of the Count Jean de Mezy."

A low laugh came from a distant corner of the room, and the red of de Mezy's face turned to purple. His hand dropped to the hilt of his sword, but Le Moyne whispered to him and he became more collected.

"In Quebec," he said, throwing back his shoulders and raising his chin, "an officer of His Majesty, King Louis, does not accept an insult. We preserve our honor with the edge of our swords, and for that reason I intend to let a good quantity of the hot blood out of you with mine. There is a good place near the St. Louis gate, and the hour may be as early as you wish."

"He is but a boy," interposed Willet.

"But I know the sword," said Robert, who had made up his mind, and who was measuring his antagonist. "I will meet you tomorrow morning just after sunrise with the small sword, and my seconds will confer with yours tonight."

He stood up that they might see his size. Although only a boy in years, he was as large and strong as de Mezy, and his eyes were clearer and his muscles much firmer. A hum of approval came from the spectators, who now numbered more than a score, but the approval was given for different reasons. Some, and they belonged to the honnetes gens, were glad to see de Mezy rebuked and hoped that he would be punished; others, the following of Bigot, Cadet, Pean and their corrupt crowd, were eager to see the Bostonnais suffer for his insolence to one of their number. But most of them, both the French of old France and the French of Canada, chivalric of heart, were resolved to see fair play.

Monsieur Berryer shrugged his shoulders, but made no protest. The affair to his mind managed itself very well. There had been none of the violence that he had apprehended. The quarrel evidently was one of gentlemen, carried out in due fashion, and the shedding of blood would occur in the proper place and not in his inn. And yet it would be an advertisement. Men would come to point out where de Mezy had sat, and where the young Bostonnais had sat, and to recount the words that each had said. And then the red wine and the white wine would flow freely. Oh, yes, the affair was managing itself very well indeed, and the thrifty Monsieur Berryer rubbed his hands together with satisfaction.

"We have beds here at the Inn of the Eagle," said Robert coolly--he was growing more and more the master of speech; "you can send your seconds this evening to see mine, and they will arrange everything, although I tell you now that I choose small swords. I hope my choice suits you."

"It is what I would have selected myself," said de Mezy, giving his antagonist a stare of curiosity. Such coolness, such effrontery, as he would have called it, was not customary in one so young, and in an American too, because Americans did not give much attention to the study of the sword. New thoughts raced through his head. Could it be possible that here, where one least expected it, was some marvelous swordsman, a phenomenon? Did that account for his indifference? A slight shudder passed over the frame of Jean de Mezy, who loved his dissolute life. But such thoughts vanished quickly. It could not be possible. The confidence of the young Bostonnais came from ignorance.

Robert had seen de Mezy's face fall, and he was confirmed in the course that he had chosen already.

"Gusgaesata," he said to Tayoga in Iroquois.

"Ah, the deer buttons!" the Onondaga said in English, then repeating it in French.

"You will pardon us," said Robert carelessly to de Mezy, "but Tayoga, who by the way is of the most ancient blood of the Onondagas, and I often play a game of ours after dinner."

His manner was that of dismissal, and the red in de Mezy's cheeks again turned to purple. Worst of all, the little dart of terror stabbed once more at his heart. The youth might really be the dreaded marvel with the sword. Such coolness in one so young at such a time could come only from abnormal causes. Although he felt himself dismissed he refused to go away and his satellites remained with him. They would see what the two youths meant to do.

Tayoga took from a pocket in his deerskin tunic eight buttons about three quarters of an inch in diameter and made of polished and shining elk's horn, except one side which had been burned to a darker color. From another pocket he drew a handful of beans and laid them in one heap. Then he shook the buttons in the palm of his hand, and put them down in the center of the table. Six white sides were turned up and taking two beans from the common heap he started a pile of his own. He threw again and obtained seven whites. Then he took four beans. A third throw and all coming up white twenty beans were subtracted from the heap and added to his own pile. But on the next throw only five of the whites appeared, and as at least six of the buttons had to be matched in order to continue his right of throwing he resigned his place to Robert, who threw with varying fortune until he lost in his turn to Tayoga.

"A crude Indian game," said de Mezy in a sneering tone, and the two satellites, Nemours and Le Moyne, laughed once more. Robert and Tayoga did not pay the slightest attention to them, concentrating their whole attention upon the sport, but Willet said quietly:

"I've seen wise chiefs play it for hours, and the great men of the Hodenosaunee would be great men anywhere."

Angry words gathered on the lips of de Mezy, but they were not spoken. He saw that he was at a disadvantage, and that he would lose prestige if he kept himself in a position to be snubbed before his own people by two strange youths. At length he said: "Farewell until morning," and stalked out, followed by his satellites. Others soon followed but Robert and Tayoga went on with their game of the deer buttons. They were not interrupted until Monsieur

113

Berryer bowed before them and asked if they would have any more refreshment.

"No, thank you," said Robert, and then he added, as if by afterthought, although he did not take his eyes from the buttons: "What sort of a man at sword play is this de Mezy?"

"Very good! Very good, sir," replied the innkeeper, "that is if his eyes and head are clear."

"Then if he is in good condition it looks as if I ought to be careful."

"Careful, sir! Careful! One ought always to be careful in a duel!"

"In a way I suppose so. Monsieur Berryer. But I fancy it depends a good deal upon one's opponent. There are some who are not worth much trouble."

Monsieur Berryer's eyes stood out. Robert had spoken with calculated effect. He knew that his words uttered now would soon reach the ears of Jean de Mezy, and it was worth while to be considered a miraculous swordsman. He had read the count's mind when he stood at his elbow, shuddering a little at the thought that a prodigy with the blade might be sitting there, and he was resolved to make the thought return once more and stay.

"And, sir, you distinguish between swordsmen, and find it necessary to make preparation only for the very best? And you so young too!" said the wondering innkeeper.

"Youth in such times as ours does not mean inexperience, Monsieur Berryer," said Willet.

"It is true, alas!" said the innkeeper, soberly. "The world grows old, and there are seas of trouble. I wish no annoyance to any guests of mine. I know the courtesy due to visitors in our Quebec, and I would have stopped the quarrel had I been able, but the Count Jean de Mezy is a powerful man, the friend and associate of the Intendant, Monsieur Bigot."

"I understand, Monsieur Berryer," said Robert, with calculated lightness; "your courtesy is, in truth, great, but don't trouble yourself on our account. We are fully able to take care of ourselves. Come, Tayoga, we're both tired of the game and so let's to bed."

Tayoga carefully put away the deer buttons and the beans, and the three rose.

CHAPTER X
THE MEETING

Only four or five men, besides themselves, were left in the great room of the Inn of the Eagle. The looks they gave the three were not hostile, and Robert judged that they belonged to the party known in Quebec as honnêtes gens and described to him already by de Galisonnière. He thought once of speaking to them, but he decided not to put any strain upon their friendliness. They might have very bitter feelings against Bigot and his corrupt following, but the fact would not of necessity induce them to help the Bostonnais.

"I thought it would be best to go to bed," he said, "but I've changed my mind. A little walk first in the open air would be good for all of us. Besides we must stay up long enough to receive the seconds of de Mézy."

"A walk would be a good thing for you," said Willet—it was noteworthy that despite his great affection for the lad, he did not show any anxiety about him.

"Your wrist feels as strong as ever, doesn't it, Robert?" he asked.

Young Lennox took his right wrist in his left hand and looked at it thoughtfully. He was a tall youth, built powerfully, but his wrists were of uncommon size and strength.

"I suppose that paddling canoes during one's formative period over our lakes and rivers develops the wrists and arms better than anything else can," he said.

"It makes them strong and supple, too," said the hunter. "It gives to you a wonderful knack which with training can be applied with equal ability to something else."

"As we know."

"As we know."

They went out and walked a little while in the streets, curious eyes still following them, a fact of which they were well aware, although they apparently took no notice of it. Willet observed Robert closely, but he could not see any sign of unsteadiness or excitement. Young Lennox himself seemed to have forgotten the serious business that would be on hand in the morning. His heart again beat a response to Quebec which in the dusk was magnificent and glorified. The stone buildings rose to the size of castles, the great river showed like silver through the darkness and on the far shore a single light burned.

A figure appeared before them. It was de Galisonnière, his ruddy face anxious.

"I was hoping that we might meet you," said Robert.

"What's this I hear about a quarrel between you and de Mézy and a duel in the morning?"

"You hear the truth."

"But de Mézy, though he is no friend of mine, is a swordsman, and has had plenty of experience. You English, or at least you English in your colonies, know nothing about the sword, except to wear it as a decoration!"

Robert laughed.

"I appreciate your anxiety for me," he said. "It's the feeling of a friend, but don't worry. A few of us in the English colonies do know the use of the sword, and at the very head of them I should place David Willet, whom you know and who is with us."

"But de Mézy is not going to fight Willet, he is going to fight you."

"David Willet has been a father to me, more, in truth, than most fathers are to their sons. I've been with him for years, Captain de Galisonnière, and all the useful arts he knows he has tried long and continuously to teach to me."

"Then you mean that the sword you now wear at your thigh is a weapon and not an ornament?"

"Primarily, yes, but before we go further into the matter of the sword,

I wish to ask you a favor."

"Ask a dozen, Lennox. We've been companions of the voyage and your quarrel with de Mézy does not arouse any hostility in me."

"I felt that it was so, and for that reason I ask the favor. We are strangers in Quebec. We did not come here to seek trouble with anybody, and so I ask you to be a second for me in this affair with de Mézy. Dave and Tayoga, of course, would act, but at the present juncture, ours being an errand of peace and not of war, I'd prefer Frenchmen."

"Gladly I'll serve you, Lennox, since you indicate that you're a swordsman and are not going to certain death, and I'll bring with me in the morning a trusty friend, Armand Glandelet, one of our honnêtes gens who likes de Mézy as little as I do."

"I thank you much, my good friend. I knew you would accept, and if all are willing I suggest that we go back now to the Inn of the Eagle."

"A little trial of the sword in your room would not hurt," said de

Galisonnière.

"That's a good suggestion," said Willet. "A few turns will show whether your wrists and your arms and your back are all right. You come with us, of course, Captain de Galisonnière."

They went to their large room, Captain de Galisonnière procuring on the way two buttons for rapiers from Monsieur Berryer—it seemed that duels were not uncommon in Quebec—and Willet and Robert, taking off their coats and waistcoats, faced each other in the light of two large candles. The young Frenchman watched them critically. He had assisted at many affairs of honor in both Quebec and Montreal and he knew the build of a swordsman when he saw one. When Robert stood in his shirt sleeves he noted his powerful chest and shoulders and arms, and then his eyes traveling to the marvelous wrists were arrested there. He drew in his breath as he saw, from the way in which Robert flexed them for a moment or two that they were like wrought steel.

"If this lad has been taught as they indicate he has, our ruffling bully, Jean de Mézy, is in for a bad half hour," he said to himself. Then he looked at Willet, built heavily, with great shoulders and chest, but with all the spring and activity of a young man. His glance passed on to Tayoga, the young Onondaga, in all the splendor of his forest attire, standing by the wall, his eyes calm and fathomless. It occurred all at once to Captain de Galisonnière that he was in the presence of an extraordinary three, each remarkable in his own way, and, liking the unusual, his interest in them deepened. It did not matter that they were his official enemies, because on the other hand they were his personal friends.

"Now, Robert," said Willet, "watch my eye, because I'm going to put you to a severe test. Ready?"

"Aye, ready, sir!" replied Robert, speaking like a pupil to his master. Then the two advanced toward the center of the room and faced each other, raising their slim swords which flashed in the flame of the candles like thin lines of light. Then Willet thrust like lightning, but his blade slipped off Robert's, and young Lennox thrust back only to have his own weapon caught on the other.

"Ah," exclaimed the gallant Frenchman. "Well done! Well done for both!"

Then he held his breath as the play of the swords became so fast that the eye could scarcely follow. They made vivid lines, and steel flashed upon steel with such speed that at times the ringing sound seemed continuous. Willet's agility was amazing. Despite his size and weight he was as swift and graceful as a dancing master, and the power of his wrist was wonderful. The amazement of young de Galisonnière increased. He had seen the best swordsmanship in Quebec, and he had seen the best swordsmanship in Paris, but he had never seen better swordsmanship than that shown in a room of the Inn of the Eagle by a man whom he had taken to be a mere hunter in the American wilderness.

De Galisonnière was an artist with the sword himself, and he knew swordsmanship when he saw it. He knew, too, that Lennox was but little inferior to Willet. He saw that the older man was not sparing the youth, that he was incessantly beating against the strongest parts of his defense, and that he was continually seeking out his weakest. Robert was driven around and around the room, and yet Willet did not once break through his guard.

"Ah, beautiful! beautiful!" exclaimed the Frenchman. "I did not know that such swordsmen could come out of the woods!"

His eyes met those of the Onondaga and for the first time he saw a gleam in their dark depths.

"Their swords are alive," said Tayoga. "They are living streaks of flame."

"That describes it, my friend," said de Galisonnière. "I shall be proud to be one of the seconds of Mr. Lennox in the morning."

Willet suddenly dropped the buttoned point of his rapier and raised his left hand.

"Enough, Robert," he said, "I can't allow you to tire yourself tonight, and run the risk of stiffening in the wrist tomorrow. In strength you are superior to de Mézy, and in wind far better. You should have no trouble with him. Watch his eye and stand for a while on the defensive. One of his habits, will soon wear himself down, and then he will be at your mercy."

"You are a wonderful swordsman, Mr. Willet," said de Galisonnière, frank in his admiration. "I did not think such skill, such power and such a variety in attack and defense could be learned outside of Paris."

"Perhaps not!" said Willet, smiling. "The greatest masters of the sword in the world teach in Paris, and it was there that I learned what I know."

"What, you have been in Paris?"

"Aye, Captain de Galisonnière, I know my Paris well."

But he volunteered nothing further and Louis de Galisonnière's delicacy kept him from asking any more questions. Nevertheless he had an intensified conviction that three most extraordinary people had come to Quebec, and he was glad to know them. Jean de Mézy, count of France, and powerful man though he might be, was going to receive a punishment richly deserved. He detested Bigot, Cadet, Pean and all their corrupt crowd, while recognizing the fact that they were almost supreme in Quebec. It would be pleasing to the gods for de Mézy to be humiliated, and it did not matter if the humiliation came from the hands of a Bostonnais.

"Would you mind trying a round or two at the foils with me?" he said to Willet. "Since you don't have to fight in the morning you needn't fear any stiffening of the wrist, and I should like to learn something about that low thrust of yours, the one well beneath your opponent's guard, and which only a movement like lightning can reach. You used it five times, unless my eye missed a sixth."

"And so you noticed it!" said Willet, looking pleased. "I made six such thrusts, but Robert met them every time. I've trained him to be on the watch for it, because in a real combat it's sure to be fatal, unless it's parried with the swiftness of thought."

"Then teach me," said de Galisonnière eagerly. "We're a fighting lot here in Quebec, and it may save my life some day."

Willet was not at all averse, and for nearly an hour he taught the young Frenchman. Then de Galisonnière departed, cautioning Robert to sleep well, and saying that he would come early in the morning with his friend, Glandelet.

"His advice about sleeping was good, Robert," said Willet. "Now roll into bed and off with you to slumberland at once."

Robert obeyed and his nerves were so steady and his mind so thoroughly at peace that in fifteen minutes he slept. The hunter watched his steady breathing with satisfaction and said to Tayoga:

"If our bibulous friend, Count Jean de Mézy, doesn't have a surprise in the morning, then I'll go back to the woods, and stay there as long as I live."

"Will Lennox kill him?" asked Tayoga.

"I hadn't thought much about it, Tayoga, but he won't kill him. Robert isn't sanguinary. He doesn't want anybody's blood on his hands, and it wouldn't help our mission to take a life in Quebec."

"The man de Mézy does not deserve to live."

Willet laughed.

"That's so, Tayoga," he said, "but it's no part of our business to go around taking the lives away from all those who don't make good use of 'em. Why, if we undertook such a job we'd have to work hard for the next thousand years. I think we'd better fall on, ourselves, and snatch about eight good hours of slumber."

In a few minutes three instead of one slept, and when the first ray of sunlight entered the room in the morning Tayoga awoke. He opened the window, letting the fresh air pour in, and he raised his nostrils to it like a hound that has caught the scent. It brought to him the aromatic odors of his beloved wilderness, and, for a time, he was back in the great land of the Hodenosaunee among the blue lakes and the silver streams. He had been educated in the white man's schools, and his friendship for Robert and Willet was strong and enduring, but his heart was in the forest. Enlightened and humane, he had nevertheless asked seriously the night before the question: "Will Lennox kill him?" He had discovered something fetid in Quebec and to him de Mézy was a noxious animal that should be destroyed. He wished, for an instant, that he knew the sword and that he was going to stand in Lennox's place.

Then he woke Robert and Willet, and they dressed quickly, but by the time they had finished Monsieur Berryer knocked on the door and told them breakfast was ready. The innkeeper's manner was flurried. He was one of the honnêtes gens who liked peace and an upright life. He too wished the insolent pride of de Mézy to be humbled, but he had scarcely come to the point where he wanted to see a Bostonnais do it. Nor did he believe that it could be done. De Mézy was a good swordsman, and his friends would see that he was in proper condition. Weighing the matter well, Monsieur Berryer was, on the whole, sorry for the young stranger.

But Robert himself showed no apprehensions. He ate his excellent breakfast with an equally excellent appetite, and Monsieur Berryer noticed that his hand did not tremble. He observed, too, that he had spirit enough to talk and laugh with his friends, and when Captain de Galisonnière and another young Frenchman, Lieutenant Armand Glandelet, arrived, he welcomed them warmly.

The captain carried under his arm a long thin case, in which Monsieur Berryer knew that the swords lay. Lieutenant Armand Glandelet was presented duly and Robert liked his appearance, his age apparently twenty-three or four, his complexion fair and his figure slender. His experience in affairs of honor was not as great as de Galisonnière's, and he showed some excitement, but he was one of the honnêtes gens and he too wished, the punishment of de Mézy. Perhaps he had suffered from him some insult or snub which he was not in a position to resent fully.

"Is your wrist strong and steady and without soreness, Mr. Lennox?" asked Captain de Galisonnière.

"It was never more flexible," replied Robert confidently. "Shall we go to the field? I should like to be there first."

"A praiseworthy attitude," said Captain de Galisonnière. "The sun is just rising and the light is good. Come."

Keeping the long, thin case under his arm, he went forth, and the rest followed. Monsieur Berryer also came at a respectful distance, and others fell into line with him. Robert walked by the side of Willet.

"Don't forget that low thrust," said the hunter, "and watch his eye. You feel no apprehensions?"

"None at all, thanks to you. I'm quite sure I'm his master."

"Then it's a good morning for a fight, and the setting is perfect. You'll remember this day, Robert. What a wonderful situation has the Quebec of the French that was the Stadacona of the Mohawks! A fine town, a great rock and the king of rivers! The St. Lawrence looks golden in the early sunlight, and what a lot of it there is!"

"Yes, it's a great stream," said Robert, looking at the golden river and the far shores, green and high.

"Here we are," said de Galisonnière, passing beyond some outlying houses. "It's a good, clear opening, pretty well surrounded by trees, with plenty of sunlight at all points, and as you wished, Mr. Lennox, we're the first to arrive."

They stood together, talking with apparent unconcern, while the morning unfolded, and the golden sunlight over the river deepened. Although he had been trained with the sword for years, it would be Robert's first duel, and, while he approached it with supreme confidence, he knew that he could find no joy in the shedding of another's blood. He felt it a strange chance that such an affair should be forced upon him, and yet this was a dueling city. The hot young spirits of France had brought their customs with them into the North American wilderness, and perhaps the unsought chance, if he used it as he thought he could, would not serve him so ill after all.

De Mézy, with his seconds, Nemours and Le Moyne, was approaching among the trees. It appeared that the seconds for both had arranged everything at a meeting the night before, and nothing was left for the two principals but to fight. Robert saw at a single glance that de Mézy's head was clear. Some of the mottled color had left his cheeks, but the effect was an improvement, and he bore himself like a man who was strong and confident. He and his seconds wore dark blue cloaks over their uniforms, which they laid aside when they saw that Robert and his friends were present.

Nemours stepped forward and asked to speak with Captain de Galisonnière.

"Count Jean de Mézy," he said, "is an experienced swordsman, a victor in a dozen duels, a man of great skill, and he

121

does not wish to take an advantage that might seem unfair to others. He considers the extreme youth of his opponent, and if by chance his friend, Mr. Willet, should know the sword, he will meet him instead."

It was, on the whole, a handsome offer, better than they had expected from de Mézy, and Galisonnière looked with inquiry, first at young Lennox and then at Willet. But Robert shook his head.

"No," he said, "Captain de Mézy's offer does him credit, but I decline it. I am his inferior in years, but his equal in stature and strength, and I have had some experience with the sword. Mr. Willet would gladly take my place, but I can support the combat myself."

Nemours stepped back, and Robert resolved that de Mézy's offer should not have been made wholly in vain. It would save the Frenchman some of his blood, but Nemours and de Galisonnière were now choosing the positions in such a manner that neither would have the sun in his eyes but merely his shoulder against the disc. Robert took off his coat and waistcoat and Willet folded them over his own arm. De Mézy prepared in like manner. Nemours gazed at young Lennox's shoulders and arms, and the muscles swelling beneath his thin shirt, and he was not quite so sure of his principal's victory as he had been.

Then the two faced each other and Robert looked straight into his opponent's eyes, reading there the proof that while outwardly de Mézy might now show no signs of dissipation, yet drink and lost hours had struck a blow at the vital organism of the human machine. He was more confident than ever, and he repeated to himself Willet's advice to be cautious and slow at first.

"Your positions, gentlemen!" said de Galisonnière, and they stood face to face. The turf was short and firm, and the place was ideal for their purpose. Among the trees the eager eyes of Monsieur Berryer and a score of others watched.

"Ready!" said de Galisonnière, and then, after a pause of two or three moments, he added:

"Proceed!"

Robert had not looked straight into his opponent's eye so long for nothing. He knew now that de Mézy was choleric and impatient, that he would attack at once with a vigorous arm and a furious heart, expecting a quick and easy victory. His reading of the mind through the eye was vindicated as de Mézy immediately forced the combat, cutting and thrusting with a fire and power that would have overwhelmed an ordinary opponent.

Robert smiled. He knew now beyond the shadow of a doubt that he was de Mézy's master. Not in vain did he have those large and powerful wrists, firm and strong as wrought steel, and not in vain had he been taught for years by the best swordsman in America. He contented himself with parrying the savage cuts and thrusts, and gave ground slowly, retreating in a circle. De Mézy's eyes blazed at first with triumph. He had resented Robert's refusal of his offer to substitute Willet, and now, the victory which he had regarded as easy seemed to be even easier than he had hoped. He pushed the combat harder. His sword flashed in a continuous line of light, and the whirring of steel upon steel was unceasing. But the face of Nemours, as he watched with an understanding eye, fell a little. He saw that the breathing of young Lennox was long and regular, and that his eye was still smiling.

Robert continued to give ground, but he never took his eye from that of de Mézy, and at last the count began to feel that something lay behind that calm, smiling gaze. The drink and the multitude of lost hours came back to demand their price. Something bit into his bone. Was it physical weakness or a sudden decay of confidence? He did not see any sign of weariness in his young opponent, and putting forth every effort of his muscles and every trick and device he knew he could not break through that shining guard of circling steel.

The strange apprehension that had suddenly found a place in de Mézy's mind began to grow. The slow retreat of his young antagonist was becoming slower and then it ceased entirely. Now the leaping sword before him began to drive him back, and always the calm smiling eyes probed into his, reading what he would keep hidden deep in his heart. They saw the terror that was growing there. The disbelief in his antagonist's prowess was now fast turning into a hideous contradiction, and all the while drink and the lost hours that had clamored for their price were taking it.

De Mézy began to give back. His breath grew shorter and he gasped. The deep mottled red returned to his cheeks, and terror took whole possession of him. He had struck down his man before and he had laughed, but he had never faced such a swordsman as this strange youth of the woods, with his smiling eyes and his face which was a mask despite the smile.

Nemours and Le Moyne turned pale. They saw that their leader had never once passed the bar of steel before him, and that while he panted and grew weary Lennox seemed stronger than ever. They saw, too, that the youth was a swordsman far surpassing de Mézy and that now he was playing with his enemy. He struck down his opponent's guard at will, and his blade whistled about his body and face. Nemours' hand fell to his own hilt, but the watchful Willet saw.

"Be careful," the hunter said in a menacing tone. "Obey the rules or

I'll know the reason why."

Nemours' hand fell away from the hilt, and he and Le Moyne exchanged glances, but stood helpless. De Mézy had been driven backward in an almost complete circle. His wrist and arm ached to the shoulder, and always he saw before him the leaping steel and the smiling mask of a face. He caught a glimpse of the blue sky and the shining river, and then his eyes came back to the one that held his fate. Well for de Mézy that he had made the offer that morning to substitute Willet for Lennox, since youth, with the hot blood of battle pulsing in its veins, may think too late of mercy. But Robert remembered. His revenge was already complete. All had seen the pallid face of de Mézy, and all, whether they knew anything of the sword or not, knew that he lay at the mercy of his foe.

"Strike and make an end!" gasped de Mézy.

The sword flashed before his eyes again, but the blade did not touch him. Instead his own sword was torn from his weakening grasp, and was flung far upon the grass. Young Lennox, turning away, sheathed his weapon.

"Well done, Robert!" said Willet.

De Mézy put his hand to his face, which was wet with perspiration, and steadied himself. He had grown quite dizzy in the last few moments, and the pulses in his head beat so heavily that he could neither see nor think well. He was conscious that he stood unarmed before a victorious foe, but he did not know Robert had put away his sword.

"Why don't you strike?" he muttered.

"Mr. Lennox is satisfied," said Nemours. "He does not wish the combat to go further."

"Unless Captain de Mézy insists on another trial," said de Galisonnière, smiling a little, "but if he will take the advice of a countryman of his he will let the matter rest where it is. Enough has been done to satisfy the honor of everybody."

He and Nemours exchanged significant glances. It was quite evident to de Mézy's seconds that he was no match for Robert, and that another trial would probably result in greater disaster, so Nemours and Le Moyne, in behalf of their principal, promptly announced that they were satisfied, and de Galisonnière and Glandelet said as much for theirs. Meanwhile Monsieur Berryer and the other spectators, who had now risen to the number of two score, continued to watch from the shelter of the trees. They had seen the result with protruding eyes, but they had not understood when the

124

young victor thrust his sword back in its sheath. They could not hear the talk, but it was quite clear that the duel was over, and they turned away, somewhat disappointed that one of their own had lost the combat, but somewhat pleased, too, that he had not lost his own life at the same time.

"Shake hands, gentlemen," said de Galisonnière blithely. "Although no blood was shed it was a hot battle and I hope when you two meet again it will be in friendship and not in enmity. You are a fine swordsman, Lennox, and it was honorable of you, de Mézy, when you didn't know his caliber, to offer to take on, because of his youth, the older man, Mr. Willet."

Robert came back and offered his hand frankly. De Mézy, whose head was still ringing from his uncommon exertions and chagrin, took it. It was bitter to have lost, but he still lived. In a manner as he saw it, he had been disgraced, but time and the red wine and the white would take away the sting. He still lived. That was the grand and beautiful fact. Many more joyous days and nights awaited him in the company of Bigot and Cadet and Pean, powerful men who knew how to exercise their power and how to live at the same time. He should be grateful for a little while, at least, to the young Bostonnais, and he shook the proffered hand as heartily as his own damp, limp fingers would admit.

"May your stay in Quebec be as pleasant as you wish," he said, a bit thickly.

"Thanks," said Robert, who read the man's mind thoroughly.

De Galisonnière put away the unstained swords, quite satisfied with the affair, himself and everybody. An important follower of Bigot had been humbled, and yet he had not suffered in such a manner that he could call for the punishment of the one who had humbled him. The very youth of the Bostonnais would disarm resentment against him.

De Mézy's party with formal bows drew away, and Robert and his friends returned to the Inn of the Eagle.

CHAPTER XI
BIGOT'S BALL

"You needn't expect any trouble from the authorities," said de Galisonnière, when they sat once more in the great room at the inn. "Dueling is of course frowned upon theoretically, but it's a common practice, and since no life has been lost, not even any wound inflicted, you'll hear nothing of it from the government. And de Mézy, I imagine, will say as little about it as possible. He rather fancies himself as a swordsman, and he will not want everybody in Quebec to know that he was defeated and disarmed by a boy. Still, it will spread."

He and Glandelet took a courteous leave, and Robert thanked them for their services. He liked them both, especially de Galisonnière, and he was sorry that fate should put them on opposing sides in the war that all of them felt was surely coming.

"The French count gave you the hand of friendship, but not the spirit of it," said Tayoga, who had not spoken at all while they were at the dueling ground. "He was grateful to you for sparing his life, but his gratitude will go like the wind, and then he will hate you. And he will have the powerful friends, of whom the captain spoke, to plot against you and us."

"That's so, Tayoga," said the hunter, gravely, "I'm sorry the Governor General wasn't here when we arrived. It was an unlucky chance, because it would have been better for us to have given him our letters and have departed at once."

Robert, in his heart, knew that it was true, and that dangers would soon cluster about them, but he was willing to linger. The spell of Quebec had grown stronger, and he had made an entrance into its world in most gallant fashion, sword in hand, like a young knight, and that would appeal to the warlike French.

They deemed it wise to stay in the inn for a while, but two or three hours later Willet went out, returning soon, and showing some excitement.

"An old friend has come," he said.

"A friend!" said Robert. "I know of no friend to expect."

"I used the word 'friend' in exactly the opposite sense. It's an enemy.

I'm quite sure nobody in the world hates us more."

"Tandakora!"

"None other. It's the sanguinary Ojibway, his very self. I saw him stalking along the streets of Quebec in the most hideous paint that man ever mixed, a walking monument of savage pride, and I've no doubt in my mind either why he came here."

"To get some sort of revenge upon us."

"That's it. He'll go before the Governor General, and charge that we attacked him in the gorge and slew good, innocent men of his."

"Tandakora is cunning," said Tayoga. "The Great Bear is right. He will lie many times against us, and it is likely that the Frenchmen, de Courcelles and Jumonville, will come also and tell that they met us in the woods, although they said smooth words to us when we left them."

"And we don't know what kind of a net they'll try to weave around us," said Willet. "I say again I wish we'd delivered our letters and were out of Quebec."

But Robert could not agree with the hunter and Tayoga. He was still glad of the lucky chance that had taken away the Governor General. There was also a certain keen delight in speculating what their enemies would do next. Conscious of right and strength he believed they could foil all attempts upon them, and while the question was still fresh in his mind Father Philibert Drouillard came in. Wrapped closely in his black robe he looked taller, leaner, and more ascetic than ever, and his gaze was even stronger and more penetrating. Now it rested upon Robert.

"I had a fair opinion of you," he said. "Coming with you in the Frontenac down the river I judged you, despite your weapons and the fact that you belong to another race than mine, a gentle youth and full of the virtues. Now I find that you have been fighting and fighting with intent to kill."

"Hold hard, Father," said Willet in a good-humored tone. "Only half of that is true. Your information is not full. He has been fighting, but not with intent to kill. He held the life of Count Jean de Mézy on the point of his sword, but gave it back to him, such as it was."

The deep eyes of the priest smoldered. Perhaps there was a distant and fiery youth of his own that the morning's deed recalled, but his menacing gaze relaxed.

"If you gave him back his life when you could have taken it, you have done well," he said. "As the hunter intimates, it is a life of little value, perhaps none at all, but you did not on that account have any right to take it. And I say more, that if the misadventure had to happen to any Frenchman here in Quebec I am glad it happened to one of the wicked tribe of Bigot."

"Your man Bigot, powerful though he may be, seems to have plenty of enemies," said the hunter.

"He has many, but not enough, I fear," said the priest gloomily. "He and his horde are a terrible weight upon the shoulders of New France. But I should not talk of these things to you who are our enemies, and who may soon be fighting us."

He quit the subject abruptly, and talked in a desultory manner on irrelevant matters. But Robert saw that Quebec itself and the struggle between the powerful Bigot ring and the honnêtes gens was a much greater weight on his mind than the approaching war with the English colonies.

After a stay of a half hour he departed, saying that he was going to visit a parish farther down the river, and might not see them again, but he wished them well. He also bade them once more to beware of Tandakora.

"A good man and a strong one," said Willet, when, he left. "I seem to feel a kindred spirit in him, but I don't think his prevision about not seeing us again is right, though his advice to look out for Tandakora is certainly worth following."

They saw the Ojibway warrior twice that afternoon. Either he concealed the effects of the wound in his shoulder or it had healed rapidly, since he was apparently as vigorous as ever and gave them murderous glances. Tayoga shrugged his shoulders.

"Tandakora has followed us far," he said, "but this is not the ground that suits him. The forest is better than a city for the laying of an ambush."

"Still, we'll watch him," said Willet.

The evening witnessed the arrival at the Inn of the Eagle of two new guests to whom Monsieur Berryer paid much deference, Colonel de Courcelles and Captain de Jumonville, who had been on an expedition in behalf of His Majesty, King Louis, into the forests of the south and west, and who, to the great surprise of the innkeeper, seemed to be well acquainted with the three.

Robert, Tayoga and Willet were having their dinner, or supper as it would have been called in the Province of New York, when the two Frenchmen dressed in their neat, close-fitting uniforms and with all the marks of travel removed, came into the large room. They rose at once and exchanged greetings. Robert, although he did not trust them, felt that they had no cause of quarrel with the two, and it was no part of his character to be brusque or seek trouble.

De Courcelles gave them a swift, comprehensive glance, and then said, as if they were chance visitors to Quebec:

"You've arrived ahead of us, I see, and as I learn, you find the

Marquis Duquesne away. Perhaps, if your letters are urgent, you would care to present them to the Intendant, Monsieur Bigot, a man of great perception and judgment."

Robert turned his examining look with interest. Was he also one of Bigot's men, or did he incline to the cause of the honnêtes gens? Or, even if he were not one of Bigot's followers, did he prefer that Robert's mission should fail through a delivery of his letters to the wrong man? Bigot certainly was not one with whom the English could deal easily, since so far as Robert could learn he was wrapped in the folds of a huge conceit.

"We might do that," the youth replied, "but I don't think it's quite proper. I make no secret of the fact that I bear letters for the Governor General of Canada, and it would not be pleasing to the Governor of the Province of New York for me to deliver them to someone else."

"It was merely a suggestion. Let us dismiss it."

He did not speak again of the immediate affairs that concerned them so vitally, but talked of Paris, where he had spent a gay youth. He saw the response in the glowing eyes of Robert, and exerted himself to please. Moreover his heart was in his subject. Quebec was a brilliant city for the New World, but Paris was the center of the whole world, the flower of all the centuries, the city of light, of greatness and of genius. The throne of the Bourbons was the most powerful in modern times, and they were a consecrated family.

Robert followed him eagerly. Both he and de Courcelles saw the Bourbons as they appeared to be before the fall, and not as the world has seen them since, in the light of revelation. The picture of Paris and its splendors, painted by one who loved it, flung over him a powerful spell, and only the warning words Willet had spoken recalled to him that the Bourbon throne might not really be made for all time.

De Courcelles and Jumonville, who had no permanent quarters in Quebec, would remain two days at the inn, and, on the whole, Robert was glad. He felt that the three could protect themselves from possible wiles and stratagems of the two Frenchmen, and that they meant to attempt them he believed he had proof later, as de Courcelles suggested they might call in the course of the evening upon the Intendant, Bigot, who was then at his palace. They need not say anything about their mission, but good company could be found there, and they might be sure of a welcome from the Intendant. Again Robert declined, and de Courcelles did not press the matter. He and Jumonville withdrew presently, saying they had a report to make to the commandant of the garrison, and the three went to bed soon afterward.

Tayoga, who slept lightly, awoke after midnight and went to a window. The Onondaga, most of the three, distrusted Quebec. It was never Quebec to him. It was Stadacona of the Ganeagaono, the great warrior nation of the Hodenosaunee who stood beside the Onondagas, their lost Stadacona, but their Stadacona still. In his heart too burned the story of Frontenac and how he had ravaged the country of the Hodenosaunee with fire and sword. He was here in the very shrine and fortress of the ancient enemies of the great Iroquois. He had taken the education of the white man, he had read in his books and he knew much of the story of the human race, but nothing had ever disturbed his faith that a coming chief of the clan of the Bear, of the nation Onondaga, of the mighty League of the Hodenosaunee was, by right, and in fact, a prince among men.

But while Tayoga learned what civilization, as the European races called it, had to offer, it did not make him value any the less the arts and lore of his own forest. Rather, they increased in size and importance by comparison. He had seen how the talk of de Courcelles had lighted a fire in the soul of Lennox, he had seen how even Willett, the wary, had been stirred, but he, Tayoga, had been left cold. He had read the purpose behind it all, and never for an instant did he let himself put any faith in de Courcelles or Jumonville.

The air of the room was heavy and fetid to Tayoga. His free spirit detected poison in the atmosphere of Quebec, and, for the moment, he longed to be in the great, pure wilderness, pure at least to one of his race. He opened the window more widely and inhaled the breeze which was coming from the north, out of vast clean forests, that no white man save the trapper had ever entered.

He looked upward, at first toward the blue sky and its clustering stars, and then, turning his eyes to the open space near the inn, caught sight of two shadowy figures. The Onondaga was alert upon the instant, because he knew those figures, thin though they seemed in the dusk. One was Tandakora, the Ojibway, and the other was Auguste de Courcelles, Colonel in the French army, a pair most unlike, yet talking together earnestly now.

Tayoga was not at all surprised. He had pierced the mind of de Courcelles and he had expected him to seek Tandakora. He watched them a full five minutes, until the Ojibway slipped away in the darkness, and de Courcelles turned back toward the inn, walking slowly, and apparently very thoughtful.

Tayoga thought once of going outside to follow Tandakora,

but he decided that no good object would be served by it and remained at the window, where the wind out of the cold north could continue to blow upon him. He knew that the Indian and de Courcelles had entered into some conspiracy, but he believed they could guard against it, and in good time it would disclose itself.

There might be many hidden trails in a city like Quebec, but he meant to discover the one that Tandakora followed. He remained an hour at the window, and then without awaking his comrades to tell what he had seen went back to his bed. Nor did he say anything about it when they awoke in the morning. He preferred to keep Tandakora as his especial charge. A coming chief of the clan of the Bear, of the nation Onondaga, of the great League of the Hodenosaunee, would know how to deal with a savage Ojibway out of the western forests.

At breakfast, Robert wondered what they would do during the coming day, as it was not advisable to go much about Quebec owing to the notoriety the duel had brought to them. Monsieur Berryer, suave, deferential and full of gossip, informed them that the fame of young Mr. Lennox as a master of the sword had spread through the city in a few hours. Brave and skillful young Frenchmen were anxious to meet him and prove that where Count Jean de Mézy had failed they might succeed.

"The young gentleman will not lack opportunities for honor and glory in

Quebec," said Monsieur Berryer, rubbing his fat, white hands.

"In view of our errand here you must let all these opportunities go, Robert," said Willet. "If we show ourselves too much some of these hot young French knights will force a fight upon you, not because they hate you, but from sporting motives. But it would be just as bad for you to lose your life in a friendly duel as in one full of hate."

Robert chafed, nevertheless. The Inn of the Eagle was a good inn, but he did not wish to spend an entire day within its walls. Young Captain Louis de Galisonnière solved the problem, arriving just after breakfast with a note addressed to Mr. Robert Lennox, which proved to be an invitation for all three of them from Monsieur François Bigot, Intendant of Canada, to attend a dinner given by him that evening at his palace. The letter was full of polite phrases. The Intendant had heard of young Mr. Lennox's surpassing skill with the sword, and of his success with Count Jean de Mézy, who wielded a good blade himself. But neither the Intendant nor those associated with him bore any ill will. It was well known that Mr. Lennox was accredited with letters to the Marquis Duquesne, but in the absence of the Governor General it would be the pleasure of the Intendant to show courtesy to the messenger of the Governor of the Province of New York and his comrades.

It was a full and abounding letter, swarming with polite phrases, and it appealed to Robert. Bigot might be corrupt, but he belonged to the great world, and Robert felt that since he had come to Quebec he ought to see the Intendant, his palace and what was done within its walls. It was true that they had evaded suggestions to meet him, but a formal invitation was different. He passed the letter to Willet, who read it and handed it to Tayoga.

"We'll have to go, Robert," said the hunter. "It's evident that Bigot wants us, and if we don't accept he may make trouble for us. Yes, it's wiser to go."

Robert's eyes shone and Willet noticed it.

"You'd have been disappointed if I had counseled a negative," he said.

"I would," said Robert frankly. "I'm looking forward to the dinner with the Intendant. Will you be there, Captain de Galisonnière?"

"Yes, and I'm glad you've accepted. Mr. Willet was right when he said it was wisdom to go. The Intendant is the most powerful man in Canada. 'Tis said that the Governor General, the Marquis Duquesne, will return to France before long, and hence he lets a part of his authority slip into the hands of Monsieur Bigot. You understand the dual nature of our government in Canada. The Governor General is the immediate personal representative of the King, but the Intendant is supreme over the courts, finance, commerce and all the civil affairs of the country. So a mighty power is lodged in his hands and it's also true here, as well as elsewhere, that he who holds the purse holds more than the sword."

"Will Colonel de Courcelles and Captain de Jumonville be there?" continued Robert.

"Undoubtedly. They belong to the military arm, of course, but they are both favorites of Bigot, and they neglect no opportunity to strengthen their position with him. Be careful what you say before them."

Robert thanked him for his caution, although it was not needed, as he had already resolved to be very wary in the presence of de Courcelles and Jumonville, and the Onondaga also made a mental note of it, knowing that de Courcelles was willing to plot in the dusk with a savage Ojibway.

De Galisonnière did not stay long, and after his departure Robert and his friends reconsidered their determination, deciding that it was best to brave Quebec and whatever it should have to offer in the full light of day. The hunter's apprehensions that a quarrel might be forced upon them were not justified, as Canadian and French politeness held true, and they were received only with curiosity and interest.

They gazed again at the great stone buildings and also took a brief view of the Intendant's palace, where they expected to dine in the evening. It was a palace in extent, but not in beauty, a great rambling building of both timber and masonry, with a green lawn and flower gardens near by. It was said that Bigot and his predecessors had spent huge sums on the interior decoration, but that Robert expected soon to see for himself.

Returning to the Inn of the Eagle late in the afternoon, they began to array themselves for Bigot's dinner, not wishing the Bostonnais to appear at a disadvantage before the noblesse of Quebec. Monsieur Berryer sent them a barber, Gaston, who not only shaved the two white faces, but who powdered and arranged their queues, and also manicured their nails and gave their coats and waistcoats a rakish set, which he assured them was quite the latest mode in Paris. Robert took all his advice. He was very particular about his attire, knowing that however much the jealous might criticize fine dress it always had its effect.

The hunter watched Robert as he and Gaston arranged the new Paris styles with a look that was almost paternal. The fine youth had exceeded Willet's best hopes. Tall, straight, frank and open, he had the sound mind in the sound body which is the sum of excellence, and the hunter was glad to see him particular. It was a part of his heritage, and became him.

They were not to leave the Inn of the Eagle until after dusk, and Willet suggested that they should not start until late, as they could walk to the palace in a few minutes. But Robert said boldly that they would not walk. It was fitting for the messengers of the Governor of New York to ride and he would have Monsieur Berryer to call a caleche. Willet assented with a laugh.

"You're right, Robert," he said, "but I ride so little in carriages that

I didn't think of it."

The night was rather dark, but when the three in the caleche approached the palace they saw many men holding torches, and many people back of them watching. The entertainments of François Bigot were famous in Quebec for lavish splendor, and the uninvited usually came in numbers to see the guests go in.

"Be on your guard tonight, Robert," whispered Willet. "This is a society to which you're not used, although I'll not deny that you could soon learn it. But the French think we English, whether

English English or American English, are inferior in wit and quickness to themselves, and there may be some attempts at baiting the bear before we leave."

Robert felt his breath coming a little more quickly, and in the dusk, Willet did not see the glow that appeared in his eyes. They might try to "bait the bear" but he would be ready. The new powers that he had found in himself not only accepted the challenge, but craved it. He was conscious that he was not deficient in wit and quickness himself, and if any follower of François Bigot, or if the great Bigot himself tried to make sport of him he might find instead that the ruffler was furnishing sport for the Bostonnais. So it was with a beating heart but no apprehension that he alighted from the caleche with his friends, and went into the palace to meet the Intendant.

The interior of the great building was a singular mixture of barbaric and civilized splendor, the American forests and the factories of France alike being drawn upon for its furnishings. The finest of silken tapestries and the rarest of furs often hung close together. Beyond the anterooms was a large hall in which the chosen guests danced while the people might look on from galleries that surrounded it. These people, who were not so good as the guests, could dance as much as they pleased in a second hall set aside exclusively for their use. In another and more secluded but large room all kinds of games of chance to which Bigot and his followers were devoted were in progress. In the huge dining-room the table was set for forty persons, the usual number, until the war came, when it was reduced to twenty, and Bigot gave a dinner there nearly every evening, unless he was absent from Quebec.

Robert felt as soon as he entered the palace that he had come into a strange, new, exotic atmosphere, likely to prove intoxicating to the young, and he remembered the hunter's words of warning. Yet his spirit responded at once to the splendor and the call of a gayer and more gorgeous society than any he had ever known. Wealth and great houses existed even then in New York and upon occasion their owners made full use of both, but there was a restraint about the Americans, the English and the Dutch. Their display was often heavy and always decorous, and in Quebec he felt for the first time the heedless gayety of the French, when the Bourbon monarchy had passed its full bloom, and already was in its brilliant decay. Truly, they could have carved over the doorway, "Leave all fear and sorrow behind, ye who enter here."

There were lights everywhere, flaming from tall silver candlesticks, and uniforms, mostly in white and silver, or white with black or violet facings, were thick in the rooms. Ladies, too, were present, in silk or satin billowing in many a fold, their powdered hair rolled high in the style made fashionable by Madame Jeanne Poisson de Pompadour. From an inner room came the music of a band softly playing French songs or airs from the Florentine opera. The air was charged with odors of perfume.

It was intoxicating, and yet it was pleasant. No, "pleasant" was not the word, it was alluring, it played upon the senses, it threw a glow over the rooms and the people, and the youth saw everything through a tawny mist that heightened and deepened the colors. He was glad that he had come. Nor was "glad" the word either. Seeing what he now saw and knowing what he now knew, he would have blamed himself bitterly had he stayed away.

"Welcome, Mr. Lennox, my brave and generous opponent of the morning," said a voice, and, looking through the tawny mist, he saw the man whom he had fought and spared, Count Jean de Mézy, in a wonderful coat, waistcoat and knee breeches of white satin, heavily embroidered, white silk stockings, and low white shoes with great silver buckles, and a small gold-hilted sword hanging at his thigh. The cheeks, a trifle too fat, were mottled again, but his manner like his costume was silken. One would have thought that he and not Robert was the victor in that trial of skill by the St. Louis gate.

"Welcome, Mr. Lennox," he said again in a tone that showed no malice. "The Intendant's ball will be all the more brilliant for the presence of yourself and your friends. What a splendid figure the young Onondaga chief makes!"

Tayoga bowed to the compliment, which was rather broad but true, and de

Mézy ran on:

"We are accustomed here to the presence of Indian chiefs. We French have known how to win the trust and friendship of the warriors and we ask them to our parlors and our tables as you English do not do, although I will confess that the Iroquois hitherto have come into Canada as enemies and not as friends."

"Quebec was once the Stadacona of the Ganeagaono, known to you as the Mohawks," said Tayoga in his deep musical voice, "and there is no record that they ever gave or sold it to Onontio."

De Mézy was embarrassed for a moment, but he recovered himself quickly and laughed.

"You have us there!" he cried, "but it was long, long ago, when Cartier came to Quebec. Times change and ownerships change with them. We can't roll back the past."

Tayoga said no more, content to remind the French at

135

intervals that a brother nation of the Hodenosaunee still asserted its title to Quebec.

"You are not the only member of the great red race present," said de Mézy to Tayoga. "We have a chief from the far west, a splendid type of the forest man. What size! What strength! What a mien! By my faith, he would make a stir in Paris!"

"Tandakora, the Ojibway!" said Robert.

"Yes, but how did you know?"

"We have met him—more than once. We have had dealings with him, and we may have more. He seems to be interested in what we're doing, and hence we're never surprised when we see him."

De Mézy looked puzzled, but at that moment de Courcelles and de Jumonville, wearing uniforms of white and silver, came forward to add their greeting to those of the count. They were all courtesy and the words dropped from their lips like honey, but Robert felt that their souls were not like the soul of de Galisonnière, and that they could not be counted among the honnêtes gens. But the three Frenchmen were ready now to present the three travelers to Monsieur François Bigot, Intendant of Canada, great and nearly all powerful, and Robert judged too that they had made no complaint against his friends and himself.

Bigot was standing near the entrance to the private dancing room, and about him was a numerous company, including ladies, among them the wife of Pean, to whom the gossip of the time gave great influence with him, and a certain Madame Marin and her sister, Madame de Rigaud, and others. As the three approached under the conduct of the three Frenchmen the group opened out, and they were presented in order, Robert first.

The youth was still under the influence of the lights, the gorgeous rooms and the brilliant company, but he gazed with clear eyes and the most eager interest at Bigot, whose reputation had spread far, even in the British colonies. He saw a man of middle years, portly, his red face sprinkled with many pimples, probably from high living, not handsome and perhaps at first repellent, but with an expression of vigor and ease, and an open, frank manner that, at length, attracted. His dress was much like de Mézy's, but finer perhaps.

Such was the singular man who had so much to do with the wrecking of New France, a strange compound of energy and the love of luxury, lavish with hospitality, an untiring worker, a gambler, a profligate, a thief of public funds, he was also kindly, gracious and devoted to his friends. A strange bundle of contradictions and disjointed morals, he represented in the New World the glittering decadence that marked the French monarchy at home. Now he was smiling as de Mèzy introduced Robert with smooth words.

"Mr. Robert Lennox of Albany and New York," he said, "the brilliant young swordsman of whom I spoke to you, the one who disarmed me this morning, but who was too generous to take my life."

Bigot's smiling gaze rested upon Robert, who was conscious, however, that there was much penetration behind the smile. The Intendant would seek to read his mind, and perhaps to learn the nature of the letters he brought, before they were delivered to their rightful owner, the Marquis Duquesne. Quebec was the home of intrigue, and the Intendant's palace was the heart of it, but if Robert's pulse beat fast it was with anticipation and not with fear.

"It was fortune more than skill," he said. "The Count de Mézy credits me with too much knowledge of the sword."

"No," said Bigot, laughing, "Jean wouldn't do that. He'd credit you with all you have, and no more. Jean, like the rest of us, doesn't relish a defeat, do you, Jean?"

De Mézy reddened, but he forced a laugh.

"I suppose that nobody does!" he replied, "but when I suffer one I try to make the best of it."

"That's an honest confession, Jean," said Bigot, "and you'll feel better for making it."

He seemed now to Robert bluff, genial, all good nature, and the youth stood on one side, while Willet and Tayoga were presented in their turn. Bigot looked very keenly at the Onondaga, and the answering gaze was fierce and challenging. Robert saw that Tayoga was not moved by the splendor, the music and the perfumed air, and that he did not forget for an instant that this gay Quebec of the French was the Stadacona of the Mohawks, a great brother nation of the Hodenosaunee.

Bigot's countenance fell a little as he met the intensely hostile gaze, but in a moment he recovered himself and began to pay compliments to Willet and the Iroquois. Robert felt the charm of his manner and saw why he was so strong with a great body of the French in New France. Then his eyes wandered to the others who stood near like courtiers around a king, and he noticed that foremost among them was a man of mean appearance and presuming manner, none other, he soon learned, than the notorious Joseph Cadet, confederate of Bigot, in time to become Commissary General of New France, the son of a Quebec butcher, who had begun life as a pilot boy, and who was now one of the most powerful men in those regions of the New World that paid allegiance to the House of Bourbon. Near him stood Pean, the Town Mayor of Quebec, a soldier of energy, but deep in corrupt bargains with Cadet, and just beyond Pean was his partner, Penisseault, and near them were their wives, of whom scandal spoke many a true word, and beyond them were the Commissary of Marine, Varin, a Frenchman, small and insignificant of appearance, the Intendant's secretary, Deschenaux, the son of a shoemaker at Quebec, Cadet's trusted clerk, Corpron and Maurin, a humpback.

A strange and varied company, one of the strangest ever gathered in any outlying capital of a diseased and dying monarchy. Robert, although he knew that it was corrupt and made a mockery of many things that he had been taught to reverence, did not yet understand how deadly was the poison that flowed in the veins of this society. At present, he saw only the glow and the glitter. All these people were connected closely. The Canadians intermarrying extensively were a great family, and the Frenchmen were bound together by the powerful tie, a common interest.

"Don't believe all you see, Robert," whispered Willet. "You're seeing the surface, and it's hollow, hollow! I tell you!"

"But we have nothing like it at home," said Robert. "We're lucky to come."

De Mézy had left them, but de Courcelles was near, and he saw that they were not neglected. Robert was introduced to officers and powerful civilians and the youngest and handsomest of the ladies, whose freedom of language surprised him, but whose wit, which played about everything, pleased a mind peculiarly sensitive to the charm of light and brilliant talk.

He had never before been in such an assembly, one that contained so much of rank and experience in the great world. Surrounded by all that he loved best, the people, the lights, the colors, and the anticipation of what was to come, the Intendant shone. One forgot his pimply face and portly figure in the geniality that was not assumed, and the ease of his manners. He spoke to Robert more than once, asked him many questions about Albany and New York, and referred incidentally, too, to the Iroquois, but it was all light, as if he were asking them because of interest in his guest, or merely to make conversation.

The hues of everything gradually grew brighter and more brilliant to Robert. The music from the next room steeped his senses, and he began to feel the intoxication of which Willet had warned him. Many of the guests were of the noblest families of France, young officers who had come to Quebec, where it was reported promotion was rapid and sure, or where younger sons, with the aid of such powerful men as Bigot and Cadet, could make fortunes out of the customs or in the furnishing of supplies to the government. Robert found himself talking much, his gift of speech responding readily to the call. He answered their jests with a jest, their quips with a quip, and when they were serious so was he. He felt that while there may have been an undercurrent of hostility when he entered the palace it had all disappeared now, and he was a favorite, or at least they took a friendly interest in him, because he was a new type and they did not think him brusque and rude, as the French believed all Bostonnais to be.

And through this picturesque throng stalked the two Indians, Tayoga and Tandakora. The Ojibway wore a feather headdress, and a scarlet blanket of richest texture was draped around his body, its hem meeting his finely tanned deerskin leggings, while his feet were encased in beaded moccasins. Nevertheless he looked, in those surroundings, which belonged so thoroughly to an exotic civilization, more gigantic and savage than ever. Robert was well aware that Bigot had brought him there for a political purpose, to placate and win the western tribes, and to impress him with the power and dignity of France. But whatever he may have felt, the Ojibway, towering half a head above the tallest white man, save Willet, was grim and lowering. His left arm lay in a fold of his blanket, and, as he held it stiffly, Robert knew that his wound was yet far from healed. He and Tayoga were careful to keep away from each other, the Onondaga because he was a guest and was aware of the white man's amenities, and the Ojibway because he knew it was not the time and place for his purpose.

They went in to dinner presently and the table of François Bigot was splendid as became the powerful Intendant of New France, who had plenty of money, who was lavish with it and who, when it was spent, knew where to obtain more with ease and in abundance. Forty guests sat down, and the linen, the silver and the china were worthy of the King's palace at Versailles. A lady was on Robert's right and Colonel de Courcelles was on his left. Willet and Tayoga were farther down on his own side of the table, and he could not see them, unless he leaned forward, which he was too well mannered to do. Bigot sat at the foot of the table and at its head was Madame Pean, a native of Canada, born Mademoiselle Desméloizes, young, handsome and uncommonly vivacious, dressed gorgeously in the latest Parisian style, and, as Robert put it to himself, coruscating with talk and smiles.

The dinner progressed amid a great loosening of tongues and much wit. The perfume from the flowers on the table and the continuous playing of the band made the air heavier and more intoxicating. It seemed to Robert that if these people had any cares they had dismissed them all for the time. Their capacity for pleasure, for snatching at the incense of the fleeting moment, amazed him. War might be coming, but tonight there was no thought of it.

Bigot toasted the two Bostonnais and the young Iroquois chief who were his guests in a flowery speech and Robert responded. When he rose to his feet he felt a moment of dizziness, because he was so young, and because he felt so many eyes upon him. But the gift of speech came to his aid—he was not the golden-mouthed for nothing. The heavy sweet odor of the roses was in his nostrils, inspiring him to liquid words, and everything glittered before him.

He had the most friendly feeling for all in the room except Tandakora, and a new thought coming into his mind he spoke it aloud. He was, perhaps, in advance of his time, but he told them that New France and the British colonies could dwell in peace, side by side. Why should they quarrel? America was vast. British and French were almost lost in its forests. France and England together could be stowed away in the region about the Great Lakes and the shades of the wilderness would encompass them both. The French and British were great races, it was useless to compare them and undertake to say which was the greater, because each was great in its own way, and each excelled in its own particulars, but the two combined were the sum of manly virtues and strength. What the British lacked the French supplied, and what the French lacked the British supplied. Together they could rule the world and spread enlightenment.

He sat down and the applause was great and hearty, because he had spoken with fervor and well. His head was singing, and he was confused a little, after an effort that had induced emotion. Moreover, the band had begun to play again some swaying, lilting dance tune, and his pulses beat to its measure. But he did lean forward, in spite of his manners, and caught Willet's approving look, for which he was very glad. He received the compliments of the lady on his right and of de Courcelles, then the band ceased presently and he became conscious that Tayoga was speaking. He had not heard Bigot call upon him, but that he had called was evident.

Tayoga stood up, tall, calm and dignified. He too had the oratorical power which was afterward displayed so signally by the Seneca who was first called by his own people Otetiani and was later known as Sagoyewatha, but who was known to the white men as Red Jacket.

"I speak to you not as a Frenchman nor as an Englishman," said Tayoga, "but as a warrior of the clan of the Bear of the nation Onondaga, of the great League of the Hodenosaunee. Most of this land belonged to our fathers before ever Englishmen or Frenchmen crossed the great water and put foot upon these shores. Where you sit now was Stadacona, the village of our brother race, the Mohawks. Frenchmen or Englishmen may make war upon one another, or they may make peace with one another, but the Hodenosaunee cannot be forgotten. There are many beautiful rivers and lakes and forests to the south and west, but they do not belong to either Onontio or Corlear. The laws of the fifty sachems who sit in council in the vale of Onondaga run there, and those who leave them out, be they French or English, reckon ill. There was a time when Frontenac came raiding their villages, burning and slaying, but we did not know the use of firearms then. Now we do know their use and have them, and in battle we can meet the white man on equal terms, be he English or French. I have been to the white man's school and I have learned that there are other great continents beyond the sea. I do not know what may happen in them, nor does it matter, but in this vast continent which you call America the wars and treaties of the English and the French are alike unavailing, unless they consider the wishes of the Hodenosaunee."

He spoke in a manner inexpressibly haughty, and when he had finished he swept the table from end to end with his challenging glance, then he sat down amid a deep silence. But they were French. They understood that he had tossed a glove among them, their quick minds saw that the challenge was intended not alone for them, but for the English as well, unless the rights of the Hodenosaunee were respected, and such a speech at such a time appealed to their gallant instincts. After a moment or two of silence the applause burst forth in a storm.

"'Twas a fair warning," said de Courcelles in Robert's ear, "and 'twas meant for us both."

It was on Robert's tongue to reply that the English were included for the sake of courtesy, as they were the friends of the Hodenosaunee and always kept faith with them, but second thought stopped the words on his lips. Then the band began again, playing a warm song of the south from the Florentine opera, and the talk increased. It seemed to Robert that everybody spoke at once, and his senses were again steeped in the music and the perfumed air, and the sound of so many voices. Presently he realized that some one across the table was speaking to him.

"The Onondaga said bold words in behalf of his league, but can he prove them true?" the voice was saying.

There was something provocative in his tone, and Robert looked closely at the speaker. He saw a tall man of at least forty-five, thin but obviously very powerful and agile. Robert noticed that his wrists were thick like his own and that his fingers were long and flexible. His face was freckled, his nose large and curved, giving to his face an uncommonly fierce appearance, and his eyes were black and set close together. It was a strong countenance and, when Robert looked at him, the black brows were drawn together in a frown. His words undoubtedly had a challenge in them, and the youth replied:

"When Tayoga speaks he speaks from his head as well as his heart, and I who am his sworn brother, although we are of different races, know that he doesn't boast when he refers to the power of the Hodenosaunee."

"And may it not be possible, sir, that you have been deceived by your friendship?"

Robert looked at him in surprise. The man's manner was pointed as if he were making an issue, and so he did not answer just then, but de Courcelles by his side leaned forward a little and said:

"Perhaps, Mr. Lennox, you have not yet been introduced formally to the chevalier, Chevalier Pierre Boucher, who has been only a year from Paris, but who is already a comrade good and true."

"No, I don't think I've been deceived," replied Robert, keeping his temper, and bowing to the introduction. "The Hodenosaunee, better known to you as the Iroquois, are a very powerful league, as many of the villages of Canada can tell."

The man's face darkened.

"Is it wise," he asked, "to remind us of the ferocious deeds the Iroquois have done upon us,"

But de Courcelles intervened.

"Peace! Peace, chevalier!" he said in a good-humored tone. "Mr. Lennox meant no innuendo. He merely stated a fact to prove a contention."

The chevalier subsided into silence, but Robert saw a significant look pass between them, and instantly he became keen and watchful. What did it mean? Willet's warning words came back to him. The more he studied Boucher the less he liked him. With his thin face, and great hooked nose, and long, bony fingers like talons, he reminded him of some great bird of prey. He noticed also that while the others were drinking wine, although he himself did not, the chevalier was the only one within his view who also abstained.

The dinner was long. One or two of the ladies sang to the music, another danced, and then de Galisonniére, in a full, round tenor voice, sang "The Bridge of Avignon."

"Hier sur le pont d'Avignon
J'ai oui chanter la belle
Lon, la,
J'ai oui chanter la belle,
Elle chantait d'un ton si doux
Comme une demoiselle
Lon, la,
Comme une demoiselle."

It was singularly appealing, and for a moment tears came to the eyes of all those who were born in France. They saw open fields, stone fences, and the heavy grapes hanging in the vineyards, instead of the huge rivers, the vast lakes and the mighty wilderness that curved almost to their feet. But it was only for a moment. This was Quebec, the seat of the French power in America, and they were in the Intendant's palace, the very core and heart of it. The laughter that had been hushed for a thoughtful instant or two came back in full tide, and once more the Chevalier Pierre Boucher spoke to Robert.

"The songs of our France are beautiful," he said. "None other have in them so much of poetry and haunting lament."

The youth detected as before the challenging under note in a remark that otherwise would have seemed irrelevant, and an angry contradiction leaped swiftly to his lips, but with the recollection of Willet's warning look he restrained himself again.

"France has many beautiful things," he replied quietly.

"Well spoken, Mr. Lennox! A compliment to us from one of another race is worth having," said de Courcelles. But Robert thought he saw that significant look pass for a second time between de Courcelles and Boucher. The long dinner drew to its close and the invited guests passed into the private ballroom, where the band began to play dance music. In the other ballroom, the one intended for the general public, the people were dancing already, and another band was playing.

Now Bigot was in his element, swelling with importance and good humor, easy, graceful, jesting with men and women, wishing the world well, knowing that he could milk from the royal treasury the money he was spending tonight, and troubled by no twinges of conscience. Cadet hovered near his powerful partner and Pean, Maurin, Penisseault and Corpron were not far away. Robert looked with interest at the ballroom which was decorated gorgeously. The balcony was filled already with spectators who would watch the lords and ladies dance. There was no restraint. No Father Drouillard was present to give rebuke and all the honnêtes gens were absent, unless a few young officers like de Galisonnière, who sympathized with them, be excepted.

They began to dance to light, tripping music, and to Robert all the women seemed beautiful and graceful now, and all the men gay and gallant. He could dance the latest dances himself, and meant to do so soon, but for the present he would wait, standing by the wall and looking on. Willet came to him, and evidently intended to whisper something, but de Courcelles, by the youth's side, intervened laughingly.

"No secrets, Mr. Willet," he said. "No grave and serious matters can be discussed at the Intendant's ball. It is one of our rules that when we work we work and when we play we play. It is a useful lesson which you Bostonnais should learn."

Then Jumonville came and began to talk to the hunter in such direct fashion that he was compelled to respond, and presently he was drawn away, leaving Robert with de Courcelles.

"You at least dance, do you not?" asked de Courcelles.

"Yes," replied Robert, "I learned it at Albany."

"Shall I get you a partner?"

"In a little while, if you will be so good, Colonel de Courcelles, but just now I'd rather see the others dancing. A most brilliant assemblage. I never beheld its like before."

"Brilliant for Quebec," said a voice at his elbow, "but you should go to Paris, the very heart and center of the world, to see great pleasure and great splendor in the happiest combination."

It was the grim and freckle-faced Boucher, and again Robert detected that challenging under note in his voice. In spite of himself his blood grew hot.

"I don't know much about Paris," he said. "I've never been there, although I hope to go some day, but Quebec affords both pleasure and splendor in high degree tonight."

"You don't mean to say that Quebec, much as we French have labored to build it up here in the New World, can compare with Paris?"

Robert stared at him in astonishment. Both manner and tone were now certainly aggressive, and as far as he could see aggressive about nothing. Why should anyone raise an issue between Quebec and Paris, and above all at such a time, there at Bigot's ball? He refused to be drawn into a controversy, and shrugging his shoulders a little, he turned away without an answer. He heard Boucher's voice raised again, but de Courcelles laughingly waved him down.

"Come! come, my Pierre," he said. "You're too ready to suspect that someone is casting aspersions upon that beloved Paris of ours. Perhaps you and I shall have the pleasure of showing the great city to Mr. Lennox some day."

He hooked his hand in Robert's arm and drew him away.

"Don't mind Boucher," he said. "He has a certain brusqueness of manner at times, although he is a good soul. He can't bear for anyone to suggest that another city, even one of our own, could possibly rival Paris in any particular. It's his pet devotion, and we won't disturb him in it. There's your friend, Tayoga, standing by the wall with his arms folded across his chest. What a splendid savage!"

"He's not a savage. Tayoga was educated in our schools and he has both the white man's learning and the red man's. He has the virtues, too, of both races, and few, very few of their vices."

"You're an enthusiast about your friend."

"And so would you be if you knew him as well as I do. That little speech he made showed his courage and the greatness of his soul."

"Spoken at such a time, its appeal was strong. I don't want to boast of my race, Mr. Lennox, but the French always respond to a gallant act."

"I know it, and I know, too, that if we English, and Americans or Bostonnais, as you call us, do go to war with you we could not possibly have a more enterprising or dangerous foe."

Colonel de Courcelles bowed to the compliment, and then with a nod indicated Tandakora, also standing against the wall, huge, sullen and looking like a splash of red flame, wrapped in his long scarlet blanket.

"He, at least, is a savage," he said.

"That I readily admit," said Robert.

"And as you know by the charges that he made against you to me, he wishes you and your comrades no good."

"I know by those charges and by events that have occurred since. Tandakora is a savage through and through, and as such my comrades and I must guard against him."

"But the Ojibway is a devoted friend of ours," said a harsh voice over his shoulders.

He turned and saw the lowering face of Boucher, and once more he was amazed. De Courcelles did not give the youth time to answer. Again he laughingly waved Boucher away.

"Pierre, my friend," he said, "you seem to be seeking points of issue tonight. Now, I refuse to let you and Mr. Lennox quarrel over the manners, habits and personal characteristics of Tandakora. Come, Mr. Lennox, I'm about to present you to a lady with whom you are going to dance."

Robert went away with him and he saw that Boucher, who was

145

left behind, was frowning, but he danced with the lady and others, and as the excitement of the moment mounted again to his head he forgot all about Boucher. He saw too that de Galisonnière had abandoned his restraint, and had plunged into the gayety with all the enthusiasm and delight of one to whom pleasure was natural. After a while de Courcelles hooked his arm again in Robert's and said: "Come, I'll show you something."

He led the way down a narrow passage, and then into a large apartment, well lighted, though not so brilliantly as the ballroom. A clicking sound had preceded their entrance, and Robert was aware that he was in the famous gambling room of Monsieur Bigot. Nearly twenty men, including the Intendant himself, Cadet and Pean, were there, gambling eagerly with cards or dice.

And standing by one of the tables, a frown on his freckled face, Robert also saw the man, Boucher.

CHAPTER XII
THE HUNTER AND THE BRAVO

Robert turned away, not wishing to meet Boucher again, as he felt that the man would say something provocative, and, standing on one side with de Courcelles, he watched the players. The air was heated, and the faces of the men were strained and eager. It was all unwholesome to the last degree, and he felt repulsion, yet it held him for the time with a fascination due to curiosity. He saw Boucher begin to play and as the latter held his cards, noticed again his thick and strong, but supple wrists. Uncommon wrists they were, and Robert knew that an uncommon amount of power was stored in them.

Bigot presently observed Robert, and asked him to play, but the lad declined, and he was brave enough to say that he never played. Bigot laughed and shook his head.

"Ah, you Puritan Bostonnais!" he said; "you'll never learn how to live."

Then he went back to his game.

"I think," said Robert, upon whom the heat and thick air were beginning to tell, "that I'd like to go outside and breathe a little fresh air."

"It is like a hothouse in here," said de Courcelles.

"It's but a step from this room to a little garden, where we can find all the cool air we want."

"Then show the way," said Robert quickly. He was eager to escape from the room, not alone for the sake of air, but because the place choked him. After a period of excitement and mental intoxication the reaction had come. The colors growing dimmer, the perfume in the air turned to poison, and he longed for the clean out-of-doors.

De Courcelles opened a small door and they stepped out. Robert did not notice that Boucher instantly put down his cards and followed. Before them was a grassy lawn with borders of rose bushes, and beyond, the vast sweep of the hills, the river and the far shore showed dimly through the dusk. The air, moved by a light wind, was crisp, fresh and pure, and, as Robert breathed it deeply, he felt his head grow clear and cool. Several men were walking in the garden. One of them was Jumonville, and the others he did not know.

"A wonderful site and a wonderful view," said Robert.

"But from Montmartre in Paris one may see a far greater city," said Boucher at his elbow.

Robert turned angrily upon him. He felt that the man, in some manner, was pursuing him, and that he had stood enough.

"I did not speak to you, Monsieur Boucher," he said.

"But I spoke to you, my young sprig of a Bostonnais."

He spoke with truculence, and now de Courcelles did not interfere. The others, hearing loud and harsh words, drew near. Jumonville came very close and regarded Robert with great intentness, evidently curious to see what he would do. The youth stared at Boucher in amazement, but he exercised his utmost self-control.

"I know that you spoke to me, Monsieur Boucher," he said, "but as I do not see any relevancy in your remarks I will ask you to excuse me. I came here merely for the air with Colonel de Courcelles."

He turned away, expecting de Courcelles to resume the walk with him, but the figure of the Frenchman stiffened and he did not move. All at once a wind of hostility seemed to be blowing. Somewhere in the dusk, somebody laughed lightly. Robert's face blazed, but he was still master of himself.

"And so you would leave after speaking to me in a manner that is an insult," sneered Boucher.

"You were the first to give an insult."

"If you think so I am ready to return satisfaction."

Boucher folded his arms across his chest, his powerful wrists crossed, and stared at Robert, his lips wrinkling in ugly fashion. It was a look like that which Tandakora had given him, and there in the background was the huge and sinister figure of the Indian, wrapped in his blanket of flame. He also saw de Mezy and he too was sneering in insolent triumph. De Courcelles, from whom he had a right at that time to expect friendship, or at least support, had drawn farther away.

"I am a guest here," said Robert, "and I seek no trouble. I don't wish to mar the hospitality of Monsieur Bigot by being a party to a quarrel in his garden."

Again that light laugh came from a point somewhere in the dusk and again Robert's face blazed, but he still held himself under firm control.

"You were ready enough to fight Count Jean de Mezy this morning," said Boucher, "knowing that he was not in condition and that you had a skill with the sword not suspected by him."

The truth of it all flashed upon Robert with the certainty of conviction. The entire situation had been arranged and de Courcelles was one of its principals. He had been brought into the garden that a fight might be forced upon him there. Boucher was a bravo and undoubtedly a great swordsman. He understood now the secret of those thick flexible wrists and of the man's insulting manner. His blood became ice in his veins for a moment or two, but it was good for him, cooling his head and quickening his mind. His heart beat with regularity and steadiness.

"I thank you, Monsieur de Courcelles," he said, "for your action in this matter, which I now understand. It's true that it departs in some respects from what I have understood to be the code and practice of a French gentleman, but doubtless, sir, it's your right to amend those standards as you choose."

De Courcelles flushed, bit his lip and was silent.

"Very pretty! Very pretty!" sneered Boucher, "but French gentlemen are the best judges of their own manners and morals. You have your sword, sir, and I have mine. Here is a fine open space, well lighted by the moon, and no time is better than the present. Will you draw, sir?"

"He will not," said a voice over Robert's shoulder, which he instantly recognized as that of the hunter. He felt suddenly as if a great wall had been raised for his support. He was no longer alone among plotting enemies.

"And why will he not, and what affair is it of yours?" asked Boucher, his manner threatening.

Willet took a step forward, his figure towering and full of menace. Just behind him was Tayoga. Robert had never seen the hunter look taller or more charged with righteous wrath. But it was an anger that burned like a white hot flame, and it was alive with deadly menace.

"He will not draw because he was brought here to be assassinated by you, bully and bravo that you are," replied Willet, plumbing the very depths of Boucher's eyes with his stern gaze. "I like the French, and I know them to be a brave and honest people. I did not think that in a gathering of French gentlemen enough could be found to form a treacherous and murderous conspiracy like this."

Nobody laughed in the dusk. The silence was intense. A cool wind blew across Robert's face, and he felt anew that an invincible champion stood by his side. Boucher broke the silence with a contemptuous laugh.

"Out of the way, sir," he said. "The affair does not concern you. If he does not draw and defend himself I will chastise him with the flat of my sword."

"You will not," said the hunter, in his cool, measured tones. "You will fight me, instead."

"My quarrel is not with you."

"But it soon will be."

Near Willet was a rose bush with fresh earth heaped over its roots. Stooping suddenly he picked up a handful and flung it with force into the bravo's face. Boucher swore under his breath, stepped back, and wiped away the earth.

"You've earned the precedence, sir," he said, "though I reserve the right to attend to Mr. Lennox afterward. 'Tis a pity that I should have to waste my steel on a common hunter. I call all of you to witness that this quarrel was forced upon me."

"Your pity does you credit," said the hunter, "but it's not needed. 'Twere better, sir, if you have such a large supply of that commodity that you save a little of it for yourself. And as for your attending to Mr. Lennox afterward, that meeting, I think, will not occur."

A long breath came from the crowd. This strange hunter spoke in a confident tone, and so he must know more than a little of the sword. De Galisonniere had just come into the garden, and was about to speak, but when he saw that Willet was face to face with Boucher he remained silent.

"Robert," said the hunter, "do you give me full title to this quarrel of yours?"

"Yes, it is yours," replied the youth, knowing that the hunter would not be denied, and having supreme confidence in him.

"And now, Monsieur Boucher," continued Willet, "the quicker the better. Mr. Lennox will be my second and I recommend that you choose for yours one of three gentlemen, Colonel de Courcelles, Count de Mezy or the Captain de Jumonville, all of whom conspired to lead a boy into this garden and to his death."

The faces of the three became livid.

"And," said the hunter, "if any one of the three gentlemen whom I have mentioned should feel the need of satisfaction after I have attended to Monsieur Pierre Boucher, I shall be very glad to satisfy him."

De Mezy recovering himself, and assuming a defiant manner, took the part of Boucher's second. Willet removed his coat and waistcoat and handed them to Robert, beside whom Tayoga was now standing. Then he drew his sword and balanced it a moment in his hand, before he clasped it lightly but firmly by the hilt.

Another long breath came from the crowd which had increased. Every man there was aware that something uncommon was afoot. Who and what Boucher was most of them knew, but the hunter was an unknown quantity, all the more interesting because of the mystery that enshrouded him. And the interest was deepened when they saw his swift, easy motion, his wonderful lightness for so large a man, and the manner in which the hilt of his sword fitted into his hand, as if they had long been brothers.

"I call you all to witness once again," said Boucher, "that this quarrel was forced upon me, and that I had no wish to slay a wandering hunter of the Bostonnais."

Willet made no reply for the present. He took his position and Boucher took his. The seconds gave the word, their swords clashed together, and they stepped back, each looking for an opening in the other's guard. Then it dawned upon the bravo that a swordsman stood before him. But he had not the slightest fear. He knew his own skill and strength.

"It's strange that a hunter should know anything about the sword," he said, "but it seems that you do and the fact pleases me much. I would not have it said that I cut down an ignorant man."

"And yet it might be said," replied the hunter. "Do you remember the boy, Gaston Lafitte, whom you fought behind the Luxembourg near twenty years ago?"

The face of Boucher suddenly went deathly white, and, for a moment, he trembled.

"Who are you, you mumming hunter?" he cried. "I know no Gaston Lafitte."

"There you lie, Boucher. You knew him well enough and you can't forget him if you would. Your face has shown it. It was well that you had powerful friends then, or you would soon be completing your twentieth year in the galleys."

The blood rushed back into Boucher's face until it was a blazing red, and he attacked savagely. Few men could have stood before that powerful and cunning offense, but Willet met him at every point. Always the flashing steel was turned aside, and the hunter, cool, patient and wary, looked like one who, in absolute faith, bided his time.

A gasp came from the spectators. The omens had foretold something unusual, but here was more than they had expected or had hoped. The greatest swordsman whom France could send forth had been checked and held by an unknown hunter, by a Bostonnais, among whom one would not look for swordsmanship. They stopped for breath and Boucher from under his dark brows stared at the hunter.

"Mummer," he said. "You claim to know something of me. What other lie about me can you tell?"

"It's not necessary to tell lies, Pierre Boucher. There was

151

Raoul de Bassempierre whom you compelled to fight you before he was fairly recovered of a sickness. His blood is still on your hands. Time has not dried it away. Look! Look! See the red bubbles standing on your wrists!"

Boucher, again as white as death, looked down hastily, and then uttered a fierce oath. The hunter laughed.

"It's true, Boucher," he said, "and everyone here knows it's true. Why speak of lies? I don't carry them in my stock, and I've proved that I don't need them. Come, you wish my death, attack again, but remember that I'm neither the untrained boy, Gaston Lafitte, nor Raoul de Bassempierre, wasted from illness."

Boucher rushed at him, and Robert thought he could hear the angry breath whistling through his teeth. Then he grew cooler, steadied himself and pushed the offense. His second attack was even more dangerous than the first, and he showed all the power and cunning of the great swordsman that he was. Willet slowly gave ground and the spectators began to applaud. After all, Boucher was a Frenchman and one of themselves, although it was not the best of the French who were gathered there in the garden that night-- except de Galisonniere and one or two others.

Robert watched the hunter and saw that his breathing was still regular and easy, and that his eye was as calm and confident as ever. Then his own faith, shaken for a moment, returned. Boucher was still unable to break through that guard of living steel, and when they paused a second time for breath each was still untouched.

"You are a swordsman, I'll admit that," said Boucher.

"Yes, a better than the raw lad, Gaston Lafitte, or Raoul de Bassempierre who was ill, and a better than a third whom I recall."

"What do you mean, mummer?"

"There was a certain Raymond de Neville who played at dice with another whom I could name. Neville said that the other cheated, but he was a great swordsman while Neville was but an indifferent fencer, and the other slew him. Yet, they say Neville's charges were true. Shall I name that man, Boucher?"

Boucher, livid with rage, sprang at him.

"Mummer!" he cried. "You know too much. I'll close your mouth forever!"

Now it seemed to Boucher that a very demon of the sword stood before him. His own fierce rush was met and he was driven back. The ghosts of the boy, Gaston Lafitte, of the sick man Raoul de Bassempierre, and of the indifferent swordsman, Raymond de Neville who had been cheated at cards, came back, and they helped Willet wield his weapon. His figure broadened and grew. His blade was no longer of steel, it was a strip of lightning that played around the body and face of the dazzled bravo. It was verily true that the hands of four men grasped the hilt, the ghosts of the three whom he had murdered long ago, and Willet who stood there in the flesh before him.

A reluctant buzz of admiration ran through the crowd. Many of them had come from Paris, but they had never seen such swordsmanship before. Whoever the hunter might be they saw that he was the master swordsman of them all. They addressed low cries of warning to Boucher: "Have a care!" "Have a care!" "Save your strength!" they said. But de Galisonniere stood, tight-lipped and silent. Nor did Robert and Tayoga feel the need of saying anything to their champion.

Now Boucher felt for the first time in his life that he had met the better man. The great duelist who had ruffled it so grandly through the inns and streets of Paris looked with growing terror into the stern, accusing eyes that confronted him. But he did not always see Willet. It was the ghosts of the boy, Gaston Lafitte, of the sick man Raoul de Bassempierre and of the indifferent swordsman, Raymond de Neville, that guided the hunter's blade, and his forehead became cold and wet with perspiration.

De Galisonniere had moved in the crowd, until he stood with Robert and Tayoga. He was perhaps the only one of the honnetes gens in the garden, and while he was a Frenchman, first, last and all the time, he knew who Boucher was and what he represented, he understood the reason why Robert had been drawn into the garden and he was willing to see the punishment of the man who was to have been the sanguinary instrument of the plot.

"A miracle will defeat the best of plans," he said to de Courcelles.

"What do you mean, de Galisonniere?" asked de Courcelles with a show of effrontery.

"That an unknown hunter should prove himself a better swordsman than your great duelist and bravo, Boucher."

"Why do you call him my duelist and bravo, de Galisonniere?"

"I understand that you brought young Lennox into the garden, apparently his warm friend on the way, and then when he was here, stood aside."

"You must answer for such insinuations, Captain de Galisonniere."

"But not to you, my friend. My sword will be needed in the coming war, and I'm not called upon to dull it now against one who was a principal in a murderous conspiracy. I may be over particular about those with whom I fight, de Courcelles, but I am what I am."

"You mean you will not fight me?"

"Certainly not. A meeting would cause the reasons for it to be threshed out, and we are not so many here in Canada that those reasons would not become known to all, and you, I fancy, would not relish the spread of such knowledge. The Intendant is a powerful man, but the Marquis Duquesne is the head of our military life, and he would not be pleased to hear what one of his officers so high in rank has done here tonight."

All the blood left de Courcelles' face, and he shook with anger, but he knew in his heart that de Galisonniere spoke the deadly truth. Besides, the whole plan had gone horribly wrong. And it had been so well laid. Who could have thought that a wandering hunter would appear at such a time, take the whole affair into his hands, and prove himself a better swordsman than Boucher, who was reputed not to have had his equal in France. It was the one unlucky chance, in a million! Nay, it was worse! It was a miracle that had appeared against them, and in that de Galisonniere had told the truth. Rage and terror stabbed at his heart, rage that the plan laid so smoothly had failed, and terror for himself. No, he would not challenge de Galisonniere.

"You will notice, de Courcelles," said the young Captain, "that Boucher is approaching exhaustion. Perhaps not another man in the world could have withstood his tremendous offense so well, but the singular hunter seems to be one man in a world, at least with the sword. Now, the seconds will give them a little rest before they close once more, and, I think, for the last time."

"For God's sake, de Galisonniere, cease! It's bad enough without your unholy glee!"

"'Bad enough' and 'unholy glee,' de Courcelles! Not at all! It's very well, and my pleasure is justified. I fear that villany is not always punished as it should be, and seldom in the dramatic manner that leaps to the eye and that has the powerful force of example. Ah, a foul blow before the seconds gave the word! Boucher has gone mad! But you and I won't trouble ourselves about him, since he will soon pay for it. I think I see a change in the hunter's eye. It has grown uncommonly stern and fierce. He has the look of an executioner."

De Galisonniere had read aright. When the treacherous blow was dealt and turned aside barely in time, Willet's heart hardened. If Boucher lived he would live to add more victims to those who had gone before. The man's whole fiber, body and mind, was poison, nothing but poison, and the murdered three whom Willet had known cried upon him to take vengeance. He began to press the bravo and Boucher's followers were silent. De Galisonniere was not the only one who had marked the change in the hunter's eye.

"You will note, de Courcelles," said he, "that your man, Boucher, has thrown his life away."

"He's not my man, de Galisonniere!"

"You compel me to repeat, de Courcelles, that your man, Boucher, has thrown away his own life. It's not well to deal a foul blow at a consummate swordsman. But I suppose it's hard for a murderer to change his instincts. Ah, what a stroke! What a stroke! It was so swift that I saw only a flash of light! And so, our friend, Boucher, has sped! And when you seek the kernel of the matter, de Courcelles, it was you who helped to speed him!"

De Courcelles, unable to bear more, strode away. Boucher was lying upon his back, and the bravo had fought his last fight. Willet looked down at him, shook his head a little, but he did not feel remorse. The ghosts of the untrained boy, Gaston Lafitte, of the sick man, Raoul de Bassempierre, and of Raymond de Neville, who had been murdered at dice, guided his hand, and it was they who had struck the blow. Robert helped him to put on the waistcoat and coat, as a group of men, Bigot, Cadet, and Pean at their head, invaded the garden.

"What's this! What's this!" exclaimed Bigot, staring at the motionless prostrate figure with the closed eyes.

Then de Galisonniere spoke up, and Robert was very grateful to him.

"It was done by Mr. Willet, as you see, sir, and if ever a man had justification he has it. The quarrel was forced upon him, and, during a pause, Boucher struck a foul blow, which, had it not been for Mr. Willet's surpassing skill, would have proved mortal and would have stained the honor of all Frenchmen in Quebec. Colonel de Courcelles will bear witness to the truth of all that I have said, will you not, de Courcelles?"

"Yes," said de Courcelles, though he shook in his uniform with anger.

"And so will Count Jean de Mezy. He too is eager to give testimony and support me in what I say. Is it not so, de Mezy?"

"Yes," said de Mezy, the purple spots in his face deepening.

"Then," said the Intendant, "I see nothing left to do but bury Boucher. He was but a quarrelsome fellow with none too good a record in France. And keep it from the ladies at present."

He returned with his courtiers to the house, and the dancing continued, but Robert felt that he could not stay any longer. Such cynicism shocked him, and paying his respects to Bigot and his friends, he left with Tayoga and the hunter for the Inn of the Eagle.

"It was a great fight," said Tayoga, as they stood outside and breathed the cool, welcome air again. "What Hayowentha was with the bow and arrow the Great Bear is with the sword."

"I don't like to take human life," said the hunter, "and it scarcely seems to me that I've done it now. I feel as if I had been an instrument in the hands of others, giving to Boucher the punishment deferred so long."

"There will be no trouble about it," said Tayoga. "I read the face of Bigot and no anger was there. It may be that he was glad to get rid of the man Boucher. The assassin becomes at times a burden."

But Willet remained silent and thoughtful.

"I've a feeling, Robert," he said, "that our mission to Quebec will fail. We've passed through too much, and all the signs are against us. As for me, I'm going to get ready for war."

"Maybe the Governor General will arrive tomorrow," said Robert, "and if so we can give him our letters and go. I was glad to come to Quebec, and I'll be equally glad to leave."

"And we can see the lodges of the Hodenosaunee again," said Tayoga, his eyes glistening.

"Yes, Tayoga, and glad I'll be to be once more among your great people, the hunters of the hills."

It was about two o'clock in the morning, when Robert went to bed, and he slept very late. Willet awoke shortly after dawn, dressed himself and went to the window, where he stood, gazing absently at the deepening sunlight on the green hills, although he saw the incidents of the heated night before far more vividly. He was a man who did not favor bloodshed, though it was a hard and stern age, and the slaying of Boucher, who would have added another to his victims, did not trouble him even the morning after. In his mind was the thought, expressed so powerfully, that the mills of God grind slowly, but they grind exceeding small. However, his anxiety to be away from Quebec had grown with the hours. The dangers were too thick, and they also had a bad habit of increasing continually.

When Robert awoke he found the hunter and Tayoga awaiting him.

"I've ordered breakfast," said Willet, "and it will be ready for us as soon as you dress. After that I'll have to comply with some formalities, owing to last night's affair, and then if the Governor General arrives this afternoon, we can deliver our letters and depart. It seems strange, Robert, that we should be here such a little while and that both you and I should fight duels. Perhaps it will be Tayoga's turn today, and he too will have to fight."

"Not unless Tandakora seeks me," said the young Onondaga.

"Did you see what became of him last night, Tayoga?" asked Willet.

"I watched him all the time you and the Frenchman were fighting, and I watched also when we came back to the inn. He would willingly have thrown a tomahawk in the dark at the head of any one of us, but he knew I watched and he did not dare."

"And that Ojibway savage is another of our troubles. He's gone clean mad with his hate of us."

Their late breakfast was served by Monsieur Berryer himself with much deference and some awe. The large room also held many more guests than usual at such an hour, but most of them ate little, only an egg or a roll, perhaps, or they dallied over a cup of coffee, reserving most of their attention for Willet, whom they regarded covertly, but with extraordinary interest. The youth with him had shown himself to be a fine swordsman, as Count Jean de Mezy could testify, but the elder man, who had appeared to be a hunter, and who claimed to be one, was such a master of the weapon as had never before appeared in New France. And it was said by the French officers that his equal could not be found in old France either. The interest aroused by his fame was increased by the mystery that enshrouded him, and they gave him an attention that was not at all hostile. In truth, it was strongly compounded with admiration. A man who had removed Pierre Boucher as he had done, was to be regarded with respect. Boucher had given every promise of becoming a public danger in Quebec, and perhaps they owed gratitude to the hunter, Bostonnais though he was.

Late in the afternoon they had word that the Marquis Duquesne had come and would receive them. Again they arrayed themselves with the greatest care, and took their way to the Castle of St. Louis. They found a man very different in appearance and manner from the Intendant, Bigot. Tall, austere, belonging to a race that was reckoned very noble in France, the Marquis Duquesne was not popular in New France. He had none of the geniality and easy generosity of Bigot, as he spent his own money, but he had shown a military energy and foresight which the British governors to the south were far from imitating. While Canada did not love him, it respected him and his boldness, and his daring and foresight had deeply impressed the powerful Indian tribes whose friendship and alliance were so important in the coming war.

The manner of the Marquis was high, when he received the three in his chamber of audience, but it was not deficient in courtesy. He looked intently at each of them in turn.

"You come, so I am told, from the Governor of New York," he

said, "and judging from what I have heard he has chosen messengers who are able to make a stir. Two days in Quebec and already you have fought two duels, one of them ending fatally."

"My lord," said Willet, gravely, "they were not of our seeking."

"That also, I hear. They tell me, too, Mr. Willet, that you are an incomparable swordsman, and it must be true, or you would not have been able to defeat Boucher. But that matter is adjusted. You will not be held here because of his death. It seems that the Intendant, Monsieur Bigot himself, does not wish to carry it further. But the letters from the Governor of New York?"

"Mr. Lennox has them," said Willet.

Robert bowed and took from an inner pocket of his waistcoat the letters he had carried through so many dangers. They were contained in a small deerskin pouch, and were only two in number. Bowing again, he handed them to the Governor General, who said:

"Pray be seated, and excuse me for a few minutes while I read them."

He read slowly, stopping at times to consider, and when he had finished he read them over again.

"Do you and Mr. Willet know the contents of these letters?" he said to Robert.

"We do," replied the youth. "They were read to us by the Governor of New York before he sealed them. If we were robbed of them on the way to Quebec, and he knew the way was dangerous, we were to continue our journey and deliver the message to you verbally."

"Their nature does credit to both the heart and head of the Governor of New York. He makes a personal appeal to me to use all my influence against the war seemingly at hand. He says that England and France have nothing to gain by attacking each other in the American woods, which are large enough to hide whole European kingdoms. But he wishes the letters to be a secret with him and me and you three who have brought them. You understand that?"

Robert bowed once more.

"The second letter explains and amplifies the first, contains, I should say, his afterthoughts. As I said, 'tis a noble act, but what can I do? A war may look to many men like a sudden outburst, but it is nearly always the result of conditions that have been a long time in the growth. Your hunters, your traders and your surveyors pressed forward into the Ohio country, which is ours."

He looked at them as if he expected them to challenge the French claim to the Ohio regions, but they were wisely silent.

"The letters do not demand an immediate reply," he

continued. "His Excellency prays me to consider. Perhaps I shall send one later through a trusted messenger by sloop or schooner to New York, and naturally, I shall choose one of my own officers."

"Naturally, my lord," said Robert. "We did not expect to take back the answer."

The Marquis Duquesne looked at him very keenly.

"You speak as if you were relieved at not having the errand," he said. "Perhaps there is something else on your mind which you wish to do and with which such a mission would interfere."

Robert was silent and the Marquis laughed.

"I will not press the question, because I've no right to do so," he said. "But I will let it remain an inference."

Then his eye rested upon Tayoga, at whom he looked long and searchingly, and the eye of the Onondaga met him with an answering gaze, fixed and unfaltering.

"Captain de Galisonniere has told me," said the Marquis, "that you are a young chief, or coming chief, of the Iroquois, that despite your youth you have thought much and have influence with your people. How do the Iroquois feel toward the French who wish them so well?"

"They do not forget that this Quebec is the Stadacona of one of their great warrior nations, the Mohawks," replied Tayoga.

The Marquis started and flushed.

"Quebec is ours," he said slowly, after taking due thought. "You cannot undo what was done two centuries ago."

"The nations of the Hodenosaunee do not forget, what are two centuries to them?"

"When you return to the Long House in the vale of Onondaga, and the fifty sachems meet in council, tell them Onontio has only kindness in his heart for them. The war clouds that hang over England and France grow many and thick, and my children are brave and vigilant. They know the ways of the forest. They travel by day and by night, and they strike hard. The English are not a match for them."

"If I should tell them what Onontio tells to me they would say: 'Go back to Quebec, which is by right the Stadacona of our great warrior nation, the Mohawks, and say to Onontio that his words are like the songs of birds, but we, the Hodenosaunee, do not forget. We remember Frontenac, and we remember Champlain, the first of the white men to come among us with guns, the use of which we did not know, killing our warriors.'"

"Time makes changes, Tayoga, and the Iroquois must change too."

Tayoga, was silent, but his haughty face did not relax a

particle. The Marquis was about to say more upon the subject, but he had a penetrating mind and he saw that his words would be wasted.

"We shall see what we shall see," he said. "My master, His Majesty King Louis, keeps his promises. Mr. Lennox, as I take it, still clinging to my inference, it will be some time before you see the Governor of New York again. But, when you do see him, and if my letter has not then reached him, tell him it is coming by ship to New York. As for you and your comrades, I wish you a safe journey whithersoever you go. An aide-de-camp will give the three of you, as you go out, passports which will be your safe conduct until you reach the borders of Canada. Of course, I cannot speak with certainty concerning anything that will happen to you beyond that point. Mr. Willet, I am sorry that a sword such as yours is not French."

Willet bowed, and so did Robert. Then the three withdrew, receiving their safe conducts as they went. At the inn they made hurried preparations for departure, deciding that they would cross at once to the south side of the St. Lawrence and travel on foot through the woods until they reached the Richelieu, where in a secret cove a canoe belonging to Willet lay hidden. The canoe would take them into Lake Champlain and then they could proceed by water to the point they wished.

Robert wrote a note of thanks to the Intendant for his courtesy, expressing their united regrets that the brevity of time would not permit them to pay a formal call, and as it departed in the hands of a messenger, de Galisonniere came to say farewell.

"It's likely," he said, "that if we meet again it will be on the battlefield. I see nothing for it but a war, but if we do meet, Mr. Willet, you must promise that you will not use that sword against me."

"I promise, Captain de Galisonniere," said Willet, smiling, "but if the war does come, and I hope it may not, it will be fought chiefly in the woods, and there will be little need for swords. And now we wish to thank you for your great kindness and help."

He shook hands with them all, showing some emotion, and then left hastily. The three deferred their departure, concluding to spend the night at the inn, but before dawn the next morning they crossed the St. Lawrence and began their journey.

CHAPTER XIII
THE BOWMEN

Robert looked back and saw the roofs and spires of Quebec sitting on its mighty rock, and he remembered how much had happened during their short stay there. He could recall the whole time, hour by hour, and he knew that he would never forget any part of it. The town was intense, glowing, vivid in the clear northern sunlight, and he had seen it, as he so often had longed to do. A quality in his nature had responded to it, but at the last his heart had turned against it. The splendor of that city into which he had enjoyed such a remarkable introduction had in it something hot and feverish.

"You're thinking a farewell to Quebec, Robert," said the hunter. "It looks grand and strong up there, but I've an idea there'll be a day when we'll come again."

"Americans and English have besieged it before," said Robert, "but they've never taken it."

"Which proves nothing, but we'll turn our minds now to our journey into the south. It's good to breathe this clean air again, and the sooner we reach the deep woods the better I'll like it. What say you, Tayoga?"

The nostrils of the Onondaga expanded, as he inhaled the odors of leaf and grass, borne on the gentle wind.

"I have lived in the white man's house in Albany," he said, "and in our own log house in the vale of Onondaga, and I know the English and the French have many things that the nations of the Hodenosaunee have not, but we can do without most of them. If the great chiefs were to drink and dance all night as Bigot and his friends do, then indeed would we cease to be the mighty League of the Hodenosaunee."

They traveled all that day on foot, but at a great pace, showing their safe conduct twice to French soldiers, and so thin was the line of settlements along the St. Lawrence that when night came they were beyond the cultivated fields and had entered the deep woods. The three, in addition to their weapons, carried on their backs packs containing blankets and food, and as Willet and Tayoga put them down they drew long breaths of relief like those of prisoners escaped.

161

"Home, Tayoga! Home!" said the hunter, joyfully. "I've nothing against cities in general, but I breathed some pretty foul air in Quebec, and it's sweet and clean here. There comes a time when you are glad no house crosses your view and you are with the world as it was made in the beginning. Don't these trees look splendid! Did you ever see a finer lot of tender young leaves? And the night sky you see up there has been washed and scrubbed until it's nothing but clean blue!"

"Why, you're only a boy, Dave, the youngest of us three," laughed Robert. "Here you are singing songs about leaves and trees just as if you were not the most terrible swordsman in the world."

A shadow crossed Willet's face, but it was quick in passing.

"Let's not talk about Boucher, Robert," he said. "I don't regret what I did, knowing that it saved the lives of others, but I won't recall it any oftener than I can help. You're right when you term me a boy, and I believe you're right, too, when you say I'm the youngest of the three. I'm so glad to be here that just now I'm not more'n fifteen years old. I could run, jump, laugh and sing. And I think the woods are a deal safer and friendlier than Quebec. There's nobody, at least not here, lying around seeking a chance to stick a rapier in your back."

He unbuckled his sword and laid it upon the grass. Robert put his beside it.

"I don't think we'll need to use 'em again for a long time," said the hunter, "but they're mighty fine as decorations, and sometimes a decoration is worth while. It impresses. Now, Tayoga, you kindle the fire, and Robert, you find a spring. It's pleasant to feel that you're again on land that belongs to nobody, and can do as you please."

Robert found a spring less than a hundred yards away, and Tayoga soon kindled a fire near it with his flint and steel, on which the hunter warmed their food. Each had a small tin cup from which he drank clear water as they ate, and Robert, elastic of temperament, rejoiced with the hunter.

"You are right, Dave," he said. "These are splendid trees, and every leaf on 'em is splendid, too, and the little spring I found is just about as fine a spring as the forest holds. I slept in a good bed at the Inn of the Eagle, but when I scrape up the dead leaves here, roll myself in my blanket and lie on 'em I think I'll sleep better than I did between four walls. What did you think of the Marquis Duquesne, Dave?"

"A man of parts, Robert. He has more military authority than any of our Governors have, and if war comes he'll be a dangerous opponent."

"And it will come, Dave?"

"Looks like a certainty. You see, Robert, the King of France and the King of England sitting on their golden thrones, only three or four hundred miles apart, but three or four thousand miles from us, have a dyspeptic fit, make faces at each other, and here in the woods we must fall to fighting. Even Tayoga's people—and the King of France and the King of England are nothing to them—must be drawn into it."

"Both Kings claim the Ohio country, which they will never see, and of which they know nothing," said Tayoga, with a faint touch of sarcasm, "but perhaps it belongs to the people who live in it."

"Maybe so, Tayoga! Maybe!" said Willet briskly, "but we'll not look for trouble or unpleasant thoughts now. We three are too glad to be in the woods again. Tayoga, suppose you scout about and see that no enemy's near. Then we'll build up the fire, till it's burning bright, and rejoice."

"It is well!" said Tayoga, as he slipped away among the trees, making no sound as he went. Robert meanwhile gathered dead wood which lay everywhere in abundance, and heaped it beside the fire ready for use. But as Tayoga was gone some time he sat down again with his back to a tree, taking long deep breaths of the cool fresh air, and feeling his pulses leap. The hunter sat in a similar position, gazing meditatively into the fire. Robert heard a rattling of bark over his head, but he knew that it was a squirrel scuttling up the trunk of the tree, and pausing now and then to examine the strange invaders of his forest.

"Do you see the squirrel, Dave?" he asked.

"Yes, he's about twenty feet above you now, sitting in a fork. He's a fine big fellow with a bushy tail curved so far over his back that it nearly touches his head. He has little red eyes and he's just burning up with curiosity. The firelight falls on him in such a way that I can see. Perhaps he has never seen a man before. Now he's looking at you, Robert, trying to decide what kind of an animal you are, and forming an estimate of your character and disposition."

"You're developing your imagination, Dave, but since I saw what you said and did in Quebec I'm not surprised."

"Encouraged by your motionless state he's left the fork, and come a half dozen feet down the trunk in order to get a better look at you. I think he likes you, Robert. He lies flattened against the bark, and if I had not seen him descending I would not notice him now, but the glow of the coals still enables me to make out his blazing little red eyes like sparks of fire. Now he is looking at me, and I don't think he has as much confidence in my harmlessness as

163

he has in yours. Perhaps it's because he sees my eyes are upon him and he doesn't like to be watched. He's a saucy little fellow. Sit still, Robert! I see a black shadow over your head, and I think our little friend, the squirrel, should look out. Ah, there he goes! Missed! And our handsome young friend, the gray squirrel, is safe! He has scuttled into his hole higher up the tree!"

Robert had heard a rush of wings and he had seen a long black shadow pass.

"What was it, Dave?" he asked.

"A great horned owl. His iron beak missed our little squirrel friend just about three inches. Those three inches were enough, but I don't think that squirrel will very soon again stay out at night so late. The woods are beautiful, Robert, but you see they're not always safe even for those who can't live anywhere else."

"I know, Dave, but I'm not going to think about it tonight, because I've made up my mind to be happy. Here comes Tayoga. Is any enemy near, Tayoga?"

"None," replied the Onondaga, sitting down by the fire. "But the forest is full of its own people, and they are all very curious about us."

"That's true," said Willet, "a squirrel over Robert's head was so inquisitive that he forgot his vigilance for a few moments and came near losing his life as the price of his carelessness. I'm not surprised to hear you say, Tayoga, they're all looking at us. I've felt for some time that we're being watched, admired and perhaps a little feared. It's a tribute to the enormously interesting qualities of us three."

"That is, Dave, because we're human beings we're kings in the forest among the animals."

"You put it right, Robert. They look up to us. Is anything watching us among the leaves near by, Tayoga?"

"A huge bald-headed eagle, Great Bear, is sitting on a bough in the center of a mass of green leaves. He is looking at us, and while he is full of curiosity and some admiration he fears and hates us more."

"What is he saying to himself, Tayoga?"

"You can read his words to himself by the look in his eyes. He is saying that he does not like our appearance, that we are too large, that we have created here something hot and flaming, that we behave with too much assurance, going about just as if the forest was ours, and paying no attention to its rightful owners."

"He has got a grievance, and perhaps it's a just one," laughed Robert.

"No, it is not," said Tayoga, "because there is plenty of room in the forest for him and for us, too. I can read his eyes quite well. There is much malice and anger in his heart, and I will give him some cause for rage."

He picked up a live coal between the ends of two sticks, and holding it firmly in that manner, walked a little distance among the trees. Then swinging the sticks he hurled the coal far up among the boughs. There was an angry screech and whirr and Robert saw a swift shadow passing between his eyes and the sky.

"His heart can burn more than ever now," laughed Tayoga, as he returned to the fire.

"You've hurt his dignity, Tayoga," said Robert.

"So I have, but why should he not suffer a loss of pride? He is ruthless and cruel and when he has his way he makes desolation about him."

"What else is watching us, Tayoga?"

"A beast upon the ground, and his heart is much like that of the eagle in the air. He is crouched in a thicket about twenty yards away, and his lips are drawn back from his sharp fangs. His nostrils twitch with the odor of our food, and his yellow eyes are staring at us. Oh, he hates us because he hates everything except his own kind and very often he hates that. He wants our food because he's hungry—he's always hungry—and he would try to eat us too if he were not so much afraid of us."

"Tayoga, one needs only a single glance to tell that this animal you're talking about is a wolf."

"It is so, Dagaeoga. A very hungry and a very angry wolf. He is cunning, but he does not know everything. He thinks we do not see him, that we do not know he is there and that maybe, after awhile, when we go to sleep, he can slip up and steal our food, or perhaps he can bring many of his brothers, and they can eat us before we awake. Now, I will tell him in a language he can understand that it's time for him to go away."

He picked up a heavy stick and threw it with all his might into the bushes on their right. It sped straighter to the target than he had hoped, as there was a thud, a snarling yelp, and then the swift pad of flying feet. Tayoga lay back and laughed.

"The Spirit of Jest guided my hand," he said, "and the stick struck him upon the nose. He will run far and his wrath and fear will grow as he runs. Then he will lie down again in some thicket, and he will not dare to come back. Now, we will wait a little."

"Anything more looking at us?" asked Robert after awhile.

"Yes, we have a new visitor," replied Tayoga in a low tone.

"Speak only in a whisper and do not move, because the animal that is looking at us has no malice in its heart, and does not wish us harm. It has come very softly and, while its eyes are larger, they are mild and have only curiosity."

"A deer, I should say, Tayoga."

"Yes, a deer, Lennox, a very beautiful deer. It has been drawn by the fire, and having come as near as it dares it stands there, shivering a little, but wondering and admiring."

"We won't trouble it, Tayoga. We'll need the meat of a deer before long, but we'll spare our guest of tonight."

"He is staring very straight at us," said Tayoga, "but something has stirred in the brushwood—perhaps it's another wolf—and now he has gone."

"We seem to be an attraction," said Willet, "and so I suppose we'd better give 'em as good a look as we can."

He cast a great quantity of the dry wood on the fire, and it blazed up gayly, throwing the red glow in a wide circle, and lighting up the pleasant glade. The figures of the three, as they leaned in luxurious attitudes, were outlined clearly and sharply, a view they would not have allowed had not Tayoga been sure no enemy was near.

"Now let the spectators come on," said Willet genially, "because we won't be on display forever. After a while we'll get sleepy, and then it will be best to put out the fire."

The flames leaped higher and the glowing circle widened. Robert, leaning against a tree, with his blanket wrapped around him and the cushion of dead leaves beneath him, felt the grateful warmth upon his face, and it rejoiced body and mind alike. Tayoga and the hunter were in a similar state of content, and they were silent for a while. Then Robert said:

"Who's looking at us now, Tayoga?"

"Two creatures, Dagaeoga, that belong upon the ground, but that are not now upon it."

"Your answer sounds like a puzzle. If they're not now upon the ground they're probably in the air, but they're not birds, because birds don't belong on the ground. Then they're animals that have climbed trees."

"Dagaeoga's mind is becoming wondrous wise. In time he may be a sachem among his adopted people."

"Don't you have sport with me, Tayoga, because bear in mind that if you do I will pay you back some day. Have these creatures a mean, vicious look?"

"I could not claim, Dagaeoga, that they are as beautiful as the deer that came to look at us but lately."

"Then I make so bold as to say, Tayoga, that they have tufted ear tips, spotted fur, and short tails, in brief a gentleman lynx and a lady lynx, his wife. They are gazing at us with respect and fear as the wolf did, and also with just as much malice and hate. They're wondering who and what we are, and why we come into their woods, the pair of bloodthirsty rabbit slayers."

"Did I not say you would be a sachem some day, Dagaeoga? You have read aright. An Onondaga warrior could not have done better. The two lynxes are on a bough ten feet from the ground, and perhaps in their foolish hearts they think because they are so high above the earth that we cannot reach them."

"You're not going to shoot at 'em, Tayoga? We don't want to waste good bullets on a lynx."

"Not I, Dagaeoga, but I will make them acquainted with something they will dread as much as bullets. It's right that those who come to look at us should be made to pay the price of it."

"So you think that Monsieur and Madame Lynx have looked long enough at the illustrious three?"

"Yes, Dagaeoga. It is time for them to go. And since they do not go of their own will I must make them go."

He snatched a long brand from the fire, and whirling it around his head, and shouting at the same time, he dashed toward an old dead tree some distance away. Two stump-tailed, tuft-eared animals, uttering loud ferocious screams, leaped from the boughs and tore away through the thickets, terror stabbing at their hearts, as the circling flame of red pursued them. Tayoga returned laughing.

"They will run and they will run," he said, throwing down his brand.

"You don't give 'em much chance to see us, Tayoga," said the hunter. "Since we're on exhibition tonight you might have let 'em look and admire a while longer."

"So I could, Great Bear, but I do not like the lynx. Its habits are unpleasant, and its scream is harsh. Hence, I drove the two of them away."

"I suppose you're right. I don't dare care much about 'em either. Now we'll rest and see what other visitors come to admire."

Tayoga sat down again. Their packs were put in a neat heap near the three, Robert's and Willet's swords, and Tayoga's bow and arrows in their case resting on the top. Robert threw more wood on the fire, and contentedly watched the great, glowing circle of light extend its circumference.

"We knew we'd find peace and rest here," said Willet, "but we

167

didn't know we'd be watched and admired like people on the stage at a theater."

"Have you seen many plays, Dave?" asked Robert.

"A lot, especially in London at Drury Lane and other theaters."

"And so you know London, as well as Paris?"

"Well, yes, I've been there. Some day, Robert, I'll tell you more about both Paris and London and why I happened to be in such great cities, but not now. We'll keep our minds on the forest, which is worth our attention. Don't you hear a tread approaching, Tayoga?"

"Yes, Great Bear, and it's very heavy. A lord of the forest is coming."

"A moose, think you, Tayoga?"

"Yes, Great Bear, a mighty bull, one far beyond the common size. I can tell by his tread, and I think he is angry, or he would not march so boldly toward the fire."

"Then," said the hunter, "we'd better stand up, and be ready with our weapons. I've no wish to be trodden to death by a mad bull moose, just when I'm feeling so happy and so contented with the world."

"The Great Bear's advice is good," said Tayoga, and the three took it. The approaching tread grew heavier, and the largest moose that Robert had ever seen, pushing his way through the bushes, stood looking at the fire, and those who had built it. He was a truly magnificent specimen, and Tayoga had been right in calling him a lord of the forest, but his eyes were red and inflamed and his look was menacing.

"Mad! Quite mad!" whispered the hunter. "He sees us, but he doesn't admire us. He hates us, and he isn't afraid of us."

The three moved softly and discreetly into a place where both trees and bushes were so dense that the moose could not get at them.

"What troubles him?" asked Robert.

"I don't know," said the hunter. "He may be suffering yet from a wound by an Indian arrow, or he may have a spell of some kind. We can be certain only that he's raging mad, every inch of him. Look at those great sharp hoofs of his, Robert. I'd as soon be struck with an axe."

The moose, after some hesitation, rushed into the glade, leaped toward the fire, leaped back again, pawed and trampled the earth in a terrible convulsion of rage, and then sprang away, crashing through the forest. They heard the beat of his hoofs a long time, and when the sound ceased they returned and resumed their seats by the fire.

"That moose was a great animal," said Tayoga with irony, "but his mind was the mind of a little child. He did nothing with his strength and agility but tear the earth and tire himself. Now he runs away among the trees, scratching his body with bushes and briars."

"At any rate, he was an important visitor, Tayoga," said the hunter, "and since we've had a good look at him we're glad he's gone away. I think it likely now that all who wanted to look at us have had their look, and we might go to sleep. How are your leaves, Robert?"

"Fine and soft. They make a splendid bed, and I'm off to slumberland."

He pushed up the leaves at one end of his couch high enough to form a pillow, and stretched himself luxuriously. The night was turning cold, but he had his blanket, and there was the fire. He felt as comfortable as at the Inn of the Eagle in Quebec, and freer from plots and danger.

They were allowing the fire to die now, but the coals would glow for a long time, and Robert looked at them sleepily. His feeling of coziness and content increased, and presently he slept. The hunter soon followed him, but Tayoga slept not at all. His subtle Indian instinct warned him not to do so. For the Onondaga the forest was not free now from danger, and he would watch while his white friends slept.

Tayoga arose, after a while, and taking a stick, scattered the coals of the fire. But he did it in such a manner that he made no noise, the hunter and young Lennox continuing to sleep soundly. Then he watched the embers, having lost that union which is strength, die one by one. The conquered darkness came back, recovering its lost ground, slowly invading the glade, until it was one in the dusk with the rest of the forest. Then Tayoga felt better satisfied, and he looked at the sleepers, whose faces he could still discern, despite the absence of the fire, a fair moonlight falling.

Robert and the hunter slept peacefully, but their sleep was deep. The youth was weary from the long march in the woods, but as he slept his strong healthy tissues rapidly regained their vitality. The Onondaga looked at the two longer than usual. These comrades of his were knitted to him by innumerable labors and dangers shared. In him dwelled the soul of a great Indian chief, the spirit that has animated Pontiac, and Little Turtle, and Tecumseh and Red Cloud and other dauntless leaders of his race, but it had been refined though not weakened by his white education. Gratitude and truth were as frequent Indian traits as the memory of injuries, and

169

while he was surcharged with pride because he was born a warrior of the clan of the Bear, of the nation Onondaga, of the great League of the Hodenosaunee, he felt as truly as any knight ever felt that he must accept and fulfill all the duties of his place.

Standing in a dusk made luminous by a silvery moonlight he was a fitting son of the forest, one of its finest products. He belonged to it, and it belonged to him, each being the perfect complement of the other. His face cut in bronze was lofty, not without a spiritual cast, and his black eyes flamed with his resolve. He looked up at the heavens, fleecy with white vapors, and shot with a million stars, the same sky that had bent over his race for generations no man could count, and his soul was filled with admiration. Then he made his voiceless prayer:

"O, Tododaho, first and greatest sachem of the Onondagas, greatest and noblest sachem of the League, look down from your home on another star, and watch over your people, for whom the storms gather! Let the serpents in your hair whisper to you of wisdom that you in turn may whisper it to us through the winds! Direct our footsteps in the great war that is coming between the white nations and save to us our green forests, our blue lakes and our silver rivers! Remember, O, Tododaho, that although the centuries have passed since Manitou took you from us, your name still stands among us for all that is great, noble and wise! I beseech you that you give sparks of your own lofty and strong spirit to your children, to the Hodenosaunee in this, their hour of need, and I ask too, that you help one who is scarcely yet a warrior in years, one who invokes thee humbly, even, Tayoga, of the clan of the Bear, of the nation Onondaga, of thy own great League of the Hodenosaunee!"

He bent his head a little to listen. All the legends and beliefs of his race, passed from generation to generation, crowded upon him. Tododaho leaning down from his star surely heard his prayer. Tayoga shivered a little, not from cold or fear, but from emotion. The mystic spell was upon him. Far above him in the limitless void little wreaths of vapor united about a great shining star, taking the shape of a man, the shape of a great chief, wise beyond all other chiefs that had ever lived, and he distinctly saw the wise serpents, coil on coil, in Tododaho's hair. They were whispering in his ear, and bending his head a little farther he heard the words of the serpents which the rising wind brought, repeated, from the lips of Tododaho:

"Fear not, O young warrior of the Onondagas! Tododaho leaning down from his star hears thy pious appeal! Tododaho, for more than four hundred years, has watched over the great League, night and day! Let the fifty sachems, old in years and wisdom, walk in the straight path of truth, and let the warriors follow! Let them be keepers of the faith, friends to those who have been their friends, sage in council, brave in battle, and they shall hold their green forests, their blue lakes and their silver rivers! And to thee, Tayoga, I say, thou shalt encounter many dangers, but because thy soul is pure, thou shalt have great rewards!"

Then the wind died suddenly. The leaves hung motionless. The vapors about the great shining star dissolved, the face of Tododaho, with the wise serpents, coil on coil in his hair, disappeared, and the luminous heavens were without a sign. But they had spoken.

Tayoga trembled, but again it was from emotion. Tododaho had sent his words of promise on the wind, and they had been whispered in his ear. Great would be his dangers but great would be his rewards. He was uplifted. His heart exulted. His deeds would be all the mightier because of the dangers, and he would never forget that he had the promise of Tododaho, greatest, wisest and noblest of the chiefs of the Hodenosaunee, who had gone to a shining star more than four hundred years ago.

He sat down under one of the trees and sleep remained far from him. He still listened with all the power of his sensitive hearing for any sound that might come in the forest, and after awhile he took his bow and quiver from their case, putting his quiver over his shoulder. He covered his rifle with the leaves, and holding the bow in his hand stole away among the trees.

The faintest of sounds had come to him, and Tayoga did not doubt its nature. It was strange to the forest and it was hostile. The mystic spell was still upon him, and it heightened his faculties to an extraordinary degree. He had almost the power of divination. A hundred yards, and he crouched low behind the trunk of a great oak. Then as the moonlight fell upon a small opening just ahead he saw them, Tandakora and two warriors.

The Ojibway was in full war paint, and the luminous quality of the moon's rays enlarged his huge form. He towered like Hanegoategeh, the Evil Spirit, and the figures upon his shoulders and chest stood out like carving. He and the two warriors also carried bows and arrows, and Tayoga surmised that they had meant to slay in silence. His heart burned with rage and he felt, too, an unlimited daring. Did he not have the promise of Tododaho that he should pass through all dangers and receive great rewards? He felt himself a match for the three, and he did not need secrecy and silence. He raised his voice and cried:

171

"Stand forth, Tandakora, and fight. I too have only waano (the bow) and gano (the arrow), but I meet the three of you!"

Tandakora and the two warriors sprang back and in an instant were hidden by the trees, but Tayoga had expected them to do so, and he dropped down, moving silently to another and hidden point, where he waited, an arrow on the string. He knew that Tandakora had recognized his voice, and would make every effort, his shoulder healed enough for use, to secure such a prize. The Ojibway would believe, too, that three must prevail against one, and he would push the attack. So the Onondaga remained motionless, but confident.

Nearly ten minutes of absolute silence followed, but his hearing was so acute that he did not think any of the three could move without his knowledge. Then a slight sliding sound came. One of the warriors was passing to the right, and that, too, he had expected, as they would surely try to flank him. He moved back a little, and with the end of his bow shook gently a bush seven or eight feet away. In an instant, an arrow, coming from the night, whistled through the bush. But Tayoga drew back the bow quick as lightning, fitted an arrow to the string and shot with all the power of his arm at a bronze body showing among the leaves at the point whence the arrow had come.

The shaft sang in the air, and so great was its speed and so short the range that it passed entirely through the chest of the warrior, cutting off his breath so quickly that he had no time to utter his death cry. There was no sound but that of his fall as he crashed among the leaves. Nor did Tayoga utter the usual shout of triumph. He sank back and fitted another arrow to the string, turning his attention now to the left.

It had been the Onondaga's belief that Tandakora would remain in front, sending the warriors on either flank, and now he expected a movement on the left. He did not have to make any feint of his own to draw the second warrior, who must have been lacking somewhat in skill, as he presently saw a dim figure in the bushes and his second arrow sped with the same speed and deadly result that had marked the first. Fitting his third arrow to the string, he called:

"Stand forth, Tandakora, and show yourself like a man! Then we shall see who shoots the better!"

But being a knight of the woods, and to convince the Ojibway that it was no trick, he showed himself first. Tandakora shot at once, but Tayoga dropped back like a flash, and the arrow cut the air, where his feathered head had been. Then all his Indian nature, the training and habit of generations, leaped up in him and he began to taunt.

"You shot quickly, Tandakora," he called, "and your arm was strong, but the arrow struck not! You followed us all the way from Stadacona, and you thought to have our scalps! The Great Bear and Lennox did not suspect, but I did! The warriors who came with you are dead, and you and I alone face each other! I have shown myself and I have risked your arrow, now show yourself, Tandakora, and risk mine!"

But the Ojibway, it seemed, had too much respect for the bow of Tayoga. He remained close, and did not disclose an inch of his brown body. The Onondaga did not show himself again, but crouched for a shot, in case the opportunity came. He knew that Tandakora was a great bowman, but he had supreme confidence in his own skill against anybody. Nothing stirred where his enemy lay and no sound came from the little camp, which was beyond the reach of the words they had uttered.

A quarter of an hour, a half hour, an hour passed, and neither moved, showing all the patience natural to the Indian on the war path. Then Tayoga shook a bush a few feet from him, but Tandakora divined the trick, and his arrow remained on the string. Another quarter of an hour, and seeing some leaves quiver, Tayoga, at a chance, sent an arrow among them. No sound came back, and he knew that it had been sped in vain.

Then he began to move slowly and with infinite care toward the right, resolved to bring the affair to a head. At the end of twenty feet he rustled the bushes a little once more and lay flat. An arrow flew over his head, but he did not reply, resuming his slow advance after his enemy's shaft had sped. Another twenty feet and he made the bushes move again. Tandakora shot, and in doing so he exposed a little of his right arm. Tayoga sent a prompt arrow at the brown flesh. He heard a cry of pain, wrenched in spite of his stoical self from the Ojibway, and then as he sank down again and put his ear to the ground came the sound of retreating footsteps.

The affair, unfinished in a way, so far as the vital issue was concerned, was concluded for the present, at least. Ear and mind told Tayoga as clearly as if eye had seen. His arrow had ploughed its path across Tandakora's arm near the shoulder, inflicting a wound that would heal, but which was extremely painful and from which so much blood was coming that a quick bandage was needed. Tandakora could no longer meet Tayoga with the bow and arrow and so he must retreat. Nor was it likely that his first wound was yet more than half healed.

The Onondaga waited until he was sure his enemy was at least a half mile away, when he rose boldly and approached the place

173

where Tandakora had last lain hidden. He detected at once drops of dark blood on the leaves and grass, and he found his arrow, which Tandakora had snatched from the wound and thrown upon the ground. He wiped the barb carefully and replaced it in his quiver. Then he followed the trail at least three miles, a trail marked here and there by ruddy spots.

Tayoga did not feel sorry for his enemy. Tandakora was a savage and an assassin, and he deserved this new hurt. He was a dangerous enemy, one who had made up his mind to secure revenge upon the Onondaga and his friends, but his fresh wound would keep him quiet for a while. One could not have an arrow through his forearm and continue a hunt with great vigor and zest.

Tayoga marked twice the places where Tandakora had stopped to rest. There the drops of blood were clustered, indicating a pause of some duration, and a third stop showed where he had bound up his wound. Fresh leaves had been stripped from a bush and a tiny fragment or two indicated that the Ojibway had torn a piece from his deerskin waistcloth to fasten over the leaves. After that the trail was free from the ruddy spots, but Tayoga did not follow it much farther. He was sure that Tandakora would not return, as he had lost much blood, and for a while, despite his huge power and strength, exertion would make him weak and dizzy. Evidently, the bullet in his shoulder, received when they were on their way to Quebec, had merely shaken him, but the arrow had taken a heavier toll.

Tayoga returned to the camp of the three. All the fire had gone out, and Willet and Robert, wrapped in their blankets, still slept peacefully. The entire combat between the bowmen had passed without their knowledge, and Tayoga, quietly returning the bow and quiver to their case, and taking his rifle instead, sat down with his back against a tree, and his weapon across his knees. He was on the whole satisfied. He had not removed Tandakora, but he had inflicted another painful and mortifying defeat upon him. The pride of the Indian had been touched in its most sensitive place, and the Ojibway would burn with rage for a long time. Tayoga's white education did not keep him from taking pleasure in the thought.

He had no intention of going to sleep. Although Tandakora would not return, others might come, and for the night the care of the three was his. It had grown a little darker, but the blue of the skies was merely deeper and more luminous. There in the east was the great shining star, on which Tododaho, mightiest of chiefs, lived with the wise serpents coiled in his hair. He gazed and his heart leaped. The vapors about the star were gathering again, and for a brief moment or two they formed the face of Tododaho, a face that smiled upon him. His soul rejoiced.

"O Tododaho," were his unspoken words. "Thou hast kept thy promise! Thou hast watched over me in the fight with Tandakora, and thou hast given me the victory! Thou hast sent all his arrows astray and thou hast sent mine aright! I thank thee, O, Tododaho!"

The vapors were dissolved, but Tayoga never doubted that he had seen for a second time the face of the wise chief who had gone to his star more than four hundred years ago. A great peace filled him. He had accepted the white man's religion as he had learned it in the white man's school, and at the same time he had kept his own. He did not see any real difference between them. Manitou and God were the same, one was the name in Iroquois and the other was the name in English. When he prayed to either he prayed to both.

The darkness that precedes the dawn came. The great star on which Tododaho lived went away, and the whole host swam into the void that is without ending. The deeper dusk crept up, but Tayoga still sat motionless, his eyes wide open, his ecstatic state lasting. He heard the little animals stirring once more in the forest as the dawn approached, and he felt very friendly toward them. He would not harm the largest or the least of them. It was their wilderness as well as his, and Manitou had made them as well as him.

The darkness presently began to thin away, and Tayoga saw the first silver shoot of dawn in the east. The sun would soon rise over the great wilderness that was his heritage and that he loved, clothing in fine, spun gold the green forests, the blue lakes and the silver rivers. He took a mighty breath. It was a beautiful world and he was glad that he lived in it.

He awoke Robert and Willet, and they stood up sleepily.

"Did you have a good rest, Tayoga?" Robert asked.

"I did not sleep," the Onondaga replied.

"Didn't sleep? Why not, Tayoga?"

"In the night, Tandakora and two more came."

"What? Do you mean it, Tayoga?"

"They were coming, seeking to slay us as we slept, but I heard them. Lest the Great Bear and Dagaeoga be awakened and lose the sleep they needed so much, I took my bow and arrows and went into the forest and met them."

Robert's breath came quickly. Tayoga's manner was quiet, but it was not without a certain exultation, and the youth knew that he did not jest. Yet it seemed incredible.

"You met them, Tayoga?" he repeated.

"Yes, Dagaeoga."

"And what happened?"

"The two warriors whom Tandakora brought with him lie still in the forest. They will never move again. Tandakora escaped with an arrow through his arm. He will not trouble us for a week, but he will seek us later."

"Why didn't you awake us, Tayoga, and take us with you?"

"I wished to do this deed alone."

"You've done it well, that's sure," said Willet, "and now that all danger has been removed we'll light our fire and cook breakfast."

After breakfast they shouldered their packs and plunged once more into the greenwood, intending to reach as quickly as they could the hidden canoe on the Richelieu, and then make an easy journey by water.

CHAPTER XIV
ON CHAMPLAIN

The three arrived at the Richelieu without further hostile encounter, but they met a white forest runner who told them the aspect of affairs in the Ohio country was growing more threatening. A small force from Virginia was starting there under a young officer named Washington, and it was reported that the French from Canada in numbers were already in the disputed country.

"We know what we know," said Willet thoughtfully. "I've never doubted that English and French would come into conflict in the woods, and if I had felt any such doubts, our visit to Quebec would have driven them away. I don't think our letters from the Governor of New York to the Governor General of Canada will be of any avail."

"No," said Robert, soberly. "They won't. But I want to say to you, Dave, that I'm full of gladness, because we've reached our canoe. Our packs without increasing in size are at least twice as heavy as they were when we started."

"I can join you in your hosannas, Robert. Never before did a canoe look so fine to me. It's a big canoe, a beautiful canoe, a strong canoe, a swift canoe, and it's going to carry us in comfort and far."

It was, in truth, larger than the one they had used coming up the lakes, and, with a mighty sigh of satisfaction, Robert settled into his place. Their packs, rifles, swords and the case containing Tayoga's bow and arrows were adjusted delicately, and then, with a few sweeps of the Onondaga's paddle, they shot out into the slow current of the river. Robert and Willet leaned back and luxuriated. Tayoga wanted to do the work at present, saying that his wrists, in particular, needed exercise, and they willingly let him. They were moving against the stream, but so great was the Onondaga's dexterity that he sent the canoe along at a good pace without feeling weariness.

"It's like old times," said Willet. "There's no true happiness like being in a canoe on good water, with the strong arm of another to paddle for you. I'm glad you winged that savage, Tandakora, Tayoga. It would spoil my pleasure to know that he was hanging on our trail."

"Don't be too happy, Great Bear," said Tayoga. "Within a week the Ojibway will be hunting for us. Maybe he will be lying in wait on the shores of the great lake, Champlain."

"If so, Tayoga, you must have him to feel the kiss of another arrow."

Tayoga smiled and looked affectionately at his bow and quiver.

"The Iroquois shaft can still be of use," he said, "and we will save our ammunition, because the way is yet far."

"Deer shouldn't be hard to find in these woods," said Willet, "and when we stop for the night we'll hunt one."

They took turns with the paddle, and now and then, drawing in under overhanging boughs, rested a little. Once or twice they saw distant smoke which they believed was made by Canadian and therefore hostile Indians, but they did not pause to investigate. It was their desire to make speed, because they wished to reach as quickly as they could the Long House in the vale of the Onondaga. It was still possible to arrive there before St. Luc should go away, because he would have to wait until the fifty sachems chose to go in council and hear him.

On this, their return journey, Robert thought much of the chevalier and was eager to see him again. Of all the Frenchmen he had met St. Luc interested him most. De Galisonniere was gallant and honest and truthful, a good friend, but he did not convey the same impression of foresight and power that the chevalier had made upon him, and there was also another motive, underlying but strong. He wished to match himself in oratory before the fifty chiefs with Duquesne's agent. He was confident of his gifts, discovered so recently, and he knew the road to the mind and hearts of the Iroquois.

"What are you thinking so hard about, Robert?" asked Willet.

"Of St. Luc. I think we'll meet him in the vale of Onondaga. Do you ever feel that you can look into the future, Dave?"

"Just what do you mean?"

"Nothing supernatural. Don't the circumstances and conditions sometimes make you think that events are going to run in a certain channel? At the very first glance the Chevalier de St. Luc interested me uncommonly, and even in our exciting days in Quebec I thought of him. Now I have a vision about him. His life and mine are going to cross many times."

The hunter looked sharply at the lad.

"That's a queer idea of yours, Robert," he said, "but when you think it over it's not so queer, after all. It seems to be the rule that queer things should come about."

"Now I don't understand you, Dave."

"Well, maybe I don't quite understand myself. But I know one thing, Robert. St. Luc is always going to put you on your mettle, and you'll always appear at your best before him."

"That's the way I feel about it, Dave. He aroused in me an odd mixture of emotions, both emulation and defiance."

"Perhaps it's not so odd after all," said Willet.

Robert could not induce him to pursue the subject. He shied away from St. Luc, and talked about the more immediate part of their journey, recalling the necessity of finding another deer, as their supplies of food were falling very low. Just before sunset they drew into the mouth of a large creek and made the canoe fast. Tayoga, taking bow and quiver, went into the woods for his deer, and within an hour found him. Then they built a small fire sheltered well by thickets, and cooked supper.

The Onondaga reported game abundant, especially the smaller varieties, and remarkably tame, inferring from the fact that no hunting parties had been in the region for quite a while.

"We're almost in the country of the Hodenosaunee," he said, "but the warriors have not been here. All of the outlying bands have gone back toward Canada or westward into the Ohio country. This portion of the land is deserted."

"Still, it's well to be careful, Tayoga," said the hunter. "That savage, Tandakora, is going to make it the business of his life to hunt our scalps, and if there's to be a great war I don't want to fall just before it begins."

That night they dressed as much of their deer as they could carry, and the next day they passed into Lake Champlain, which displayed all of its finest colors, as if it had been made ready especially to receive them. Its waters showed blue and green and silver as the skies above them shifted and changed, and both to east and west the high mountains were clothed in dark green foliage. Robert's eyes kindled at the sight of nature's great handiwork, the magnificent lake more than a hundred miles long, and the great scenery in which it was placed. It had its story and legend too. Already it was famous in the history of the land and for unbroken generations the Indians had used it as their road between north and south. It was both the pathway of peace and the pathway of war, and Robert foresaw that hostile forces would soon be passing upon it again.

They saw the distant smoke once more, and kept close to the western shore where they were in the shadow of the wooded heights, their canoe but a mote upon the surface of the water. In so small a vessel and almost level with its waves, they saw the lake as one cannot see it from above, its splendid expanse stretching away from north to south, until it sank under the horizon, while the Green Mountains on the east and the great ranges of New York on the west seemed to pierce the skies.

"It's our lake," said Robert, "whatever happens we can't give it up to the French, or at least we'll divide it with the Hodenosaunee who can claim the western shore. If we were to lose this lake no matter what happened elsewhere I should think we had lost the war."

"We don't hold Champlain yet," said the hunter soberly. "The French claim it, and it's even called after the first of their governors under the Company of One Hundred Associates, Samuel de Champlain. They've put upon it as a sign a name which we English and Americans ourselves have accepted, and they come nearer to controlling it than we do. They're advancing, too, Robert, to the lake that they call Saint Sacrement, and that we call George. When it comes to battle they'll have the advantage of occupation."

"It seems so, but we'll drive 'em out," said Robert hopefully.

"But while we talk of the future," said Tayoga in his measured and scholastic English, "it would be well for us also to be watchful in the present. The French and their Indians may be upon the lake, and we are but three in a canoe."

"Justly spoken," said Willet heartily. "We can always trust you, Tayoga, to bring us back to the needs of the moment. Robert, you've uncommonly good eyes. Just you look to the north and to south with all your might, and see if you can see any of their long canoes."

"I don't see a single dot upon the water, Dave," said the youth, "but I notice something else I don't like."

"What is it, Robert?"

"Several little dark clouds hanging around the crests of the high mountains to the west. Small though they are, they've grown somewhat since I noticed them first."

"I don't like that either, Robert. It may mean a storm, and the lake being so narrow the winds have sudden and great violence. But meanwhile, I suppose it's best for us to make as much speed southward as we can."

Tayoga alone was paddling them, but the other two fell to work also, and the canoe shot forward, Robert looking up anxiously now and then at the clouds hovering over the lofty peaks. He noticed that they were still increasing and that now they fused together. Then all the crests were lost in the great masses of vapor which crept far down the slopes. The blue sky over their heads turned to gray with amazing rapidity. The air grew heavy and damp. Thunder, low and then loud, rolled among the western mountains. Lightning blazed in dazzling flashes across the lake, showing the waters yellow or blood red in the glare. The forest moaned and rocked, and with a scream and a roar the wind struck the lake.

The water, in an instant, broke into great waves, and the canoe rocked so violently that it would have overturned at once had not the three possessed such skill with the paddle. Even then the escape was narrow, and their strength was strained to the utmost.

"We must land somewhere!" exclaimed Willet, looking up at the lofty shore.

But where? The cliff was so steep that they saw no chance to pull up themselves and the canoe, and, keeping as close to it as they dared, they steadied the frail vessel with their paddles. The wind continually increased in violence, whistling and screaming, and at times assuming an almost circular motion, whipping the waters of the lake into white foam. Day turned to night, save when the blazing flashes of lightning cut the darkness. The thunder roared like artillery.

Willet hastily covered the ammunition and packs with their blankets, and continued to search anxiously for a place where they might land.

"The rain will be here presently," he shouted, "and it'll be so heavy it'll come near to swamping us if we don't get to shelter first! Paddle, lads! paddle!"

The three, using all their strength and dexterity, sent the canoe swiftly southward, still hugging the shore, but rocking violently. After a few anxious minutes, Robert uttered a shout of joy as he saw by the lightning's flash a cove directly ahead of them with shores at a fair slope. They sent the canoe into it with powerful strokes, sprang upon the bank, and then drew their little craft after them. Selecting a spot sheltered on the west by the lofty shore and on either side to a certain extent by dense woods, they turned the canoe over, resting the edges upon fallen logs which they pulled hastily into place, and crouched under it. They considered themselves especially lucky in finding the logs, and now they awaited the rain that they had dreaded.

It came soon in a mighty sweep, roaring through the woods, and burst upon them in floods. But the canoe, the logs and the forest and the slope together protected them fairly well, and the contrast even gave a certain degree of comfort, as the rain beat heavily and then rushed in torrents down to the lake.

"We made it just in time," said Willet. "If we had stayed on the water I think we'd have been swamped. Look how high the waves are and how fast they run!"

Robert as he gazed at the stormy waters was truly thankful.

"We have many dangers," he said, "but somehow we seem to escape them all."

"We dodge 'em," said Willet, "because we make ready for 'em. It's those who think ahead who inherit the world, Robert."

The storm lasted an hour. Then the rain ceased abruptly. The wind died, the darkness fled away and the lake and earth, washed and cleansed anew, returned to their old peace and beauty, only the skies seemed softer and bluer, and the colors of the water more varied and intense.

They launched the canoe and resumed their journey to the south, but when they had gone a few hundred yards Robert observed a black dot behind them on the lake. Willet and Tayoga at once pronounced it a great Indian canoe, containing a dozen warriors at least.

"Canadian Indians, beyond a doubt," said Tayoga, "and our enemies. Perhaps Tandakora is among them."

"Whether he is or not," said Willet, "they've seen us and are in pursuit. I suppose they stayed in another cove back of us while the storm passed. It's one case where our foresight couldn't guard against bad luck."

He spoke anxiously and looked up at the overhanging forest. But there was no convenient cove now, and it was not possible for them to beach the canoe and take flight on land. A new danger and a great one had appeared suddenly. The long canoe, driven by a dozen powerful paddles, was approaching fast.

"Hurons, I think," said Tayoga.

"Most likely," said the hunter, "but whether Hurons or not they're no friends of ours, and there's hot work with the paddles before us. They're at least four rifleshots away and we have a chance."

Now the three used their paddles as only those can who have life at stake. Their light canoe leaped suddenly forward, and seemed fairly to skim over the water like some great aquatic bird, but the larger craft behind them gained steadily though slowly. Three pairs of arms, no matter how strong or expert, are no match for twelve, and the hunter frowned as he glanced back now and then.

"Only three rifleshots now," he muttered, "and before long it will be but two. But we have better weapons than theirs, and ours can speak fast. Easy now, lads! We mustn't wear ourselves out!"

Robert made his strokes slower. The perspiration was standing on his face, and his breath was growing painful, but he remembered in time the excellence of Willet's advice. The gain of the long canoe increased more rapidly, but the three were accumulating strength for a great spurt. The pursuit and flight, hitherto, had been made in silence, but now the Hurons, for such their paint proved them to be, uttered a long war whoop, full of anticipation and triumph, a cry saying plainly that they expected to have three good scalps soon. It made Robert's pulse leap with anger.

"They haven't taken us yet," he said.

Willet laughed.

"Don't let 'em make you lose your temper," he said. "No, they haven't taken us, and we've escaped before from such places just as tight. They make faster time than we can, Robert, but our three rifles here will have a word or two to say."

After the single war whoop the warriors relapsed into silence and plied their paddles, sure now of their prey. They were experts themselves and their paddles swept the water in perfect unison, while the long canoe gradually cut down the distance between it and the little craft ahead.

"Two rifle shots," said the hunter, "and when it becomes one, as it surely will, I'll have to give 'em a hint with a bullet."

"It's possible,'" said Robert, "that a third power will intervene."

"What do you mean?" asked Willet.

"The storm's coming back. Look up!"

It was true. The sky was darkening again, and the clouds were gathering fast over the mountains on the west. Already lightning was quivering along the slopes, and the forest was beginning to rock with the wind. The air rapidly grew heavier and darker. Their own canoe was quivering, and Robert saw that the long canoe was rising and falling with the waves.

"Looks as if it might be a question of skill with the paddles rather than with the rifles," said Willet tersely.

"But they are still gaining," said Tayoga, "even though the water is so rough."

"Aye," said Willet, "and unless the storm bursts in full power they'll soon be within rifle shot."

He watched with occasional keen backward looks, and in a few minutes he snatched up his rifle, took a quick aim and fired. The foremost man in the long canoe threw up his arms, and fell sideways into the water. The canoe stopped entirely for a moment or two, but then the others, uttering a long, fierce yell of rage, bent to their paddles with a renewed effort. The three had made a considerable gain during their temporary check, but it could not last long. Willet again looked for a chance to land, but the cliffs rose above them sheer and impossible.

"We are in the hands of Manitou," said Tayoga, gravely. "He will save us. Look, how the storm gathers! Perhaps it was sent back to help us."

The Onondaga spoke with the utmost earnestness. It was not often that a storm returned so quickly, and accepting the belief that Manitou intervened in the affairs of earth, he felt that the second convulsion of nature was for their benefit. Owing to the great roughness of the water their speed now decreased, but not more than that of the long canoe, the rising wind compelling them to use their paddles mostly for steadiness. The spray was driven like sleet in their faces, and they were soon wet through and through, but they covered the rifles and ammunition with their blankets, knowing that when the storm passed they would be helpless unless they were kept dry.

The Hurons fired a few shots, all of which fell short or wide, and then settled down with all their numbers to the management of their canoe, which was tossing dangerously. Robert noticed their figures were growing dim, and then, as the storm struck with full violence for the second time, the darkness came down and hid them.

"Now," shouted Willet, as the wind whistled and screamed in their ears, "we'll make for the middle of the lake!"

Relying upon their surpassing skill with the paddle, they chose a most dangerous course, so far as the risk of wreck was concerned, but they intended that the long canoe should pass them in the dusk, and then they would land in the rear. The waves were higher as they went toward the center of the lake, but they were in no danger of being dashed against the cliffs, and superb work with the paddles kept them from being swamped. Luckily the darkness endured, and, as they were able to catch through it no glimpse of the long canoe, they had the certainty of being invisible themselves.

"Why not go all the way across to the eastern shore?" shouted Robert. "We may find anchorage there, and we'd be safe from both the Hurons and the storm!"

"Dagaeoga is right," said Tayoga.

"Well spoken!" said Willet. "Do the best work you ever did with the paddles, or we'll find the bottom of the lake instead of the eastern shore!"

But skill, strength and quickness of eye carried them in safety across the lake, and they found a shore of sufficient slope for them to land and lift the canoe after them, carrying it back at least half a mile, and not coming to rest until they reached the crest of a high hill, wooded densely. They put the canoe there among the bushes and sank down behind it, exhausted. The rifles and precious ammunition, wrapped tightly in the folds of their blankets, had been kept dry, but they were wet to the bone themselves and now, that their muscles were relaxed, the cold struck in. The three, despite their weariness, began to exercise again vigorously, and kept it up until the rain ceased.

Then the second storm stopped as suddenly as the first had departed, the darkness went away, and the great lake stood out, blue and magnificent, in the light. Far to the south moved the long canoe, a mere black dot in the water. Tayoga laughed in his throat.

"They rage and seek us in vain," he said. "They will continue pursuing us to the south. They do not know that Manitou sent the second storm especially to cover us up with a darkness in which we might escape."

"It's a good belief, Tayoga," said Willet, "and as Manitou arranged that we should elude them he is not likely to bring them back into our path. That being the case I'm going to dry my clothes."

"So will I," said Robert, and the Onondaga nodded his own concurrence. They took off their garments, wrung the water out of them and hung them on the bushes to dry, a task soon to be accomplished by the sun that now came out hot and bright. Meanwhile they debated their further course.

"The long canoe still goes south," said Tayoga. "It is now many miles away, hunting for us. Perhaps since they cannot find us, the Hurons will conclude that the storm sank us in the lake!"

"But they will hunt along the shore a long time," said Willet. "They're nothing but a tiny speck now, and in a quarter of an hour they'll be out of sight altogether. Suppose we cross the lake behind them--I think I see a cove down there on the western side--take the canoe with us and wait until they go back again."

"A wise plan," said Tayoga.

In another hour their deerskins were dry, and reclothing themselves they returned the canoe to the lake, the Hurons still being invisible. Then they crossed in haste, reached the cove that Willet had seen, and plunged into the deep woods, taking the canoe with them, and hiding their trail carefully. When they had gone a full three miles they came to rest in a glade, and every one of the three felt that it was time. Muscles and nerves alike were exhausted, and they remained there all the rest of the day and the following night, except that after dark Tayoga went back to the lake and saw the long canoe going northward.

"I don't think we'll be troubled by that band of Hurons any more," he reported to his comrades. "They will surely think we have been drowned, and tomorrow we can continue our own journey to the south."

"And on the whole, we've come out of it pretty well," said Willet.

"With the aid of Manitou, who so generously sent us the second storm," said Tayoga.

They brought the canoe back to the lake at dawn, and hugging the western shore made leisurely speed to the south, until they came to the neighborhood of the French works at Carillon, when they landed again with their canoe, and after a long and exhausting portage launched themselves anew on the smaller but more splendid lake, known to the English as George and to the French as Saint Sacrement. Now, though, they traveled by night and slept and rested by day. But Lake George in the moonlight was grand and beautiful beyond compare. Its waters were dusky silver as the beams poured in floods upon it, and the lofty shores, in their covering of dark green, seemed to hold up the skies.

"It's a grand land," said Robert for the hundredth time.

"It is so," said Tayoga. "After Manitou had practiced on many other countries he used all his wisdom and skill to make the country of the Hodenosaunee."

The next morning when they lay on the shore they saw two French boats on the lake, and Robert was confirmed in his opinion that the prevision of the French leaders would enable them to strike the first blow. Already their armed forces were far down in the debatable country, and they controlled the ancient water route between the British colonies and Canada.

On the second night they left the lake, hid the canoe among the bushes at the edge of a creek, and began the journey by land to the vale of Onondaga. It was likely that in ordinary times they would have made it without event, but they felt now the great need of caution, since the woods might be full of warriors of the hostile tribes. They were sure, too, that Tandakora would find their trail and that he would not relinquish the pursuit until they were near the villages of the Hodenosaunee. The trail might be hidden from the Ojibway alone, but since many war parties of their foes were in the woods he would learn of it from some of them. So they followed the plan they had used on the lake of traveling by night and of lying in the bush by day.

Another deer fell to Tayoga's deadly arrow, and on the third day as they were concealed in dense forest they saw smoke on a high hill, rising in rings, as if a blanket were passed rapidly over a fire and back again in a steady alternation.

"Can you read what they say, Tayoga?" asked Willet.

"No," replied the Onondaga. "They are strange to me, and so it cannot be any talk of the Hodenosaunee. Ah, look to the west! See, on another hill, two miles away, rings of smoke also are rising!"

"Which means that two bands of French Indians are talking to each other, Tayoga?"

"It is so, Great Bear, and here within the lands of the Hodenosaunee! Perhaps Frenchmen are with them, Frenchmen from Carillon or some other post that Onontio has pushed far to the south."

The young Onondaga spoke with deep resentment. The sight of the two smokes made by the foes of the Hodenosaunee filled him with anger, and Willet, who observed his face, easily read his mind from it.

"You would like to see more of the warriors who are making those signals," he said. "Well, I don't blame you for your curiosity and perhaps it would be wise for us to take a look. Suppose we stalk the first fire."

Tayoga nodded, and the three, although hampered somewhat by their packs, began a slow approach through the bushes. Half the distance, and Tayoga, who was in advance, putting his finger upon his lips, sank almost flat.

"What is it, Tayoga?" whispered Willet.

"Someone else stalking them too. On the right. I heard a bush move."

Both Willet and Robert heard it also as they waited, and used as they were to the forest they knew that it was made by a human being.

"What's your opinion, Tayoga?" asked the hunter.

"A warrior or warriors of the Hodenosaunee, seeking, as we are, to see those who are sending up the rings of smoke," replied the Onondaga.

"If you're right they're likely to be Mohawks, the Keepers of the Eastern Gate."

Tayoga nodded.

"Let us see," he said.

Putting his fingers to his lips, he blew between them a note soft and low but penetrating. A half minute, and a note exactly similar came from a point in the dense bush about a hundred yards away. Then Tayoga blew a shorter note, and as before the reply came, precisely like it.

"It is the Ganeagaono," said Tayoga with certainty, "and we will await them here."

The three remained motionless and silent, but in a few minutes the bushes before them shook, and four tall figures, rising to their full height, stood in plain view. They were Mohawk warriors, all young, powerful and with fierce and lofty features. The youngest and tallest, a man with the high bearing of a forest chieftain, said:

"We meet at a good time, O Tayoga, of the clan of the Bear, of the nation Onondaga, of the great League of the Hodenosaunee."

"It is so, O Daganoweda, of the clan of the Turtle, of the nation Ganeagaono, of the great League of the Hodenosaunee," replied Tayoga. "I see that my brethren, the Keepers of the Eastern Gate, watch when the savage tribes come within their territory."

The brows of the young Mohawk contracted into a frown.

"Most of our warriors are on the great trail to the vale of Onondaga," he said. "We are but four, and, though we are only four, we intended to attack. The smoke nearer by is made by Hurons and Caughnawagas."

"You are more than four, you are seven," said Tayoga.

Daganoweda understood, and smiled fiercely and proudly.

"You have spoken well, Tayoga," he said, "but you have spoken as I expected you to speak. Onundagaono and Ganeagaono be the first nations of the Hodenosaunee and they never fail each other. We are seven and we are enough."

He took it for granted that Tayoga spoke as truly for the two white men as for himself, and Robert and the hunter felt themselves committed. Moreover their debt to the Onondaga was so great that they could not abandon him, and they knew he would go with the Mohawks. It would also be good policy to share their enterprise and their danger.

"We'll support you to the end of it," said Willet quietly.

"The English have always been the friends of the Hodenosaunee," said Daganoweda, as he led the way through the undergrowth toward the point from which the smoke come. Neither Robert nor Willet felt any scruple about attacking the warriors there, as they were clearly invaders with hostile purpose of Mohawk territory, and it was also more than likely that their immediate object was the destruction of the three. Yet the two Americans held back a little, letting the Indians take the lead, not wishing it to be said that they began the battle.

Daganoweda, whose name meant "Inexhaustible," was a most competent young chief. He spread out his little force in a half circle, and the seven rapidly approached the fire. But Robert was glad when a stick broke under the foot of an incautious and eager warrior, and the Hurons and Caughnawagas, turning in alarm, fired several bullets into the bushes. He was glad, because it was the other side that began the combat, and if there was a Frenchman with them he could not go to Montreal or Quebec, saying the British and their Indians had fired the first shot.

All of the bullets flew wide, and Daganoweda's band took to cover at once, waiting at least five minutes before they obtained a single shot at a brown body. Then all the usual incidents of a forest struggle followed, the slow creeping, the occasional shot, a shout of triumph or the death yell, but the Hurons and Caughnawagas, who were about a dozen in number, were routed and took to flight in the woods, leaving three of their number fallen. Two of the Mohawks were wounded but not severely. Tayoga, who was examining the trail, suddenly raised his head and said:

"Tandakora has been here. There is none other who wears so large a moccasin. Here go his footsteps! and here! and here!"

"Doubtless they thought we were near, and were arranging with the other band to trap us," said Willet. "Daganoweda, it seems that you and your Mohawks came just in time. Are the smoke rings from the second fire still rising? We were too far away for them to hear our rifles."

"Only one or two rings go up now," replied Tayoga. "Since they have received no answer in a long time they wonder what has happened. See how those two rings wander away and dissolve in the air, as if they were useless, and now no more follow."

"But the warriors may come here to see what is the matter, and we ought to be ready for them."

Daganoweda, to whom they readily gave the place of leader, since by right it was his, saw at once the soundness of the hunter's advice, and they made an ambush. The second band, which was about the size of the first, approached cautiously, and after a short combat retired swiftly with two wounded warriors, evidently thinking the enemy was in great force, and leaving the young Mohawk chieftain in complete possession of his victorious field.

"Tayoga, and you, Great Bear, I thank you," said Daganoweda. "Without your aid we could never have overcome our enemies."

"We were glad to do what we could," said Willet sincerely, "since, as I see it, your cause and ours are the same."

Tayoga was examining the fleeing trail of the second band as he had examined that of the first, and he beckoned to his white comrades and to Daganoweda.

"Frenchmen were here," he said. "See the trail. They wore moccasins, but their toes turn out in the white man's fashion."

There was no mistaking the traces, and Robert felt intense satisfaction. If hostile Indians, led by Frenchmen, were invading the territory of the Hodenosaunee, then it would be very hard indeed for Duquesne and Bigot to break up the ancient alliance of the great League with the English. But he was quite sure that no one of the flying Frenchmen was St. Luc. The chevalier was too wise to be caught in such a trap, nor would he lend himself to the savage purposes of Tandakora.

"Behold, Daganoweda," he said, "the sort of friends the French would be to the Hodenosaunee. When the great warriors of the Six Nations go to the vale of Onondaga to hear what the fifty sachems will say at their council, the treacherous Hurons and Caughnawagas, led by white men from Montreal and Quebec, come into their land, seeking scalps."

The power of golden speech was upon him once more. He felt deeply what he was saying, and he continued, calling attention to the ancient friendship of the English, and their long and bitter wars with the French. He summoned up again the memory of Frontenac, never dead in the hearts of the Mohawks, and as he spoke the eyes of Daganoweda and his comrades flashed with angry fire. But he did not continue long. He knew that at such a time a speech protracted would lose its strength, and when the feelings of the Mohawks were stirred to their utmost depths he stopped abruptly and turned away.

"'Twas well done, lad! 'twas well done!" whispered Willet.

"Great Bear," said Daganoweda, "we go now to the vale of Onondaga for the grand council. Perhaps Tayoga, a coming chief of the clan of the Bear, of the great nation Onondaga, will go with us."

"So he will," said Willet, "and so will Robert and myself. We too wish to reach the vale of Onondaga. An uncommonly clever Frenchman, one Chevalier Raymond de St. Luc, has gone there. He is a fine talker and he will talk for the French. Our young friend here, whom an old chief of your nation has named Dagaeoga, is, as you have heard, a great orator, and he will speak for the English. He will measure himself against the Frenchman, St. Luc, and I think he will be equal to the test."

The young Mohawk chieftain gave Robert a look of admiration.

"Dagaeoga can talk against anybody," he said. "He need fear no Frenchman. Have I not heard? And if he can use so many words here in the forest before a few men what can he not do in the vale of Onondaga before the gathered warriors of the Hodenosaunee? Truly the throat of Dagaeoga can never tire. The words flow from his mouth like water over stones, and like it, flow on forever. It is music like the wind singing among the leaves. He can talk the anger from the heart of a raging moose, or he can talk the otter up from the depths of the river. Great is the speech of Dagaeoga."

Robert turned very red. Willet laughed and even Tayoga smiled, although the compliment was thoroughly sincere.

"You praise me too much, Daganoweda," said young Lennox, "but in a great cause one must make a great effort."

"Then come," said the Mohawk chieftain. "We will start at once for the vale of Onondaga."

They struck the great trail, waagwenneyu, and traveled fast. The next day six Mohawks from their upper castle, Ganegahaga on the Mohawk river near the mouth of West Canada Creek, joined them and they continued to press on with speed, entering the heart of the country of the Hodenosaunee, Robert feeling anew what a really great land it was, with its green forests, its blue lakes, its silver rivers and its myriad of creeks and brooks. Nature had lavished everything upon it, and he did not wonder that the Iroquois should guard it with such valor, and cherish it with such tenderness. As he sped on with them he was acquiring for the time at least an Indian soul under a white skin. Long association and a flexible mind enabled him to penetrate the thoughts of the Iroquois and to think as they did.

He knew how the word had been passed through the vast forest. He knew that every warrior, woman and boy of the Hodenosaunee understood how the two great powers beyond the sea and their children here, were about to go into battle on the edge of their country. And what must the Hodenosaunee do? And he knew, too, that as the Six Nations went so might go the war in America. He had seen too much to underrate their valor and strength, and on that long march his heart was very anxious within him.

CHAPTER XV
THE VALE OF ONONDAGA

The heavens favored their journey. They were troubled by no more storms or rain, and as the soft winds blew, flowers opened before them. Game was abundant and they had food for the taking. As they drew near the vale they were joined by a small party of Oneidas, and a little later were met by an Onondaga runner who spoke with great respect to Tayoga and who gave them news.

The Frenchman, St. Luc, and the Canadian, Dubois, who had come with them, were in the vale of Onondaga, where they had been received as guests, and had been treated with hospitality. The fifty sachems, taking their own time, had not yet met in council, and St. Luc had been compelled to wait, but he had made great progress in the esteem of the Hodenosaunee. Onontio could not have sent a better messenger.

"I knew that he would do it," said Willet. "That Frenchman, St. Luc, is wonderful, and if anybody could convert the Hodenosaunee to the French cause he's the man. Oh, he'll ply 'em with a thousand arguments, and he'll dwell particularly on the fact that the French have moved first and are ready to strike. We haven't come too soon, Robert."

But the runner informed them further that it would yet be some time before the great council in the Long House, since the first festival of the spring, the Maple Dance, was to be held in a few days, and the chiefs had refused positively to meet until afterward. The sap was already flowing and the guardians of the faith had chosen time and place for this great and joyous ceremony of the Hodenosaunee, joyous despite the fact that it was preceded by a most solemn event, the general confession of sins.

The eyes of Tayoga and of the Mohawks and Oneidas glistened when they heard.

"We must be there in time for all," said Tayoga.

"Truly we must, brother," said Daganoweda, the Mohawk.

And now they hastened their speed through the fertile and beautiful country, where spring was attaining its full glory, and, as the sap began to run in the maples, so the blood leaped fresh and sparkling even in the veins of the old. A band of Senecas joined them, and when they came to the edge of the vale of Onondaga they were a numerous party, all eager, keen, and surcharged with a spirit which was religious, political and military, the three being inseparably intertwined in the lives of the Hodenosaunee.

They stood upon a high hill and looked over the great, beautiful valley full of orchards and fields and far to the north they caught a slight glimpse of the lake bearing the name of the Keepers of the Council Fire. Smoke rose from the chimneys of the solid log houses built by this most enlightened tribe, flecking the blue of the sky, and the whole scene was one of peace and beauty. The eyes of Tayoga, the Onondaga, and of Daganoweda, the Mohawk, glistened as they looked, and their hearts throbbed with fervent admiration. It was more than a village of the Onondagas that lay before them, it was the temple and shrine of the great league, the Hodenosaunee. The Onondagas kept the council fire, and ranked first in piety, but the Mohawks, the Keepers of the Eastern Gate, were renowned even to the Great Plains for their valor, and they stood with the Onondagas, their equals man for man, while the Senecas, known to themselves and their brother nations as the Nundawaono, were more numerous than either.

"We shall be in time for the great festival, the Maple Dance," said Tayoga to the young Mohawk.

"Yes, my brother, we have come before the beginning," said Daganoweda, "and I am glad that it is so. We may not have the Maple Dance again for many seasons. The shadow of the mighty war creeps upon the Hodenosaunee, and when the spring returns who knows where the warriors of the great League will be? We are but little children and we know nothing of the future, which Manitou alone holds in his keeping."

"You speak truth, Daganoweda. The Ganeagaono are both valiant and wise. It is a time for the fifty sachems to use all the knowledge they have gathered in their long lives, but we will hear what the Frenchman, St. Luc, has to say, even though he belongs to the nation that sent Frontenac against us."

"The Hodenosaunee can do no less," said the Mohawk, tersely.

Robert could not keep from hearing and he was glad of the little affair with the two hostile bands, knitting as it did their friendship with the Mohawks. But he too, since he had penetrated the Iroquois spirit and saw as they did, felt the great and momentous nature of the crisis. While the nations of the Hodenosaunee might decide whether English or French were to win in the coming war they might, at the same time, decide the fate of the great League which had endured for centuries.

They descended into the vale of Onondaga, but at its edge, in a great forest, the entire group stopped, as it became necessary there for Tayoga, Willet and Robert to say a temporary farewell to the others who would not advance into the Onondaga town until the full power of the Hodenosaunee was gathered. The council, as Robert surmised and as he now learned definitely, had been called by the Onondagas, who had sent heralds with belts eastward to the Oneidas, who in turn had sent them yet farther eastward to the Mohawks, westward to the Cayugas whose duty it was to pass them on to the Senecas yet more to the west. The Oneidas also gave belts to the Dusgaowehono, or Tuscaroras, the valiant tribe that had come up from the south forty years before, and that had been admitted into the Hodenosaunee, turning the Five Nations into the Six, and receiving lands within the territory of the Oneidas.

Already great numbers of warriors from the different nations, their chiefs at their head, were scattered about the edges of the valley awaiting the call of the Onondagas for participation in the Maple Dance, and the great and fateful council afterward. And since they did not know whether this council was for peace or for war, every sachem had brought with him a bundle of white cedar fagots that typified peace, and also a bundle of red cedar fagots that typified war.

"Farewell, my friends," said Daganoweda, the Mohawk, to Tayoga, Robert and Willet. "We rest here until the great sachems of the Onondagas send for us, and yet we are eager to come, because never before was there such a Maple Dance and never before such a council as these will be."

"You speak true words, Daganoweda," said Robert, "and the Great Bear and I rejoice that we are adopted sons of the Iroquois and can be here."

Robert spoke from his heart. Not even his arrival at Quebec, great as had been his anticipations and their fulfillment, had stirred in him more interest and enthusiasm. The feeling that for the time being he was an Iroquois in everything except his white skin grew upon him. He saw as they saw, his pulses beat as theirs beat, and he thought as they thought. It was not too much for him to think that the fate of North America might turn upon the events that were to transpire within the vale of Onondaga within the next few days. Nor was he, despite his heated brain, and the luminous glow through which he saw everything, far from the facts.

Robert saw that Willet, despite his years and experience, was deeply stirred also, and the dark eyes of Tayoga glittered, as well they might, since the people who were the greatest in all the world to him were about to deliberate on their fate and that of others.

The three, side by side, their hearts beating hard, advanced slowly and with dignity through the groves. From many points came the sound of singing and down the aisles of the trees they saw young girls in festival attire. All the foliage was in deepest green and the sky was the soft but brilliant blue of early spring. The air seemed to be charged with electricity, because all had a tense and expectant feeling.

For Robert, so highly imaginative, the luminous glow deepened. He had studied much in the classics, after the fashion of the time, in the school at Albany, and his head was filled with the old Greek and Roman learning. Now he saw the ancient symbolism reproduced in the great forests of North America by the nations of the Hodenosaunee, who had never heard of Greece or Rome, nor, to him, were the religion and poetry of the Iroquois inferior in power and beauty, being much closer kin than the gods of Greece and Rome to his own Christian beliefs.

"Manitou favors us," said Tayoga, looking up at the soft blue velvet of the sky. "Gaoh, the spirit of the Winds, moves but gently in his home, Dayodadogowah."

He looked toward the west, because it was there that Gaoh, who had the bent figure and weazened face of an old man, always sat, Manitou having imprisoned him with the elements, and having confined him to one place. In the beautiful Iroquois mythology, Gaoh often struggled to release himself, though never with success. Sometimes his efforts were but mild, and then he produced gentle breezes, but when he fought fiercely for freedom the great storms blew and tore down the forests.

"Gaoh is not very restless today," continued Tayoga. "He struggles but lightly, and the wind from the west is soft upon our faces."

"And it brings the perfume of flowers and of tender young leaves with it, Tayoga," said Willet. "It's a wonderful world and I'm just a boy today, standing at its threshold."

"And even though war may come, perhaps Manitou will smile upon us," said Tayoga. "The Three Sisters whom Hawenneu, who is the same to the white man as Manitou, gave to us, the spirit of the Corn, the spirit of the Squash and the spirit of the Bean will abide with us and give us plenty. The spirits in the shape of beautiful young girls hover over us. We cannot see them, but they are there."

He looked up and shadows passed over their heads. To the mystic soul of the young Onondaga they were the spirits of the three sisters who typified abundance, and Robert himself quivered. He still saw with the eyes and felt with the heart of an Iroquois.

Both he and Tayoga were conscious that the spirits were everywhere about them. All the elements and all the powers of nature were symbolized and typified. The guardians of fire, earth, water, healing, war, the chase, love, winter, summer and a multitude of others, floated in the air. The trees themselves had spirits and identity and all the spirits who together constituted the Honochenokeh were the servants and assistants of Hawenneyu. To the eyes of Tayoga that saw not and yet saw, it was a highly peopled world, and there was meaning in everything, even in the fall of the leaf.

Tayoga presently put his fingers to his lips and uttered a long mellow whistle. A whistle in reply came from a grove just ahead, and fourteen men, all of middle years or beyond, emerged into view. Though elderly, not one among them showed signs of weakness. They were mostly tall, they held themselves very erect, and their eyes were of uncommon keenness and penetration. They were the fourteen sachems of the Onondagas, and at their head was the first in rank, Tododaho, a name that never ceased to exist, being inherited from the great chief who founded the League centuries before, and being passed on from successor to successor. Close to him came Tonessaah, whose name also lasted forever and who was the hereditary adviser of Tododaho, and near him walked Daatgadose and the others.

Tayoga, Robert and Willet stopped, and the great chief, Tododaho, a man of splendid presence, in the full glory of Iroquois state costume, gave them welcome. The sight of Tayoga, of lofty birth, of the clan of the Bear, of the nation Onondaga, was particularly pleasing to his eyes. It was well that the young warriors, who some day would be chiefs to lead in council and battle, should be present. And the coming of the white man and the white lad, who were known to be trusted friends of the Hodenosaunee, was welcome also.

The three, each in turn, made suitable replies, and Robert, his gift of golden speech moving him, spoke a little longer than the others. He made a free use of metaphor and allegory, telling how dear were the prosperity and happiness of the Hodenosaunee to his soul, and he felt every word he said. Charged with the thoughts and impressions of an Iroquois, the fourteen chiefs were the quintessence of dignity and importance to him, and when they smiled and nodded approval of his youthful effort his heart was lifted up. Then he, Tayoga and Willet bowed low to these men who in very truth were the keepers of the council fire of the Hodenosaunee, and whose word might sway the destinies of North America, and, bowing, passed on that they might rest in the Long House, as became three great warriors who had valiantly done their duty in the forest when confronted by their enemies, and who had come to do another and sacred duty in the vale of Onondaga.

Young warriors were their escort into one of the great log houses, which in their nature were much like the community houses found at a later day in the far southwest. The building they entered was a full hundred and twenty feet in length and about forty feet broad, and it had five fires, each built in the center of its space. The walls and roof were of poles thatched with bark, and there were no windows, but over each fire was a circular opening in the roof where the air entered and the smoke went out. If rain or storm came these orifices were covered with great pieces of bark.

On the long sides of the walls extended platforms about six feet wide, covered with furs and skins where the warriors slept. Overhead was a bark canopy on top of which they placed their possessions. About a dozen warriors were in the house, all lying down, but they rose and greeted the three. Berths were assigned to them at once, food and water were brought, and Robert, weary from the long march, decided that he would sleep.

"I think I'll do the same," said Willet, "and then we'll be fresh for what's coming. Tayoga, I suppose, will want to see his kin first."

Tayoga nodded, and presently disappeared. Then Robert and Willet took their places upon the bark platforms and were soon asleep, not awakening until the next morning when they went forth and found that the excitement in the valley had increased. Tayoga came to them at once and told them that Sanundathawata, the council of repentance, was about to be held. The dawn was just appearing, and as the sun rose the sachems of the Onondagas would proceed to the council grove and receive the sachems of the allied nations.

"You will wish to see the ceremony," he said.

"Of course, of course!" said Robert, eagerly, who found that with the coming of a new day he was as much an Iroquois in spirit as ever. Nor could he see that Willet was less keen about it and the three proceeded promptly to the council grove where a multitude was already hastening. There was, too, a great buzz of talk, as the Iroquois here in the vale, the very heart of their country, did not show the taciturnity in which the red man so often takes refuge in the presence of the white.

The fourteen Onondaga chiefs, Tododaho at their head and Tonessaah at his right, were gathered in the grove, and the warriors of the allied nations approached, headed by their chiefs, nine for the Mohawks, ten for the Oneidas, nine for the Cayugas, and eight for the Senecas, while the Tuscaroras, who were a new nation in the League, had none at all, but spoke through their friends, the Oneidas, within whose lands they had been allowed to settle. And when the roll of the nations of the Hodenosaunee was called it was not the Onondagas, Keepers of the Council Fire, who were called first, although they were equal in honor, and leaders in council, but the fierce and warlike Mohawks. Then came the Onondagas, after them the numerous Senecas, followed by the Oneidas, with the Cayugas next and the sachemless Tuscaroras last, but filled with pride that they, wanderers from their ancient lands, and not large in numbers, had shown themselves so valiant and enduring that the greatest of all Indian leagues, the Hodenosaunee, should be willing to admit them as a nation.

Behind the sachems stood the chiefs, the two names not being synonymous among the Iroquois, and although the name of the Mohawks was called first the Onondagas were masters of the ceremonies, were, in fact, the priests of the Hodenosaunee, and their first chief, Tododaho, was the first chief of all the League. Yet the Senecas, who though superior in numbers were inferior in chiefs, also had an office, being Door Keepers of the Long House, while the Onondagas were the keepers in the larger sense. The eighth sachem of the Senecas, Donehogaweh, had the actual physical keeping of the door, when the fifty sachems met within, and he also had an assistant who obeyed all his orders, and who, upon occasion, acted as a herald or messenger. But the Onondaga sachem, Honowenato, kept the wampum.

The more Robert saw of the intertwined religious, military and political systems of the Hodenosaunee, the more he admired them, and he missed nothing as the Onondaga sachems received their brother sachems of the allied tribes, all together being known as the Hoyarnagowar, while the chiefs who were elective were known collectively as the Hasehnowaneh.

Robert, Willet, and Tayoga, who was yet too young to have a part in the ceremonies, stood on one side with the crowd and watched with the most intense interest. Among the nine Mohawk sachems they recognized Dayohogo, who had given Robert the name Dagaeoga, and the lad resolved to see him later and renew their friendship.

Meanwhile the thirty-six visiting sachems formed themselves in a circle, with Tododaho, highest of the Onondagas in rank, among them, and facing the sun which was rising in a golden sea above the eastern hills. Presently the Onondaga lifted his hand and the hum and murmur in the great crowd that looked on ceased. Then starting towards the north the sachems moved with measured steps around the circle three times. Every one of them carried with him a bundle of fagots, and in this case half of the bundle was red and half white. When they stopped each sachem put his bundle of fagots on the ground, and sat down before it, while an assistant sachem came and stood behind him. Tododaho took flint and steel from his pouch, set fire first to his own fagots and then to all the others, after which he took the pipe of peace, lighted it from one of the fires, and, drawing upon it three times, blew one puff of smoke toward the center of the heavens, another upon the ground, and the last directly toward the rising sun.

"He gives thanks," whispered Tayoga, to Robert, "first to Manitou, who has kept us alive, next to our great mother, the Earth, who has produced the food that we eat and who sends forth the water that we drink, and last to the Sun, who lights and warms us."

Robert thought it a beautiful ceremony, full of idealism, and he nodded his thanks to Tayoga while he still watched. Tododaho passed the pipe to the sachem on his right, who took the three puffs in a similar manner, and thus it was passed to all, the entire act requiring a long time, but at its end the fourteen Onondaga sachems and the thirty-six visiting sachems sat down together and under the presidency of Tododaho the council was opened.

"But little will be done today," said Tayoga. "It is merely what you call at the Albany school a preliminary. The really great meeting will be after the Maple Dance, and then we shall know what stand the Hodenosaunee will take in the coming war."

Robert turned away and came face to face with St. Luc. He had known that the chevalier was somewhere in the vale of Onondaga, but in his absorption in the Iroquois ceremonies he had forgotten about him. Now he realized with full force that he had come to meet the Frenchman and to measure himself against him. Yet he could not hide from himself a certain gladness at seeing him and it was increased by St. Luc's frank and gay manner.

"I was sure that we should soon meet again, Mr. Lennox," he said, "and it has come to pass as I predicted and hoped. And you too, Mr. Willet! I greet you both."

He offered a hand to each, and the hunter, as well as Robert, shook it without hesitation.

"You reached Quebec and fulfilled your mission?" he said, giving Robert a keen look of inquiry.

"Yes, but not without event," replied the youth.

"I take it from your tone that the event was of a stirring nature."

"It was rather a chain of events. The Ojibway chief, Tandakora, whom we first saw with you, objected to our presence in the woods."

St. Luc frowned and then laughed.

"For that I am sorry," he said. "I would have controlled the Ojibway if I could, but he is an unmitigated savage. He left me, and did what he chose. I hope you do not hold me responsible for any attacks he may have made upon you, Mr. Lennox."

"Not at all, Monsieur, but as you see, we have survived everything and have taken no hurt. Quebec also, a great and splendid city, was not without stirring event, not to say danger."

"But not to heralds, for such I take you and Mr. Willet and Tayoga to have been."

"A certain Pierre Boucher, a great duelist, and if you will pardon me for saying it, a ruthless bravo, also was disposed to make trouble for us."

"I know Boucher. He is what you say. But since you are here safe and unhurt, as you have just reminded me, you escaped all the snares he set for you."

"True, Monsieur de St. Luc, but we have the word that the fowler may fall into his own snare."

"Your meaning escapes me."

"Boucher, the duelist and bravo, will never make trouble for anybody else."

"You imply that he is dead? Boucher dead! How did he die?"

"A man may be a great swordsman, and he may defeat many others, but the time usually comes when he will meet a better swordsman than himself."

"Yourself! Why, you're but a lad, Mr. Lennox, and skillful as you may be you're not seasoned enough to beat such a veteran as Boucher!"

"That is true, but there is another who was."

He nodded toward the hunter and the chevalier's eyes opened wide.

"And you, a hunter," he said, "could defeat Pierre Boucher, who has been accounted the master swordsman! There is more in this than meets the eye!"

He stared at Willet, who met his gaze firmly. Then he shrugged his shoulders and said:

"I'm not one to pry into the secrets of another, but I did not think there was any man in America who was a match for Boucher. Well, he is gone to another world, and let us hope that he will be a better man in it than he was in this. Meanwhile we'll return to the business that brings us all here. I speak of it freely, since every one of us knows it well. I wish to bring in the Hodenosaunee on the side of France. The interests of these red nations truly lie with His Majesty King Louis, since you British colonists will spread over their lands and will drive them out."

"Your pardon, Chevalier de St. Luc, but it is not so. The

English have always been the good friends of the Six Nations, and have never broken treaties with them."

"No offense was meant, Mr. Lennox. But we do not wish to waste our energies here debating with each other. We will save our skill and strength for the council of the fifty, where I know you will present the cause of the British king in such manner that its slender justification will seem better than it really is."

Robert laughed.

"A stab and praise at the same time," he said. "No, Monsieur de St. Luc, I have no wish to quarrel with you now or at any other time."

"And while we're in the vale of Onondaga we'll be friends."

"If you wish it to be so."

"And you too, Mr. Willet?"

"I've nothing against you, Chevalier de St. Luc, although I shall fight the cause of the king whom you represent here. On the other hand I may say that I like you and I wish nothing better than to be friends with you here."

"Then it is settled," said St. Luc in a tone of relief. "It is a good way, I think. Why be enemies before we must? I shall see, too, that my good Dubois becomes one of us, and together we will witness the Maple Dance."

St. Luc's manner continued frank, and Robert could not question his sincerity. He was glad that the chevalier had proposed the temporary friendship and he was glad, too, that Willet approved of it, since he had such a great respect for the opinion of the hunter. St. Luc, now that the treaty was made, bore himself as one of their party, and the dark Canadian, Dubois, who was not far away, also accepted the situation in its entirety. Tayoga, too, confirmed it thoroughly and now that St. Luc was with him on a footing of friendship Robert felt more deeply than ever the charm of his manner and talk. It seemed to him that the chevalier had the sincerity and honesty of de Galisonniere, with more experience and worldly wisdom, his experience and worldly wisdom matching those of de Courcelles with a great superiority in sincerity and honesty.

The three quickly became the five. St Luc and Dubois being accepted were accepted without reserve, although Dubois seldom spoke, seeming to consider himself the shadow of his chief. The next day the five stood together and witnessed the confessions of sins in the council grove, the religious ceremony that always preceded the Maple Dance.

Tododaho spoke to the sachems, the chiefs and the multitude upon their crimes and faults, the necessity for repentance and of resolution to do better in the future. Robert saw but little difference between his sermon and that of a minister in the Protestant faith in which he had been reared. Manitou was God and God was Manitou. The Iroquois and the white men had traveled by different roads, but they had arrived at practically the same creed and faith. The feeling that for the time being he was an Iroquois in a white man's skin was yet strong upon him.

Many of the Indian sachems and chiefs were men of great eloquence, and the speech of Tododaho amid such surroundings, with the breathless multitude listening, was impressive to the last degree. Its solemnity was increased, when he held aloft a belt of white wampum, and, enumerating his own sins, asked Manitou to forgive him. When he had finished he exclaimed, "Naho," which meant, "I have done." Then he passed the wampum to Tonessaah, who also made his confession, and all the other sachems and chiefs did the same, the people, too, joining with intense fervor in the manifestation.

A huge banquet of all that forest, river and field afforded was spread the next morning, and at noon athletic games, particularly those with the ball, in which the red man excelled long before the white man came, began and were played with great energy and amid intense excitement. At the same time the great Feather Dance, religious in its nature, was given by twelve young warriors and twelve young girls, dressed in their most splendid costumes.

Night came, and the festival was still in progress. What the Indian did he did with his whole heart, and all his strength. Darkness compelled the ball games to cease, but the dancing went on by the light of the fires and fresh banquets were spread for all who cared. Robert knew that it might last for several days and that it would be useless until the end for either him or St. Luc to mention the subject so dear to their hearts. Hence came an agreement of silence, and all the while their friendship grew.

It is true that official enemies may be quite different in private life, and Robert found that he and St. Luc had much in common. There was a certain kindred quality of temperament. They had the same courage, the same spirit of optimism, the same light and easy manner of meeting a crisis, with the same deadly earnestness and concentration concealed under that careless appearance. It was apparent that Robert, who had spent so much of his life in the forest, was fitted for great events and the stage upon which men of the world moved. He had felt it in Quebec, when he came into contact with what was really a brilliant court, with all the faults and vices of a court, one of the main objects of which was pleasure, and he felt it anew, since he was in the constant companionship of a man who seemed to him to have more of that knightly spirit and chivalry for which France was famous than any other he had ever met. St. Luc knew his Paris and the forest equally well. Nor was he a stranger to London and Vienna or to old Rome that Robert hoped to see some day. It seemed to Robert that he had seen everything and done everything, not that he boasted, even by indirection, but it was drawn from him by the lad's own questions, back of which was an intense curiosity.

Robert noticed also that Willet, to whom he owed so much, never intervened. Apparently he still approved the growing friendship of the lad and the Frenchman, and Tayoga, too, showed himself not insensible to St Luc's charm. Although he was now among his own people, and in the sacred vale of which they were the keepers, he still stayed in the community house with Robert and sought the society of his white friends, including St. Luc.

"I had thought," said Robert to the hunter the third morning after their arrival, "that you would prefer for us to show a hostile face to St. Luc, who is here to defeat our purpose, just as we are here to defeat his."

"Nothing is to be gained by a personal enmity," replied the hunter. "We are the enemies not of St. Luc, but of his nation. We will meet him fairly as he will meet us fairly, and I see good reasons why you and he should be friends."

"But in the coming war he's likely to be one of our ablest and most enterprising foes."

"That's true, Robert, but it does not change my view. Brave men should like brave men, and if it is war I hope you and St. Luc will not meet in battle."

"You, too, seem to take an interest in him, Dave."

"I like him," said Willet briefly. Then he shrugged his shoulders, and changed the subject.

The great festival went on, and the agents of Corlear and Onontio were still kept waiting. The sachems would not hear a word from either. As Robert understood it, they felt that the Maple Dance might not be celebrated again for years. These old men, warriors and statesmen both, saw the huge black clouds rolling up and they knew they portended a storm, tremendous beyond any that North America had known. France and England, and that meant their colonies, too, would soon be locked fast in deadly combat, and the Hodenosaunee, who were the third power, must look with all their eyes and think with all their strength.

While the young warriors and the maidens sang and danced without ceasing, the sachems and the chiefs sat far into the night, and as gravely as the Roman Senate, considered the times and their needs. Runners, long of limb, powerful of chest, and bare to the waist, came from all points of the compass and reported secretly. One from Albany said that Corlear and the people there and at New York were talking of war, but were not preparing for it. Another, a Mohawk who came out of the far east, said that Shirley, the Governor of Massachusetts, was thinking of war and preparing for it too. A third, a Tuscarora, who had traveled many days from the south, said that Dinwiddie, the Governor of Virginia, was already acting. He was sending men, led by a tall youth named Washington, into the Ohio country, where the French had already gone to build forts. An Onondaga out of the north said that Quebec and Montreal were alive with military preparations. Onontio was giving to the French Indians muskets, powder, bullets and blankets in a profusion never known before.

The red fagots were rapidly displacing the white, and the secret councils of the fifty sachems were filled with anxiety, but they hid all their disquietude from the people, and much of it from the chiefs. But, to their eyes, all the heavens were scarlet and the world was about to be in upheaval. It was a time for every sachem to walk with cautious steps and use his last ounce of wisdom.

On the fourth night a powerful ally of St. Luc's arrived, although the chevalier had not called him, and did not know until the next day that he had come. He was a tall, thin man of middle years, wrapped in a black robe with a cross upon his breast, and he had traveled alone through the wilderness from Quebec to the vale of Onondaga. He carried no weapon but under the black robe beat a heart as dauntless as that of Robert, or of Willet, or of Tayoga, and an invincible faith that had already moved mountains.

Onondaga men and women received Father Philibert Drouillard, and knelt for his willing blessing. Despite the memories of Champlain and Frontenac, despite the long and honored alliance with the English, the French missionaries, whom no hardships could stop, had made converts among the Onondagas, an enlightened nation with kindly and gentle instincts, and of all these missionaries Father Drouillard had the most tenacious and powerful will. And piety and patriotism could dwell together in his heart. The love of his church and the love of his race burned there with an equal brightness. He, too, had seen the clouds of war gathering, thick and black, and knowing the power of the Hodenosaunee, and that they yet waited, he had hastened to them to win them for France. He was burning with zeal and he would have gone forth the very night of his arrival to talk, but he was so exhausted that he could not move, and he slept deeply in one of the houses, while his faithful converts watched.

Robert encountered the priest early the next morning, and the meeting was wholly unexpected by him, although the Frenchman gave no sign of surprise and perhaps felt none.

"Father Drouillard!" he exclaimed. "I believed you to be in Canada! I did not think there was any duty that could call you to the vale of Onondaga!"

The stern face of the priest relaxed into a slight smile. This youth, though of the hostile race, was handsome and winning, and as Father Drouillard knew, he had a good heart.

"Holy Church sends us, its servants, poor and weak though we may be, on far and different errands," he said. "We seek the wheat even among the stones, and there are those, here in the vale of Onondaga itself, who watch for my coming."

Robert recalled that there were Catholic converts among the Onondagas, a fact that he had forgotten for the time, and he realized at once what a powerful factor Father Drouillard would be in the fight against him.

"The Chevalier de St. Luc has been here for some time," he said, "waiting until the fifty sachems are ready to hear him in council, when he will speak for France. Mr. Willet and I are also waiting to speak for England. But the Chevalier de St. Luc and I are the best of friends, and I hope, Father Drouillard, that you, who have come also to uphold the cause of France, will not look upon me as an enemy, but as one, unfitting though he may be, who wishes to do what he can for his country."

Father Drouillard smiled again.

"Ah, my son," he said, "you are a good lad. You bore yourself well in Quebec, and I have naught against you, save that you are not of our race."

"And for that, reverend sir, you cannot blame me."

Father Drouillard smiled for the third time. It was not often that he smiled three times in one day, and again he reflected that this was a handsome and most winning lad.

"Peace, my son!" he said. "Protestant you are and Catholic am I, English you are and French am I, but no ill wind can ever blow between you and me. We are but little children in the hands of the Omnipotent and we can only await His decree."

Robert told Willet a little later that Father Drouillard had come, and the hunter looked very grave.

"Our task has doubled," he said. "Now we fight both St. Luc and Father Drouillard, the army and the church."

CHAPTER XVI
THE GREAT TEST

While Robert and Willet had been glad hitherto that the council of the fifty sachems had delayed its meeting, they were anxious, now that Father Drouillard had come, to hasten it. That the army and the church, that is the French army and the French church, were in close alliance, they soon had full proof. The priest and the chevalier were much together, and Robert caught an occasional flash of exultation in St. Luc's eyes.

The new influence was visible also among a minority of the Onondagas. The faith of the converts was very strong, and Father Drouillard was to them not only a teacher but an emblem also, and through him, a Frenchman, they looked upon France as the chosen country of the new God whom they worshiped. And Father Drouillard never worked harder than in those fateful days. His thin face grew thinner, and his lean figure leaner, but the fire in his eyes burned brighter. The fifty sachems said nothing. Whether they were for the priest or against him, they never interfered with his energies, because without exception they respected one who they knew sought nothing for himself, who could endure hardship, privation and even torture as well as they, and who also had the gift of powerful and persuasive speech.

The other nations too, except one, listened to him, though less than the Onondagas. The fierce and warlike Mohawks would have none of him, nor would they allow St. Luc to speak to them. Never could a single Mohawk warrior forget that Stadacona was theirs, though generations ago it had become French Quebec. They recalled with delight the numerous raids they had made into Canada, and their many wars with the French. Robert saw that one nation, and it was the one standing on an equality with the Onondagas, was irreconcilable. When the council met the nine sachems of the Mohawks, and their names would be called first, would prove themselves to the last man the bitter and implacable enemies of the French. So, feeling that he was right and loving his own country as much as the priest and the chevalier loved theirs, he deftly worked upon the minds of the Mohawks. He talked to the fiery young chief, Daganoweda, of lost Stadacona that he had seen with his own eyes. He spoke of its great situation on the lofty cliffs above the grandest of rivers, and he described it as the strongest fortress in America.

The spirit of the young Mohawk responded readily. Robert's appeal was not made to prejudice. He felt that truth and right were back of it. As he saw it, the future of the Hodenosaunee lay with the English, the French could never be their real friends, the long breach between Quebec and the vale of Onondaga could not be healed.

He had an able and efficient assistant in Tayoga, who was devoted to the alliance with the English and the Americans, and who was constantly talking with the sachems and chiefs. Willet, too, who had a long acquaintance with all the nations of the Hodenosaunee, and who had many friends among them, used all his arts of persuasion, which were by no means small, and thus the battle for the favor of the Iroquois went on. The night before the council was to be held, Tayoga, his black eyes flashing, came to Robert and the hunter and they talked together for a long time.

The great council was held the next day in the grove devoted to that purpose, the entire ceremony being Greek in its simplicity and dignity, and in its surroundings. The fifty sachems, arrayed in their finest robes, sat once more in a half circle, save that Tododaho, the Onondaga, was slightly in front of the others, with Tonessaah at his elbow. The nine Mohawk chiefs, fierce and implacable, sat close together, and long before the appeals of England and France were begun Robert knew how they would vote.

The effort that he would make had already taken definite shape in his mind. He would be moderate, he would not ask the Hodenosaunee to fight for the English and Americans, he would merely ask the great nations to refuse the alliance of the French, and if they could not find it in their hearts to take up the tomahawk for their old friends then to remain at peace in their villages, while English and French fought for the continent.

Spring was now far advanced. Robert had never seen the forest in deeper green and he had never looked up to a bluer sky than the one that bent over them, as they walked toward the council grove. His heart was beating hard, but it was with excitement, not with fear. He knew that a great test was before him, but his mind responded to it, in truth sprang forward to meet it. The breeze that came down from the hills seemed to whisper encouragement in his ears, and the words that he would speak were already leaping to his lips.

A great crowd, men, women and children, was gathered about the grove, and like the sachems they were clothed in their best. Brilliant red, blue or yellow blankets gleamed in the sun's rays, and the beads on leggings and moccasins of the softest tanned deerskin, flashed and glittered. Robert, with his memories of the Albany school still fresh, thought once more of the great Greek and Roman assemblies, where all the people came to hear their orators discuss the causes that meant most. And then his pulse leaped again and his confidence grew.

Tododaho spoke first, and when he rose there was a respectful silence broken only by the murmurs of the wind or the heavy breathing of the multitude. In a spirit of love and exhortation he addressed his people, all of the six great nations. He told them that the mighty powers beyond the sea, England and France, who with their children divided nearly the whole world between them, were about to begin war with each other. The lands occupied by both bordered upon the lands of the Hodenosaunee, and the storm of battle would hover over all their castles and over the vale of Onondaga. It was well for them to take long and anxious thought, and to listen with attention to what the orators of the English and the French would have to say.

Then Father Drouillard spoke for France. He made an impressive figure, wrapped in his black robe, his eyes burning like coals of fire in his thin, dead white face. Near him on the right, his Onondaga converts were gathered, and he frequently looked at them as he told the fifty sachems that France, the greatest and strongest son of Holy Church, was their best friend, and their fitting ally. Such was the thread of his discourse. He struck throughout the priestly note. He appealed not alone to their sense of right in this world, but to the deeds they must do to insure their entrance into the world to come. France alone could lead them in the right path, she alone thought of their souls.

The priest spoke with intense fervor, using the tongue of the Indians with the greatest clearness and purity. His sincerity was obvious. Neither Robert nor Willet could doubt it for an instant, and they saw, too, that it was making an impression. Deep murmurs of approval came often from the converts, and now and then the whole multitude stirred in agreement. But the fifty sachems, all except the nine Mohawks, sat as expressionless as stones. The Mohawks did not move, but the stern, accusing gaze they bent upon the priest never relaxed. As Robert had foreseen, the most eloquent orator might talk a thousand years, and he could never bring them a single inch toward France.

Willet followed the priest. He attempted no flights. He left the future to itself and emphasized the present and the past. He recalled the facts, so well known, that the English had always been their friends, and the French always their enemies. The English had kept their treaties with the Hodenosaunee, the French could not be trusted.

The hunter, too, received applause, much of it, and when he

208

finished he took his position in the audience beside Tayoga. Then the Chevalier de St. Luc stood before the fifty sachems, as gallant and as handsome a figure as one could find in either the Old World or the New, clothed in a white uniform faced with gold, his hair powdered and tied in a knot, his small sword, gold hilted, by his side.

The chevalier knew the children of the forest, and Robert recognized at once in him an antagonist even more formidable than he had expected. His appeal was to the lore of the woods and to valor. The French adapted themselves to the ways of the forest. They practiced the customs of the Indians, lived with them and often married their women. They could grow and flourish together, while the Englishmen and the Bostonnais held themselves aloof from the red men, and pretended to be their superiors. The French soldier and the Indian warrior had much in common, side by side they were invincible, and together they could drive the English into the sea, giving back to the red races the lands they had lost.

He was a graceful and impassioned speaker, and he, too, made his impression. The principal point of his theme, that the French alone fraternized with the Indians, was good and all were familiar with the fact. He returned to it continually, and when he sat down the applause was louder than it had been for either Willet or the priest. It was evident that he had made a strong appeal, and the Onondaga and Seneca sachems regarded him with a certain degree of favor, but the nine fierce and implacable Mohawk sachems did not unbend a particle.

Then Robert rose. Despite the fewness of his years, the times and hard circumstance had given him wisdom. He was surcharged, too, with emotion. He was yet an Iroquois for the time being, despite his white face. He still saw as they saw, and felt as they felt, and while he wished them to take the side of Britain and the British colonies, or at least not join the side of France and the French colonies, he was moved, too, by a deep personal sympathy. The fortunes of the Hodenosaunee were dear to him. He had been adopted into the great League. Tayoga, as the red people saw it, was his brother in more than blood.

He trembled a little with emotion as he looked upon the grave half-circle of the fifty sachems, and the clustering chiefs behind them, and then upon the people, the old men, the warriors, the women and the children. As he saw them, they were friendly. They knew him to be one of them by all the sacred rites of adoption, they knew that he had fought by the side of the great young warrior Tayoga of the clan of the Bear, of the nation Onondaga, of the mighty League of the Hodenosaunee, and after the momentary silence a deep murmur of admiration for the lithe, athletic young figure, and the frank, open face, ran through the multitude.

He spoke with glowing zeal and in a clear, beautiful voice that carried like a trumpet. After the first minute, all embarrassment and hesitation passed away, and his gift shone, resplendent. The freshness and fervor of youth were added to the logic and power of maturer years, and golden words flowed from his lips. The Indians, always susceptible to oratory, leaned forward, attentive and eager. The eyes of the fifty sachems began to shine and the fierce and implacable Mohawks, who would not relax a particle for any of the others, nodded with approval, as the speaker played upon the strings of their hearts.

He dwelled less upon the friendship of the English than upon the hostility of the French. He knew that Champlain and Frontenac were far away in time, but near in the feelings of the Hodenosaunee, especially the Mohawks, the warlike Keepers of the Eastern Gate. He said that while the French had often lived with the Indians, and sometimes had married Indian women, it was not with the nations of the Hodenosaunee, but with their enemies, Huron, Caughnawaga, St. Regis, Ojibway and other savages of the far west. Onontio could not be the friend of their foes and their friends also. Manitou had never given to any man the power to carry water on both shoulders in such a manner.

The promises of the French to the great nations of the League had never been kept. He and Willet, the hunter whom they called the Great Bear, and the brave young warrior, Tayoga, whom they all knew, had just returned from the Stadacona of the Mohawks, which the French had seized, and where they had built their capital, calling it Quebec. They had covered it with stone buildings, palaces, fortresses and churches, but, in truth and right, it was still the Stadacona of the Mohawks. When Tayoga and Willet and he walked there, they saw the shades of the great Mohawk sachems of long ago, come down from the great shining stars on which they now lived, to confound the French, and to tell the children of the Ganeagaono never to trust them.

Stirred beyond control, a fierce shout burst from the nine Mohawk sachems. It was the first time within the memory of the council that any of its members had given evidence of feeling, while a question lay before it, but their cry touched a common chord of sympathy. Applause swept the crowd, and then, deep silence coming again, the orator continued, his fervor and power increasing as he knew now that all the nations of the Hodenosaunee were with him.

He enlarged upon his theme. He showed to them what a

victorious France would do. If Quebec prevailed, the fair promises the priest and the chevalier had made to the Hodenosaunee would be forgotten. Even as the Mohawks had lost Quebec and other villages they would lose now their castles, the Upper, the Lower and the Middle, the Cayugas and the Oneidas would be crushed, and with them their new brethren the Tuscaroras. The French would burst with fire and sword into the sacred vale of Onondaga itself, they would cut down the council grove and burn the Long House, then their armies would go forth to destroy the Senecas, the Keepers of the Western Gate.

The thousands, swayed by uncontrollable emotion, sprang to their feet and a tremendous shout burst from them all. St. Luc, seeing the Hodenosaunee slipping from his hands and from those of France, leaped up, unable to contain himself, and cried:

"Do not listen to him! Do not listen to him! What he says cannot come to pass!"

The people were in a turmoil, and the council strove in vain for order, but the young speaker raised his hand and silence came again.

"The Chevalier de St. Luc and Father Drouillard, who have spoken to you in behalf of France, are brave and good men," he said, "but they cannot control the acts of their country. They tell you what I say cannot come to pass, but I tell you that it can come to pass, and what is more it has come to pass. Behold!"

He took from beneath his deerskin tunic a tomahawk, large and keen, and held it up. Its shining blade was stained red with the blood of a human being. The silence was now so intense that it became heavy and oppressive. Everyone in the crowd expected something startling to follow, and they were right.

He swung the tomahawk about in a circle that all might see it, and the blood upon its blade. His feeling for the dramatic was strong upon him, and he knew that the right moment had come.

"Do you know whose tomahawk this is?" he cried.

The crowd was silent and waiting.

"It is the tomahawk of Tandakora, the Ojibway, the friend and ally of the French."

A fierce shout like a peal of thunder from the crowd, and then the same intense, waiting silence.

"Do you know whose blood stains the tomahawk of Tandakora, the Ojibway, the friend and ally of the French?"

A deep breath from the crowd.

"It is the blood of Hosahaho, the Onondaga. You knew him well, one of your swiftest runners, a skillful hunter, a great warrior, one who lived a truthful and upright life before the face of Manitou.

211

But he is gone. Three nights ago, Tandakora, the Ojibway, the friend and ally of the French, with a band of his treacherous men, foully murdered him in ambush. But other Onondagas came, and Tandakora and his band had to flee so fast that he could not regain his tomahawk. It has been brought to the vale of Onondaga by those who saw Tandakora, but who could not overtake him. It was given by them to Tayoga, whom all of you know and honor, and he has given it to me as proof of the faith of Onontio. Tandakora and Onontio are brothers. What Tandakora does Onontio does also, and the bright blood of Hosahaho, the Onondaga, that stains the tomahawk of Tandakora, the Ojibway, was shed by Onontio as well as Tandakora. Behold! Here are the promises of Onontio, written red in the blood of your brother!"

An immense tumult followed, but presently Tododaho, first among the sachems, rose and stilled it with uplifted hands. Turning his eyes upon Robert, he said:

"You have spoken well, O Dagaeoga, and you have shown the proof of your words. Never will the great nations of the Hodenosaunee be the friends of the French. There is too much blood between us."

Then, turning to Chevalier de St. Luc and Father Drouillard, he said:

"Go you back to Quebec and tell Onontio that he cannot come to us with promises in one hand and murder in the other. Our young men will guard you and see that you are safe, until you pass out of our lands. Go! Through me the fifty sachems speak for the great League of the Hodenosaunee."

The chevalier and the priest, disappointed but dignified, left the vale of Onondaga that night, and St. Luc said to Robert that he bore him no ill will because of his defeat.

Several weeks later, as Robert, Willet, and Tayoga were on their way to Albany, they heard from an Oneida runner that the English colonials from Virginia, under young Washington, and the French had been in battle far to the west.

"The war has begun," said Willet solemnly, "a war that will shake both continents."

"And the Hodenosaunee will not help Onontio," said Tayoga.

"And the French may lose Quebec," said Robert looking northward to the city of his dreams.

www.ingramcontent.com/pod-product-compliance
Lightning Source LLC
Chambersburg PA
CBHW030450250626
47154CB00003BA/1208